THE BLACK DRAGON

A Medieval Romance
Part of the Executioner Knights Series

By Kathryn Le Veque

KATHRYN LE VEQUE
NOVELS

ARE YOU SIGNED UP FOR KATHRYN'S BLOG?

You'll get the latest news and information on exclusive giveaways, exclusive excerpts, coming releases, sales, free books, cover reveals and more.

Kathryn's blog followers get it all first. No spam, no junk.

Get the latest info from the reigning Queen of English Medieval Romance!

Sign Up Here

kathrynleveque.com

Welcome to the world of THE BLACK DRAGON!

Addax al-Kort was not born in England.

As the heir to the throne of a defunct distant kingdom (near present day Pakistan), Addax came to England with a trade caravan when he was very young. He became a page for a powerful knight and worked his way through the ranks and protocols of Medieval England to become a full-fledged English knight serving William Marshal. Addax is part of the brotherhood of Executioner Knights serving the Marshal, but he has a great talent for the tournament circuit. Competing under a standard emblazoned with a black dragon, he becomes quite rich.

But something changes the course of his life forever.

A man he thought was a friend.

Addax and Maximillian de Grey, a fellow competitor, are close friends, so close that Addax leaves the tournament circuit to go with his friend to help secure his new legacy when he marries a woman of his father's choosing. Unfortunately, that's where the trouble begins, for Maximillian is not a noble man when it comes to women. He doesn't want a wife and he makes that abundantly clear. He has mistresses, openly, in front of his new wife, and steps on everything that marriage stands for.

But the new wife isn't any ordinary woman. Emmeline de Witt is a sweet, beautiful woman who doesn't deserve what Maximillian is dishing out. Addax is put in the position of comforting his friend's wife simply out of duty and a sense of compassion, but the inevitable happens. When the woman Addax loves is abused by her husband, will he look the other way because of the sanctity of marriage? Or will he fight for the woman who has captured his heart, no matter what happens to him in the end? He's a man of honor, above all... but will honor be what he chooses?

Addax has lost everything in his life – his throne, his identity, his family. But Emmeline... *Emmy*... gives him hope that he can know joy once again. In her, he can see his destiny.

Or his death.

HOUSE OF KITARA (AL-KORT)

Motto: *a nullo victa*

Conquered By None

AUTHOR'S NOTE

I can't tell you how excited I am to finally be writing Addax al-Kort's story. He's my very first non-English-born knight!

Let me qualify that statement a little. My first non-English/Scottish/Welsh/Irish-born hero was Brogan d'Aurilliac from *Valiant Chaos*. He was born in, what is today, Germany. But Brogan wasn't a knight, merely a soldier. Addax al-Kort is a full-fledged knight and very entrenched with some of the greatest warlords England has ever seen (de Velt, de Lohr).

Technically, he should be ruling over them.

Since Addax and his story has appeared in other books, I'm not giving anything away by saying Addax was a prince to his people. His father was the King of Kitara and Addax was his heir. Where is the kingdom of Kitara, exactly? The best I can describe it is in the southern end of modern-day Pakistan. Kitara encompassed almost the entire southern portion of the country with borders that extended into India. The Indus River runs through Kitara and its capital was Larkana, which is the site of the ancient city of Mohenjo-daro, one of the greatest ancient cities in the world. Mohenjo-daro's contemporaries were ancient Egypt, Mesopotamia, Minoan Crete, etc., so Addax comes from very ancient bloodlines. He is the embodiment of ancient peoples and their contribution to the world at large. His people helped form civilization as we know it today. But, as with most ancient civilizations, they disappear seemingly overnight. They vanish due to upheaval or natural disasters, and in Addax's case, it was an upheaval. But you'll find out more about that in this story.

Now, we've got some cameos in this tale, mostly by William

de Wolfe about eight or ten years before he met Jordan. If you have read *The Wolfe*, then you know that William was in his early thirties when he met her, so in this story, he's about twenty-three. He's been a seasoned knight for several years, and he's essentially in his prime, so welcome to William before the advent of Jordan!

Also take note that in this story, we once again have the House of de Grey. That house appears in a few of my stories, and it is, indeed, a real Medieval family. Although they were mostly in the north of England, the truth is that it was a very large family, so it's spread around throughout the country. In *Lion of Hearts*, a de Lohr novel, we discovered that the de Lohrs are even related to the House of de Grey, but in this novel, the de Grey mentioned is just another offshoot of the family.

One of the main things I wanted to mention is that we are, once again, in Berwick Castle. I've had a lot of stories set in, near, or around Berwick. Why? I have no idea. Any author will tell you that sometimes, stories simply write themselves, and Berwick has been at the heart of several of mine. It has also had a couple of major families in charge of it because around the time this story is set, Berwick belongs to the Crown of England. Probably more than any other castle in England, Berwick has belonged to the Scots, the English, back to the Scots, back to the English, and so on. It wasn't built by a great family, but by King David of Scotland back in the twelfth century. The English got a hold of it at one point, and King Richard sold it back to the Scots to fund his quest to the Levant.

But to the point—in the early part of the thirteenth century, it belongs to Jax de Velt. Who better to keep it from the Scots than the Dark Lord himself? His son, Cole, was garrison commander for years. All during the Executioner Knights' heyday, Cole is the commander. But then it was lost, and we don't see it again until Patrick de Wolfe is garrison commander in his novel, *Nighthawk*. More than that, in the Dragonblade series, the novel *The Savage Curtain* sees the hero, Stephen of Pembury, once again take command of it about 1333 AD. We know that Atty (Patrick) had it from 1267 through the early part of the fourteenth century, but somehow, the Scots got it again until the Dragonblade boys helped the English get it back.

That brings the questions—did Cole de Velt actually lose Berwick to the Scots? Worse still, what happened that Atty and the de Wolfe family lost it to the Scots again? I've got this worked out in outlines of other books that haven't yet been published, but the gist of it is that it wasn't exactly lost—not really—but more used as a bargaining chip. But why didn't it go back to de Velt and instead to de Wolfe? All part of the "bargaining chip." Rest assured that neither Cole nor Atty "lost" it. Of course they couldn't. Not those two, nor their families, but the castle changed hands many, many times in the course of its life, passing from de Velt to Scots, back to de Wolfe, back to Scots, and then back to Stephen of Pembury. Clearly, it's a very popular place!

And that's the tale of Berwick Castle in the Le Veque Medieval Universe!

Also, one more thing to note in this tale—William Marshal, Earl of Pembroke, passed away in 1219 (for a man who had spent his entire life fighting, surprisingly, he died peacefully of old age), so the care and feeding, so to speak, of the Executioner Knights would fall to his eldest son, also William Marshal. However, the Marshals and their lands in Ireland were having a lot of trouble in the years following the original William's death, which is why control of the EKs was turned over to Christopher de Lohr and Peter de Lohr. The 1220s are a transitional period for them as Christopher and Peter take control, but not without collaboration from the Earls of Pembroke, who still remain active and involved. Because William Marshal's sons all died in quick succession until only Anselm was left, when he passed, full control went to Peter de

Lohr because Christopher was quite elderly at that point (and that is mentioned in *Lion of Twilight*, a de Lohr novel).

Some random final facts: (and I know this author's note was long), but some of this book talks about silver/lead mining in Medieval England. Yes, that was a thing. Of course, it's not at the scale of today, but it did happen. Believe it or not, silver can be extracted from lead ores and other metals. I read a lot about metals for this book, and silver can be extracted from a few things. Another random fact is, YES, Medieval women did have tweezers and, according to artwork from the period, they did indeed pluck their eyebrows. They also used razors, cosmetics, and other beauty routines/implements that women still use today.

The usual pronunciation guide:

Deira—DAIR-uh

Kitara—kit-TAR-uh

Addax—ADD-x (it sort of sounds like "Attics" if you say it properly)

Emmeline—Emma-line (not "lyn," but "line")

Amare—uh-MAR-ay

Kiya—KY-uh

Essien—ess-EE-in

There are some great cameos in this story, so keep an eye out for the Terrible Trio—William de Wolfe, Paris de Norville, and Kieran Hage. They've got some great moments!

Happy Reading!

PROLOGUE

Year of Our Lord 1190
The fall of the kingdom of Kitara

T HE SMELL OF smoke was heavy in the air.
But it wasn't just the smoke—it was the smell of burning flesh and burning dreams, all of it going up in flame as the enemy rolled in from the north on a clear night with a million stars as witness. A witness to the death and destruction that usually followed the army from the north and their fearless leader.

Temüjin.

The great khan of the Mongols and his massive army had breached the outer perimeter of Kitara.

But it wasn't entirely a surprise. King Amare, tall and powerful, with eyes the color of jade and skin as smooth as polished stone, watched the fire from Larkana Palace, the residence of more than two dozen generations of his family. But tonight would see that legacy come to an end, because the royal family of Kitara had been betrayed from within. Amare was so emotionally wounded by the betrayal that it was difficult for him to face the task ahead. One of desperation, one of reckoning.

But it had to be done.

He had to kill his brother.

Prince Ekon was four years younger than Amare and had coveted the throne since he was a young boy. There had been numerous attempts on Amare's life over the years, and the general belief was that most of them had been orchestrated by Ekon, who simply denied the accusations and threw himself on his brother's mercy. It wasn't mercy he wanted, but fragility. He played on his brother's one weakness—his love for his family.

Even for those who betrayed him.

Amare knew this. He was well aware of his brother's ploys. He was well aware of the man's movements, his subversion, and even his attempts to seduce Amare's own wife. Rumor had it that the youngest child, a beautiful daughter named Adanya, was Ekon's child. Since Amare and Ekon looked quite similar to one another and the daughter had the same green eyes, perhaps the truth would never be known, even though Amare's wife vehemently denied anything illicit. Given that Amare loved her, and she had always been quite loyal, he believed her. But the rumors continued, and Amare ignored them.

The price of his ignorance, however, would be high. Ekon had taken a journey some time ago into the north after he'd tried to assassinate one of Amare's generals. Amare had sent him north as a diplomat, trying to give him a useful position in the hopes that would satisfy him, but it didn't. The intent of Ekon's journey was to seek trade with the tribes to the north and the vast empire that was established there, but Ekon had done something quite different. Rather than establish ties for his brother's kingdom, he'd managed to ally himself with the most feared warlord in the world.

A man he promised his fealty, should he remove Amare from the throne.

And that was why Temüjin had come.

Amare and his loyalists had known of the approach of his army for a couple of weeks now, ever since the outposts began reporting the movement of the enormous army southward. Amare had listened to the reports in horror, and when he sent for Ekon, his brother was nowhere to be found. As the days passed and the army drew closer, Amare knew that his brother could be found somewhere in the approaching army, and he further knew that, given the size of the force, his own army, which was trained and sizable, would be facing a suicide mission.

And so would his people.

But Amare would have the last word.

It was, therefore, with a heavy heart that Amare ordered his own city burned before the Mongols could get to it. His army was out there right now, helping the villagers flee and burning their homes behind them. When Amare had been told, by a double agent, that Ekon was indeed with the approaching army and was promised Kitara's throne, Amare knew he had to destroy everything. He'd rather do that than let his brother have it.

Ekon would be the king of ashes.

"My love!" a woman gasped as she came rushing into the throne room. "What are you doing here? The caravan is ready to take us by river out to the sea. We must hurry!"

Amare turned to look at his wife. Kiya was such a lovely creature, so graceful and beautiful and kind. She had been an arranged marriage, a princess of her people in the land of the pharaohs, but the moment Amare set eyes on her was the moment he fell in love with her. Before he could answer, however, two young boys ran up behind her, throwing themselves at him. Amare laughed softly as he collected his sons, Addax and Essien. He was a warm and loving father, but tonight, he was perhaps a little more loving and warm.

He knew it would be the last time he ever held his sons.

"Addax," he said, giving the boys a squeeze before he set them to their feet. "Essien, look at me. I have something very important to ask you."

Addax was nearly five years of age, and Essien was not quite three. They were very young, that was true, but they were big for their age and quite brilliant. At least, Amare thought so. They could ride and hunt, and already, Addax could read. The boys were still trying to climb back into his arms as he held them at bay, looking them in the face.

"Es, stop climbing," he commanded softly. "Stand still. That's good. Something very important is happening tonight, and you must be part of it."

Addax, the less squirmy of the two, was watching his father seriously. "An army is coming, Abba," he said. "We have come to help you fight."

Abba. That meant father. It would be the last time he ever heard it from his sons, and Amare smiled at his brave boy. "And you are very courageous," he said. "I am honored to have you by my side. But I have an even more important task for you."

Addax cocked his head curiously. "What, *Pita?*"

Pita. Father. Amare wasn't sure he could keep his composure knowing it would be the last time he heard it from his son. But time was not his friend on this night—it was passing more quickly than usual—so he pulled his boys against him one last time, hugging them fiercely.

But his heart was breaking.

"You must get your mother to safety," he said, indicating Kiya as she stood behind the boys and tried not to weep. "You must go with her and protect her. Will you do this for me?"

Addax and Essien looked at their mother before Addax returned his attention to his father. "But what about you?" he asked. "Who will help you fight?"

Amare forced a smile. "I have the entire army to help me fight," he said, making it sound as if it was nothing at all. "But your mother does not command an army. She has a few servants, but you are her very best warrior. Will you please do this for me?"

Essien nodded solemnly, but Addax was still hesitant. "She has Bobo and Rani to help her," he said. "But you need me."

He was referring to the old women who served his mother, but Amare nodded sincerely. "Indeed, I do need you," he said. "I will always need you, Addax, and right now I need you to take care of your mother. Promise me."

Addax sighed heavily before finally nodding. When Amare saw that he had his heir's agreement, he quickly removed a small dagger that was hanging at his side. He held it up in front of the boy.

"You will take this with you," he said. "My *pita* gave it to me, and now, I give it to you. It has been passed down from father to son for many generations of our family, and now it belongs to you, Addax. Use it to protect your mother. Use it to remember me."

Addax's dark eyes glittered at the sight of the *ejadar* dagger. The dragon blade. Every King of Kitara kept it at his side, a symbol of the al-Kort dynasty, because every King of Kitara since the dawn of the dynasty was called the *kaara ejadar.*

The Black Dragon.

Addax took the dagger silently, looking at the dragon-head hilt with the onyx eyes. It was an ancient weapon, well used, but it was still as sharp and beautiful as it had been on the day it was forged. In fact, when he put his finger on the tip of it, the weapon immediately drew blood.

"Now you are one with the dragon," Amare said softly, watching his son's expression as he realized his skin had been pierced. "Now you and the dagger are blood brothers. It will always kill for you. It will always support you. Take it with you, my son, and protect your mother and brother and sister with it. Take it with my blessing."

Addax looked up from the dagger, gazing at his father with eyes the same color as the onyx eyes on the dragon. Amare's father had possessed those dark eyes, too. There was something deep and intense and mysterious about them, but also something of great humanity. Addax may be young, but he possessed all of those things.

Amare knew he would have made a magnificent king.

"Why can you not come, too, *Pita*?" Addax asked.

It was becoming increasingly difficult for Amare to keep his composure. "Because someone must protect Kitara," he said simply. "I will see you again, but for now, you must go with your mother. Do you understand me?"

Addax nodded seriously. "But *when* will I see you again?"

"Soon," Amare said, for he could say no more. Before Addax could ask another question, he kissed the boy on the forehead and stood up, facing his beloved Kiya. "Where is Adanya?"

Kiya was verging on tears, having heard everything Amare

said to their eldest son and knowing how difficult it was for him.

"She is already at the river with her nurse," she said softly. "She is so young. She would not understand this parting. But the boys…"

Amare nodded quickly, for there was no reason for her to continue. It would be the last time their sons faced their father, so it was more important for them. And more important that Amare say what he needed to say.

"Thank you, my love, for allowing me to bid them farewell," he said. Then he cupped her face with one hand and gently kissed her mouth. "You must hurry. I sent word to your father when the army from the north approached. He will not receive the missive for some time, but you must be on your way so his ships can meet yours. The captain of your ship knows the way, and by the time your ship reaches the Red Sea, your father should be on his way to meet you. You and the children will be safe in Cairo."

Her tears started to come. "And you, my darling?" she whispered. "What about you?"

He forced a smile, kissing her again. "I must do what I was destined to do," he said bravely. "What I was meant to do. I will burn Lankara to the ground, and when there is only smoke and ashes left, I will kill my brother."

"What if he kills you first?"

Amare shrugged. "Then I will see you in paradise," he said. "But know… know that you have made my life paradise on earth, Kiya. No man has ever loved a woman more than I have loved you."

"And I love you with every breath I take," she murmured. "That will never stop, not in this world or any other."

"I know, *mere jaan*."

"Promise me, Amare. If you can escape to Egypt, promise that you will come to us."

"I promise. But if I do not… this farewell was well made. It has given me courage."

She started to weep. Weeks of being strong had reached the breaking point. But Amare shushed her softly, turning her around and hustling her toward the servants who were waiting for her. Essien grabbed her hand, holding it tightly as they rushed along, while Addax and his dagger lingered behind with his father. Amare took them to the secret palace exit, where tunnels would take them to the river beyond where ships awaited, and then the river would take them to the sea and westward. At the exit, Amare came to a halt and kissed his wife one last time, kissed Essien, and took a moment with Addax as the boy faced him with more bravery than a five-year-old should have to summon.

For a moment, Amare let himself drink in the sight of Addax, imagining the man his son would grow up to be. Of all of his regrets, the fact that he would not live to see it was probably his biggest one. Before him, he saw greatness.

He hoped his son would be able to achieve something of it, wherever life took him.

"Be strong, my son," he whispered, struggling not to weep. "In the face of whatever this life will bring you, be strong, be honest, and be loyal to those you love. Promise me."

"I promise, *Pita*."

Amare smiled weakly. "Good," he said, turning him to his mother and the rest of the escort bound for the tunnels. The servants were already dressing Essien in a disguise as a servant's child. "Hurry, now. I will see you soon."

Addax started to turn, but paused. "When?"

"As soon as God allows."

That was good enough for Addax. It was something of a definitive answer, which his father had failed to give him before now. The last vision he had of his father was as the man stood in the great stone doorway, watching his family flee. But there was nothing but courage on his face, hope that they would survive, and that gave Addax the strength he needed to do as his father had asked. He took the dragon blade dagger with him, knowing it carried the power of his ancestors.

On that dark, terrible night, Addax, his mother, brother, and sister, along with several loyal servants, fled out to sea.

But all did not go well.

A storm on the second night at sea pushed their convoy of three ships off course and into a gulf, where they were forced to dock at the city of Abu Samra. That was when the captain, who had been loyal to Amare for years and had established trade routes for him, decided to demand favors from Kiya. He'd never had a queen before, he'd said, something that confused Addax and Essien, but Addax knew instinctively that it wasn't good. When Kiya refused, he struck her.

Addax rammed the dragon-headed dagger into the man's kidney. *Protect your mother*, his father had said. So, he did.

After that, it was chaos.

Kiya and her children fled with her servants onto the streets of Abu Samra, but they became separated in the chaos. Dust and wind and terror swirled about them, and the group fractured further. The two old women, Bobo and Rami, fell afoul of a man they'd run into, and he threw them both into the sea. After hiding out for a day and a night, Addax and Essien searched for their mother and sister for days and days, until they found an old fisherman who said he saw a screaming woman and her infant daughter taken aboard another ship.

Distraught, the hungry and exhausted boys had no idea what to do when they came across one of the male servants who had accompanied them, only the man had been in a fight and left to die in an alley. He told Addax and Essien that, indeed, their mother and sister had been captured by the crew of the murdered captain and taken back aboard the ship. Now, the ship was gone.

So were their last links to their family.

Two very small boys found themselves alone in a strange land, their mother and sister vanished. There were no more servants out of the several who came with them, except for the dying old man. Therefore, Addax and Essien took up vigil next to the old servant, through heat and cold, night and day, learning to beg for food and receiving a pittance from the mosque in town. But it was enough to sustain them until the old servant finally passed away six days after they had found him.

After that, they were on their own.

But not for long.

Abu Samra was a crossroads for trade caravans throughout the region, and one day, when Addax and Essien went to the mosque to beg for more food, the holy man introduced them to a merchant who was bringing an enormous caravan from Abu Dhabi and heading for Damascus. The merchant needed small boys to run errands or complete tasks, and the holy man made it seem as if it would be a great, fruitful adventure for Addax and Essien. It was better than begging in the streets, he said, and God would smile upon those who helped themselves.

Addax did want to please God, after all.

So, they went.

Unfortunately, the merchant was not their savior. He enslaved them both, starving them and beating them, forcing them to tend camels and horses and load and unload merchandise. Addax was a little older and a little stronger than Essien, who was little more than a toddler. But he was a three-year-old who was forced to grow up very quickly as the hardships of life settled around them. It was either that or he would die, and Addax found himself being both father and mother to his younger brother. He would give Essien half of his meager rations so the child wouldn't go to bed hungry at night, crying for his mother and father.

But the caveat was that Addax went to bed hungry.

This went on for two very long years.

Two years of being beaten and abused, of hoping the next day would bring relief or even someone with some kindness for them. At one point, the merchant, a man by the name of Abiram, was given a slave girl in Basrah in exchange for goods. She was young, but pretty and strong, and Abiram used her for labor. She worked alongside Addax and Essien, her nature kind and joyful in spite of her circumstances. Finally, the two young boys had someone to show them a measure of kindness and compassion, things they craved at their young age.

Amala was her name.

But Amala's presence wasn't to last forever.

Abiram had reached the Levant with his caravan of goods, and he found ready customers in the men protecting Acre, and other cities, from the onslaught of Christian armies. One night, Abiram sold Amala to a lord for his harem, and Addax would never forget her soft weeping as she was taken away. Somehow, Addax knew that he and Essien would not survive much longer. Abiram was growing crueler, and they were growing weaker.

Once they hit the outskirts of Jerusalem, a vast and populous city, Addax made the decision to run.

It was either run or die.

When Abiram brought the caravan to a halt and ordered the boys to go into town with a message for a friend of his, they willingly went into the citadel of Jerusalem and lost themselves on the dusty, ancient streets. Instead of searching for Abiram's friend on the Street of the Merchants, they escaped the city walls to the north, running through scrub and rocks, avoiding scorpions and snakes, rushing toward another village.

It took all night.

Once they arrived, there were very few people on the streets. Everyone seemed to be inside, even on what should have been a busy morning. Addax and Essien did what they'd learned to do best—hide in the shadows, trying to remain unseen, being as unobtrusive as possible. They'd learned that from Abiram, but more so now that they had fled the man. They didn't want to be brought back to him. But they were only small boys, after all, and by midmorning, they collapsed in a grove of olive trees from sheer exhaustion, and Essien fell asleep on his older brother.

But Addax couldn't sleep.

He had to remain vigilant.

Hollow-eyed, malnourished, and quite possibly as close to death as he'd ever been, Addax wondered if he would die in this place. He wondered what would become of his brother. Before Abiram's caravan, they'd begged for food because they didn't know what else to do. Now, it seemed they were to live on the street again, and Addax didn't relish the thought. He'd once had plans to find his mother and sister and return to Kitara to fight alongside his father, but all of those events had happened over two years ago. It seemed like a thousand years had passed. His father was dead, and so were his mother and sister, more than likely. Although he didn't want to believe that, deep down, he knew it was true.

He and Essien were the only ones left.

And the dragon blade.

That dragon-headed dagger had never left his possession. Oddly, Abiram had never searched him or stripped him in all the time they'd been with him, and Addax had been able to keep the dagger sewn into the hem of his tunic. He'd done that himself with some thread that one of the other slaves loaned him. Amala had known about it, and her sewing skill had secured it tightly when his skills hadn't. The dagger was with him, even now. His father had given it to him and told him to protect his mother and brother and sister with it. He'd failed with his mother and sister, but he still had Essien. Perhaps protecting meant different things—not only brandishing the weapon, but perhaps, in this case, exchanging it for food or money.

Perhaps it had come to that.

Trading away the very last vestiges of his legacy.

As Addax pondered what he needed to do, he heard horses in the distance. He was near the road, but still somewhat protected by the grove of olive trees. Turning his head, he could see enormous warhorses ridden by men covered with steel coats and great tunics and big, square buckets of metal on their heads. The tunics they wore were red, with yellow cats on them. There were so many of them that he couldn't see where the line of them ended, all of them heading down the road and into the village.

Somewhat fearful, Addax tried to move without waking up

Essien. His brother would likely cry at the sight of so many armed, unfamiliar warriors, and that would bring attention to them. If there was one thing Addax had learned as a young lad, it was how to be quiet. Noise was never a good thing. But he couldn't move enough, knowing he could be seen from the road.

And he was.

By dogs.

Two big gray dogs found him, licking his face furiously, wagging their tails, and evidently quite happy to see him. Even the dogs had steel on them, around their necks, and Addax was absolutely terrified. The dogs were very big, but thankfully friendly, and they licked Essien, too, who awoke to a giant dog head in his field of vision that was larger than his own head. He opened his mouth to scream, but Addax slapped a hand over his lips so the sound would go no further.

Then someone was yelling for the dogs. The dogs heard their names, but they were so happy that they'd found new people that they refused to leave the boys. In fact, one dog lay across Essien, and the other sat down next to Addax. It didn't seem to matter that someone was calling for them. They'd found something, and they were proud of it. As Addax watched in terror, one of the heavily armed men on the road moved into the olive grove and dismounted.

He was heading straight for them.

"Argos!" the man boomed. "Artemis! Did you not hear me, you foolish animals?"

Addax had no idea what the man was saying. He didn't understand the language. But he was absolutely terrified as he clutched Essien, watching the big warrior as he approached. The man saw them fairly quickly, realizing his dogs had found the pair. He slowed down, pausing a moment before removing his helm. He had hair the color of gold and a beard of nearly the same color around his jaw.

Addax had never seen hair that color in his life.

"Aap kaun hain?" the man asked, not unkindly.

Who are you? Addax recognized the language because he'd spent enough time in these lands to understand, and speak, a little of it. But he was so frightened, and so hungry and exhausted, that he started to weep.

"Addax," he said. "Ana Addax."

I am Addax.

The warrior looked him over. He pointed to Essien questioningly, and Addax told the man his name. But that didn't seem to satisfy him. He didn't go away. He tried to get the dogs to come away, but they wouldn't. He finally gave up and crouched down a few feet away from them, even as other warriors saw what he was doing and reined their horses to a halt.

But the man's focus was on Addax.

"Do you understand me?" he asked in the language of the land.

Addax nodded. "Aye."

"Are you injured?"

Addax shook his head. "Nay."

"But you have bruises and blood on you."

Addax didn't know how to answer that. He was terrified to tell him the truth, so he made up something. Anything. "We… we are traveling."

"Where are you going?"

"I do not know."

The crouching warrior was joined by two more of the biggest men Addax had ever seen. One had the same gold hair, but the other man had black hair and blue eyes. They all had blue eyes. Addax had never seen that shade before, nor skin tone that color. It was quite pale.

"Where are your parents?" the crouching man asked. "Where do you belong?"

Addax shook his head. "We belong to no one," he said. "Please… will you let us go?"

The other blond warrior walked around the tree trunk, coming up on their other side. He, too, crouched down, closer to Essien. He spoke to the other man in a language Addax didn't understand.

"They've been beaten, Chris," he said quietly. "Starved, too, from the looks of it."

The man called Chris, the one with the blond beard, nodded. "I can see that," he said. "And they're clearly terrified. They are probably running from whoever did this. Why else would they be sleeping in an olive grove?"

The second blond man merely nodded and stood up. "We have some provisions we can give them," he said. "But we need to be on our way. Richard is expecting us."

The man called Chris stood up, too, but he was gazing down at the frightened boys. After a moment, he looked at the black-haired man standing next to him.

"Something tells me not to leave them here," he said.

The man with the dark hair frowned. "Why?"

"I do not know. It is a feeling I have." The man called Chris paused, looking indecisively at the boys huddling fearfully against the tree. "Those are very little boys who probably will not see another sunrise if they are not given food and help."

The man with the dark hair rolled his eyes. "So you come all this way to kill Muslims, yet you want to save these two?" he asked incredulously. "We do not have time for this. Give them some bread and let us be on our way."

With that, he turned and walked away, but the man called Chris didn't leave with him. In fact, he called after him.

"Mayhap God will be more willing to forgive me for the Muslims I've killed if I help two small children," he said loudly. But his focus returned to Addax and Essien. He'd made up his mind. He was going to help. "I cannot leave them here to die. David, pick up the one closest to you. I'll take the bigger one."

The other blond man looked confused. "And do what with them?" he said. "We bring them along like baggage?"

The man named Chris pointed to the dogs, still lying with the boys. "We bring them along like the dogs," he said. "Mayhap I will put them to work for us. In any case, I will not leave them. Pick up the smaller boy."

With a shrug, the other blond man dutifully reached down and picked up Essien, who screamed at being separated from his brother, but the man called Chris held up a hand to him.

"Hadi, hadi," he said quickly. *Quiet, quiet.* "Sawf 'usaeiduk."

I will help you.

That shut Essien up somewhat, but he was still crying. Addax found himself heaved up by the big blond man with the beard, being carried toward the warhorses that were tethered at the side of the road. No sooner were they put upon them than the warriors, men from a faraway land who spoke a strange language, were giving them water and stale bread.

But neither boy cared.

They wolfed it down.

Little did either one of them know that the food represented hope, and the Christian knights represented destiny. Hope and destiny came to Addax and Essien that day.

And they embraced it.

CHAPTER ONE

Year of Our Lord 1225
Berwick Tournament
England

O NE MORE PASS *and victory shall be mine!*

The Black Dragon was in fine form today.

The dagger given to Addax by his father, the one that had belonged to generations of his forefathers, was front and center as he made his run down the guides toward the de Birmingham knight. With all of the protection, padding, and tunics that Addax wore, he'd had a special sheath sewn into his tunic for the dagger so that the hilt was peeking out, the onyx eyes observing his success. It was lodged at his breastbone, and that was intentional. Addax always wanted the dragon dagger to see everything he did, especially in the tournaments.

He felt as if his father was watching through those onyx eyes.

And perhaps he was.

Astride his muscular, dappled Belgian warmblood, Addax lowered his lance into the cradle, preparing to aim it right at his opponent's chest. He could hear the crowd in the list screaming in excitement, the cry they took up whenever the Black Dragon was competing. It was a cry that sent chills up his spine, that fed his bravery and soothed his soul. That cry that the crowd rarely did for anyone else when he was around.

Black! they would cry. But it sounded like…

Blaaaaaaaaaaaaaaaaaaaaaaaaaaaaaaaaaaaaaaaaaaaaaaaaaa!

The horses were drawing closer to one another. Addax was focused on his opponent's neck and chest area and nothing else. He wasn't looking at his horse, or his lance, or the guides, or even the arena around him. Only at his opponent's chest. Then the horses were finally in range of one another. He dropped his lance and braced himself, leaning forward slightly so the impact wouldn't throw him off his horse.

Crash!

The de Birmingham knight toppled.

The crowd went wild.

Addax's lance was shattered, but he still had the hilt and about six feet of it left, so he held it aloft as he swung his horse around and made a run past the lists as the crowd screamed for their champion. They were throwing flowers and silken, scented scarfs, and even money and gloves. Having several men who worked for him as he rode the circuit, including two squires, he knew that anything of value would be collected by his squires and brought to him. Often, he shared anything that was tossed to him with his men, so he knew nothing would be stolen from the booty. He trusted the men who worked for him, and they knew that Addax was generous.

It was easy to be generous when one had more money than God.

Loping out of the arena, he reined his excited horse to a walk as friends and servants were there to greet him. The first face he saw was Cole de Velt, commander of Berwick's garrison and head of the de Velt empire. Cole had thousands of men at his disposal, carrying on his father's legacy by adding his own fame to it. Jax de Velt was a legend in these parts, and in England as a whole, and Addax and Cole went back many years in their friendship. Addax had spent several evenings feasting at Berwick Castle before the tournament, something he'd deeply regretted the first two days of competition because it took that long for the ache in his head to subside.

But it had been worth it.

"And *that* is how you defeat an opponent," Addax announced as his squires reached out to stop the horse. "Every man here should take note of my technique."

Cole shook his head at the arrogance, looking at the knights around him. Seasoned men, all of them, who smirked and rolled their eyes at Addax's egotistical declaration.

"You are only a battering ram," Cole said. "You may as well go around with a club and beat men off their horses for all of the technique you show."

Addax guffawed loudly as he swung his leg over the saddle and slid off. "If I thought I could get away with it, I would do exactly that," he said, moving to the group of men who had been waiting to congratulate him. "In fact, I thought about breaking some arms when I arrived. Only on those men I do not like, of course. I would spare your arm, Cole. And my brother's. And perhaps Julian and Beau's. But de Wolfe? I will break both of his arms and both of his legs, and take great delight doing it. Anything to keep him out of the arena."

That brought laughter from the group. Essien, who had grown up tall and powerful and handsome, was positioned next to Julian de Velt, Cole's younger brother, who had also competed earlier in the day. To Julian's right stood Beau de Russe, the great competitor known as Bringer of Nightmares. He had quite a brutal reputation on the tournament circuit, and had for several years. Rounding out the group was the object of Addax's ire, Sir William de Wolfe. A knight at Northwood Castle, seat of the Earl of Teviot, and the truth was that there was no one more skilled, more ruthless, or more respected than William. In the north, he'd already earned himself the nickname of the Wolfe of the Border. He was young compared to the rest of the knights in their circle, but youth had nothing to do with a man who was quickly working his way into legendary status.

And they all knew it.

"I've not faced you yet, Addax," William reminded him, a twinkle of mirth in his hazel-gold eyes. "But I will, eventually."

"And you'd better be prepared," Julian said. "De Wolfe has won at least two tournaments in the north that I know of, and probably more that I don't. You may have some serious competition."

"Pah," Addax said, frowning. "I am the Black Dragon. A dragon has no competition."

"Dragons can be tamed," William muttered.

Addax lifted a dark eyebrow. "Now you shall feel my wrath," he said. Then he started to look around. "Es? Where is that big club we always carry around to dispose of whelps like de Wolfe?"

Essien grinned. "I will not help you," he said. "If you want to beat de Wolfe, then you must do it alone."

The threats, as well as the responses, were lighthearted. There was a good deal of laughing going on, mostly because they all knew Addax wasn't serious. The man dominated the tournament circuit everywhere he went, and he'd kill anyone who tried to harm his friends, de Wolfe included. He'd proven that on multiple occasions when an opponent injured someone who meant something to him. Addax wasn't beyond vengeance to protect those he loved.

None of them were.

"My lord!"

A shout came from the direction of the arena, and they could see one of the field marshals approaching. The man was heading for Cole, mostly, because Berwick was his town and the House of de Velt had sponsored the competition. Cole waved the man over.

"Speak," he told him.

The man was an older, seasoned marshal who followed the tournament circuit. His judgment was just, and he was well respected. He focused on the enormous lord bearing the title of Baron Blackadder, an honor he'd inherited from his father.

"After the last bout, the guides must be repaired, my lord," the man said. "We had one more bout this morning, but it will take time to repair the guides."

Cole nodded. "I see," he said. "What happened? I watched al-Kort's bout, and I didn't see any damage to the guides."

"When the de Birmingham knight fell, my lord," the marshal explained. "He fell into the guide and collapsed a section of it."

Everyone looked at Addax, who merely shrugged. "Such are the perils of the game," he said. "I've fallen into the guide enough. We all have."

"The de Birmingham knight was impaled on part of the broken wood," the marshal told him. "He is in his tent, having it removed."

Addax hadn't known that, and suddenly, the victorious mood he'd been indulging in seemed to dampen. "I did not realize that he had been wounded," he said. "Is it bad?"

The marshal shrugged. "I do not know," he said. "I do not think so, for he walked from the arena under his own power."

Addax's dark eyes moved off toward the competitor's encampment. "I will see to him," he said. "De Birmingham and I have competed against one another in the past. He is a fair opponent."

With nothing more to say to that, the marshal simply bowed out. As he headed toward another group of competitors to tell them that the schedule of bouts had changed, a knight wearing a tunic emblazoned with a three-point shield with blue and white stripes approached Addax and his group. In fact, the knight intentionally bumped into Addax to catch his attention.

"My bout was next," he said loudly. "Did you truly have to break everything so the rest of us could not complete, Addax?"

Addax grinned at the man who had become one of his best friends on the tournament circuit. A member of the Northumberland de Grey family, Sir Maximilian de Grey was handsome, strong, and skilled. So very skilled in so many things. With his blond hair and dark eyes, he was also quite handsome and had no shortage of female admirers. He had the flashy style and the ego to match, as many tournament knights did, competing for prize money because it was lucrative and they had no other real means of making their fortune. But Maximilian was different. Someday, he would be a wealthy earl.

He competed for the glory and nothing more.

"I do not know why you are crying about it," Addax said. "It is not as if you have a chance against de Wolfe, whom you shall be competing against."

Maximilian shot a long glance William's way, only to see William with a lazy smile on his lips. "*You*," Maximilian demanded as he pointed at William. "You will be pulverized."

William struggled not to laugh. "Is that what you call it?"

"Do you mock me?"

"Nay," William said. "I simply question your definition of pulverizing."

"How *dare* you."

The group broke out in laughter the way Maximilian had said the word "dare." He dragged the word out, making it a long and hissed word. In fact, William turned away, unwilling to engage in any more of Maximilian's theatrics, at least before their bout, but the truth was that he, like everyone else, thought Maximilian was humorous and exciting. And he was. But he was also a serious competitor, and all jesting aside, he wasn't particularly keen to go up against the enormous, and wildly talented, de Wolfe. Maximilian had talent, but not nearly as much as some of the other competitors. Maximilian, at times, got by on sheer perseverance alone. As William and Essien headed back toward the arena, Maximilian tugged on Addax.

"I must speak with you," he said. "Walk with me."

Excusing himself from Cole and Julian and Beau, Addax followed Maximilian away from the arena and toward the smithy stalls that were crammed together on the east side of the field. This was where competitors with broken lances, armor, or even weapons had their equipment repaired, and the smell from the forge fires was strong. Smoke billowed up, black and thick, as the smithies stoked the flames. But it was nothing compared to the flame that was currently being stoked in Maximilian's chest.

He was a man with much on his mind.

"I should go and see how de Birmingham fares," Addax said, pulling off the linen cap that covered his long, dark hair against the chafe of his helm. "I knocked the man into the guide, but I truly had no idea that he'd been impaled. Did you see it?"

Maximilian was preoccupied. "See what?" he said before he thought about what Addax had said. "Oh, *that*. Aye, I saw it. He hit the guide hard, but I did not see anything impale him. Who told you that?"

"The field marshal."

Maximilian shrugged. "It cannot be too serious, for I saw the man walk from the field," he said. "But enough about him. I have troubles, Addax. Big trouble."

Addax looked at him. "What trouble?"

"My father should be here shortly."

Addax's eyebrows lifted in surprise. "The Earl of Bretherdale?" he said. "Why is that trouble? I should think that is great news. I've not seen your father in a couple of years."

Maximilian waved him off. "It is not great news because he is bringing someone with him."

"Who?"

"My betrothed."

Addax came to a halt, facing him with a confused expression on his face. "I think you had better start from the beginning," he said. "Since when are you betrothed?"

Maximilian averted his gaze. "I have been for two years," he said. "I've simply never spoken of it."

"Nay, you have not," Addax said, eyeing him. "I've known you for years, and you've never said a word about it. Nor have you *behaved* like a betrothed man, if you get my meaning."

Maximilian waved him off defensively. "I know," he said.

"But that is because I do not feel like one. This was not my doing."

"Your father?"

"Aye." Maximilian nodded. "It was his idea. My betrothed is the widow of Sir Ernest de Witt. Have you heard the name?"

Addax thought on it. "I do not think so," he said. "De Witt. *De Witt.* Nay, it does not sound familiar. Who is he?"

Maximilian sighed sharply. "You mean who *was* he," he said. "Only one of the wealthiest warlords in England. The man's family has control of most of the northern Pennines and surrounding lands, which include great lead deposits. Their lands border my father's lands, and when de Witt died, my father waited a nominal amount of time before soliciting the man's widow. Without my permission, I might add."

Addax could see how unhappy he was. "Ah," he said. "No wonder you've never spoken of it."

Maximilian shook his head firmly. "I would like to forget he did such a thing, but alas, I cannot," he said. "My father sent me a missive last month telling me that he would be here at this tournament this week and he would be bringing my bride with him. Then I received a missive from him today telling me that he will be here this morning. He says that he expects a wedding."

"The very day he arrives?"

Maximilian shrugged. "Who knows?" he said. "Knowing my father, it could be the very moment he steps off his horse. But he certainly means we should do it during his visit, considering he is bringing her with him."

A distasteful prospect, as far as Maximilian was concerned. Addax could read it all over his face, so he was careful in proceeding.

"Have you met her?" he asked.

Maximilian shook his head. "Nay," he said. "I've never met her. If she's the widow of de Witt, who was a very old and very disagreeable old man, I might add, then surely she's old and disagreeable also, although my father did say that she was his second wife, so mayhap she's a bit younger. Imagine that, Addax. I am to marry the leavings of a disagreeable old man."

Addax wasn't unsympathetic. "Then you'll simply have to focus on the good," he said. "The good is that she is wealthy. You've said so yourself."

"True."

"And a man needs heirs, Max."

Maximilian rolled his eyes. "She was married for ten years to de Witt, and there are no children," he said. "The old cow is barren."

"Did de Witt have children from his first marriage?"

"Nay, he did not, which is why his lands and wealth will go to me."

"Then mayhap the problem was not with her, but with him."

Maximilian cocked his head thoughtfully, but it was only momentary. "Pah," he said, spitting onto the ground. "The only good out of this situation is the money. I will use it to pay for a stable of mistresses."

Addax didn't exactly think that was a good idea, especially for a titled earl, as Maximilian would be when his father died, but he didn't say anything to that effect. He could see how unnerved and unhappy his friend was, so he didn't want to point out the flaws in his future plans. The man was trying to figure out a way to make himself happy in a world that would probably be filled with disappointment. Marrying an ancient, infertile woman, wealthy though she might be.

But something didn't make sense to Addax.

"Why would your father force you to marry a woman who is old and barren?" he said. "That makes no sense, not if he wants the Bretherdale line to continue. Are you sure she's older?"

Maximilian shrugged. "As I said, I have never met her," he said. "But I can only assume what I have told you based on the facts. My father brokered his contract so that I inherit the de Witt lands, which will join with the Bretherdale lands. It will be an enormous empire."

"But that doesn't explain why he wants you to marry a woman who cannot bear a child."

Maximilian sighed again. "Because she is the granddaughter of King John," he said. "More than the wealth, that is at the heart of this situation. Her mother was a royal bastard, so she has royal blood and royal connections. My father wants that for me."

Addax nodded in realization. "Now *that* makes sense."

Maximilian rolled his eyes. "Aye, it does," he said. "But hopefully, she is old and will die soon. Then I can marry a young woman and have my heirs."

"And keep the de Witt money."

"Exactly." Maximilian scratched his head irritably. "Addax, will you do something for me?"

"If I can."

"My bout is up next, and I do not wish to be distracted, not when I am to face de Wolfe," he said. "Will you greet my father when he arrives? He will be coming to the competitors' camp, straight to my encampment. Please?"

Addax was hesitant. "He will expect to see *you*, Max."

Maximilian's irritation grew. "I realize that," he said. "But I told you that I do not wish to be distracted. Would you want to be distracted, going up against de Wolfe?"

Addax shook his head. "I confess that I would not," he said. "In fact, I heard him say that Hage and de Norville would be arriving shortly, and you know how those three can be when they are together."

Maximilian shook his head as if that was the worst news he'd ever heard. Addax was speaking of Sir Kieran Hage and Sir Paris de Norville, two of the most talented young knights the north had ever seen, stationed at Northwood Castle with de Wolfe. The trio had been thick as thieves most of their lives, and even at their young age were legendary in military circles, but not always for the best of reasons. Young, brash, and with a talent for gambling, the three had quite a reputation both on and off the battlefield. They were like everyone's naughty younger brothers.

Younger brothers that needed a good spanking now and then.

"Damnation," Maximilian muttered. "Hage is a beast. He is coming just in time for the mass competition and the swords. With his size and strength, he is unbeatable in those events."

Addax grinned. "If we stay together for the mass competition, we may have a chance of victory over him," he said. "But in the swords, one on one, there is no chance. I doubt I will even compete in that."

Maximilian was rolling his eyes miserably but ended up laughing at the thought of a very big, very strong knight, who was more brawn than brains at this point in his life, sweeping through the competition as if they were all untried children.

"We shall see," he said, still pretending as if he had a

chance. "In any case, back to my father. Will you greet him for me?"

Addax's smile faded. "I suppose," he said. "If I must."

"Good," Maximilian said with relief. "Take them into the lists if they arrive in time. They can watch me compete."

"Against de Wolfe?"

"It will make me try harder knowing that my father is watching."

Addax shrugged. He wasn't sure that was a good idea, because de Wolfe was nearly as unbeatable as Addax was in the joust, but he didn't say so. He didn't want to undermine Maximilian's confidence.

"As you wish," he said. Then, hearing shouting over near the arena, he turned in that direction and shielded his eyes from the sun. "It looks as if the guides are close to being repaired. You'd better go and prepare."

Maximilian did, rushing off toward the arena where his horse and lance and men were gathered. That left Addax standing alone, wondering why he'd agreed to greet the Earl of Bretherdale in the first place. The man wasn't going to want to see him. He was going to want to see his son, who didn't seem to have any sense of responsibility when it came to greeting his father. Perhaps letting a friend greet him was Maximilian's way of telling his father just what he thought of the betrothal and the wedding plans. Whatever the case, Addax was stuck.

With a heavy sigh, he headed off to the competitors' encampment.

CHAPTER TWO

WHAT HAVE I gotten myself into?

It wasn't really a question. It was a reflection upon her future, a statement of the existing plane of time upon which she was living. It was a statement to the loss of control of her own life, something she didn't have control of anyway, not really, but something she'd lost along the way to yet one more man.

When she'd been younger, it had been her father. He had controlled everything. Then she had married her husband, and he controlled everything. As a widow, she'd regained some control at the death of her husband, but she had lost it when she agreed to another marriage. She had only agreed to another marriage because she wanted children, but the father of the man she was betrothed to took it as an invitation to dictate her life. As if she needed any help with that. She didn't, but that didn't stop a man with more power than she had from taking control.

His name was Claudius de Grey, the Earl of Bretherdale.

He was seated across the carriage from her even now as the great wagon with the wooden sides braced with iron straps lurched over a road that had seen better days. A couple of the bumps had threatened to launch her right out of her seat and onto Lord Bretherdale, but she'd held fast, at least as much as she could, because the last thing she wanted to do was end up on that man's lap.

He was the very reason why she was here.

"Hmm," he said, looking from the window at what lay ahead. "I see the tournament village now. 'Tis a fine day for competition. I am certain that my son is doing quite well, my lady. You needn't worry. He will make us both proud."

Lady Emmeline de Witt smiled politely. That same pale, polite smile that she'd been giving the man for seven days, the length of time it took for them to travel from her home to Berwick, where Bretherdale's son, a man with the grandiose name of Maximilian, was competing in a tournament circuit. She knew that Maximilian traveled with the tournament circuit, more as a hobby than anything else, and she further knew that his father hadn't seen him in a couple of years.

Now, it was her turn to see him.

To meet him.

She wasn't exactly eager about it.

"You have explained his prowess to me, my lord," she said, trying to mask her boredom on the subject. "I look forward to seeing for myself."

"Of course you do," Bretherdale said. He was a tall man with a hook nose and glorious white hair. He was also thin to the point of having a frail appearance. "All young women love the thrill of tournaments. When I was younger, I competed in them myself. I was quite good, I think."

Her polite smile turned genuine. "Did you win very much?"

He shrugged. "A little," he said, turning his attention to the distant tournament village, which was drawing closer by the second. "My father was not too keen on his heir competing in dangerous sport, so he made me give it up."

"Yet you let your heir compete," Emmeline said. "You do not have the same fears for your son that your father had for you?"

He smiled weakly. "I do," he said. "That is partly why you are here. It is time for him to give up this life of tournaments and return home with his wife. It is time for him to do his duty, and you, my lady, will be the start of it."

Emmeline didn't have anything to say to that, mostly because she could already see how much her new husband was going to resent her. She didn't even know the man, but she didn't have to in order to know how he would feel about all of this. Were she in his position, she knew that she would be quite bitter about it.

Maximilian.

Though Bretherdale lands bordered de Witt lands, she'd never met Maximilian de Grey. She'd only known about the Earl of Bretherdale because her husband had spoken of him in not particularly favorable terms. But, then again, Ernest never spoke favorably about anyone, so Emmeline took anything he said with a grain of salt. *Too ambitious,* Ernest had said, as if he himself had no ambition at all. The truth was that Ernest had not only been ambitious, but he'd been greedy, too. The mines on de Witt land were worked day and night to bring forth the ore that was so in demand throughout the country, and Ernest had no problem setting a premium price for it. He had a big army to protect his lands, even from kings who had coveted them. King John certainly had, and there had been a few skirmishes as a result. But John died and his young son had taken the throne, and they'd not heard a peep from him with regards to the riches on de Witt land.

Yet.

Those riches and that land belonged to Emmeline, but it would soon belong to Bretherdale. He had a decently sized army as well, so perhaps it was fortuitous to have their army for protection as well. She was quite certain that Bretherdale would protect his son's interests to the death, because the man had already made intimations about it on the ride north. He wanted them very badly, and for the price of a marriage, he had them. Emmeline didn't even wonder what the man's son thought, because she was certain he would feel the same. What man wouldn't want to marry into a household that produced the equivalent of more than ten thousand pounds sterling every year? Only a madman wouldn't want it, and Emmeline was the means by which Bretherdale would have it.

She was a commodity, just like the precious metals on de Witt lands.

The thoughts stayed with her as the carriage drew closer to the tournament village. Off to the north, she began to see an encampment, with clusters of colorful tents indicating the individual competing houses. Suddenly, she began to feel a little more interested in their destination—and, in truth, a little nervous. Up until this moment, it had simply been a dreaded task, a moment she wasn't looking forward to, but now that the moment was here, so was her anxiety on the matter.

If Bretherdale noticed her nerves, he didn't say anything. He was too busy yelling at the escort, telling them to look for the blue-and-white-striped tents. He thought he saw them at one point, but it turned out to be someone else, so he ordered the carriage to a halt and climbed out to hunt down his son's encampment on his own.

That left Emmeline alone in the carriage, which she didn't mind in the least. Quite honestly, she was thankful for the reprieve. She'd spent the past several days with Bretherdale right in front of her, with hardly any time to herself except when they'd stopped for the night at a tavern to sleep. That was literally the only time. Therefore, she slumped back in her seat and closed her eyes for a moment, blissful in her aloneness.

But then her eyes popped open.

Bretherdale had gone to find his son, no doubt for an introduction. Emmeline wasn't sure what she looked like after hours of travel that morning on a dusty road, but she could guess. Quickly, she found her small satchel, the one she carried all manner of personal things in, and pulled forth a small mirror made of polished silver. It gave a gloriously true reflection, and she looked at herself critically, realizing she needed to comb her hair. She'd dressed earlier that morning before they left for the tournament, and she had been well groomed at the time, but now she had hair sticking out. She thought she looked rather unkempt.

The braids were quickly undone and the comb came out.

Emmeline combed her hair and re-braided it, wrapping the braid around the back of her head and pinning it down with the big iron pins. Back on went the hairnet of delicate silver netting, and she pinned that down, too. The overall effect was proper for a widowed woman, but Emmeline hated it. She hated pinning her hair up and always had. She loved the feel of her hair down her back, but unfortunately, the proper way for a married woman to wear her hair was up, so up it went.

Next, she used a kerchief and a little of the boiled water in a bladder kept in the carriage and wiped her face, cleaning off the dust. Ernest had liked women who wore cosmetics because he thought they enhanced one's beauty, so she had lip balm and rouge, and even something to line her eyes made from kohl. All things that Ernest had given to her, things he had liked her to wear, so she dabbed the wine-colored lip balm made from tallow on her lips and took the small, fine brush to put a tiny line on the upper lid of each eye, against her eyelashes.

The effect was really quite stunning.

Tucking the cosmetics away, she was prepared to meet her new husband. As prepared as she was ever going to be, anyway. She waited patiently for Claudius to return to the carriage, but the minutes ticked away and he didn't return, so she peered from the window where he had been sitting, spying the hustle and bustle of the tournament encampment.

It was actually rather exciting.

Ernest hadn't been a social man, meaning Emmeline hadn't gotten out much. No great parties, no great events, and certainly no tournaments. Ernest wouldn't hear of it. He liked to keep to himself, and that meant his wife kept to herself also. He didn't even like her having friends to visit, so any relationship she had formed before she married had fallen by the wayside. That was simply the way it had been. Therefore, at the ripe old age of twenty years and six, she was seeing a tournament for only the second time in her life.

The energy around it was palpable.

Because Berwick was by the sea, there was a strong, salty breeze that blew in from the east. Every knight in the encampment had their banners flying high to announce who was in attendance, and those banners were snapping briskly in the sea wind. The area that the encampment was located in had been a meadow at one time, full of flowers and fat green grass, but that had all been trampled in the wake of wagons and horses and men. There must have been some rain at some point over the past couple of days, because there were small puddles of muddy water along the side of the road.

Everything felt damp and cold, but bright with the clear sky.

Emmeline watched the distant encampment for what seemed like hours when, in truth, it was only a few minutes. But it was long enough for her to become restless, so she opened the door to the carriage and climbed out. The road beneath her feet was hard-packed earth, so there was little danger of her getting her slippers or her dress dirty. That emboldened her, and she began to walk along the road, along the edge of the escort who was watching her curiously as she headed to the front. But she didn't go any further, simply watching the competitors' encampment. As she stood there, hands clasped behind her back, she could see someone approaching from off to her right.

A big, broad man wearing the finest and the latest in military garb.

Curious, Emmeline turned her attention to the man as he drew near. He wore a mail coat and a tunic over the top of it that was emblazoned with a red, three-point shield and what looked like a serpent upon it. A black serpent. He was wearing gloves, covering his enormous hands, and enormous boots that came up and over his knees. Once she finished inspecting what he was wearing, her gaze moved to his face.

A most interesting and handsome face.

As he drew closer, she realized that he had long hair. It was long and dark and luxurious from what she could see, but the front of it was sectioned into small braids along his scalp to keep it off his face. There were several rows. He had hair on his face, neatly trimmed around his mouth and against his jawline, but it was his eyes that had her attention. He had arched brows, dark and serious, and as he came onto the road toward her, she could see that his eyes were as dark as a moonless night. Truth be told, there wasn't one thing about the man that wasn't dark and brooding and handsome.

In fact, he took her breath away.

When their eyes met, he came to a halt and bowed politely.

"My lady," he said. "Forgive me my boldness in speaking to you, but I am looking for Lord Bretherdale, and I believe the standard on the carriage belongs to him. Am I incorrect?"

He had an accent she didn't recognize when he spoke, which told her he hadn't been born in England. In fact, the more she looked at him, the more she could see that he was not a product of England in any way other than the clothing he wore and the words he used. He had an otherworldly quality about him that was intriguing and alluring, like a distant star that was shrouded in mystery.

She'd never seen anyone like him.

"You are correct, my lord," she said after a moment. Then she pointed toward the encampment. "He has gone in search of his son, who is a great competitor here today. Mayhap you know him? Sir Maximilian de Grey?"

The man nodded. "I know him well," he said. "In fact, it is he who has sent me to greet his father. Would you be, perchance, Maximilian's betrothed?"

Emmeline nodded. "I am," she said. "Since there is no one to introduce us, I am Lady Emmeline de Witt. Who are you?"

Again, the man bowed politely. "Sir Addax al-Kort, at your service," he said. "My lady, if you would like to return to the carriage, I shall lead your escort to Max's encampment."

Addax al-Kort. Not a Norman or a Saxon name, but something lyrical and unfamiliar. Quickly, she climbed back into the carriage with his polite assistance, and as she claimed her seat, he shut the door. Then he whistled through his teeth very loudly and waved an arm at the escort, who pulled out.

Then he disappeared toward the front.

Emmeline stuck her head out, briefly, to watch him, but she was also watching the commanding presence that he seemed to have. Men were jumping to do his bidding as he took her escort into the encampment, heading for the northern end of it, where there were tents with the blue and white stripes that signaled the House of de Grey. As the carriage pulled around, she could even see Bretherdale there, as he'd found his son's tents.

But no son.

Emmeline could hear him yelling from where she sat.

Addax had gone to Bretherdale to evidently explain why Maximilian wasn't here to greet his father, but that only seemed to calm Bretherdale marginally. He was still quite upset. Addax gestured over toward the tournament arena, and Bretherdale simply took off in that direction. Addax started to follow, but then he remembered about the lady in the carriage. He sent a couple of men to follow Bretherdale to assist the man as he personally went for the carriage and opened the door.

"It seems Lord Bretherdale is quite anxious to see his son," he said as if to explain the old man's bad manners. "In fact, your betrothed has asked me to escort you and his father to the lists, where you can watch him compete. Will you come, my lady?"

Emmeline climbed out of the carriage with Addax's help. "I would like that, my lord," she said. "I've never seen a tournament before. This will be my first."

Addax's dark eyebrows lifted. "Truly?" he said. "You've never seen one?"

"Not one."

Now he frowned. "And you say you are from England?"

"I am."

"And not from the moon?"

Emmeline was starting to pick up on the fact that he was jesting with her, and she grinned. "Not the moon," she said. "Only from England, but I've simply never had the opportunity to attend a tournament. Is that so odd?"

"Possibly," Addax said, his dark eyes glimmering with mirth. He held out an elbow to her. "Max should be doing the honors, but it seems that I am privileged to be the first to introduce you to this brutal and exciting sport as you watch your betrothed compete."

Emmeline took his elbow, feeling rather hot in the cheeks about it. She hadn't been around a man this handsome in a very long time, if ever, and she was feeling the slightest bit giddy. If Addax was this kind and charming, she had the slightest bit of hope that her betrothed might be as well.

"If it is so brutal, why do men do it?" she asked.

Addax snorted softly. "Because men are constantly trying to prove themselves over one another," he said. "Only the strongest survive."

She considered that as they began to head over toward the village that had popped up around the enormous arena. "And you compete to prove yourself?" she said, indicating what he was wearing.

"As much as any man, I suppose," Addax said. "How much do you know about the tournament circuit?"

"Absolutely nothing, my lord."

He gestured to the village. "Then I shall explain," he said. "The tournament circuit follows a schedule of tournaments from all around the country. There are some tournaments that are established year after year, and also some that are added, for example, if a lord decides to hold an event that is open to everyone."

Emmeline picked up the edge of her skirt as they walked over a wet patch of road. "And all tournaments are not open to everyone?"

Addax shook his head. "Some are invitation only," he said. "But the tournament circuit usually allows anyone with the proper credentials to compete."

"What are the proper credentials?"

Addax gestured back at the encampment. "Knights who have been properly trained," he said simply. "Men from good backgrounds, as some tournaments require you to present your letters of patent establishing nobility, while others will simply allow any man with the means and the talent to compete. You do not see that too often, however. Usually, men who follow the tournament circuit, like me, have been doing this a very long time and have an impeccable pedigree."

"And Sir Maximilian has that pedigree?"

"Indeed, he does," Addax said. His gaze lingered on her a moment. "I understand that you have never met him, my lady."

Emmeline shook her head. "Nay," she said. "But I… I am looking forward to the introduction."

She didn't sound very convincing. Even Emmeline didn't think she sounded very convincing. But Addax didn't comment on it one way or the other. Like any good escort, he remained detached but polite. He gestured ahead to the tournament village and the smells from the cooking stalls.

"Would you like refreshments before you watch the bout?" he asked. "I believe there is time to find you something to your liking."

Emmeline could see the stalls where vendors were selling all manner of goods. "I've not eaten since before dawn," she admitted. "If it is not too much trouble, I could use something to drink."

"Then we shall find you something to drink."

"*And* eat."

He grinned at her. "And eat," he said. "I saw a man selling coffins with meat and gravy. Does that sound tempting?"

Emmeline nodded eagerly. "Aye," she said. "I have money to pay for it."

He looked at her as if gravely insulted. "You will do no such thing," he said. "It would be my pleasure to provide you with whatever you wish."

She didn't fight him on it because he seemed quite firm. "Thank you for taking the trouble, my lord," she said gratefully. "You are most kind to do so."

Addax had hold of her as they headed into the crowds around the vendor stalls. "Max is a dear friend of mine, my lady," he said. "I consider it an honor to tend to his betrothed in his stead. He asked me to because he wanted to ensure you were shown all due respect."

That brightened Emmeline. She smiled at Addax, displaying big dimples in each cheek. "That is very kind," she said. "And I am happy to have made your acquaintance, my lord."

"And yours, my lady."

Off to the left, the coffin vendor was calling, and on behalf of a famished lady, Addax answered.

CHAPTER THREE

*G*OD'S *B*ONES, *SHE'S a beauty.*

That was the first thing Addax thought when he laid eyes upon Lady Emmeline de Witt. Standing outside of the brightly painted de Grey carriage, he assumed it had to be the woman he was looking for, but even as he drew closer to her and could see her features, he was pleasantly surprised. Maximilian had made it sound as if Lady de Witt was an old and dried-up hag, but this lady was no hag.

Far from it.

In fact, the more he looked at her, the more beautiful she became. She wasn't a very young woman, to be sure. She had seen more than twenty years easily. If he had to guess, he would say around twenty and five or more, but it wasn't because she looked old. It was simply because she was a beautiful young woman who had grown into herself. She had an ageless beauty that could only be achieved with maturity. She had dark blonde hair, beautifully dressed, and eyes that were a pale shade of brown with a hint of red. They were truly stunning. But given the traveling he'd done in his life, he'd seen women adorned with cosmetics, and he could see that she wore cosmetics on her lips and eyes, which made her look like a goddess.

He suspected Maximilian might change his mind about marriage after he met her.

After procuring two meat pies, or coffins, that were filled with gravy and meat, and then purchasing two big cups of ale cut with fruit juice, he found a place for he and the lady to sit at a table under the branches of a big yew tree. Other people were sitting there, enjoying their food from various vendors, as a man wandered through the tables trying to sell necklaces made from shells from the beaches of Berwick. When he came near Addax, he was chased away as Addax sat down to a feast.

While Addax used his hands and teeth to sheer off big bites of the coffin, Emmeline wasn't quite so unmannerly about it. When Addax realized that she wasn't going to simply shove it into her mouth like he was, he quickly went to find her a wooden spoon, which she was grateful for. That made it easier, and neater, for her to eat, and she indulged heartily as Addax plowed through the rest of his coffin.

"Has your trip been pleasant so far, my lady?" he asked simply to make conversation.

She nodded as she swallowed the bite in her mouth. "The weather has been good," she answered. "There has been no trouble."

She didn't seem inclined to say more, so Addax took the lead in the conversation. "Max mentioned that your husband was Ernest de Witt," he said. "Though I did not know him, please accept my condolences on his passing."

"Thank you, my lord."

"Were you married a long time?"

It was a question he already knew the answer to, but he was simply trying to keep the conversation going out of politeness.

Emmeline nodded to his question.

"Ten years," she said. "Our home is Alston Castle."

"In the Pennines, I am told?"

"Aye, my lord."

"Where were you born?"

She put another bite in her mouth, chewing a moment before answering. "Exelby Castle," she said. "Do you know of it?"

"I've heard of it."

"My father is Mortimer de Geld, Lord Leeming," she said. "Now, may I ask you a question?"

"Of course."

"Where were *you* born?"

He looked at her, grinning. "What makes you think I was not born in London or Liverpool or even Edinburgh?"

"Were you?"

"Nay."

She smiled in return, displaying those big dimples. "If you do not wish to tell me, you do not have to," she said. "I was simply curious."

"I was born in a land very far away."

"Yet you make your life in England?"

"I do."

"And do you like it here?"

He nodded. "Very much," he said. "I have been here for many years and have made excellent friends. My brother is here with me, also."

She had stopped eating, simply listening to him and the accent in his speech. He had a deep voice and an articulate way of speaking. "I've not heard anyone speak like you," she said. "It is very melodic."

He guffawed. "I've never had anyone tell me that," he said, popping the last few crumbs of the coffin into his mouth. "I was born in a land of great deserts and great mountains and a great river. It would take you years to travel to it because it is so far away."

Emmeline's eyes reflected her fascination at the description. "How marvelous," she said. "What language do they speak there?"

"It has a few names," he said. "Zatan or Urdu. It is the language of my land."

"Do you remember how to speak it?"

He chuckled. "Of course," he said. "Because of the travels I did when I was younger, I learned to speak other languages, too. When living in a distant land, like I am in England, it is important to speak the language of the country out of respect. And in my case, it is also because no one here speaks Zatan."

From her expression, it was clear that she was fascinated by his background. "I've never met anyone who was from anywhere other than England."

"There is a very big world beyond England's borders."

"You have given me a glimpse of that," she said. "Thank you for telling me. Mayhap you will tell me more sometime, if it is not inconvenient."

He smiled at her, appreciating her genuine curiosity at his origins. He had learned to be careful when telling people where he was from, because he'd had varied reactions over the years. Some thought he was lying about it, some thought he was beneath them because he wasn't born in England, but some—like the lady—were genuinely interested without prejudice. At least, he didn't sense any, but there had been times when prejudice against his origins had been obvious. He was pleased that it didn't seem to bother the lady.

"I am certain it will not be inconvenient," he said. "But you must make sure that Max does not mind. He is to be your husband, after all."

Her brow furrowed slightly. "He would not wish for me to speak with you?"

Addax shook his head. "I did not mean it like that," he said. "I simply meant that I am certain he will want you to himself now that you have arrived. I do not wish to impose on his time. I suspect the two of you have much to discuss."

Emmeline understood. She was about to say so when the sound of a distant horn caught her attention. It caught Addax's, too, because he was on his feet before the horn finished sounding.

"Come, my lady," he said. "The bout is about to begin, and you do not want to miss it."

Emmeline bolted to her feet, taking a last big gulp of the watered ale before quickly rushing to Addax's side.

"Nay, I do not," she said. "You are very kind to be my escort, my lord. I realize that Sir Maximilian asked you to assume the role, but you are still kind to do it. You could have refused."

Addax cocked a dark eyebrow as he extended his elbow to her. "No one refuses Max," he muttered. "You will learn that, my lady. You will learn."

He seemed to be jesting for the most part, but there was some seriousness to it. Since Emmeline didn't know Maximilian, she felt some trepidation at his comment, but she didn't say anything. They were headed to the tournament field, and soon enough, she would see the man she was soon to marry.

You will learn, he'd said.

She had a suspicion that she was about to.

CB

MAXIMILIAN HAD JUST spent ten minutes listening to his father shout at him.

"You knew when you came here that I was competing in the tournament," he shouted in return. "You did not ask if this would be convenient for me. You simply came and expected me to be available to cater to your every whim. Well, I cannot. I *will* not. I am preparing for my bout, so we can fight about this later."

He was bustling about, adjusting armor and his stirrups, as his father followed along behind him.

"You could not even greet us?" he scolded. "Instead, we are met by Addax? I like the man, but that was a shameful thing to do to your future wife."

Maximilian whirled on his father, his features tense with anger. "Go into the lists and watch my bout," he said, jabbing a finger toward the arena. "Go and watch. We will speak when I am finished."

Claudius was furious. He moved closer to his son and lowered his voice so Maximilian's men wouldn't hear him.

"When you are finished, we are going straight to the nearest church, and you *will* marry Lady de Witt," he muttered. "I am tired of waiting for you to do your duty, so you will do it now so that I may witness it. I've come all this way on a journey my physic advised me against taking, but I am here and you will marry. Do you understand me?"

Maximilian almost brushed him off, but something his father said caught his attention. "Your physic advised you not to come?" he said. "Why?"

Claudius was still angry and perhaps not as restrained as he should have been. "Something I am certain you will care nothing about," he said. "But if you are curious, then I will tell you that the physic believes I am suffering from a weakness of the heart. I would like to see you wed before I die."

Maximilian looked at his father with an expression close to concern, but he couldn't quite manage it. After a moment, he shook his head.

"You once told me when I was younger than you had an ailment that was going to kill you, so I should behave well to honor you," he said. "Do you remember telling me that? Then I came back from fostering because you said that you had been poisoned and were on your deathbed. I spent a month sitting beside your bed while you recovered from bad food."

Claudius lost some of his rage, but not all of it. He had a flair for the dramatics that Maximilian was well aware of, but he would not acknowledge that. "All things that were true at the time," he said quietly. "I sincerely believed that I was dying. But my heart... It *is* weakening, Max, whether or not you choose to believe it."

Maximilian didn't have time for his father's histrionics. He simply grunted and turned back to his steed, mounting the animal as he prepared to move out. The field marshals were waving him over, so without another word, he spurred his horse toward the field, leaving his father behind. Disgusted at his stubborn son but also feeling uncertain due to the man's disbelief over the heart revelation, Claudius headed toward the lists.

Maximilian was well aware that he'd been rude to his father. He didn't much care. He knew the man had come to see him married, and, knowing it was something Maximilian had no interest in doing, he'd made up another lie about his health. As

Maximilian had pointed out, it wasn't the first time Claudius had done that to create leverage in a situation.

Maximilian didn't know whether to believe him or not.

But this time, his father had brought someone with him who was directly involved in the situation. Someone meant to force Maximilian into submission. The widow was here, and she was with Addax, more than likely already in the lists. He didn't have any real interest in seeing her, but on second thought, perhaps he needed to simply so he could be prepared when they were introduced. He donned his helm at the mouth of the arena but didn't lower the visor because he was looking at the lists. He was looking for Addax.

The man wasn't difficult to find. Then he spied the woman sitting beside him.

A young, beautiful woman.

Maximilian was peering so closely at her that he almost missed the start of his bout.

CB

"SEE THE GREEN shield on that tunic?" Addax said, pointing to de Wolfe as he took up position on the west side of the arena. "The knight is William de Wolfe, and he serves the Earl of Teviot, so he is wearing Teviot's standard. They call him the Wolfe, not simply because it is his name, but because he is as cunning and deadly as a wolf."

Emmeline was listening to him intently, looking at the man he was pointing at. A very big man with a big lance, seated upon a big horse as the chaos of the tournament field went on around them.

"He seems quite fearsome," she said.

"He is," Addax said, turning to the eastern side of the arena, where Maximilian was making an appearance. "And that knight is your betrothed, Maximilian. With the blue-and-white shield."

Emmeline's head snapped in that direction. She could see a knight astride a fat horse, with several servants and squires following him.

So that's him, she thought to herself.

Her apprehension returned.

As Emmeline watched, a few of Maximilian's men broke away and headed toward the lists, yelling to the crowd and demanding they give encouragement to their liege. The crowd responded by howling, like dogs, and when de Wolfe lifted a hand to acknowledge them, they went mad and cheered. Emmeline looked around curiously at the people around her, some of them bearing small banners with the same colors de Wolfe was wearing.

"What are they saying?" she asked Addax.

He glanced over his shoulder as well, watching the crowd in their excitement. "Since de Wolfe is called the Wolfe, they are howling like wolves," he said. "Evidently, they have already chosen him as their champion of this bout."

She looked at him. "Do they do that for every favorite competitor?"

He shrugged. "Mostly."

"Do they do it for you?"

He nodded. "Every time I compete," he said without a hint of boasting. It was fact. "You see, every competitor has a moniker, something that makes them more appealing to the crowd."

"Why is that?"

He glanced at her, grinning. "Would you cheer for a man named John de Vere with the same enthusiasm you would cheer a man called the Wolfe or the Bringer of Nightmares?" he asked. "People come to the tournament to give them a taste of something beyond their daily lives, my lady. They come to see glory and greatness and excitement not easily found. Giving a knight a nickname is to make him something fabled and immortal, don't you think?"

She nodded. "I do," she said. "What do they call you?"

"The Black Dragon."

Emmeline smiled. "I like that," she said. "It sounds very mythical and strong."

"Thank you, my lady."

"What do they call my betrothed?"

Addax's gaze moved over to Maximilian, who was undoubtedly upset that the crowd's favor had gone to de Wolfe. "Your betrothed is known as the King of Chaos," he said. "We have other competitors known as the Curse, Hades' Wrath, and the like. My brother is known as the God of Vengeance. Those sound more exciting than boring Christian names, don't they?"

Emmeline nodded with some enthusiasm. "They do," she said. "It sounds to me that the tournament is more than simply a man proving his prowess."

He looked at her. "What do you mean?"

She shrugged, watching Maximilian as he prepared to take his lance. "It is about entertainment, too."

He grinned. "Very astute," he said. "It very much is about entertainment. The more you entertain, the more people will return and spend their money. And the bigger the purses become."

"Then this is a financial endeavor."

His gaze lingered on her for a moment. "You know something of business, my lady?"

Emmeline smiled weakly. "Given what my husband's family has done for generations, I have helped my husband manage the mining operations on our lands," she said. "He taught me how to determine how much product is mined and how much it should be sold for, so I do know something about making money."

Addax smiled in return. "Impressive," he said. "To address your statement, aye, this is a financial endeavor for many of us. There is much money to be made, and men who cannot make their fortune any other way compete for just that purpose—to earn a fortune."

"Including you?"

"Including me."

"And has it been successful?"

His smile grew. "Verily," he said. "Now, let us see how successful it will be for Max."

That bout was finally ready to begin. On the field, the marshals were moving away from the guides, and someone dropped a big yellow flag. Suddenly, the horses were charging toward one another and the crowd were on their feet. Because they were on their feet, Addax and Emmeline were forced to stand. The roar of the crowd grew to a crescendo as the lances were lowered. The knights drew closer, and there was a deafening crash as de Wolfe's lance made contact with Maximilian's left arm and shoulder. Splinters from a broken lance went flying, and Maximilian was booted off his horse, flipping over the back of it and ending up laid out in the dirt on his stomach.

The spectators went wild.

"Damnation!"

Emmeline and Addax heard the curse, turning to see that Claudius had come up behind them just in time to see his son splayed out in the dust. Before Emmeline could greet the man, he reached out and grabbed her by the arm.

"Come with me," he said. "Come along, now. Get moving."

Emmeline was trying, but she was standing on the hem of her dress. Addax was trying to help her follow Claudius, who was tugging on her enough to pull her off balance. Addax was forced to steady her, following the woman and Claudius from the lists as the man mumbled angrily to himself.

Addax wasn't sure why he was following, only that he didn't like the way Claudius was behaving. The man was furious, clearly at Maximilian, but he was taking it out on Emmeline, who was doing her best to be obedient. He followed the pair out of the lists, into the street that surrounded the arena, and back into the area where the competitors were. Just as they arrived, Maximilian was coming in from the arena under his own power, but his men walked on either side of him, making sure he wouldn't fall. Addax headed toward him, intercepting him before his father could get to him.

"Are you well?" he asked. "Did you break anything?"

Maximilian was pale. "I am well," he said gloomily. "I just had the wind knocked out of me, but nothing is broken."

"That is good."

"De Wolfe cheated!"

Addax shook his head. "He did not," he said. "I was in the lists, Max. I saw the run, and it was clean."

Not having Addax's support in such an accusation shut Maximilian down fairly quickly, but he was still shaken and embarrassed.

"I could not see well through my visor," he said, shifting tactics because *he* certainly wasn't going to take responsibility for his failure. "But I *could* see the lady in the stands with you, and it was very distracting. You should not have put her in my line of sight."

Addax lifted an eyebrow. "Aye, she was there," he said sarcastically. "Her and hundreds of other people screaming and waving their hands, so you cannot single her out as the sole distraction. Accept it, Max—you were simply bested. It has happened to all of us."

That was true, but Maximilian didn't want to hear it. Upset that Addax wasn't supporting his complaints, he spied his father as the man headed in his direction, dragging the lady with him. Before Claudius could say a word, Maximilian pointed a finger at him.

"Had you not come to harass me right before my bout, I would not have been unseated," he said angrily. "This is *your* fault."

Claudius frowned. "*My* fault?" he repeated, aghast. "You have been on the tournament circuit for years, and the best you can do is fall flat on your face on the first run? I am ashamed of you."

"Good," Maximilian said dramatically. "I am glad you are ashamed. Mayhap you'll go home now, and take that woman with you. I never wanted you here in the first place."

He was looking straight at Emmeline, who realized that she had been caught in the midst of two angry men. When she saw Maximilian looking at her, she quickly curtsied and averted her gaze. She didn't say a word, but Claudius had much to say.

"Still your tongue, boy," he hissed. "You were raised better than that. Lady de Witt has come at my invitation, and you will show her all due respect. Now, greet her properly or you'll not like my reaction."

Maximilian knew he'd been rude, but he was so angry at his

father that he didn't care. He removed his gauntlets, a wry smile creasing his lips.

"Is that so?" he said. Then he slapped his gloves onto his saddle and faced Emmeline. "My lady, I am sorry you have come. I truly am. I did not ask my father to come, but he has pulled you into his scheme, and if I have offended you, then I am sorry. You have not exactly caught me at my best."

It was an apology. Sort of. Addax, who had been watching the scene carefully, came to stand next to Maximilian.

"Lady de Witt has never been to a tournament, Max, so rest assured that she probably does not know that falling from your horse is a sign of failure," he said. "I have been explaining things to her, and she is quite eager to learn. Mayhap you would be willing to teach her, since you are so well versed in the rules of a tournament."

He was looking at Emmeline, silently encouraging her to agree with him, but it took her a moment to catch on.

"I found it all quite exciting, my lord," she said to Maximilian. "I thought you looked splendid astride your horse. A Spanish jennet, is it not?"

Maximilian was prepared to brush her off, but her recognition of horseflesh had him give her a second look. "Aye," he said. "He is a jennet. Do you know much about horses, my lady?"

Emmeline nodded. "I have several," she said. "Do you only ride one horse when you compete, or do you ride different horses for different events?"

She was focused on him in a positive way, and it seemed to calm him down quickly. He forgot about his enraged father and went to her, looking her over as if only just seeing her for the first time.

"It depends," he said. "If the field conditions are bad, then I have heavier-boned horses that I will ride because their legs are stronger. But if it is dusty and dry, the jennet is an excellent choice."

"Do you train them yourself, then?"

Maximilian nodded. "Mostly," he said. "My lady, would you like to accompany me to the village? I've not eaten all morning."

Even though Emmeline had already stuffed herself, she nodded. "With pleasure, my lord."

Maximilian extended an elbow to her, and they began to head off toward the village, with Emmeline talking about horses as they lost themselves in the crowd. Addax watched them go, breathing a sigh of relief, before looking to Claudius. The man was also watching them go, probably with the same relief that Addax was feeling.

"She has a good way about her," Addax said to him. "I think she and Max will get along well enough."

Claudius scratched his cheek. "They'd better," he muttered. Then he looked at Addax. "You have been a gracious host today, even if my son has not."

Addax dipped his head in thanks. "My pleasure, my lord," he said. "If I can be of further service, you need only ask."

Claudius considered that statement. "I do have something more for you," he said. "Are you familiar with Berwick?"

Addax nodded. "I am, my lord."

"Do you know St. Andrews?"

Addax turned to point northeasterly, toward the town. "I do, my lord," he said. "You can see the bell tower from here."

"A grand cathedral," Claudius said. "I've visited it several times. When do you compete next, Addax?"

Addax glanced over at the arena as they prepared for another bout. "This afternoon at some point," he said. "They've not yet announced the schedule."

Claudius took a few steps in his direction, putting a hand on Addax's broad shoulder. "When they do and you know for sure, come and see me," he said. "I am afraid I will need your help with Max."

"What help, my lord?"

"I will take the lady to the church. You will bring Max."

When Addax realized what he meant, he couldn't help the sigh that escaped his lips. "My lord, I am afraid that is asking a good deal of me," he said. "I know how Max feels about this marriage. It should be you bringing him to the church."

"I will have the lady."

"You are the only one who can force him to comply, my lord. I cannot force him."

He had a point. Thwarted in his plan to force Addax to handle Maximilian, Claudius had to concede.

"Very well," he said. "You can take the lady. Come and see me when the schedule is announced, and we shall have a wedding before you ride again."

With that, he headed off in the direction of the village to ensure that his son was behaving himself with his betrothed, but all Addax could think of was the fact that this was a bad situation for all concerned. Maximilian didn't want to marry, Claudius was determined that he should, and poor Emmeline was caught in the middle. Poor, sweet, beautiful Emmeline.

Addax couldn't help but feel sorry for the lady.

She didn't deserve what Maximilian was going to undoubtedly dish out.

CHAPTER FOUR

*A*LREADY, *I CAN see he's unpleasant.*

That was because the man seated across from Emmeline, the one she was to marry, seemingly had no sense of decorum. He'd asked such a blunt question that she wasn't sure she heard it correctly.

She asked him to repeat it.

"How old *are* you?"

There it was again, that tasteless demand, and she couldn't avoid answering it. "I have seen twenty years and six, my lord," she said steadily. "And you?"

Maximilian had a coffin in one hand and a cup of strong ale in the other. "Older than you are," he said before he swigged the ale. "Are you are truly that old and have never had children?"

"Nay, my lord."

"Why not?"

"Because God has not seen fit to bless me."

Maximilian wasn't sure what that meant. He took a big bite of his coffin, and gravy dripped out on his chin. "You *did* have relations with your husband, didn't you?" he said. "Or did you ban him from your bed because he was so old? Is that why there were no children?"

Emmeline's patience was becoming increasingly thin at his line of questioning. "I cannot tell you why there were not any children, only that we had none," she said. "Is there anything else you would like to know that I can tell you? Mayhap you would like to know about the mining operations on our lands?"

He swallowed the bite in his mouth. "I have no interest in those," he said. "As long as they continue to produce and my coffers continue to fill, that is all I care about. In fact, you should know how this marriage is going to work, my lady."

Emmeline cocked her head curiously. "Work, my lord?"

He nodded as he took another bite. "Understand that I have no interest in being married," he said. "This is all my father's idea. He wants the Bretherdale lands to join with the de Witt lands because it will make for a grand empire for me, but in order to do this, I must marry. Do you understand so far?"

"I understand."

"And you understand that I did not ask for you."

"Again, I understand."

He eyed her. "Then you know I am only doing this to please my father," he said. "It's not as if I have a choice in the matter, so I must make the best of it, I suppose."

Emmeline was quickly coming to see Maximilian de Grey for what he was—petty, selfish, apathetic, and rude. Her hope for a husband with the polite qualities that Addax had was gone. The man in front of her didn't care a thing about her or their impending marriage. Now she was faced with the very thing she'd feared—a man who didn't want her and didn't care if she knew it.

"As I have said repeatedly, I understand the situation completely," she said, unwilling to be submissive to a man who didn't care for her feelings. She'd already had one marriage like that, and was beyond frustrated that she was to have another. "Since we are being honest with one another, this marriage wasn't my idea, either. Your father came to me. He courted me with promises of a countess title. You see, my lord, Ernest de Witt had no interest in a wife. That is why we had no children, so my interest in this marriage is to, indeed, bear children. I want them. Beyond that, and the usual trappings of marriage, I expect nothing. Just so we are both clear on our expectations."

Maximilian stared at her, surprised by such a bold statement. Then he broke out in a weak grin. "Honesty," he said. "How refreshing. Since you are being honest, I will be also. You are too old for me, my lady. I like my women younger. I also like them with blonde hair, as opposed to whatever color you seem to have. And I like blue eyes. In short, I like my women looking pale and angelic, but you are pretty enough, so I suppose that is something. I will give you children, and you will give me an heir, but that is where it ends. This is a business arrangement and nothing more. Are we agreed?"

With each successive word that came out of his mouth, Emmeline hated this more. She'd taken a stand to rebut his callousness, and now she found herself wishing she hadn't. He'd taken her statement and added to it, expecting their marriage to be in name only. She'd already had that. Everything Maximilian wanted, she'd already had with Ernest. But neither one of them could back out. That same question she'd asked herself numerous times before this moment came back to haunt her.

What have I gotten myself in to?

It was a sickening realization.

"I hope we can at least be civil to one another," she said stiffly.

He nodded. "I don't see why not," he said. "As long as you do not interfere in my business or shame me in any way, I will be quite civil and generous to you."

"As you wish, my lord."

He smiled brightly. "Excellent," he said. "Mayhap this will not be so terrible after all."

She smiled thinly. "One can hope."

He chuckled, pushing his cup of ale toward her. "Let us drink to that, my lady," he said. "Or may I call you Emmeline? It is my right, you know."

She simply nodded as she took the cup and drank deeply. She needed it. Just as she drained the cup, Claudius walked up.

"There you are," he said. "I've been looking for you both."

Maximilian was still beaming. "Here we are," he said. "Papa, I think everything will work out as you hoped. The lady and I have come to an arrangement that I believe will make us all happy."

That wasn't the news that Claudius had been expecting. "Oh?" he said, surprised as he looked between his son and Emmeline. "Then… then this is agreeable for you both?"

Maximilian answered before Emmeline could. "It is," he said, taking the cup back from Emmeline and realizing it was empty. "The lady and I have come to an agreement. You may put your mind at ease."

Claudius couldn't believe what he was hearing. He looked at Emmeline. "Is this true, my lady?"

Emmeline felt defeated. Worn out and defeated. She'd waited two years to discover she was going to have exactly the same marriage she'd had before, and the realization was almost more than she could bear. Looking into Claudius' hopeful face made her want to cry.

"As he says, my lord," she said, averting her gaze.

Claudius stared at her for a moment longer before breaking out into a broad smile. "I cannot tell you how pleased I am to hear this," he said. "Truthfully, I thought I would be fighting with Max all the way to the church, but if there are no objections, then let us proceed to St. Andrews and have the priests perform a mass. Let us seal this marriage and be done with it. What a great day this shall be!"

Emmeline didn't think she had any great days ahead of her now. The fact that Claudius called this a great day was from his perspective, not from hers.

For her, it was a sentence to eternal misery.

ॐ

"HE IS BEING married *now*?"

Addax nodded. "Now."

Cole's eyebrows lifted. "Is this to the de Witt widow?"

Addax looked at him in surprise. "How did you know that?"

"Because I saw Claudius de Grey."

Addax waggled his brows. "Ah," he said. "Max only told me today. It seems that he has been betrothed for at least two years to a very wealthy widow."

He was standing next to the pen that the smithies used for the horses they were shoeing, as he'd just brought his steed over because he thought one of the animal's shoes was loose. Essien had come with him, but Cole found them as he headed back to the castle to collect his wife, who wanted to see the more advanced rounds of the joust. Now, it was Cole, Essien, and Addax standing at the rail of the pen, discussing Maximilian's impending marriage.

"Aye, I know about her wealth," Cole said. "But I did not

know the marriage was today."

"Nor did Max until his father sent word," Addax said. "It seems that Bretherdale brought the lady with him. He's not taking any chances on Max trying to back out of this betrothal."

"He's forcing it on him, is he?"

"Very much so."

Cole fell silent a moment, watching one of the smithies come to collect a horse. When the man led a bay stallion away, Cole returned his attention to Addax.

"I was just returning to the castle to collect Cori because she wants to see the champions compete this afternoon, but I will ask her if we may feast tonight to celebrate Max's marriage," he said. "Do you think he would like that?"

Addax nodded. "Anything to do with drink and food will please him," he said. "I am certain that his father will appreciate your generosity."

"Good," Cole said. "Then I will discuss it with my wife when I return. But before I go, there is something I must discuss with you, Addax. Es, you will hear this, because it may involve you at some point."

Essien had been inside the pen, looking at a black warm-blood that a knight had turned over in payment for a debt he owed one of the smithies. "I suspect this has something to do with a mission," he said, bending over to look at the horse's right fetlock. "When you have that tone in your voice, it usually does."

Cole leaned against the railing. "You are a prophet," he said, but returned his attention to Addax. "You have not been called into service for at least two years."

Addax's dark eyes were steady on him. "You know the situation," he said. "I spent time in the Earl of Hereford's ranks and, as of a little over two years ago, was his garrison commander at Wigmore Castle. But then there was the incident involving your youngest brother on the tournament circuit."

Cole held up a hand to silence him. "I know," he said. "You did what you were asked to do. You remained in the circuit, watching Cassian until he surrendered his position on the circuit and married Hereford's daughter."

"He really didn't need my guidance."

"I felt otherwise at the time. And so did Hereford."

"How is your brother, by the way?"

Cole shrugged. "At Pelinom Castle, our family's seat," he said. "With me at Berwick, Cassian has taken command of Pelinom, and Julian remains at Felkington Castle."

"That is his wife's family home, correct?"

"Correct," Cole said. "But the point is that you did me a great favor by shadowing Cassian on the tournament circuit until he could give up his wandering ways and marry Hereford's daughter and return to Pelinom. That is why I advocated for you to Hereford when you wanted to remain on the circuit. In my mind, you had earned the right to do what you wanted to do. It was your time, Addax. I hope it was productive."

Addax nodded. "It was," he said. "It continues to be, but much like Es, I am suspicious of this conversation. What do you want me to do, Cole?"

Cole smiled thinly. "Not me," he said. "This directive comes from Hereford himself, Christopher de Lohr. You know he is mostly in command of the Executioner Knights these days, a group you and I are still very much a part of."

The Executioner Knights.

The greatest group of spies, assassins, and agents that the world had ever seen, an organization started by William

Marshal, Earl of Pembroke, back in the days when Henry II was battling against everyone, including his sons. The goal of the Executioner Knights was always to protect the reigning king, even from family members who would be happier with the king in a grave, and that was a goal that had never changed. It had been particularly challenging when John was king, because he was at war with the entire world, and there wasn't one agent in William Marshal's arsenal, William included, that had a fondness for him.

But… he was the king.

And they had saved him, time and time again.

Now, John's young son, Henry, sat upon the throne, and Henry was far less contentious than his father had been. It made the duties of the Executioner Knights somewhat easier, and William Marshal had been at young Henry's side until his death about six years earlier. After that, his son, also William Marshal, took the helm of the Executioner Knights, but with the death of his father, he had all he could handle protecting his own lands and interests, especially in Ireland, so the command of the Executioner Knights had fallen to the Earl of Hereford and Worcester, Christopher de Lohr, and his eldest son, Peter.

Men who were at the core of England's politics.

Christopher de Lohr had a special place in Addax's heart. Had it not been for Christopher, neither Addax nor Essien would have made it out of the Holy Land alive. It had been Christopher who had come upon them in that olive grove all those years ago and taken pity on two small, starving boys. Christopher, his brother David, and their men had taken the two young children under their wing, nurturing them back to health.

That had been the beginning of Addax's life.

He would never forget the kindness of a man who didn't have to show him any kindness at all. Christopher had been an important man, serving his king, but the compassion he'd shown two small children had been exemplary. When Addax had been a child serving the merchant who abused him and his brother, he remembered hearing unflattering things about the Christian knights who had come to the Levant to purge the Muslim infidels. He had heard of their evils and their unsavory goals. Perhaps some men had felt that way, but Addax never had, and he never would. He looked at those Christian knights as his saviors, and they were.

Nurturing two small children back to health had only been the beginning.

Once Addax and his brother had regained their health, the knights put them to work, but not in a brutal sense. They were given chores and tasks to complete. They drew water, washed horses, cleaned shoes or clothing or swords, or anything else the English wanted them to clean. They brought food and ran messages and did anything that they were told, and the trade-off for their hard work was that the knights taught them how to read and write. Eventually, the knights taught them how to use the sword and how to fight, how to ride horses and fight on horseback. They'd started them on the road to the life they had today, and that was why Addax would do anything for Christopher de Lohr.

All the man had to do was ask.

"What does de Lohr want?" Addax asked after a moment.

Cole faced him. "You wanted to know how I knew about Max's betrothed?" he muttered. "Because our spies in Scotland tell us that Alexander himself, the King of Scotland, is eyeing the de Witt deposits for their own use. They have been in communication with Bretherdale, who wants those lands so he can sell the lead to the Scots. They can extract silver and other metals from it to make weapons."

Addax frowned. "Is *that* why Bretherdale has been pushing this betrothal?"

Cole nodded. "Exactly," he said. "We believe this all has to do with Berwick. You know the Scots want it back, and the lead that Bretherdale sells them would give them the resources they need to outfit an army. It was just rumors, really, but when I heard Bretherdale was here, it led me to believe that the Scots are closer to this goal than we thought."

Addax was looking at him with great trepidation. "I am certain Max does not know of this," he said. "Not to insult my friend, but he simply isn't that astute, nor does he care about politics. You've never seen a more reluctant man to marry."

Cole nodded. "He has never been implicated," he said. "Only his father."

"But the lady must not know, either. She wasn't exactly thrilled at the marriage either."

"This is all Bretherdale," Cole said. "The Scots have offered a handsome price, plus lands in Scotland."

Addax could hardly believe it. "So he forces the marriage, gains control of the mining operations, and sells the product to Scotland so they can take Berwick?" he said incredulously. "Berwick is *your* seat, Cole."

"I know, but you and I both know it has been contested for generations. It just happens to be mine at the moment."

"Then what do you want from me?"

Cole scratched his head in thought. "Max is going to return to the de Witt lands at some point," he said. "Do you know of his plans?"

Addax shook his head. "I do not," he said. "I can find out."

"Carefully," Cole warned. "But I would be more interested in Bretherdale's plans. Is he returning home immediately after this marriage? If so, he returns with the legal right to make decisions over his son's lands. He could do nothing while they did not belong to his family, but he certainly can now."

"Then the feast tonight is a perfect setting for me to sit with Bretherdale, congratulate him on his son's wedding, and discuss his future plans without him becoming suspicious," Addax said. "And I shall find out what Max intends."

"I will," Essien said. He'd been listening to the entire conversation. "It might look suspicious if you go from father to son, discussing future plans, Addax. Let me work on Max, and you can work on the father."

Addax nodded. "Very well," he said. "I'll see what I can get out of Bretherdale."

Cole was in agreement, but he wasn't finished on the subject. "Addax, would you be opposed to returning home with Bretherdale?" he said. "If he plans to sell to the Scots, then we must know before he does it."

Addax shrugged. "I am not opposed, but we would have to think of a plausible reason why I must go with him."

"Fair enough," Cole said. "Let us see how the evening goes, and we will speak tomorrow morning."

They began to hear the horns from the tournament field again, catching Addax's attention. "I have not seen the schedule for this afternoon's bouts," he said, changing the subject. "Es, will you see to my horse? Have the smithy check that shoe immediately. I will go to the field and see where my bout falls."

"And I must collect my wife," Cole said, heading for his horse. "She would never forgive me if she missed Addax's run."

Addax was already moving away. "I may ask for a favor from the lovely Corisande, Cole," he said. "Do not be jealous."

Cole made a face at him as he mounted his steed. "Arrogant whelp," he said. "What makes you think she would give you one?"

Addax laughed. "I cannot ask an unmarried woman," he said as he headed down the road, walking backward to speak to Cole. "She will expect a marriage proposal. I can only ask married women, so your wife is to be favored. By me."

Cole waved him off as he turned for the road that led to the castle, leaving Addax laughing as he headed toward the field. But the laughter, the jesting, was only a disguise for the serious situation they'd just discussed. Bretherdale had forced Max to marry so he could sell the de Witt metals to the Scots.

Damn, if that wasn't an ambitious plan.

And one that could very easily blow the north wide open if the Scots took Berwick.

Addax the secret agent was going back on the job.

CHAPTER FIVE

Berwick Castle

*F*INALLY, I HAVE *what I need.*

That was what Claudius was thinking. All of the bargaining and arguing and patience would finally come to fruition now that Maximilian had married Lady de Witt. Or, more appropriately, Lady de Grey. Along with her came her dead husband's mines.

And Claudius was going to get rich off them.

He had what he wanted.

Of course, he'd never let on about it, and most especially not to his son. Maximilian would want a cut of his father's hard-earned bargain. He'd raised a greedy son, hence the need for the tournament competition with its big purses, but Claudius had earned this money on his own. All Maximilian had to do was marry the de Witt widow and everything was set in place.

There was certainly no hard work in that.

Truth be told, Claudius could have married her himself. He'd considered it, but what he'd told his son was true—the physic told him that his heart was weakening, and once he passed away, he would have a widow who held both an earldom and the very wealthy de Witt lands. Although Maximilian would inherit the earldom, he probably would not want to marry his father's widow, which would put the de Witt lands in jeopardy if she married somebody else. Therefore, it simply made sense to him for Maximilian to marry Lady Emmeline from the start.

Just as he had planned.

Soon, the Scots would know, too.

Now, Claudius sat in the great hall of Berwick Castle, an enormous place that could easily house a thousand men. It was a two-story building with a soaring vaulted ceiling, and on either end of the hall, stone rosette windows had been sunk deep into the walls. There was a dais on the north end, slightly raised, and then the vast floor where there were at least twenty smaller tables that, at this moment, were filled with soldiers feasting happily.

The guests of honor were sitting at the dais, and that included Cole and his wife, plus Maximilian and Emmeline and several friends from the tournament circuit. In fact, there were many knights and even officials from the tournament circuit feasting upon venison and fish and great sides of beef. The wine was very good, and Claudius had had two full measures of it, which left him feeling quite good. His mood was light because now he had everything he planned for, and there was nothing that could stop him from carrying out his deal with the Scots.

His connections to the Scots went way back because, much like his son, he had a penchant for gambling and women, and there was a particular gambling den in Carlisle that some of the wealthier Scots would visit from time to time. This included the nobility, and Claudius had made an acquaintance of one of

King Alexander's closest confidants as he and the man rolled the dice. It had been a drunken conversation with Lord Gavinton during one of those games that brought him to this point.

After he'd had too much to drink, Claudius had mentioned de Witt and his vast mining operation, something they made a great deal of money from. He'd expressed his envy at such a thing. That had led one of his Scot companions to mention the resurgence of Scottish pride and how the Scots were eyeing Berwick once again. That wasn't anything unusual, considering Berwick had belonged to Scotland as much as it had belonged to England, but one thing led to another, and it soon became apparent that Claudius might hold the key to a Scots rebellion.

And that was how the plan took root.

A plan that was going to make him rich.

Even now, there were Scots in Berwick, waiting for Claudius to contact them and tell them that the marriage had taken place. They were Gavinton's men, ready to take the word back to their lord that everything was falling into place. Soon, they would be able to purchase the lead ore, and silver extracted from it, that would feed into the rebellion that was aiming for Berwick. Claudius found himself looking up at the ceiling of the great hall, realizing he was sitting in Berwick with the English when it would, someday soon, belong to the Scots.

He found that quite ironic.

But what did he care, so long as he got rich over it?

As Claudius sat at the end of the dais, smiling strangely and keeping good company with the copious amounts of wine he was drinking, Addax was trying not to pay too much attention to him. The man seemed content to sit by himself, which he thought was rather odd. Addax was seated with Essien, Cole,

Julian, Beau, and Maximilian, listening to Maximilian drunkenly bash de Wolfe for knocking him off his horse. The particular horse he'd been unseated from was an expensive animal that de Wolfe now owned, per the rules of the tournament, and Maximilian was deeply unhappy about it. While de Wolfe was in the tournament village greeting his comrades that had just arrived from Northwood Castle, Maximilian was plotting his revenge, but Addax thought the man was paying a little too much attention to his vengeance and not enough to his bride, who wasn't present at the table.

She hadn't been for a while.

"Where is Lady de Grey, Max?" he finally asked, simply to shut Maximilian up. "This is a wedding feast, after all. She should be here."

Maximilian took another gulp of the tart red wine Cole had generously provided. "I do not know where she is," he said. "With Lady de Velt, I think. When we came back from the church, Cole's wife took her away, and I've not seen her since."

Addax frowned. "Why should she do that?"

As Maximilian shrugged, Cole leaned toward Addax and lowered his voice. "Because she was upset," he said. "Cori will take good care of her."

Addax looked at him. "What is she upset about?"

"Because I consummated the marriage at the church," Maximilian said loudly, watching the surprise in the expressions of his friends. "I married the woman as my father wanted me to, and he wanted it consummated immediately, so the priests provided us with a small room. I think it was a storeroom, but in any case, I consummated the marriage as my father expected. That woman really *is* my wife."

Addax thought his explanation to be distasteful. "You consummated it in a *storeroom*?" he repeated. "You could not have simply taken her back to your encampment or rented a room in town?"

Maximilian grew defensive. "What difference does it make?" he said. "My father wanted it consummated, so I did. It was not difficult, to tell you the truth. The lady has ripe breasts and buttocks that can fill a man's hands. She turned to the wall, and I took her like a dog mounts a bitch."

He smacked his hands together, imitating the sound that a man's body made against a woman's when they made love. Addax rubbed his forehead as if to rub away the vision Maximilian was trying to convey, and when Maximilian saw him, he laughed and put an arm around Addax's shoulders.

"Truly, it was nothing at all," he said. "I have no idea why she is being so dramatic about it, but it does not matter. I've a couple of women waiting for me back in the village. Cole has already said the lady can sleep here tonight, so she will go to sleep and I will go about my business."

Addax looked at Cole, who was eyeing Maximilian with increasing displeasure. Cole happened to love and respect his wife, and the bilge Maximilian was spouting about the woman he'd just married didn't sit well with him.

"It is your wedding night, Max," he said. "Don't you think you should spend it with your wife?"

Maximilian shook his head. "Nay," he said. "The lady and I have an agreement. I will give her children, and she will give me my freedom."

"Did you truly make an agreement with her, or did you simply tell her the way of things?"

Maximilian's head snapped to Cole. He was starting to sense judgment. "May I remind you that I did not want to be married?" he said, throwing a finger in Claudius' direction. "My father demanded it, so I complied. How I conduct my marriage is none of your affair, Cole."

Cole didn't reply. He simply looked away, glancing at his brother as the two of them exchanged silent words of disgust. Julian, too, had a wife he loved, so Maximilian's barbaric treatment of his wife wasn't sitting well with him either. As the de Velt brothers turned to their own quiet conversation, because they didn't want to say something to Maximilian that would start an argument, Addax and Essien exchanged looks that suggested the friend they'd known and loved had a darker side to him when it came to his very own wife. As far as Addax was concerned, that was a character flaw. He wasn't happy to see it in Maximilian. Still, it was a wedding feast.

Sort of.

He lifted his cup.

"To Lady de Grey," he said. "May she bear many fine sons for the House of de Grey."

Forgetting about Cole and his judgmental attitude, Maximilian lifted his cup to the toast. "She'd better," he said. "The woman had better give me several sons who look just like me."

"I do not think she has any control over that, Max."

Maximilian shrugged before draining his cup and slamming it down on the tabletop. "She is worthless to me if she does not," he said, standing up. "But enough talk of her. I want to thank you, lads, for attending my wedding feast, but my bride is not here, and I see no reason to remain. I will see you all tomorrow at the tournament field. The sword matches, is it not?"

Addax looked at him in surprise. "You are leaving?"

Maximilian was already departing the table. "I shall see you in the morning!"

He called out the last few words over his shoulder as he walked briskly from the hall. A few of the soldiers called out to him, congratulating him, and he took it all in stride. As if the marriage, and this night, meant something to him. When he was gone, Cole turned to Addax.

"I have never known Max to be such a horse's arse," he said. "But I do not ride the circuit like you do. Is that apathy indicative of his true character? Or just his personal rebellion against his father?"

Addax cast a long glace at Claudius down the table. "I've never seen that side of him before," he muttered. "But I suspect his father has."

With that, he left his chair and headed down to the end of the table, where Claudius was very quickly becoming drunk. Very drunk. He looked at Addax as the man sat down next to him, immediately moving to pour him a cup of wine out of the pitcher he was hoarding.

"Addax," he said. "It is a great day, is it not? Celebrate with me."

Addax took the cup but didn't drink from it. He had been looking at Claudius through new eyes ever since Cole told him about the Scots and de Witt lands. But it also occurred to Addax that now might be a good time for him to endear himself to Claudius. It might gain him an invitation to Raisbeck Castle, seat of the Earl of Bretherdale.

It was time for the spy to begin the game.

"It is a joyous day when two people are wed," he said, forcing a smile. "You have waited a long time for this particular union, so I'm told."

Claudius was already into his fourth cup of wine. "Two years," he said, smacking his lips. "Two long years. Did Max tell you this?"

Addax nodded and took just a sip of wine. He wanted to be clearheaded. "He did," he said. "He seems to be quite reluctant."

Claudius rolled his eyes. "He is young," he said. "He does not understand the need for a man to build a legacy. But I do, which is why I arranged the betrothal."

"Is that so?"

Claudius wagged a finger at him. "He'll be rich," he said. "Quite rich. Ernest de Witt and his father before him made their money from mining on their lands. Lead that carries silver ore."

"Oh?" Addax said, playing dumb. "I'd not heard that. In the Pennines, I'm told. Is that right?"

Claudius nodded. "They have most of the north Pennines," he said. "Their western border abuts my eastern border, but my lands do not have the riches that they do. Believe me, I've looked. So did my father. He was friendly with Ernest de Witt's father. He remembered when they first found the precious metals on de Witt lands."

Addax nodded as if it was all very interesting. "And now it is yours."

"Indeed," Claudius said. "It belongs to Bretherdale. Max does not understand that merging our land with de Witt will make Bretherdale quite wealthy. Nay, he simply wants to play with his horses and his swords and try to push men around with his lance. He does not understand that with this marriage, he will someday rule an empire. He will be terribly wealthy."

Addax pretended to be impressed. "As you said, he is still young," he said. "He will understand it someday."

"I hope he does."

"How many mines are there?"

Claudius took another drink of wine. "Eleven lead mines," he said. "De Witt, who was an unpleasant man, was also a strangely generous one. He pays his mine workers well, so they worked hard for him."

"You will continue that, of course."

Claudius shrugged. "I suppose," he said. "I am more interested in gaining a good price for selling the metal."

"Who did de Witt sell it to?"

Claudius waved a hand. "His widow tells me that he had a list of people he sold to," he said. "Jewelers, bankers, and more. But I… I will add my own people to that list."

"You have already secured customers? Max should be very grateful for that."

"This is not for Max."

There was something that hung in the air between them with that statement. Not for Max, who had just married the widow? Addax was wondering if Claudius was going to confess right there that he intended to sell to the Scots. Would it really be so easy to get a confession out of the man, a confession that linked him to a Scots rebellion? Unwilling to tip his hand and ask questions that might make even a drunken Claudius suspicious, Addax pretended to be mildly disinterested in the statement.

"Then I wish you well, whatever it is," he said. "Speaking of Max, would you like me to find him and bring him back? This is his wedding feast, after all. It would not look good for him were his new bride to attend the feast without her husband being present."

With a yawn, Claudius looked around the hall as if just now realizing Maximilian was missing. When it became clear that his son was nowhere to be found, he frowned.

"Damnation," he muttered. "Where did he go?"

Addax shook his head. "I think I know," he said. "I will fetch him for you, my lord."

Claudius angrily settled down to finish his cup of wine. "Thank you, Addax," he said. "Your assistance is appreciated."

"It is my pleasure, my lord."

With that, Addax stood up and left the table. His plan of ingratiating himself to the earl was in its infancy, but with enough service and politeness toward the man, he might very well earn an invitation to Raisbeck. What Cole had asked him to do would take time. There were no instant answers.

This was only the beginning.

With that thought on his mind, Addax headed out of the great hall and into the cold night beyond.

⟡

I KNOW THIS hell.

Emmeline knew it all too well. The hell of a cruel, distant husband, only now it was worse. Maximilian wasn't like Ernest, a man whose manhood couldn't grow stiff enough to penetrate his wife. Horror of horrors, in that small storeroom that Maximilian had demanded to satisfy the consummation of his wife, he had dropped his breeches and taken her hands, putting them on his male member. He was stiff and hard almost immediately. Then he'd turned her around, bent her over, thrown up her skirts, and entered her from behind. No foreplay, no kisses, no touching—no anything that would have helped her prepare for the moment.

He simply took her, climaxed quickly, and then told her to pull her skirt down.

That was it.

It had been one of the worst moments of her life.

That was saying something. Emmeline had had plenty of bad moments over the years, but that one was horrific. Embarrassing and horrific. Once again, she was married to a man who didn't care for her. A man who wasn't even kind to her. Ernest had mostly ignored her, and that was probably the best she could hope for from Maximilian. Ignoring her and letting her go about her life.

Her miserable, depressing life.

This wasn't what she wanted.

She wanted out.

Lady de Velt had been incredibly sweet to her. Corisande was gentle and kind and had helped Emmeline bathe and change into a dress that wasn't covered in layers of dust from travel. She'd even combed and braided her hair for her. Emmeline had tried not to let her shocked and sour mood show on the outside. God knew, she tried to be kind and pleasant in return. But inside, she was torn to shreds by a life that had veered so far out of her control that she didn't recognize it any longer. Happiness, something that had always been so elusive to her, was just a tease. It was a tease fed by hope, but after her marriage that afternoon, the hope was gone.

Finally, she was broken.

Maximilian hadn't been cruel, but he hadn't been considerate, either. He'd treated her like any other possession he had, because that's what she was, essentially—a possession. Most men didn't deliberately mistreat a possession, because it was something important to purchase in the first place. In Emmeline's case, it was something important to marry. Not even some*one*, but some*thing*.

She didn't want to be a some*thing* for the rest of her life.

She simply couldn't face it.

Dressed in a dark blue silk that showed off her narrow torso and full breasts, she wandered out of her borrowed chamber in the keep of Berwick Castle. The distress she felt was overwhelming. She didn't know where she was going, only that she had to get some fresh air. Her wedding feast was going on in the great hall, and she had no intention of going there. She didn't want to see her new husband or his father, the man who'd orchestrated the entire thing. She didn't want to look at him, either, knowing he was the one who had trapped her into this. She knew it was for the money. She'd known that from the start. But Claudius had promised that she would be a countess someday, a title befitting the bastard granddaughter of King John.

She'd wanted something, too, so perhaps Claudius wasn't completely to blame, but she realized that she had wanted a happy life with a man who was kind to her. Perhaps he might even grow fond of her. Perhaps they would laugh together and work alongside one another, building a life that would hopefully include a family. Aye, she did it for the children, too.

Perhaps she was just as guilty as Claudius.

But hope for that pleasant future was dead.

Dead.

Perhaps she'd be better off dead, just like her dreams. She couldn't run from this marriage. She couldn't have it annulled. There was nothing she could do to escape it other than the ultimate escape. Maximilian would have the mines, and the money, and he could do as he pleased, and she didn't have to live a solitary life as her husband was out favoring other women. Ernest may not have been interested in her, but at least he hadn't chased other women. She didn't have to worry about the shame of a husband who needed more than one woman.

But now, she did.

This is a business arrangement and nothing more.

She simply couldn't face it.

Emmeline found her way out of the keep, but that wasn't a simple task because Berwick's keep was quite large and several stories. There were numerous stairwells, but only one door that she could find. It spilled out into the enormous bailey, lit by dozens of torches as men walked their rounds on the battlement. The moon was full overhead, with scattered clouds, and off to the west, the River Tweed snaked alongside the town and out to the sea.

There was a great deal of noise and music coming from the great hall. The doors were open, ventilating what was probably a steamy, smelly hall, and she could see people milling about. But her attention kept being pulled toward the river, and beneath the full moon, she found herself wandering in that direction. There was a door, guarded by an iron gate, that led up to the battlements, but there was also a wall that stretched down the side of the hill and out into the river to create a protected jetty.

Emmeline had seen that steep wall from her chamber.

It was a wall, with steps on the top of it, that led all the way down to the river. A river that would offer icy death to someone who couldn't swim. She'd never learned. Perhaps plunging into the cold water wouldn't hurt so much when her life slipped away. It would sweep her out to sea, and Maximilian would never find her.

Not that he would look for her.

It was devastating to realize that no one in the world cared whether she lived or died.

With tears in her eyes, Emmeline headed to the iron gate,

unlocked at this hour as the soldiers went about their rounds. She made her way up a dark spiral stairwell and found herself on the top of the wall. The portion of the wall that went down the slope was to her right, and she found herself going down the steep staircase, heading toward the river as it reflected the moonglow off the gentle waters. It would have been a beautiful night and a beautiful sight, but all Emmeline could think of was the darkness that awaited her.

Of a life wasted.

As Emmeline took the stairs, she thought on her useless life. She'd been born to a bastard daughter of King John, a woman who had married a simple knight, and they'd lived a quiet life with their daughter and three sons. Emmeline had been the eldest, bright and lovely, and her life had been relatively bucolic, but in spite of their royal connection, they hadn't lived that kind of life. No real extravagance. No parties, no grand feasts. Her parents, her mother in particular, weren't thrilled with the royal connection, so Emmeline—or Emmy, as she'd been known in her youth—had fostered in two homes of lesser nobility, and she'd had a penchant for sums and writing. She loved to write about characters from the Bible—only, in her stories, she would give them great adventures, or she'd change the dynamics. David and Goliath became friends, Adam and Eve made friends with the animals and had a farm of sorts, and Moses built a castle somewhere in the Holy Land.

Emmeline had a great imagination.

But it was an imagination, and a mind, that had been prone to bouts of sadness. Melancholy, her mother had called it. Melancholy so deep that it was beyond tears. It was something that had, at times, crippled her, sitting in dark rooms, staring from windows, and it was a melancholy that had only grown worse when she married Ernest. The past ten years with an apathetic, older husband and an unhappy life had made it a struggle to go on at times. That was the truth of it.

And that was why she'd hoped her marriage to Maximilian might be better.

But it wasn't.

Now, she was heading down the steep stairs, looking at the ribbon of the River Tweed and thinking that it was perhaps a fitting end for her. She was well acquainted with darkness and sadness. The icy drink of no return. The river was the physical embodiment of every darkness she had known, so she was familiar with it. There was a comfort in it.

It called to her.

And she answered.

CHAPTER SIX

*I*T'S A GLORIOUS *night.*

That was what Addax was thinking as he drew in a breath of the cold night air. Compared to the stale warmth of the hall, the bailey of Berwick was quite refreshing. Addax felt as if he could finally breathe. As he stood there, inhaling deeply and wondering if he should search for Maximilian in the tournament encampment or one of the taverns in town, Essien came up behind him.

"Well?" Essien said. "I saw you talking to Bretherdale. What did he have to say for himself?"

Addax looked at him. "About what?" he said with a hint of sarcasm. "A son who is treating marriage like a disease, or the fact that Bretherdale is in bed with the Scots?"

Essien grinned, gazing up at the full moon as he spoke. "Both," he said. "Honestly, I've known Max as long as you have, and although he has an irreverent streak, I've never seen him behave so callously."

Addax nodded. "I've been thinking the same thing," he said. "I adore Max, but today I've seen a side of him I've never seen before, and I do not like it."

"Did Bretherdale ask you to do something about it? He knows you and Max are close."

Addax shook his head. "He did not say a word about it," he said. "But he did speak of something coming from this marriage that would not belong to Max."

Essien looked at him. "Like what?"

Addax shook his head. "I couldn't help but remember what Cole told us," he said. "Bretherdale is planning on supplying the Scots in their assault on Berwick, and that will make Bretherdale a wealthy man. Mayhap that is what he meant."

Essien cocked his head thoughtfully. "It is possible," he said. "He said no more?"

"Nay," Addax said. "But one thing is certain—if he is to be stopped, then I must go to Raisbeck Castle, Bretherdale's seat. And I must keep abreast of any communication between him and the Scots."

"How are you going to do that?" Essien asked.

Addax looked at him. "If life has taught you and I one thing, it is how to be adaptable," he said. "Bretherdale does not have a close advisor or knight from what I know. I met the man two years ago and spent a few days with him, along with Max, and it is clear he never saw the need for a man to carry out his commands or handle his men. I am not certain why he feels that way, but I am going to find out."

"And maneuver your way into the position?"

Addax half shrugged, half nodded. It was what the agents of William Marshal, as they were still known, did best. The most talented spies in the world, and that included Addax and Essien. What Addax was intending for Bretherdale was something he'd done before—making himself indispensable to someone.

Now, he had a target.

As he pondered that very thing, he heard Essien mutter.

"Christ," the man mumbled. "Here comes trouble."

Addax looked to his brother, who was looking at the inner gatehouse of Berwick. There were actually two—the main gatehouse was reached by a bridge across a natural gully, and it sat on the edge of town. The inner gatehouse was built into the wall of Berwick, and as Addax watched, he could see three knights coming through the gatehouse as men with torches went to greet them.

He'd know that trio anywhere.

"Trouble, indeed." He grinned. "Welcome trouble."

Essien shook his head, pretending to be unhappy when the truth was that he was glad to see perhaps the greatest young knights—and the greatest troublemakers—in the north. De Wolfe was in the company of his closest friends, Paris de Norville and Kieran Hage, as Addax and Essien went to greet them.

"I told those gate guards to bar the gate if they saw you coming," Addax said loudly as he approached. "I shall have to punish them severely for disobeying."

William caught sight of them, smiling, as Paris scowled from atop his steed. "Did you truly think you could keep me out, al-Kort?" he demanded. "Go off and ride your little horsey to victory in these childish games. That seems to be what you're best at."

Addax laughed. He genuinely liked Paris—an arrogant man if there ever was one, but honorable to the bone and as loyal as a dog. He dismounted his horse and grabbed Addax by the shoulder as the man came near, and they grinned at each other in greeting. As they were good-naturedly insulting one another, Essien went to the third man in their group, Kieran Hage, and gave him a hug.

"So you think to come and win the combat competitions, do you?" Essien said. "It is not fair when you do that, Kieran. You're bigger and stronger and meaner than the rest of us. It's simply not right."

He was snorting even as he said it, because although Kieran was enormous and powerful, probably more than just about anyone else on the border, he wasn't mean by nature. For a big man bred and born to battle, he was actually quite calm of temperament. It took a great deal to anger him, and no one wanted to be around when that happened. Therefore, Essien was jesting with him.

But Kieran took it in stride.

"The truth is that I need the money," he said, eyeing de Wolfe. "You know that William still gambles from time to time, even though our liege has chastised him again and again for it, so he has all of my money."

"I thought you knew better than to play against him in any game."

"There is always hope that I can win just once."

Paris heard him. "You *do* win," he said, slapping Kieran on a broad shoulder. "You win money for William and me all of the time. In fact, we are going to set up some private wagers while we are here. Kieran will make us a fortune in the sword combat bouts."

Addax and William had joined Paris and Kieran and Essien, but Addax was shaking his head already. "Kieran, how many times have I told you not to let these two use you like that?" he said, fighting off a grin. "You are better than that, lad."

Kieran shrugged. "If I did not let them use me for their games, they would both be poor and destitute," he said. "I do it so they can eat, and I can sleep at night."

Essien burst out laughing. "You are magnanimous, my friend," he said. "They do not deserve you."

Kieran's dark eyes twinkled at William even though he spoke to Essien. "Nay, they do not," he said. "But this time, they are splitting their winnings with me, or I told them I will not do it."

William held up a hand in surrender. "I promised we would," he said. "Our prized Goliath is about to make his stunning return on the tournament circuit, and we shall take all of the purse money now that he is here. You shall all be paupers by the time we are done with you."

"Goliath" had been Kieran's moniker when competing in tournaments in the north, and never was a name more fitting. Addax was about to make a comment to that effect when Paris suddenly spoke up.

"Who is that?" he said.

Everyone looked at him, but he was looking off toward the western portion of the wall. When he gestured, all attention turned in the direction he was pointing. Under the full moon, they could see a woman on the battlements. The skirt of her garment was blowing in the breeze, creating a rather ethereal vision. Like a wraith. As they watched, she disappeared down the portion of the wall that ran down to the river.

"Why is a woman on the wall?" Kieran asked. "Is that one of de Velt's sisters?"

Addax shook his head. "His sisters are not here," he said. "But that looked like Max's new bride to me."

Essien looked at him. "I thought she was in the keep."

Addax met his gaze. "*Is* she in the keep?" he said, throwing his thumb toward the wall. In fact, his focus in general moved back to the wall, to the last place he'd seen the lady beneath the moonlight. "I do not mean to cause concern or stir up gossip, but Max and the lady married today, and from what I heard, Max wasn't exactly... kind to her."

"Who married today?" Paris asked, confused. "Max who?"

"Maximilian de Grey," Addax said. "You know him, Paris."

The light of recognition filled Paris' features. "Of course," he said. "Arrogant little Max who likes to call himself the King of Chaos. He's the king of something, but it is not chaos."

Addax started to chuckle. Paris didn't have a high opinion of a man he'd only met a few times, and probably didn't like him because their egos were so similar. But he didn't say so. Not that Paris would agree with him anyway.

He started for the western wall.

"I am going to see if that is indeed Lady de Grey," he said. "I cannot imagine why she would be on the wall walk."

"Why?" Kieran asked. "Is she not allowed to walk?"

Addax shrugged. "Of course not," he said. "But when a lady's wedding feast is happening and she chooses to be on the battlements instead of her own celebration, I think that is rather strange."

"Mayhap she couldn't sleep," Kieran said.

"Or mayhap she is distraught over her husband's behavior."

Kieran looked at him. "What did de Grey do?"

Addax's dark eyes eerily reflected the moonlight. "Nothing good, so I'm told."

The way he said it made them all think twice. Perhaps it *was* rather strange that the lady was wandering the battlements on her wedding night. They all started to walk in that direction, following Addax. All but Paris. He wanted to go into the hall and feast, because he was both hungry and thirsty, but his companions had other ideas.

"Mayhap she simply wanted to take in the night air," he called after them. "Mayhap she simply wants to be alone. If she wanted company, she would be in the hall."

The last few words were shouted after them, but they kept walking. No one was agreeing with him. With a sharp sigh, Paris followed.

Addax wasn't sure why he felt a sense of urgency, but he did. Or perhaps it was more concern than urgency. The lady couldn't attend her own wedding feast and then suddenly appeared on the battlements? *Why?* Berwick's walls were very steep in places, and quite high, so someone wandering the walls, unfamiliar with them, could be in danger. But in the back of his mind, something told him it was more than that.

She was upset that I consummated the marriage at the church.

Maximilian's words were rolling around in his head. Addax had thought them distasteful when he first heard them, more so because Maximilian seemed to have no issue with what he'd done. *A business arrangement,* he'd said. He'd treated her like an acquisition, not as a woman with heart and feeling. Addax had been privileged enough to have a couple of conversations with Lady Emmeline and found her intelligent and kind. God knew, she was beautiful. To think of Maximilian abusing a woman like that brought him real disgust, but the truth was that it really wasn't any of his business. One man simply didn't interfere with another man's marriage. But something told him to make sure Lady de Grey wasn't about to throw herself from the battlements.

He moved faster.

Slipping up a spiral stairwell in the nearest turret, he came out onto the wall and quickly headed for the last place he'd seen the lady. He heard footsteps behind him, suspecting Essien had come with him, but when he glanced over his shoulder, he could see de Wolfe as well. Further behind he could see de Norville and Hage. Everyone was coming with him, perhaps fed by his own sense of trepidation. When a damsel was in distress, the knights went to work.

Even if that damsel was married to another knight.

As Addax suspected, the stairs on the top of the wall leading down to the jetty in the river below were difficult to see at night, even beneath the full moon. He took them quickly, perhaps a little too quickly, because he could see the lady far down below, disappearing into a turret that had stairs leading down to the riverbank. There were soldiers down there, guarding the access and the boat jetty, but by the time Addax and the others reached the turret where she'd descended from the wall, they could see her by the river's edge, and no one had tried to stop her. The guards on duty were just standing by, watching her.

That made Addax move even faster.

Emerging onto the sandy, rocky shore of the riverbank with the jetty spread out in front of him to his right, he watched as the lady simply stood on the edge of the river. The River Tweed was a major river in the north, so it was wide and deep and cold, and it tended to move swiftly in places. Addax and the group came to a halt after having taken only a few steps from the turret stairs, observing her as she seemingly watched the river flow by. The guards in the area weren't paying much attention to her, but they were paying attention to five knights who had just come down from the castle. One of them approached Addax, but the second he took his focus off the lady to address the guard, the woman sloshed right into the river and submerged.

That brought the knights running.

William and Paris ran upriver, the direction it was flowing in, as Addax and Essien and Kieran ran for the spot where she had disappeared. Addax was throwing off his scabbard and clothes—anything he could get his hands on, because it would weigh him down once he jumped in—and Essien was doing the same. They were without protection this night because of the feast, but William, Paris, and Kieran were all in heavy mail. Paris and Kieran in particular because they'd been traveling. There was no way they could get it off fast enough, so Addax turned to Kieran as he ripped off the silk tunic he'd been wearing.

"Find a rope and anchor," he said quickly. "Anything you can throw to me as a lifeline for when I find her. Hurry!"

As Kieran quickly turned away in search of the requested gear, Addax plunged into that icy river right where the lady had disappeared. It was dark and freezing, and he couldn't see a thing. He was forced to use the only sense he could, the sense of touch, as he began frantically grabbing about in the water for a limb or a dress or even hair. Anything to grab hold of.

But there was nothing.

Essien went on off to his left, diving into the river with an enormous splash as Addax came up for air. He waited a moment to see if his brother came up with something before plunging in again, deeper this time. He could feel the current of the river, pushing him toward the town and the sea beyond.

Still, he found nothing.

As he came up again for air, he caught sight of William diving into the river about twenty feet to his left, closer to the bridge that spanned the river from Berwick to the shore on the other side. Addax swam out toward the middle of the river now, taking a deep breath before submerging himself and swimming as deep as he could, grabbing around in the darkness. There was nothing. But as he turned to surface, his foot brushed against something. He became slightly tangled in it.

Fabric.

Turning around even though his lungs were screaming for air, he went back the way he'd come, deeper into the river, and managed to grasp the fabric that had wrapped around his foot. Pulling as hard as he could, he found an ankle. Grabbing it, he swam with all his might to the surface before he, too, drowned. He was starting to see spots before his eyes. Just a few more feet and he could make it.

Push, man, push!

He broke the surface.

"Help!" he shouted, sputtering. "I have her!"

Essien and William immediately began heading in his direction. He couldn't stand up, so he treaded water as he pulled the lady up, righting her so he could bring her head to the surface. He ended up having to grab her by the hair to lift her head, and her ghostly-pale face came to the surface as Essien reached him. A little less winded than his brother, Essien took the lady and began to swim with her back toward the shore. He was joined by William, who was able to stand at that point, and William took her from Essien, swinging her up into his arms as he struggled out of chest-deep water toward the shore.

Kieran ran out to meet him.

The big man took the lady with ease, racing her back up to the shore, where Paris was waiting. Paris was, in fact, a fine healer and had trained for years under the tutelage of North-wood Castle's surgeon, so he had Kieran lay the lady on the shore and turn her onto her stomach. Straddling her slender body, Paris pushed on her lower back, firmly and strongly, using her diaphragm to force water out of her lungs.

Addax was the last one out of the water, exhausted and freezing, as he came around to watch Paris try to revive the lady. He'd very nearly drowned himself, so he bent over, hands braced on his knees, coughing to clear out the water that he'd swallowed.

"Is she alive?" he asked, breathing heavily.

Paris was methodical and calm as he continued to push on the lady's back. "We shall see," he said. Then he turned to Kieran beside him. "Get some blankets. Anything will do."

As Kieran turned to carry out the request, Addax called after him. "And tell those guards not to breathe a word of this," he said. "We do not want the lady's... accident made known, so tell them if they talk about it, you'll cut their tongues out."

Kieran nodded, running for the guards, who were collected over by the stair turret, watching the action unfold. There were four of them, and Kieran took them with him on the hunt for blankets, which would also make it easier to control any leak of information, because Kieran could shut it down immediately. It was bad enough that the situation had happened.

No one wanted the lady shamed.

As Kieran went about finding blankets, Paris continued his steady pressure on the lady's back. Essien and William were standing over her, watching with concern, as Addax finally caught his breath. He went around to the lady's head and knelt down, pushing her wet hair away from the right side of her face.

"My lady," he said. "Lady Emmeline? Do you hear me?"

She didn't move, and Paris continued to push. Some water was coming from her mouth, but she still wasn't moving.

Addax didn't think she'd been under long enough to truly drown, but maybe he was wrong. Or maybe they weren't trying hard enough. Reaching down, he lightly slapped her on the right cheek.

"My lady?" he said, a little louder. Then he slapped her cheek again, harder. "Emmeline, wake up. Do you hear me? Awaken!"

He slapped her again, and she seemed to stir. That had Paris pushing both fists into either side of her torso, just below the ribcage. When he did that, Emmeline suddenly lurched and began vomiting up water, coughing, gagging. Water spilled out of her, and Paris pounded on her back, helping her clear out her lungs.

"Breathe, my lady, breathe," he said steadily. "Slowly, now. Just breathe."

Emmeline was coughing and gasping at this point, disoriented. But she was aware enough to know that she didn't recognize Paris' voice, so she tried to push herself up, scrambling to escape the stranger. Addax was by her head, however, and as she fought to get up, he grasped her by the shoulders and held her fast.

"You are not in any danger, my lady, I swear it," he said, forcing her to focus on him. "Look at me—you know me. I am Sir Addax. We met earlier today. I sat with you, and together we watched Max compete in the joust. Do you remember?"

Emmeline was positively ashen. She stared at him with those beautiful, gem-colored eyes for several long moments before she finally recognized him. That seemed to calm her down a little.

"A-aye," she stammered. Her blue lips were beginning to quiver because she was so cold. "I remember."

Addax smiled. "Good," he said. "You are safe, I swear it. How do you feel?"

She wasn't sure what he meant, at least not right away. She looked at herself, noting that she was soaked, before realizing where she was. It all came back to her in a flood of despair and disappointment.

"How?" she said, gasping. "How did I end up here?"

"We pulled you out," Addax said. "Do you think you can stand? Let me return you to the keep and—"

Emmeline jerked back from him, looking up at Berwick, lit up with torches against the dark night, and she began shaking her head frantically.

"Nay," she breathed. "Go away and leave me alone! I am not going back!"

Addax had hold of her as she tried to pull away. "Calm yourself, lady," he said. "All will be well."

Her features were tight with distress. "You had no right to pull me out," she said, her voice dull and trembling. "You should have left me there!"

Addax didn't respond to the fact that she had clearly wanted to die. "Come," he said, trying to coax her with him. "Let me take you back so you can change into dry clothing. It's very cold out tonight."

"Let me go," she demanded. "Did you not hear me? I told you that I am *not* going back!"

Kieran chose that moment to reappear with an armful of dusty blankets that the guards had found in the small room at the top of the steep wall. He went to sling a blanket around her shoulders, but she balked, bolting like a new colt, as Addax held her fast. She didn't want the blanket, and she didn't want to go back to Berwick. She didn't want to be helped, and she only wanted to die, but she was spouting it out for all to hear. She was panicked by so many men she didn't know.

This wasn't even his problem.

Addax knew that none of this was his problem. He shouldn't even be involved. But there was something about the lady that he felt a connection to. Perhaps it was the fact that her life was so out of control, as his had once been. As a child, he understood that lack of control, and he understood it now. It was terrifying and gutting. Before Christopher de Lohr found him and Essien in the olive grove, he had often thought he might be better off dead.

Perhaps he needed to reach the lady in a way no one else could.

He certainly couldn't hold on to her all night.

"Leave us for a moment, please," he said, glancing at his brother as he spoke. "All of you. Leave us. But do not go far."

Essien, William, Paris, and Kieran did as he asked and wandered away, back toward the stair turret, as Addax continued to hold Emmeline in a viselike grip. He was afraid of what would happen if he let her go, so he held on as she tried to pull away.

"My lady, I want you to listen to me," he said steadily, hoping to break through her haze of fear. "Will you do that? If you do not like what I have said by the time I am finished, then I will let you go, and you can go back into the river if you wish. Do we have a bargain?"

She wouldn't look at him. "I will not bargain."

"Is your life not worth a few minutes before you end it?"

She closed her eyes, and he could see that she was starting to weep. "Just leave me alone," she whispered. "I am begging you."

Since she wouldn't bargain with him, Addax didn't let her

go. "In a moment," he said. "But first, you are going to hear me out."

"I have heard all I wish to hear from you, Sir Addax," she said. "I know you believe you are being chivalrous, but trust me when I tell you that death is the best possible outcome for me. There is no alternative."

"Because Max consummated your marriage in a storeroom?"

Her head snapped to him, and the tears overflowed. "My God," she breathed, hanging her head. "You know."

"He told me."

She sobbed softly. "He probably told everyone," she said. "Did he tell you that he pushed me against a wall and grabbed my breasts before sticking his fingers into my body? Did he tell you that he shoved his dirty hand into my mouth to silence me until it was over?"

Addax sighed faintly. "He did not."

She used her free hand to wipe the mucus that was running from her nose. "I've only ever been with a man twice in my life," she said, her words hardly recognizable because she was sobbing through them. "I know enough to know that a woman must be ready for her husband. Her body must be ready. I was obedient and compliant with him because he is now my husband, but... it was a horrible experience. My humiliation cannot even be my secret, because he has told you about it. God knows who else he has told."

Hearing about the situation from her perspective made him think that perhaps Maximilian really wasn't the man Addax had thought he was. He'd always suspected that Maximilian had a streak of integrity and honor in him, even if it wasn't something he'd really shown to Addax, but now he wasn't so sure if

Maximilian had any integrity at all. Men with honor didn't treat women so poorly. Certainly not their wives.

He wasn't sure what he could say to her about that.

"Humiliation is not worth your life, my lady," he said quietly. "You spoke of wanting children. Would you truly deny yourself that?"

She looked at him as if he'd gone mad. "Give birth to children with a father like that?" she said, incredulous. Then she shook her head. "It would be better if they were not born at all rather than brought into the world to suffer through a father like Maximilian de Grey. I could not give them life, knowing how they would suffer. It is not fair to them. Nay, Sir Knight... I have found my hell, and I do not want to live here."

She was off sobbing again, but not as loudly. Now her cries were mournful. Painful. She was working through something that had changed her life forever, knowing she'd married a man who cared nothing for the way she felt and who clearly had no respect for her.

What could Addax possibly say to her?

He could only think of one thing.

"When I was five years of age, I watched my father pass into legend," he said softly. "He was King of Kitara, my country. Unfortunately, his younger brother believed he should rule, and he betrayed my father with one of our greatest enemies. My father managed to send his family to safety while he remained behind to burn the largest city in the kingdom so his brother would only have ashes to rule over. The last I saw of my father was as he waved farewell to me and my brother, my mother, and my sister. We thought we were running to safety, but we were running to hell. My brother and I were separated from my mother and sister. At five years of age, I was responsible for my three-year-old brother. I was responsible for myself. I ended up on the streets of a faraway city where I did not speak the language. You have said that you've found your hell. I know the place well, because I found it when I was only five."

Emmeline had stopped sobbing openly, but the tears were still flowing as she listened to him speak of something deeply personal and deeply painful. Even in her distraught state, she realized that. But it also made her realize that if he understood hell, as he described it, then he should very well understand her desire to end the situation she had no hope of leaving.

"But you're here," she murmured. "You found your way out of it."

"I did."

"But did you ever consider the permanent solution to it all?"

"Death?"

"It is the only choice some of us have."

He let go of her. If she was going to run to the river, there was nothing he could do about it. If she really wanted to kill herself, he couldn't prevent it by physically restraining her. But he was hoping she would at least stay long enough to hear what he had to say.

It was important.

"I do not believe that death is ever the right choice," he said. "I will explain why. You see, the beginning of my hell was in that strange city. I begged for food for my brother and me. I found a holy man who was willing to help us. He gave me little jobs that he thought I could accomplish, and paid me a coin or two. But then a merchant came to town, and the holy man told me and my brother to go with him, that he would give us a better life. A greater lie was never told, not to anyone, because the merchant starved us and beat us. We were cold and hungry and injured all the time, but there were moments of hope and light that kept us going. Brief moments, but they were there. However, when those moments faded, Essien and I decided to flee the merchant. Running was our only choice if we wanted to live, and we did, very badly. But we were dying. Of lack of food, shelter, love... everything. We were dying. We made our way to an olive grove, where a column of English knights found us. And that was the beginning of my way out of hell."

Shivering and wet, Emmeline was nonetheless listening to him. He had her attention. "The knights saved you?" she asked.

He nodded. "We were saved by the Earl of Hereford and Worcester," he said. "He wasn't titled back then, but he was the right hand of Richard the Lionheart. He was strong and noble. He saved me and made it possible for the life I have today, and I am grateful for it every single day. There isn't one sunrise I don't give thanks for or one sunset I am not appreciative of. Had I not known the hell I suffered through, how could I know the wonderful life I have today? What I am trying to tell you is that there is always hope, my lady. You do not know what the future holds, and you must not give up. God could have something completely wonderful for you that you will never know if you jump into that river again. Isn't the hope of something glorious tomorrow worth living through the hell you must endure today?"

Emmeline had stopped sniffling. She was looking at him intently, absorbing his words, using them to counter the darkness that had tried to overtake her. The thoughts of death and despondency were balanced out by the truth of Addax's words.

Isn't the hope of something glorious tomorrow worth living through the hell you must endure today?

Perhaps it was.

But the truth was that she simply didn't know.

"I endured one terrible marriage," she finally said. "I endured being treated like an afterthought, used as a whipping post for every problem that arose. I hoped this marriage would be different, but instead, I can already see that it will be worse. How can I believe in a glorious future when all I can see before me is an apathetic husband who does not care whether I live or die?"

Addax could see her point, but he wasn't going to give in to it. Instead, he stood up, picked up the blanket that Kieran had tried to put around Emmeline's shoulders, and swung it over her. He pulled it tightly, and she grasped it because she was truly cold. At least she was letting him cover her.

That was something.

"My lady, I will do something for you if you do something for me," he said. "Are you willing to listen?"

Gazing up at him, she nodded unsteadily. "What is it?"

Addax gestured toward the keep. "I would like for you to go back to your chamber and get out of your wet clothing," he said. "Ask Lady de Velt for a hot bath. Tell her that you went to the river to get a breath of fresh air and accidentally tumbled in. She need not know the truth. While you are doing that, I am going to find your husband and have a talk with him."

Emmeline eyed him warily. "What sort of talk?"

"That is between me and Max."

"About me?"

Addax shrugged, but it was more like a nod. That was the only answer he gave, and Emmeline sighed heavily.

"He will take it out on me," she said. "I can just tell that he is that sort of man. If he thinks I have complained to you, he will punish me for it."

Addax reached down and pulled her to her feet. "Nay, he will not," he said. "Trust me, my lady. He will *not* punish you."

Emmeline wasn't so certain. Addax encouraged her to start walking, back the way they'd come, but she was so cold that her legs were having difficulty working. He ended up picking her up, carrying her back to the knights who were still waiting at the turret. Addax paused in front of them.

"My lady, allow me to introduce you to some of the finest knights in England," he said. "Beginning on my left, this is my brother, Essien al-Kort. Standing next to him is William de Wolfe, Paris de Norville, and Kieran Hage. They are noble and true, and if you have any trouble at all, they will surely assist you. They are no longer strangers to you."

The men dipped their heads politely at Emmeline, who was feeling just the least bit self-conscious. She was trying hard to look them in the eye but couldn't seem to manage it.

"I would like to apologize for the trouble I have caused you all," she said. "It was never my intention, and I am very sorry."

"How are you feeling?" Paris asked. "Any pain in your chest or ribs?"

She shook her head. "Only my throat," she said. "For what you did... all of you... I can only offer my gratitude that you should be so concerned over a woman you did not know."

Addax could feel her trembling in his arms. It almost superseded the sensation of her being in his arms, her life and warmth, because she felt damn good to him, but he fought that idea. It was an unhealthy one, and a shameful one. Emmeline was another man's wife, as much as he was sorry to admit it, so he carefully set her on her feet.

"It was no trouble, my lady," he said. "We were happy to do it. Now, Essien is going to escort you to the keep, where you will tell Lady de Velt that you fell into the river and require a hot bath and dry clothes. You need not tell her more than that. Are you clear?"

Emmeline kept her gaze averted, nodding her head. "Aye," she said. "But Sir Essien does not need to escort me. I can go alone."

"You will not go alone," Addax said, gesturing to Essien to take the lady in hand. "My brother is more than happy to escort you. He will tell you tales of jousts where he was unseated and fell, face-first, into horse shite. It was up his nose and stuck in his teeth. Es, regale the lady with tales of your exploits while I speak with our friends. Go along, now."

Essien rolled his eyes that his brother should bring up such a disgusting moment for him, but it had Emmeline's attention. She was looking up at him in concern.

"Did you truly fall face-first into horse dung?" she said, as if she couldn't believe it.

Essien looked at her, trying not to appear exasperated. "I did," he said. "And it wasn't the first time."

"There were others?"

Essien began to pull her along, toward the stairs, and they could hear him speaking of a horse he'd owned who did nothing but fart through an entire tournament because it had eaten something that upset its digestion. As the voices faded, Addax turned to William, Paris, and Kieran.

"Now," he growled. "We are going to find Max and tell him what his behavior has caused. What he did to the lady was shameful."

It was William who spoke first. "What *happened*, Addax?"

he said. "You have hinted that Max has behaved poorly toward his new wife, but you did not say what he did."

Addax paused. "I am aware of that," he said. "Max is my friend, you understand. We have been close friends. But he has behaved in a way I did not think he was capable of behaving toward his new wife."

"How?"

"Cold," Addax said after a moment. "Cold and callous."

"But why?"

Addax lifted a dark eyebrow. "His father arranged the betrothal, and he wanted nothing to do with it," he said. "He took his frustration with his father out on his betrothed, including consummating the marriage in a small room at St. Andrews. According to the lady, he was not gentle about it, and I'm sure he did it just to spite his father, but the damage is done. You saw the results of that."

Now the lady's actions were starting to make much more sense. William simply shook his head in disgust, looking at Paris, who clearly disapproved of the behavior as well. It wasn't unusual for a man to abuse his wife, or do what he pleased with her, but Addax wasn't friends with anyone like that because he personally wasn't an abusive man. He didn't like to be around men like that because he believed in fair treatment for all, and gentle treatment for women. It was how he'd watched his father treat his mother, and it had stayed with him after all these years.

Unfortunately, some men didn't think the way he did.

But William did.

"In that case, I cannot disagree with the distasteful nature of Max's behavior," William said quietly. "But the fact remains that the lady *is* his wife, Ad. We cannot interfere in his marriage, right or wrong."

Addax shrugged. "At the very least, he should know what happened," he said. "That poor woman felt there was no other choice but to kill herself after he humiliated her. Do you think she is going to tell him such a thing?"

William shook his head. "Nay," he said. "But what is this woman to you that you would defend her so?"

Addax pondered that question seriously. "She is nothing to me, truly, beyond a polite woman that I've only met today," he said. "But she tried to kill herself because of Max's behavior toward her."

"Why does this even matter to you?"

Addax realized how he was coming across—like an avenging angel. But there were deep-seated reasons for why he felt strongly about powerless women. Being unable to help his mother and sister those years ago was something that remained with him, that gave him a more passionate sense of justice for women who could not defend themselves.

All he knew was that he had to help.

"Something the lady said… how she has descended into hell with no way out… has resonated with me," he finally said. "Nay, it is not any of my affair, and I should not concern myself. But I have for one very good reason—I understand what it is like to be helpless. It happened to me, and I had no one to advocate for me until de Lohr came around. I suppose I understand her desolation. Sometimes we all need a little help, don't we?"

Since they all knew Addax and Essien's tale of how they'd come to England, no one questioned him. Addax was, if nothing else, a man of great feeling when it came to the downtrodden. He was also a man of great intuition, so it wasn't unusual for him to take interest in someone weaker and desolate. He was compassionate that way.

A man who should have been king.

"Very well," William said. "If you feel strongly about it. Where is Max now?"

Addax looked off in the direction of the town of Berwick. "My suspicions are that he is in his favorite tavern, the Blankenship," he said. "If he is not there, there are a couple of other taverns he could be at. The Plow and the Sow is one of them, though that one usually contains the dregs of society, and Max somehow finds it entertaining. If he is not in town, however, then he will be in the tournament encampment with some camp followers. Truly, he will not be difficult to find."

"Then let us find him."

They did.

CHAPTER SEVEN

The Plow and the Sow Tavern
Berwick

W RONG TAVERN!
The thought crossed Addax's mind as they walked into a brawl.

Strangely enough, the exterior of the unassuming tavern had been quiet as they approached it, the third tavern they'd visited on their hunt for Maximilian. Kieran opened the door and walked through, only to be hit in the face by a chair that someone had thrown. Kieran may be enormous and powerful, but a chair straight into his forehead was enough to knock him sideways. As he toppled over, William and Paris charged in, followed by Addax and Essien. As Paris went to pull Kieran back to his feet, William and Addax and Essien tried to stay out of the way of flying furniture.

"Mayhap this is not such a good idea," William said, ducking when a three-legged stool came sailing at his head. "Surely Max is not here."

Addax had to put up an arm to deflect a cup that nearly smashed into his nose. "That was my initial thought when we entered, but now I am not so certain," he said, trying to get a look at the men in the room, but it was one giant, undulating mass of flying fists. "Let us make sure before we move on."

Kieran was up now, shaking off the stars that were still dancing in front of his eyes. He was surprisingly enraged by the chair to the head, and he pushed Paris away when the man tried to get a look at the gash on his forehead.

"Who threw that?" he demanded, clenching fists that were the size of a man's head. "I'll make sure he does not do it again."

William and Addax looked at Kieran, surprised by his anger. "It wasn't personal," William said, putting a hand on Kieran's shoulder. "But you should let Paris tend that gash."

Kieran ignored him, his dark eyes searching the room for whoever had it out for him. Two men were fighting off to his left, and they were unfortunate enough to stumble into him, so he picked up one and literally threw him into a group of fighting men. When the other tried to escape, Kieran grabbed the man by the neck and flung him toward a doorway that led back to the kitchen. Both William and Addax winced as the man smacked into the wall, headfirst.

They could hear the skull crack.

"Feel better?" William asked.

Kieran took a deep breath, composing himself, and nodded. "Much," he said. "Now, let's see if we can locate Max in this mess."

"*Addax!*"

Someone was shouting. Addax turned toward the sound of his name, seeing the very man they'd been searching for. Maximilian was off to his right, tucked back in the corner. He was part of the fight because, as Addax watched, Maximilian brained some man with a pewter cup. He hit him twice, on the top of the head, and the man went down.

Addax, Essien, Kieran, William, and Paris headed in Maximilian's direction.

"Max, get out of here," Addax said, waving the man toward him. "What in the hell are you doing?"

Maximilian was fairly drunk. He kept tripping as he tried to move toward Addax, shoving men aside who got in his way.

"They are trying to kill me," Maximilian declared. Then he noticed William behind Addax, and his features lit up with outrage. "*You!* I have something to say to you!"

William was not amused. "And I do not care."

"You should *not* have won our bout today!"

Addax rolled his eyes as he grabbed Maximilian. "Shut your lips," he hissed. "If de Wolfe throws a punch at your head, he will kill you, so do yourself a favor and shut your mouth."

Maximilian didn't seem to care that he was in mortal danger. Addax was pulling him through the fight, but that meant William and Paris and Kieran had to get involved in it because men were turning on them, trying to fight the newcomers. Essien was already involved in it, beating back a man who had come at him with a broken table leg. All of them were fighting off men trying to do them harm as they moved Maximilian toward the entry door, which was no simple feat, considering Maximilian didn't want to leave.

But Addax wasn't going to let him stay.

They reached the door, and Addax thrust Maximilian through the open panel and into the darkened street beyond. Maximilian ended up falling into the dirt with the momentum Addax had given him, sprawling for a moment until he rolled onto his back and sat up. It was then that he realized Addax was standing over him.

The man didn't look pleased.

"What was all that about?" Maximilian demanded. "No need to throw me around like that, lad. I came willingly."

"Shut up," Addax snapped. "Shut your mouth and listen to me. Are you listening?"

Maximilian was genuinely puzzled. "Are you angry with me?" he asked. "Why are you angry with me? What have I done?"

Addax was indeed angry with him. Angrier than he thought he'd be. Something about Maximilian living it up in a tavern as his new bride tried to kill herself didn't sit well with him.

"I thought I knew you well," he finally said. "As it turns out, I do not know you at all. Are you truly the apathetic and abusive type?"

Maximilian scowled. "What are you talking about?"

Addax sighed sharply. "Tell me again what happened today when you married Lady de Grey."

Maximilian had to think about that. "The priest gave us a blessing in the presence of my father," he said. "I told you that I consummated the marriage immediately. Why do you ask?"

By this time, Essien and William had come out of the tavern, followed by Paris and a bleeding Kieran. They came up behind Addax as he stood over Maximilian, sitting on his arse in the dirt.

But Addax only had eyes for Maximilian.

"Because however you thought you behaved today, however polite or husbandly you thought you were, the truth was that the lady thought differently," Addax said. "The woman you marry isn't a whore to be taken, Max. She's not someone to treat like you would treat an unruly horse. This is the woman who is going to bear your sons, and you should treat her with respect. Do you understand me?"

Maximilian didn't. He scowled at Addax as he slowly and unsteadily stood up. "*What* happened, Addax?" he demanded. "Why are you telling me these things?"

Addax found that he was trying to control his anger so he wouldn't lash out at Maximilian, but the man seemed truly dense.

"Because your wife tried to kill herself tonight," he said. "She would have, had we not seen her walking toward the river. We managed to save her life, but when I asked her why she would do such a thing, she discussed her humiliation when you consummated your marriage. You yourself told me that it was swift and emotionless. Is that what kind of man you truly are, Max? Someone who has no knowledge on how to treat a woman with respect?"

Maximilian's eyes were wide with astonishment. "She... she did that?" he said. "She jumped in the river?"

"She jumped in the river."

"Did anyone see it?"

"We *all* saw it."

Maximilian's wide eyes looked from Addax to William to Essien and back to Addax. Then his mouth popped open and his eyes narrowed.

"My God," he muttered. "She *shamed* me. She shamed me in front of my friends!"

Addax shook his head. "Nay, Max," he said. "You have done that quite ably all by yourself. She's done nothing but react to your cruelty. I thought you should know so the next time you see Lady de Grey, mayhap you should apologize for your actions."

Maximilian wasn't too keen on that advice. "Apologize?" he

gasped. "I'll beat her within an inch of her life!"

"I would suggest you do not, not unless you want men you consider your friends to think you despicable and cowardly. Only the weak beat women."

Maximilian hadn't considered that. In fact, he hadn't considered that his friends wouldn't think like he did. Or support his actions. These were men he'd known for years. He considered Addax one of his closest friends. But the man wasn't supporting him in this. Not in the least. If anything, Addax was furious with him, and Maximilian wasn't sure how to react to that. It had never happened before.

He tried to regroup.

"You know that I never wanted to marry her in the first place," he said. "None of this is what *I* wanted."

"But it is what your father wanted," Addax said steadily. "Do not punish the lady because you are angry with your father. That is not a good look for you, Max. It makes you appear spoiled and cruel and petty. Is that truly the man you are? Because I will be very disappointed if I am only now coming to know who you truly are."

Maximilian was starting to twitch with anger. He had never had a disagreement with Addax, not ever, and it seemed to him that the man was siding against him. Perhaps they were *all* siding against him. He looked to Essien and then to William. He singled out William.

"Is that what you think?" he said. "Is that why you used unfair tactics against me in the joust today?"

William simply looked at him. He wasn't going to dignify his anger with a response. Instead, he turned to Addax.

"I am going to take Kieran back to the castle and have his gash tended," he said. "I'll let you deal with Max's little tantrum."

He turned to Paris and Kieran, but Maximilian wasn't going to let the insult go lightly. "Tantrum, is it?" he said. "Just wait until I get you in the mass competition. I'll show a tantrum, de Wolfe. Just you wait!"

William's back was turned to him, but he glanced over his shoulder. "You'll go down again, Max," he said. "There hasn't been a game invented yet that you can best me in."

Furious, Maximilian charged at him, perhaps to push him or strike him. Maximilian wasn't even sure. But the drink he'd imbibed all evening was causing him to behave foolishly, even with men he respected. William caught the movement out of the corner of his eye, and he threw up an arm to protect himself, but his balled fist struck Maximilian on the side of the head. The man went down, falling awkwardly on his right arm.

Maximilian started howling.

"My arm!" he cried, cradling his right arm against his chest. "It is broken!"

Addax had enough. He bent over and pulled Maximilian to his feet, assisted by Essien, as they waved on William.

"Go," Addax told him. "I will tend to him."

But William paused. "I did not mean to break your arm, Max," he said. "But I will not let you strike me."

Maximilian ignored him, howling about his broken arm, as William gave up trying to reason with him. As he and Paris and Kieran headed for the castle, Addax and Essien had a miserable Maximilian between them.

"Christ, Max, calm yourself," Addax muttered. "You are screaming like a woman."

In great pain, Maximilian yanked himself free of Addax's grip. "Enough," he snarled. "I have listened to you call me names and belittle me ever since we left the tavern, but it stops now. Clearly, you are upset because you were forced to pull Lady de Grey out of the river, and you believe I am the cause of all of the trouble, but I tell you that it was not my fault. I did not do anything to the woman that a husband is not allowed to do, so did you ever stop to think that she is the one being dramatic and trying to gain your sympathy?"

Standing a few feet away, Addax simply looked at him. "Max, the woman was genuinely distraught," he said. "Have you ever treated a woman kindly—*any* woman? What I mean to say is that women are delicate creatures. What you may not consider brutal, she very well may. You did not think that consummating the marriage in a storeroom was an issue, but she very much did. Did you even think to talk to her about it afterward? I understand your father wanted the marriage consummated right away, but did you even explain that to her? Did you tell her what you were going to do, and how you were going to do it, so she was at least prepared? If you had, she might not have been so frightened by it."

Maximilian clearly couldn't see what he was talking about. "But she understands this is only a business arrangement," he said. "Furthermore, she has been married before. She *knows* how a marriage works. I must explain everything to her still?"

"Mayhap if you do, you will have the marriage that you want," Addax said. "You cannot expect her to read your mind if she does not even know you. *Talk* to the woman, Max. Then you can avoid things like this, but for her to try to throw herself in the river... That should be an indication that you should have done something differently."

By this time, Maximilian had calmed down a little. Addax was making some sense about Lady de Grey, about the situation in general, and given that Maximilian wasn't a complete idiot, he could understand that Addax wasn't completely condemning him. Perhaps the man wasn't so much against him as much as he was actually trying to help him.

But this marriage had Maximilian greatly confused.

"Very well," he said. "But this has all been quite overwhelming. If my father hadn't told me about his heart, I might not have gone through with it. But I am certain that is why he told me, because my father is not beyond manipulation in such ways."

Addax's brow furrowed. "What about your father's heart?"

"He said that the physic told him that it is weakening," he said. "That is why my father wanted me to marry Lady de Witt now. At least, that is what he has told me, but my father has lied about his health before in order to get what he wants. I'm not entirely sure it is true, but it is possible. He doesn't exactly look well."

Addax was starting to understand more about the dynamics of the situation. "So you did what your father wished, only you literally threw a tantrum doing it," he said, lifting a hand to ease Maximilian when the man opened his mouth to protest yet another insult. "Max, it's as I've said before—you are punishing her for your father's actions, and it simply isn't fair. She was a widow, probably pushed into this by your father, so she is as much a pawn in this as you are. The least you could do is be civil to her, because if you are not, your reputation as a wife-beater will get around. Men will distance themselves, and you will probably sacrifice a few friendships as a result."

"Including yours?"

"Probably."

Maximilian sighed heavily, looking to Essien, who had the

same expression his brother had. Maximilian knew he would sacrifice Essien's friendship as well, only Essien wouldn't be so discreet about it. The man wasn't the diplomatic sort like Addax could be. But the gist was that Maximilian didn't want to sacrifice any friendships he'd cultivated over the years because he was angry at his father. He had come to a crossroads, and he didn't want to choose the wrong path, at least for his own reputation.

With that realization, he was forced to back down.

"Then I suppose I have no choice but to apologize to her," he finally said. "I still do not think I did anything that was not within my right, but if it upset her so terribly, then I am sorry. It was not my intention to cause her grief."

Addax visibly breathed a sigh of relief. "I knew you were a better man than that, Max," he said. "Anger sometimes causes us to do things we would not normally do."

Maximilian was still cradling his right arm against his chest. "Like attacking de Wolfe," he said. Then he rolled his eyes. "God, I do not know what I was thinking. I should not have done it."

Addax smiled faintly, putting a hand on his shoulder. "You can apologize to him, too, once we've had the arm looked at," he said. "Come along, now. You've had a busy day, old man."

Maximilian couldn't disagree. With an aching arm and a swimming head, he allowed Addax and Essien to lead him back to the castle, where the surgeon did indeed diagnose a broken arm. With that turn of events, Maximilian was out of the rest of the tournament, and perhaps tournaments for a few months to come.

It had been a busy day, indeed.

CHAPTER EIGHT

St. Andrews Church
Berwick

*J*UST A LITTLE *further...*

The world, as dawn approached, was damp and cold and covered in the mist that had rolled in from the sea overnight. The streets of Berwick smelled heavily of human habitation and rubbish, the dirt slick with things that stuck to one's shoes and refused to come off.

Claudius found himself on one of those streets, a heavily traveled one, as he headed toward the cathedral of St. Andrews. *Just a little further,* he told himself. Being out on the dark street made him nervous, but he had a rendezvous to make.

He didn't want to be late.

St. Andrews Cathedral was an enormous structure built upon the foundation of an even older church, one that had been used by the Saxons and the Picts of days past. It was square in nature, constructed with the brown stone that was quarried down by Middlesbrough. It had seen years of warfare, of Scots, of English, and even the occasional Northman from time to time, because the Danes weren't strangers to Berwick either.

The old church had seen a great deal in its lifetime, looking up on Berwick with its weathered walls and warped doors.

And it smelled.

Because the climate could be terrible this time of year, the priests allowed the homeless and destitute to sleep in the sanctuary, so it smelled like a sewer. Claudius entered from the main door, which was unlocked at this hour, but there were still groups of people sleeping inside. Since Claudius had told Lord Gavinton in the missive he sent him right before leaving Raisbeck Castle that Maximilian's marriage was to take place sometime during the second week of the following month, he had advised that Lord Gavinton send two men to Berwick to receive the confirmation. They were to appear early at the cathedral in Berwick, every morning, and Claudius would contact them once the marriage was completed. He'd further told Gavinton that he would be wearing a red cloak so the Scots would know him.

He was wearing that cloak this morning.

It was a blood-red woolen cloak that had belonged to his wife long ago. If he'd been a romantic, he would have thought the cloak carried her spirit with her, but he wasn't romantic and hadn't been particularly fond of his wife, so it was simply a garment like any other. He entered the church and hung back by the door, back where the prayer candles were softly glowing and where the stone basin of holy water was frozen over in the icy morning. A priest was trying to break up the ice with a piece of stone as Claudius stood near the prayer candles because they were the only thing giving off heat, minimal as it was.

And he waited.

People began arriving for lauds, or the first mass of the day. The people who had been sleeping inside the church didn't move aside too much to make way for parishioners, so those who had come to worship had to stand around them. The priests intoned the mass, mixing the pungent scent of incense with the smell of human habitation. Claudius stood by the candles, smelling that horrific aroma but paying little attention to the priests. He was looking for Scots.

But the Scots didn't come.

Prime, the second mass after dawn when the sun was rising, came. People filtered in and out of the church, praying with the priests or huddling together in groups as the mass was conducted. Some of the groups simply seemed to be talking amongst themselves and not paying attention to the mass. By the time prime was over, Claudius was beginning to wonder if it was time for him to leave. He would come back on the morrow, and every morning he was at Berwick, until Gavinton's men appeared. He felt stupid for thinking they would come the very first day he'd shown up in the red cloak.

As he stood there, thinking that he should probably leave, a poor man in a tattered cloak limped up to him, holding out his hand and begging for alms. Claudius brushed him off, but there were others. He moved away from the prayer candles, because they seemed to be congregating over there, and walked to the area where the holy water basin was. A few people were taking cups of the water, no doubt to bless things around their home, but even over here, he was accosted by dirty, smelly men who were begging for money. He brushed them off again, and was prepared to leave the cathedral completely until one of them spoke in a sentence in a Scots accent that had nothing to do with begging.

"Gavinton favors the generous, m'lord."

That brought Claudius to a halt. He turned to the men,

three of them, all of them dressed in the most terrible rags he'd ever seen. They smelled worse than the church did. But what they'd said... *Gavinton favors the generous...* had his attention.

It also had the attention of someone else.

☙

ADDAX WAS WATCHING.

As a courtesy, Bretherdale had been housed in the keep of Berwick. Cole thought it only appropriate, given the man's rank, but also because he wanted to keep an eye on him. Addax and Essien had watched the earl's chamber door all night, taking shifts, and it had been on Addax's shift about an hour before dawn when Claudius emerged from his darkened chamber and headed out into the icy predawn day.

Clad in a gray cloak and dressed in an ensemble to blend in to the mist that had come in overnight, Addax followed Claudius through the darkened streets until they reached St. Andrews Cathedral. Claudius slipped inside the main entrance while Addax waited outside for a few minutes, entering with a group of worshippers so he would not be noticed entering alone.

After that, he ducked back into the shadows.

The morning, from that point, was uneventful. Two masses were held as her remained in a corner of the church so he could watch Claudius' every move. The man seemed particularly nervous, milling around by the iron bank of prayer candles before moving over to the holy water basin. He looked at the face of every person who entered the church, and Addax could clearly see that the man was expecting someone.

But who?

Pulling the hood of his cloak down over his face so that only one eye was exposed, Addax moved over to the area where Claudius was. It was easy for him because there were several beggars back there, tugging at Claudius, who was pushing them away. All Addax had to do was lose himself in the beggars to keep watch over Claudius until three beggars in particular seemed to have his attention—suddenly had his attention with just a few spoken words.

"Gavinton favors the generous, m'lord."

Addax had no idea who Gavinton was, but he was about to find out.

αβ

"THEY MOVED TO an area inside the nave, which was perfect for me because I was able to position myself just around the corner. The shape of the nave amplified their voices, and they were not aware of it."

Cole was hanging on Addax's every word. "And?" he said. "What did you hear?"

Addax was seated on a cushioned chair in Cole's solar. It was around noon, and the sounds of the bailey wafted in through the lancet windows. The mist that had blanketed the land that morning had lifted, and gulls cried overhead, riding the sea breeze—but inside the solar, all attention was focused on Addax.

He propped a booted foot wearily on a nearby table.

"Evidently, someone named Lord Gavinton is Bretherdale's contact within the Scottish court," he said. "Claudius' discussion was with three of Gavinton's men, who had come to receive confirmation of Max's marriage to Lady de Witt. It's as you suspected, Cole. Bretherdale has promised the Scots raw material from the de Witt mines at reduced prices in exchange for lands in Scotland. Lands for *him*, not Max. This is all for Bretherdale."

Cole drew in a long, thoughtful breath as he sat back in his great chair, the one his mother had gifted him for a birthday. It was enormous and elaborate, like a throne, and Cole's wife thought it was ridiculous, but given that it was his mother's gift… Cole used it.

Even if he did look like Caligula when seated upon it.

"How soon is this exchange supposed to happen?" he finally asked.

Addax shrugged. "As soon as Bretherdale returns to Raisbeck, I suppose," he said. "They did not speak on that, so we can only assume."

Cole nodded, pondering the information for a moment. "I would say that makes it imperative that you somehow ingratiate yourself enough to Bretherdale that he allows you to return home with him," he said. "We must have eyes on any transactions with the Scots."

Addax yawned; having only gotten a couple hours of sleep the night before, he was exhausted. "I have a better idea," he said. "Max broke his arm last night, so he can no longer ride the tournament circuit. I suspect he'll be going home with his new bride, so I will go with him. I'll make up some excuse. But staying close to Max means I will be privy to any business dealings involving his father. Bretherdale cannot sell any ore to the Scots without Max, or his wife, knowing about it."

Cole nodded. "That sounds more reasonable to me," he said. "Max will welcome your company."

"Indeed, he will," Addax said. "I had the opportunity to speak with the new Lady de Grey yesterday. You understand that this marriage was not welcome, to either Max or the lady.

Bretherdale forced it on them both."

Cole glanced at him. "Do you mean to ask if I know what she did last night?" he said. "I know. You should have told me when it happened."

Addax knew what he meant. "There wasn't the opportunity," he said. "Who told you?"

"De Wolfe. He said you had to fish her out of the river."

Addax leaned his head back against the chair, his gaze on the bailey beyond the lancet window. "We did," he said. "But yesterday was a litany of failures on the part of Bretherdale and Max. That poor woman felt she had no other alternative."

Cole scratched his head. "Cori wants me to beat Max to a pulp," he said with a smirk. "By the way, how did he break his arm?"

Head still reclined on the chair, Addax turned to look at him. "De Wolfe did it."

Cole grinned. "How?"

"Max was drunk and tried to attack him," Addax said. "All de Wolfe had to do was shove him backward. Max fell awkwardly on his arm, so there is no great story behind it."

Cole laughed softly. "Aye, there is," he said. "The story of a man's stupidity when attacking a superior being. De Wolfe could have killed him."

"I know," Addax said, rolling his head back around so he was looking at the bailey once more. "Speaking of Lady de Grey…"

He was suddenly on his feet, heading for the solar door. Curious, Cole stood up.

"Where are you going?" he asked.

Addax opened the carved panel. "Lady de Grey is out in the bailey," he said, pointing at the window. "I want to see if Max apologized to her."

"For what?"

"For behaving poorly. I'll explain later."

Cole just waved him on, and Addax quickly headed out of the keep and into the bailey. He had seen Lady de Grey walking with another woman, who turned out to be one of Corisande's maids. As soon as Addax walked up, Lady de Grey's rather bland expression seemed to change. He could see her eyes brighten and a smile appear. Clearly, she was glad to see him, and that seemed to do something to Addax.

He realized that he was glad to see her, too.

"Sir Addax," Emmeline said. "You are not at the tournament field? I thought for certain you would be."

Addax smiled politely. "Later," he said. "Some of the sword bouts are going on this morning, and I've decided not to participate. And if anyone tells you it is because Kieran Hage is competing, they are filthy liars, and I shall beat every one of them."

He said the last several words severely, but it was meant to be humorous, and she giggled. "I do not think I know Kieran Hage, but I will take your word for it," she said.

Addax's dark eyes twinkled. "You met him last night, my lady, but it was dark and difficult to see," Addax said. Then he spread his arms wide. "The man has shoulders this broad. You cannot miss him."

"And he is fearsome in a sword fight?"

Addax rolled his eyes. "Fearsome is where he begins," he said. "Where he ends, no one knows."

"He sounds terrifying."

"He is," Addax said. "But so am I, so Kieran and I understand one another."

"Then I am relieved."

Somewhere in their conversation, Addax's polite smile had turned genuine. The lady seemed quite well this morning after her scare last night. He wanted to ask how she was feeling, but the maid was still standing there, looking at him, so he gestured to the bailey.

"If you are taking a turn about the ward, may I escort you?" he asked. "I can tell you a great deal about Berwick, and your maid probably has other duties to attend to."

Emmeline readily agreed. "I am certain she does also," she said as she looked at the maid. "You may return to Lady de Velt, Ansa. You may tell her that Sir Addax is my escort."

The maid didn't argue, but she did give Addax a long look before darting away. He waited until she was out of earshot.

"I hope she does not run back to Lady de Velt and tell her that I have demanded your company," he said. "I cannot imagine Cori would tolerate that very well."

Emmeline shrugged. "She is very protective, but not unreasonable," she said. "I have enjoyed coming to know her. She is a fine lady."

"She is," Addax agreed. "Actually, I am glad we are alone. I wanted to make sure you were well after last night's... activities."

Emmeline's warm expression faded, and she averted her gaze. "My ribs hurt a little, and so does my head," she said. Then she paused before lifting her eyes to him once again. "Sir Addax, I want to apologize to you. I have no idea what came over me last night. I'm not usually so foolish or so reckless. All I can say is that the events of the day overwhelmed me, and something took hold. Call it a demon if you will. I do not really know what it was, but it shall never take hold again. Once is enough."

He looked at her seriously. "Given the events of the day, I am not entirely sure the strongest woman in the world could have endured those events and not felt some devastation," he said. "Did Max at least apologize for being unkind?"

She nodded. "A little," she said. "He said that he'd heard what happened and if he had offended me, he was sorry for it."

"That's all?"

"He came to my chamber just for a moment, and then he left again."

"He did not stay the night?"

"Nay."

Addax frowned. "Where did he go?"

She shook her head. "I do not know," she said. "I have not seen him since."

Addax was starting to feel that disgusted sensation again when it came to Maximilian. Perhaps he'd only been sorry to Addax's face because he felt pressured, and the sentiment wasn't real.

Addax wouldn't be surprised.

"I see," he said, trying not to sound unhappy about it. "In that case, mayhap we should go and find him. I have a suspicion he might be at the tournament field. Would you like to accompany me?"

Emmeline nodded. "Thank you, I would."

"Shall I meet you at the keep once I've collected my horse?"

"No need. I shall go with you."

He headed toward the stables with Emmeline beside him. He kept glancing at her, discreetly, because she looked splendid this morning. She was dressed in a mustard-colored garment that set off the color of her eyes, and her hair was gathered at the nape of her neck, topped off by a jeweled cap that was quite stunning. She seemed in much better spirits than the last time he saw her, so perhaps it was as she'd said—a demon or something had overtaken her temporarily. A momentary madness had swept her. Everyone was allowed to have a little madness now and then, and Addax had seen enough rational people over the years have momentary failures.

But he was still baffled as to how Maximilian could ignore a woman like this.

And that was a feeling he would carry all the way to the tournament arena.

CB

HERE HE WAS again.

Truth be told, Emmeline had been hoping to see Addax this morning. After the events of the previous night, she found that she was almost desperate to apologize to the man who had saved her life. Had he not been on the lookout for her when he had, and had he not shown just the slightest bit of concern, the situation might have been much different.

She would have been dead.

It was as she had told him. The devastation she had felt realizing that she had entered into a marriage that was exactly the same as the one she'd had before was too much for her to bear. She had been so young when she married Ernest, and, to be perfectly truthful, she didn't know that marriage was supposed to be anything other than what she had with him. Polite apathy, civil indifference. No warmth, no feeling. Of course, she had seen other couples who had been affectionate toward one another, and in the course of her educational upbringing, she had read stories of love, of a man and woman loving one another and living for the mere sight of one another. Perhaps in some small way she had hoped that she and Ernest would have that kind of relationship, but it never came about, and then she'd entered into a marriage with Maximilian that had the same flavor and feel to it.

That had thrown her over the edge.

She understood that now.

After the events in the river, Emmeline had lain awake the night before, pondering her actions, mostly because they had put Addax and his friends in jeopardy. Those knights had been forced to dive into the freezing river, in the dark, looking for a woman who had briefly lost her mind. Thank God they'd found her, but the embarrassment over the fact that they had to save her kept her awake most of the night.

That was why the first words to Addax had been those of apology. He was the only person who had been kind to her since her arrival to Berwick, other than Corisande and Cole, and she didn't want the man thinking that she was absolutely crazy. Hopefully, he didn't. But even with her apology, she was still ashamed at her actions.

Shame that had been difficult to shake.

Maximilian had indeed come very late in the night to deliver a tepid apology for whatever part he played in her difficult day. As if the man didn't know. Emmeline was not a foolish young bride, not like some very young girls when they were first married, who tended to be submissive and obedient to a fault. Perhaps she'd been that way with Ernest in the beginning, but that abject obedience faded over time. She'd still obeyed him when the occasion called for it, but that had been rare as the years went on. He basically lived his life and she lived hers, and once in a while their lives would cross.

But that was where it ended.

Perhaps that was one of the most difficult things for her to accept after her marriage to Maximilian. As she had lamented the night before, she was going back to an existence that wasn't pleasant, only with Maximilian, there might be more to it. Ernest hadn't been demanding of her at all, but she suspected Maximilian might be. He was younger and more virile. To think that she would have more consummation encounters with him like the one they'd had in the church made her sick to her stomach. The only good thing that would come of it, hopefully, was a child. A child she could love unconditionally, and one that would love her unconditionally in return.

She'd never had that in her entire life.

And then there was Addax.

Her husband's friend, a man who had been pleasant from the start. She'd realized when she saw him coming across the bailey that she was happy to see him. He was quite handsome with his long black hair and dark eyes. His face was angular, with a square jaw that she found quite handsome. He had a way of smiling that made her stomach tremble, a giddy feeling she hadn't often experienced over the years, if ever. It was exhilarating. She was quite interested about his life before he came to England, and he'd been polite enough to tell her a little something about himself yesterday, but she suspected there was much more. As they rode away from the castle and toward the tournament arena, with her perched on the back of his horse, she felt rather guilty over liking the fact that she was holding the man around the waist. She felt as if she was indulging in some kind of forbidden pleasure with a man she found attractive.

The town of Berwick was busy today as the fishermen brought in their morning catches. As they traveled down the main street toward the bridge that spanned the River Tweed, she could see the boats on the riverbank as the men delivered their haul. She could also see the tournament on the opposite side of the river, spread out over a wide area. Banners snapped in the sea breeze, and there seemed to be a great crowd there today.

"Do all tournaments have the same types of games?" she asked, pointing.

Addax had to direct his horse through the crowds near the bridge, pausing when a small child darted out in front of him. "Mostly," he said. "Sometimes it can depend by the town. For example, there is a town in France that includes breaching a castle wall as part of the competition. Men are required to climb it while other men try to knock them off. Whoever is left is the winner."

"God's Teeth," she muttered. "That sounds rather violent."

"It can be," he said. "But it is also a great deal of fun."

She didn't have to see his face to know that he was grinning. "Then you have competed in France?"

"I have competed in many places."

"May I ask how you came to England?" she said. "You mentioned that the Earl of Hereford and Worcester found you in the Levant, but did he bring you to England also?"

Addax shook his head as they began to plod across the great stone bridge. "Nay," he said. "Although he was in the Levant for almost three years, and Essien and I spent nearly the entire time with him, we did not come to England with him because he was focused on his king, and Richard was being targeted by men who called themselves allies. That took all of his focus, so he arranged for my brother and me to serve some Thuringian knights. They were good men. When the crusade was over, we returned to Thuringia with them, but these knights were mercenaries. They ended up fighting a war for a Flemish lord, Count d'Acoz, and that is how my brother and I came into the count's service. That is where I had my first tournament—in Flanders."

"And you loved it?"

"I did," he said. "I had a choice—either follow the Thuringians and become a mercenary, or remain with d'Acoz and serve him in the capacity of a knight whilst also competing in tournaments to earn money. Given that I did not come with my father's wealth, I had to earn everything I have. The tournament circuit is a much less violent way of doing it than fighting someone else's battles and getting paid for it."

Coming off the bridge, they were nearing the arena now. Emmeline could see it looming up ahead. "Then how did you come to England?" she asked.

She couldn't have known that it was a complicated story, one without a simple answer, but he summarized it as best he could.

"The Flemish lord I spoke of, d'Acoz, was allied with Ajax de Velt," he said. "When de Velt, whose ancestors are Flemish, came to visit d'Acoz, I was enthralled by tales of England."

"And that was Cole's father?" she asked.

"Indeed," Addax said. "Ajax de Velt was a warlord like no other, and d'Acoz could see that I was quite interested in the life the man led and the battles he'd fought. D'Acoz has a large empire, but it is very peaceful, and I suppose I grew bored. I needed a new adventure. Therefore, with d'Acoz's permission, I swore fealty to de Velt and came to England. And I have loved it ever since."

They had reached the arena, and Addax began to head to

the west side, where the competitors gathered. But as he moved, people were calling his name, greeting him, something that didn't go unnoticed by Emmeline. The man was revered here.

"And England loves you," she observed.

Addax grinned, lifting a hand to Beau de Russe as the man headed in his direction. "I have made many good friends here," he said. "I have traveled to many a place and lived many different lives, but this is the one I like best."

"And you intend to stay here forever?"

He pondered that. "A very good question," he said. "I always hoped to use the money I have earned to hire an army and return to Kitara. But strangely enough, I am not entirely sure I view it as my home any longer."

"Mayhap that is because you've not lived there since you were a small child," Emmeline said. "Didn't you tell me that you were five years of age when you left?"

"Aye."

"Then it must seem more like a dream," she said. "Years and distance have made it a faraway land, just beyond your grasp. But this place, at this moment, is clearly where you live."

She made some sense, and Addax looked around, at the people, the horses, the excitement of the tournament field, and the beauty that was the north of England.

Years and distance have made it a faraway land.

That was very true. Kitara did seem like a dream he'd had once, only that wasn't a context he'd ever put it in. But Emmeline had.

He appreciated her wisdom.

"I do indeed live here," he said. "And I have my brother with me, so the only family I have is here. I wish I had my mother and sister, but alas…"

He trailed off, unable to finish that statement. It has always been a painful thing for him. By that point he'd reached Beau, who greeted Emmeline politely. Addax had to ask the man where Maximilian was, twice, before he received an answer, and even then, Beau was trying to be discreet about it, but Emmeline heard one word:

Lists.

Because of the sword bouts on this day, the arena floor had been divided up into what was effectively four pens. Spectators were allowed on the arena floor to watch knights face off against one another in what was essentially a sword fight. They were not allowed to stab each other, but nearly everything else was permitted. If a man was disarmed or fell down, he was disqualified, and the victor would remain while the next challenger entered the pen. Then the process would start all over again. As Addax dismounted his horse and helped Emmeline slide to the ground, he introduced her to Beau, whom she'd not yet met. As Beau politely acknowledged her, they could hear the cheers of the crowd going up.

"The sword fights are bloody today," Beau said. "We've seen some fairly serious injuries."

Emmeline looked at the knight. Beau was very tall, and had quite large hands. He was blond and somewhat fair, but he had dark, smoky eyes that gave him a rather mysterious look. She remembered that Addax had told her that he was called Bringer of Nightmares and was quite formidable on the tournament circuit.

Looking at the man up close, she could well believe that.

"And you have not competed in the sword fights, my lord?" she asked him.

Beau grinned. "Not me, my lady," he said. "As soon as I

heard that Kieran Hage was entering, I withdrew."

Emmeline tilted her head in Addax's direction. "Your friend said the same thing," she said, eyes twinkling with mirth as Addax laughed softly. "Is he really so terrifying?"

Beau crooked a finger at her. Curious, she followed him, with Addax trailing behind her. They walked onto the arena floor, which was crowded with people around the four pens. Beau took Emmeline and Addax over to the pen on the southwest side, where a knight had nearly had his arm cut off. The victorious knight was working up the crowd as his competitor was helped off, but that didn't last long. As Emmeline and Addax watched, the biggest man they'd ever seen—at least the widest—entered the pen.

He was ready for the bout.

Emmeline recognized the men accompanying the enormous knight as William de Wolfe and Paris de Norville. She remembered them from the night before. As she watched, the victorious knight faced the enormous newcomer, and a field marshal started the bout with the wave of a flag.

It was nearly over before it began.

The enormous knight, which she learned from Beau was the legendary Kieran Hage, closed in on the victorious knight and, within three very heavy blows, knocked the sword right out of the man's hands. The weapon clamored to the ground, and the knight, rather than throw up his hands and surrender, as was expected, began to run around the pen to keep away from Kieran. Fortunately, Kieran didn't chase him because he'd already won the bout, but the now-defeated knight wasn't apt to surrender so easily. He began to insult Kieran, calling him names even as the field marshal declared Kieran the winner.

But that didn't quiet the defeated knight.

He kept up a steady stream of jibes and insults even as the field marshal told him to get out of the pen. He did, but he was going to make sure Kieran knew what he thought of him. Kieran was over near the pen exit, simply standing there and watching as the defeated knight was practically dragged out of the pen. But as the defeated knight came close to the victor, Kieran's enormous fist shot out and clobbered the defeated man right in the face.

He went down, and the crowd went wild.

William and Paris stood there and laughed as Kieran was awarded the beautiful sword that he'd knocked out of the other knight's grasp. As the hapless defeated knight was carried out of the pen, no longer victorious, Kieran handed his newly acquired sword over to William as he prepared for the next competitor, who made it a little further than the previous knight had. He lasted several minutes, but in the end, Kieran's strength and skill ran him into the ground, too. After Kieran's second victory, Addax turned to Emmeline.

"Now do you see why I withdrew?" he said, his dark eyes glimmering with mirth. "I have no intention of losing my Spanish-forged sword to Hage. He'll have a collection of ten or twelve swords by the time the day is over."

Emmeline nodded in agreement. "I completely understand," she said. "Does he get to keep the swords of his opponents?"

Addax nodded. "He does," he said. "The same thing happens in the joust. If a knight is unseated by an opponent, his opponent is awarded his horse."

Emmeline was listening intently. "This is a fascinating world you are part of, Sir Addax," she said. "And an expensive one if you lose your sword or your horse."

Addax chuckled, returning his attention to Kieran as yet another knight entered his pen. "More than you know," he said. "As I said – I have no intention of losing my sword, and I most assuredly will not lose my horse."

"What if Sir Kieran jousts?"

Addax shook his head. "He will not," he said. "That is not his strength. The joust requires agility that he does not possess."

"But you do."

Addax looked down his nose at her. "Of course I do," he said. "Have you not seen me joust?"

She fought off a grin because he already seemed insulted by the answer to come—an answer he already knew. "Nay, I have not," she said. "It is my greatest regret."

She sounded quite sincere in her statement, causing Addax to grin again. "Of course it is," he said. "But tomorrow is the last day, when the champion shall be crowned, and you shall have your chance then."

"Excellent," she said. "I will be able to sleep better tonight, knowing my opportunity is not lost."

He looked at her, chuckling. He liked her sense of humor. Emmeline started to laugh in return, but, quite suddenly, her expression seemed to change. Her smile faded. She was looking at something over Addax's shoulder, and when he turned to see what it was, he immediately understood what Beau had trying to be discreet about.

Maximilian was standing at a neighboring pen with a woman on each arm.

And he was having a grand time of it.

Addax's smile vanished as he beheld the man, laughing and even kissing the women. His right arm was bandaged up, but that didn't stop him from using his left arm most effectively. He clutched one of the women closely while the other one cozied up to his right side, avoiding the wounded arm. Seeing him also told the tale of where Maximilian had been the night before.

There was no need for more of an explanation.

"Let me fetch your husband to you, my lady," Addax finally said, fighting down his irritation with Maximilian. "Remain here with Beau, and I will bring him."

But Emmeline put a hand on his arm. "Nay," she said, preventing him from moving away. "Leave him."

"*Leave* him?" Addax said, shocked. "Are you serious?"

She looked at Addax pointedly. "I am," she said. "My lord, my husband has made it clear what this marriage means to him. It is a business arrangement. Fetching him to me will not change that."

Addax looked at her, struggling to keep sympathy for her plight off his face. "What he is doing is not right," he said quietly. "He married you, and he should be here, with *you*."

Emmeline shook her head, forcing a smile. "He *unexpectedly* married me yesterday," she said. "I have had the night to think about this, Sir Addax, and I have come to a conclusion. I can either let his behavior destroy me or I can simply accept it. And I refuse to let it destroy me. It's come too close to that already."

Addax sighed faintly, thinking the entire situation was just horrible. He wondered if he could even give her any shred of hope that it wouldn't always be like this. "It is early in the marriage still," he said hesitantly. "Mayhap with time, he will change."

Emmeline snorted softly. "I doubt it," she said. "You have known him for a long time, have you not? Do you truly believe he will change?"

Addax couldn't lie to her. "I do not know," he said. "Truthfully, I never knew he was capable of behaving as he has, so I do not know anymore."

Emmeline shrugged, trying to pretend that it didn't bother her when, in fact, it did. It bothered her a great deal. But she wasn't going to let the melancholy win. She'd let it win last night, and it had almost killed her. Therefore, the best thing she could do was be brave about it.

Show courage!

"Mayhap he will change, or mayhap he won't," she said after a moment. "I suspect he will not, but in either case, the man cannot be expected to immediately amend his ways. He had a life before I became his wife, a life he was happy with and a life that does not include me at the moment. I do not wish to interfere with that because it will only make us both miserable."

Addax looked at her in disbelief. "Is this how *you* view marriage, also?" he asked. "Something that does not require any loyalty?"

Her smile faded. "Of course not," she said. "Every woman yearns for a marriage with a husband who will be faithful only to her. I yearn for that also, but Maximilian has made it clear he has no such yearnings. However, that does not mean I will not be faithful to him. I must live by my own convictions, and that means my loyalty is only to Maximilian. I would never entertain lovers."

"But, my lady, I—"

"*Nay,*" she said quickly, cutting him off. "Addax, I know you mean to help, but I still have to live with myself. My honor is important to me even if it is not important to my husband. What he chooses to do is his own decision, but I choose to be faithful to my marriage, even if he wishes to carry on with others."

Addax couldn't keep the pity off his face now. He'd never heard anything so sad or, quite honestly, so noble. "You deserve better," he said hoarsely. "You deserve a man who is worthy of your convictions. I am sorry it is not Max."

"As am I."

As they stood there in a desperately somber moment, each one of them realizing what the future held for her, Maximilian spied them from the other pen and lifted his hand, waving happily. It was a brazen, oblivious move on his part. As if he wasn't surrounded by women in full view of his wife. Emmeline forced a smile and lifted her hand in return as Addax simply turned away.

He couldn't stomach the audacity.

Addax found himself looking at Beau, who had the same expression of disgust that Addax surely must have himself. Beau had seen Maximilian, too. Maximilian, just married, who was proudly walking about with women who were not his wife. When their eyes met, Beau shook his head and walked away, heading over to William and Paris. That left Addax alone with Emmeline.

"My lady, may I ask a question?" he said when Beau was gone.

Emmeline's smile faded as she watched Maximilian walk off with his two women. "What is it?" she asked.

"Tomorrow, I compete for the championship of the joust," Addax said. "The only favor that I have carried at this tournament, so far, is a small dagger that my father gave me. It is the only thing I have of him, so I always wear it when I compete so that I feel him with me."

"Oh?" she said, her thoughts shifting from Maximilian to

the mysterious dagger. "May I see it?"

"It is with my possessions in my tent," Addax said. "But I would be glad to show it to you. It is called the *Qara Ejder*."

"What does that mean?"

"It means the *Black Dragon*," he said. "You see, my father was called *kaara ejadar* by our people, and that is the name I adopted on the tournament circuit as a way of keeping him alive. The small dagger is representative of the kingdom, and the throne, that should be mine."

Her brow furrowed. "Your father was the king?"

"He was. I was his heir."

She blinked as if shocked by the information. "You have spoken of your country before, but I failed to understand that… Are you a *king*, my lord?"

He shrugged. "I should have been," he said. "Had Kitara not been sacked by my uncle and our enemies, I would have been."

She stared at him. Then she suddenly dropped into a curtsy and lowered her gaze. "I… I am so sorry, my lord," she said, sounding nervous. "I did not realize your position. I never meant to be disrespectful."

He frowned, reaching out to pull her to her feet. "Stop that," he commanded softly. "I am not a king. At least, not in England, so please do not treat me any differently. I only told you because we were speaking of the dagger. But I must ask you a question."

Emmeline still seemed a little nervous in his presence. "Go ahead."

"May I carry your favor tomorrow to take me to victory?"

Emmeline was surprised. "Me?" she said. "You want something from… me?"

He nodded. "If you will give it."

She wasn't sure what to say to him. Her nerves at learning of his true heritage faded as she looked over the crowds of clamoring admirers. "But... but surely there are a hundred maidens who would love for you to carry their favor," she said. "Why not ask one of them?"

He shook his head. "I never carry an unmarried woman's favor, lest she think that it means more than it does," he said. "I have no desire to find myself betrothed because of a misunderstanding. It is, therefore, my routine to ask a favor from the wife of a friend. It is much less messy that way, and I am certain Max would not mind."

With that explanation, the entire mood of the conversation changed as Emmeline's features lit up with delight. "In that case, I will give you a token, of course," she said. "What should it be? A kerchief? A jewel?"

"Anything you wish."

Emmeline's gem-colored eyes glittered at him. "I will think of something," she said. "And... thank you. I am most honored that you should ask. I've never had a knight ask for my favor before."

Addax could feel something stirring in his chest. The way she was looking at him was warm and friendly. But there was something more to it. He wasn't sure what it was, but he knew it wasn't healthy. Or honorable.

But, God, it felt good.

"I am the honored one, my lady," he said. "To be clear, it does not mean that we are betrothed."

Emmeline laughed softly at his jest. "I understand completely," she said. "Does it at least mean that we are friends?"

"Absolutely."

They smiled at one another, though Addax was having

trouble looking at her. Now that the question of the favor was settled, he realized he felt rather giddy about the whole thing. Carrying the favor of this lovely woman was a proud thing, indeed, and looking at her made him want to blush. It was a strange sensation, indeed, and one he didn't want to entertain or navigate, so he simply changed the subject.

It was safer that way.

"Now, shall we watch Hage disarm another opponent, or would you like to see something else?" he asked.

Emmeline pointed toward the village. "Would it be possible to find the man who makes the coffins again?" she asked. "I find that I am rather hungry."

Addax nodded. "Of course," he said. "Let us go and be gluttons together. Just coffins?"

"Fruit pies if we can find them."

"I suspect we can."

With a grin, she looped her hand into the crook of his elbow, an innocent gesture that meant nothing other than the fact they were heading in the same direction and he was escorting her. It wasn't improper in the least, but a common action.

Still... Addax felt her hand on his arm like a branding iron.

God help him, he loved it.

CHAPTER NINE

*V*ICTORIA MEA EST!

The next day, Addax destroyed the competition.

From her vantage point in the lists, Emmeline watched him put away three challengers, his own brother included, before the final bout came against William de Wolfe himself. By the time the Wolfe appeared, the Black Dragon was running high on the fires of victory, and the crowd, seeing their two favorite competitors going against one another, was screaming nonstop.

It was a match for the ages.

Emmeline had never been part of something so energetic. The crowd was in a frenzy as the two knights lined up against each other. Addax had several men with him—Essien, Cole, Maximilian, and Beau included, while William had Paris, Kieran, and Julian as support. The men supporting the knights did nothing more than making sure the horse was properly outfitted or ensure that the knight didn't need any last-minute assistance, but the moment the field marshals waved the yellow flag, the crowd leapt to their feet as Addax and William spurred their horses forward.

Emmeline almost couldn't watch.

She was in the lists with Corisande, who had joined her for the final games, explaining the rules that Addax hadn't covered and talking about the women in the lists and their fashionable clothing. This far away from London, they often didn't see such fashion, but given that Berwick was a port city, they were more cosmopolitan than most in the north. In fact, a few of the competitors and their families had taken cogs up the coast from London, and those expensive cogs were moored in the river. Corisande was discussing that very thing when the roar of the crowd drowned her out on the first pass.

Lances splintered, but no one was unseated. No one was even injured. Addax and William returned to their sides of the field and collected another lance as the horses were checked for any splinters or damage. Once the animals had been cleared, the knights lined up again and the flag dropped.

More screaming. More flying wood. De Wolfe lost his shield.

But no one was hurt.

Emmeline breathed a sigh of relief.

"Does Lord Blackadder compete?" she asked, using Cole's proper title.

Corisande grinned. "Not if I can help it," she said, giggling. "Truthfully, he loves to compete, but he has an empire that is dependent on him, and a family, so he doesn't compete as much as he would like to. The games can be dangerous."

Emmeline puffed out her cheeks in a gesture of agreement. "How do you stand it?" she asked. "It is positively nerve-racking to watch, wondering if someone will be injured."

Corisande shook her head. "When the champions compete like this, they are so skilled that no one will be injured," she said. "They are not trying to unseat each other, but simply trying to gain points by breaking lances or disarming their opponent. Whoever earns the most points will win."

Emmeline nodded, watching William as he fussed with the hilt of a lance as Addax waited patiently on the other side of the arena. "Is the prize a big one?" she asked.

Corisande nodded. "Quite substantial," she said. "I heard Cole say that it was two years' worth of a knight's salary. Whoever wins will be quite rich."

Emmeline was fixed on Addax, sitting tall and proud on the big, dappled charger he rode. Just to see him made her heart beat a little faster, but it was a sensation she quickly chased away. "Sir Addax told me that he is from a faraway kingdom and he wishes to earn money to raise an army to return," she said. "It sounds like a noble goal. At least he doesn't want to waste it on wine and women."

She chuckled at her own joke until she realized that was exactly what her husband had been doing since their marriage. Suddenly, it didn't seem so funny.

"Addax would be the last person to do that," Corisande said, not entirely oblivious of the inference toward Maximilian. "He is one of the most honorable men you will ever meet. But I think you already know that."

Emmeline looked at her. "He has been very kind to me," she said quietly. "But so have you. I cannot thank you enough for everything you have done, Cori. It has been such an honor to come to know you."

Corisande put her arm around Emmeline's shoulders. "I hope this means that we are friends forever, Emmy," she said. "I hope you will write to me when you return home. I should like to know how you are doing."

"Of course I will write," Emmeline assured her. "And you must write to me about your children. I would like to know if—"

She was cut off when the field marshal suddenly waved the flag and the knights bolted toward one another. The crowd began to scream again as the competitors thundered across the arena floor, separated only by the colorful guides, until they came within range. The lower portion of Addax's body remained in the saddle, but the upper portion moved sharply to the right as he brought up his lance. That caused William's lance to barely graze his left shoulder, while Addax's lance exploded on William's left arm. Since William was without his shield, it was a hard hit. The crowd went mad as the competitors returned to their respective sides, but it didn't take long to realize that William had been injured.

The crowd quickly quieted down as the field marshals went over to talk to de Wolfe. He was still mounted on his steed, but there was a conversation going on. His left arm seemed to be the issue. After a brief conversation, one of the field marshals went to the center of the arena and called up to the crowd.

"The Wolfe cannot continue," he shouted. "Victory to the Black Dragon!"

The crowd roared so loudly that Emmeline had to cover her ears. Both she and Corisande stood up, watching as Addax rode over to William to make sure the man wasn't too badly injured before making his sweep in front of an adoring crowd. Women were throwing silk kerchiefs and gloves and flowers at him, flowers that had been sold in the tournament village for just this purpose, while men threw coins. Addax drew his horse to a halt in front of the lists as his squires rushed around, collecting anything of value.

Emmeline watched it all, a smile on her lips, feeling something she'd never felt before—pride. She'd given the man a token before his day began, and, miraculously, it had brought him luck. She watched him as he said something to one of his squires, and the boy picked up several of the flowers that had been thrown down, mostly roses and a purple flower called the Scottish primrose. Addax had a big bunch of them in his hand as he lifted his helmed head to the crowd and pointed right at Emmeline.

At least, it looked like he pointed at her. She looked around to see if he was pointing at someone else, but Corisande saw the gesture and realized it was for Emmeline too. She knew the lady had given him a favor, and now, he was going to return the gesture. She pulled Emmeline to her feet.

"Go to the edge of the lists, dearest," she said. "He is going to give you those flowers."

"Me?" Emmeline said, uncertain. "Are you sure?"

Corisande began to walk with her, pulling her down the stairs toward the railing. "Of course I am sure," she said, pushing a child out of the way so they could get down the steps. "You gave him a favor, didn't you? He wants to thank you."

They made it down to the edge of the lists, about eye level with Addax as he reined his horse along the rail. The crowd quieted down, watching in anticipation as Addax removed his helm and lifted his voice to the crowd.

"It has been an honor to compete before you today," he shouted in his deep, rich voice. "I would like to introduce you to the lady who brought me good fortune, your queen of beauty and honor, Lady Emmeline de Grey, wife of my good friend, the King of Chaos. Show her your appreciation."

The crowd screamed its approval as Addax handed the bunch of flowers over to Emmeline, who was both embarrassed and thrilled. She took the flowers, her cheeks flaming with the attention. Addax saw her discomfort and laughed softly.

"It was your favor that did it," he said, reaching down into the front pocket of his tunic to show her that he had pinned the favor into the pocket. "This brought me great fortune today, my lady. Thank you."

Emmeline looked at the long, slender gold brooch that she had given him. "As I told you when I gave it to you, it belonged to my father," she said. "What I did not tell you was that my mother gave it to him on their wedding day, and I was planning on giving it to Maximilian, but... but I did not. It would not mean anything to him."

The smile faded from Addax's lips as he looked down at the bar brooch. It was a pin, meant to hold tunics or cloaks, a very manly-looking piece of jewelry. He hadn't known the significance of it when she gave it to him, but he knew it now. It touched him that she would think enough of him to let him borrow it.

"I am honored, truly," he told her as he unpinned it. "I am certain I would not have won had you not loaned it to me."

He was extending it to her, but Emmeline shook her head. "Nay," she said seriously. Her eyes lingered on him for a moment. "Please keep it. I would rather you have it. Did you see what is inscribed on the back?"

He hadn't. With some uncertainty that he should keep what was clearly an intimate gift, he looked at the back of the brooch, holding it up for better light. There was one word there, and he squinted, trying to read it. But when he realized what it said, his features relaxed with appreciation.

"Worthy," he said softly. "It says 'worthy.'"

Emmeline nodded. "Exactly," she said. "My mother gave it

to my father because he was worthy of her. Now, I give it to you because you are the only one worthy of it. You have shown me such kindness and understanding since our introduction that I can't imagine giving it to any other. It would mean a great deal to me if you kept it. Mayhap you will remember me with a smile when you look at it, a woman who was very grateful that you saved her life."

Addax still wasn't sure if he should keep it, but a glance at Corisande showed that she was nodding at him, very faintly. *Keep it,* she was telling him. Truth be told, Addax very much wanted to keep it, to remind him not of saving Emmeline's life, but of Emmeline herself. Given that she had married Maximilian, it would be the only thing he ever had of her.

He was coming to regret that more and more.

"Very well," he said, tucking it back into the pocket alongside the Black Dragon dagger. "If you wish it, I will keep it."

Emmeline smiled. "Good," she said. "Thank you."

"Nay, lady, thank *you.*"

She chuckled softly, smiling at the man she couldn't seem to stop smiling at. But the crowd was dispersing around them and there were people clamoring for Addax's attention, so he waved at them and then indicated for the ladies to follow him back to the competitor area of the tournament field. The general population wasn't allowed in that area, but he made sure Emmeline and Corisande were admitted. Cole was there along with Essien and Beau and Maximilian. When Maximilian saw his wife coming, he went over to meet her.

"Good," he said. "I was going to send a servant to fetch you, but you've saved me the trouble. I spoke to my father last night, and we are going to depart for home on the morrow. I want you to be ready to leave."

Emmeline had known the day would come, but it seemed that it was coming fairly soon. Not that she'd expected to stay for months in Berwick, but she was rather enjoying it here. She was making friends. Except for Maximilian, she was seeing the positive side of things. One positive was that he hadn't come to her last night. She'd spent the evening alone, in her borrowed chamber in Berwick Castle, and he hadn't joined her at all. There had been a feast in the hall that night, which she hadn't attended, but Corisande had made sure supper was sent up to her.

After spending most of the day with Addax and his friends, watching the sword bouts and stuffing themselves with coffins and beef and fruit pies, Addax had returned her to the castle before evening fell. He had things to attend to, which was sad for her because she'd thoroughly enjoyed his company, but spending the evening alone had afforded her time to think about Addax. He wasn't the man she'd married, but she was quickly growing attached to him. She could feel it.

Hence her reason for not attending the feast.

That meant she was wide open for Maximilian's arrival, but it never came. She'd been more than grateful. In fact, she hadn't even seen the man until that morning. She knew he'd hurt himself because she'd seen the bandages on his right arm during the sword bouts, but she hadn't asked about the injury, and no one told her about it. Frankly, she didn't really care. Quickly, she was building up an indifferent attitude toward him, purely as self-defense. If he wanted a businesslike marriage, then she would give him one.

It was the only way to survive.

"As you wish," she said after a moment. "I am already packed, so it is simply a matter of loading my trunks into the carriage, but I was hoping we might spend a little more time at Berwick. Lord and Lady Blackadder have been gracious hosts."

Maximilian nodded impatiently. "I know, but there is no reason for me to remain, considering I have this bloody broken arm now," he said. "I may as well return to Alston Castle and assess my new property, at least until my arm heals. I'll rejoin the tournament circuit at that time."

Bloody broken arm. Now she knew it was broken, but how it happened, she didn't care. She wouldn't ask. In fact, he'd just outlined his plans for the next few months, and she was nearly giddy with the thought that he intended to leave her at Alston Castle while he went back to the tournament circuit. As she pondered that bit of news, others were starting to join their little circle of conversation, Cole and Addax included.

"What's this you say?" Addax said to Maximilian, pulling off his heavy gloves. "You'll rejoin the circuit for the autumn season?"

Maximilian nodded. "I think so," he said. "I shall return to my new lands for the summer and allow my arm to heal before returning in the autumn. Why not come with me, Ad? Take the summer off from getting battered and bruised on the tournament circuit."

Why not come with me?

That was the invitation Addax had been hoping for. It came to naturally, so organically, that it was an effort not to agree immediately. He didn't want to seem as if he'd been eager for the invitation, so he slowed down. He fussed with his gloves, finally shrugging as he looked at Cole.

"What do you think?" he said casually. "Should I take the summer away from my adoring throng?"

Cole chuckled. "The question is if they can stand being

away from you," he said. "But I think Max may have an excellent suggestion. Besides, he may need help with that arm the way it is. He'll need a knight riding escort to protect his wife, at the very least, with his sword arm injured. You'd be doing him a favor."

Cole was making it so very easy for Addax to agree, as if the entire situation made perfect sense. Addax had planned to ingratiate himself to Claudius, who hadn't shown his face yesterday or today so far, ever since Addax saw him in the church with the Scots, but none of that needed to happen now.

Maximilian had given him a way in.

"I could probably use the rest away from the tournament circuit," he said, trying to make it sound as if he was still relatively undecided. "How soon do you need my decision?"

"My father wants to return home tomorrow," Maximilian said.

That drew some surprise from Addax. "So soon?"

"He wants to go home."

Addax looked at Cole, at Essien, before finally nodding. "Then I suppose I could go," he said. "Es, come with us. Let us enjoy some rest away from the constant battle of the tournament field."

Essien, who was well aware of the situation with Claudius and the Scots as well, nodded to his brother's invitation.

"Sounds intriguing," he said. "But we've got squires and a smithy and soldiers who depend on our winnings for their livelihood. What about them?"

"I will put them to work at Berwick," Cole said, stepping in. He didn't want anything keeping Addax and Essien from going to Alston Castle with Maximilian. "You needn't worry about them. You can send word when you want them to rejoin you."

"Excellent," Addax said, slapping Cole on the shoulder. "In that case, I've much to plan before tomorrow, but first I intend to make sure de Wolfe wasn't seriously injured, and then I will collect my purse."

Maximilian, in particular, seemed relieved. "Many thanks, Ad," he said. "It will be a pleasure having you at Alston for the summer. Just like old times. Penrith and Carlisle aren't terribly far. There are many good taverns there."

He meant drinking and women, something Addax knew a little something about. Not particularly the women, because he wasn't a womanizer like Maximilian was, but he'd had his fair share of drink.

Then he caught a glimpse of Emmeline.

She was looking at her feet as Maximilian spoke of taverns and old times. Addax realized that he was glad to go with Maximilian, not because Cole had asked it of him, but because Emmeline would be there. He'd be able to see her every day. He'd enjoyed talking to her so much that he was looking forward to that. But *only* that.

He knew damn well it could go no further.

But that didn't stop him from being happy about it.

"It will be a summer to remember, to be sure," he finally said. "Of course, I should like Lady de Grey's approval. I have a feeling I will be taking her husband away from her more than she might like."

As Emmeline looked up from her feet, surprised that he should take her feelings into consideration, Maximilian spoke for her.

"I would not worry," he said. "What I do does not concern her."

It was a callous thing to say, but Addax didn't comment on

it. There was no use. He did, however, see that Corisande was eyeing Maximilian quite unhappily.

He could only imagine what was going on in her mind.

Like nearly everyone else in Cole's inner circle, Corisande knew how poorly Maximilian had treated Emmeline from the start. She'd been sickened to hear that the woman had tried to kill herself over it the night before. Emmeline seemed to have new resolve this morning, but there was no telling what would happen when the months and years dragged on and Maximilian deliberately ignored his wife, leaving her alone and despondent.

"Max," Corisande said casually, reaching out to take Emmeline's hand. "Why not leave Emmy here with me whilst you inspect your new acquisition? We have gotten along famously, and I would like her company."

Maximilian looked puzzled. "Emmy?"

"Your wife," Corisande said patiently. "Her friends call her Emmy. Or didn't you take the time to find that out yet?"

Cole cleared his throat loudly as his wife began slinging insults. "I think the weather should hold for your journey home," he said, turning to block Corisande's view of Maximilian and putting his hands on the man to steer him away. "This time of year can be misty in the morning, but I do not anticipate any storms. I've got a man who swears he can read the weather, and he's been accurate so far."

Maximilian was moving toward the encampment with Cole and Addax right behind him. He said something about the weather in general as Cole looked over his shoulder and cast his wife a threatening look that she promptly ignored. As the men began filtering away and Addax departed to check on de Wolfe and collect his purse, Corisande turned to Emmeline.

"He deserved that, the stupid goat," she muttered, but realized it was not her place to chastise him, and she smiled weakly.

"I apologize, dearest. But men like that make me furious. He has such a beauty in you. He needs to recognize that."

Emmeline forced a smile. "I do not think he cares," she said. "But no matter—you heard him. He is going to heal from his broken arm and return to the tournament circuit, leaving me alone at Alston. And that is a pleasing prospect for me. Out of sight, out of mind."

Corisande thought that sounded very sad, but she refrained from commenting. Everyone's life was different and everyone's marriage was different. She shouldn't have said what she did, but she'd never liked Maximilian. The man had always seemed rather foolish to her, like a child who never grew up. She didn't like him more now that she'd seen how he treated someone as sweet as Emmeline.

But there was nothing she could do about it.

"Well," she said, taking Emmeline by the hand. "I think we should return to the castle and pack your belongings. And I will have the cook make a great basket of food for you to take with you."

Emmeline's smile turned grateful. "That is very kind of you," she said. "And I promise that the first missive I send you will have pressed flowers from Alston's garden. Will you send me seeds from Berwick to plant?"

Corisande loved that idea. "I will," she said as the women began the mile trek back to the castle. "Send me things from Alston that I can plant here as well. It will remind me of you."

It was a sweet sentiment, a turn in conversation that Corisande had planned. She was trying to make Emmeline's return to Alston Castle seem as if it was nothing at all. As if she wasn't going back with a cold husband and an uncertain future. But Corisande knew better than that.

And so did Emmeline.

CHAPTER TEN

Near Alston Castle
The Pennines

ALL OF THIS belongs to me.

Maximilian couldn't help feeling arrogantly proud of the land he was envisioning. It had rained the night before, but the sun was shining on the brilliant green hills of the Pennine Mountains. Everything smelled fresh and new. It would have been a lovely day if not for the mud they traveled upon. The horses were muddy up to their knees from the splashing, and the carriage wheels were filthy, spraying muddy water on the sides of the cab. But his first vision of the de Witt lands, which were now de Grey lands, had him smiling from ear to ear.

Maximilian, in spite of his broken arm, had chosen to ride his warhorse. He wore his broadsword—on his left side, even though he was right-handed—but wearing his mail coat was out of the question because he couldn't get his arm through the sleeve. Therefore, he was essentially riding unprotected as Addax, beside him, was in full battle regalia, with Essien riding at the rear of the escort to cover their back.

"We should be there within the hour, according to my father," Maximilian said to Addax. "He has been to Alston Castle before, you know. He says that it is a grand place. But look at these lands, Ad... This is all mine. Is it not magnificent?"

Addax was looking at the vibrant green hills. "How do you know it is yours?"

"Because it is!" Claudius, who was sitting in the carriage listening to the conversation, shouted through the fortified window. "The village we just passed through, Lanehead, is the southernmost boundary."

Addax nodded, noticing cottages in the distance as the road went up a hill. "Quite magnificent, Max," he said. "Congratulations, my friend. May you be worthy of it."

Maximilian beamed. It was clear how pleased he was. As he shielded his eyes from the sun, looking off to the north and seeing sheep on the hills, the door to the carriage swung open and Emmeline stepped out onto the road from the moving carriage.

The escort was riding at a normal pace, but she was walking quickly. Clad in a brown traveling dress, with leather boots that went to her knees and a cloak billowing out behind her, she walked up to the front of the escort and continued on, moving swiftly up the road. There was some kind of settlement in the distance, as they could see, but they realized that it was a town. Emmeline was heading for the town.

Maximilian frowned.

"You!" he called after her. "My lady! Where are you going?"

Addax watched carefully, wondering how she was going to respond. The entire four-day trip had seen the relationship between Maximilian and Emmeline deteriorate to the point where they were hardly speaking to one another.

It had been a concerning thing to watch.

When Addax should have been focused on Claudius and his plans with the Scots, he found himself watching Emmeline as Maximilian treated her like just another property. Just another something that was under his control. The first night of their journey had seen them stop in the village of Charlton. There were a few cottages and a tavern, but it only had one rentable chamber, and Maximilian and Claudius took that one, leaving Emmeline to sleep in the common room. They never gave a second thought to her, which had infuriated Addax.

Though Emmeline didn't complain and didn't ask for anything other than a hot meal, Addax had gone out of his way to find her accommodations. The tavern keep referred him to a widowed woman on the end of town who had been willing to surrender her bedchamber to Emmeline for a hefty price. Emmeline was able to sleep in a warm bed with a fire to heat the chamber, something she had thanked Addax profusely for.

Maximilian hadn't cared one way or the other.

That had been a turning point for Addax, too. The man he'd known for a few years had turned out to be an incredibly callous individual when it came to the woman he married. His true character was being revealed. He didn't exactly mistreat her, but he certainly didn't show her any respect. He kept referring back to their first conversation, when they had agreed that their marriage would be a business arrangement. Addax pointed out that even in a business arrangement, courtesy was shown, but Maximilian didn't seem to think it was an issue. He went on doing exactly what he wanted to do.

That left Addax to show Lady de Grey what respect he could.

But the days grew darker.

Since Emmeline had brought her own coin, the next night they stopped, she was the first one into the only tavern in the village of Cramlington, where she promptly cornered the tavern keep and asked for his finest chamber. He, too, only had one, and it went to Emmeline, which infuriated Maximilian and Claudius. There was no widow to rent them a chamber in this village, so they were forced to sleep in the common room at the tavern, where Claudius received a black eye because he pushed someone away from the fire.

Addax thought that he rather deserved it.

The next night, Maximilian and Emmeline got into a verbal altercation when she tried to do the same thing she'd done the night before. Maximilian declared that he was not going to sleep in the common room again, and she told him that was not her concern, which caused him to grab her by the arm and hurt her. She reacted by slapping him in self-defense, and Addax had to break up the fight. He also had to talk Maximilian out of punishing her.

After that, Emmeline had been the first one to secure a room, and Maximilian and Claudius, not to be outdone, broke into her chamber and tried to throw her out, but Addax had to calm the situation down, yet again, and the three of them ended up sleeping in the same chamber—Maximilian and his father on one side and Emmeline, in the larger bed, on the other.

Addax sat outside in the corridor by the door, all night, to make sure there was no more trouble.

Therefore, after four nights of the same battles, he was quite honestly exhausted. He was starting to wonder what would have happened had he not come along, but he was also coming to see a side of Emmeline that was quite strong. After the first tumultuous day and night after her introduction to her new husband, she'd very quickly made the decision to fight back. She was going to treat Maximilian and Claudius the same way they were treating her. No submission to their whims, no bowing and scraping to Maximilian's tantrums. She simply went about her business, and if that interfered with Maximilian's business, and he fought her on it, then there was a battle. Addax had to admit that he was impressed with the way she'd come out of the melancholy she suffered on the day of their marriage. This wasn't the same woman who had tried to drown herself in the River Tweed. That Plantagenet blood she inherited from her grandfather gave her something more to draw from, something deep and powerful that defied explanation.

The woman was a fighter.

And this marriage was going to be a battle.

Therefore, Addax watched curiously as she walked on ahead of the escort and Maximilian called after her. She simply waved him off, and, as Maximilian prepared to explode at her, Addax spurred his horse forward to catch up to the lady. He was the only one she would talk to, anyway. As he drew alongside her, he slid from his horse and took up stride beside her.

"And?" he said pleasantly. "Where are we going, and how may I assist you in reaching our destination, Lady de Grey?"

Emmeline was looking straight ahead. "You can do something for me, Sir Addax."

"Anything you wish, my lady."

"Never again address me, to my face, as Lady de Grey."

"Then what shall I call you?"

"Emmeline," she said. "That is my name. Or Emmy if you wish. I will answer to either. But I do not want to be reminded that I've taken the de Grey name."

"Very well," Addax said. "Then you must address me as Addax."

"I have been."

"You have been addressing me as *Sir* Addax," he said. "We are friends, are we not? There is no need to be so formal."

She finally looked at him for the first time. "Nay, there is not," she said. "In fact, I want to thank you for coming. I know you came because Maximilian asked you to, but I wanted you to come also. Your presence has been a godsend."

Addax found himself looking into those eyes, glittering like jewels, and knew he was feeling something other than friendship. God help him, he knew it. He'd known it for a few days now. Sometimes, people came into a man's life that were meant to be part of it from the moment they met, and he felt strongly that Emmeline was one of those people for him. He'd met so many people in his life—those who had helped him, those who had persecuted him, and those who had touched him. There were very few who had touched him. But Emmeline had.

As the days went by, he felt that more and more.

And he shouldn't.

"I am glad to hear that," he finally said, looking away. "It would not be a good situation for me if you were opposed to it."

Emmeline shook her head. "I should be opposed to the man who has kept me sane through this entire debacle?" she said ironically. "Nay, Addax, I was not opposed to you coming. Mayhap with you mediating my marriage in the beginning, Maximilian and I can at least come to the point where we do not wish to kill one another. I think you can help us."

"Do you?" he said, eyeing her. "Because it is not my place to interfere in your marriage."

"You are not interfering if you are helping."

He sighed sharply. "My lady…"

"Emmeline."

"*Emmeline,*" he said. "I came at Max's request. The only reason I have interfered when it came to sleeping arrangements is because what Max and his father were doing to you was not fair. It was not right. They were not behaving chivalrously, and I cannot abide that."

"You stepped in to help me."

"I stepped in to do what was right."

"But you helped *me.*"

"What is it that you want me to say?"

She shook her head. "Nothing," she said. "There is nothing *to* say. But I know what you did. You've been doing it from the start. The moment you fished me out of the River Tweed was the moment you became my champion."

He almost argued with her but thought better of it, mostly because she was right. He *had* appointed himself her champion, as much as he told himself that he was not involved in any way. He didn't *want* to be involved in any way.

But he was.

God help him.

"You had better not say that in front of Max," he said quietly. "He is your husband, and by God and the law, *he* is your champion. Not me. I do not know how he would react knowing that you view me as your savior, so please do not say that in front of him. Max is my friend, and I should like to keep that friendship intact."

Emmeline felt as if she'd just been slapped back a little. She wasn't sure why she felt rejected, but she did. Addax had been the one person she could depend on for kindness and compassion since this whole foolish mess started, but now he was telling her that he wasn't really her champion. He was just trying to keep the peace. If it came down to it, he would choose Maximilian, his friend, over anything that had to do with her.

That meant she was alone in this, again.

Still.

She felt stupid.

"I understand," she said steadily. "I have expected too much. Maximilian was your friend long before I was, so of course he should take precedence."

"I did not mean—"

She cut him off as she started to walk faster, moving away from him. "I said that I understand, Sir Addax," she said, back to addressing him formally. "Your loyalty is with Maximilian and not with me. I should not have assumed for a moment that our friendship was more important. I can see that I have imposed upon you, and for that, I apologize. Please return to Maximilian now. I can walk alone."

Addax watched her walk up ahead, sensing her clipped manner, hearing her brusque tone. He hadn't meant to hurt her feelings, but she was indeed assuming too much. Assuming he had any kind of a stake in her marriage with Maximilian, which he didn't. Assuming their friendship was more than an acquaintance, but the truth was that it wasn't as much as he wanted it to be. Since the day he met her, in spite of the bumps along the way, he'd come to know a witty, deeply introspective young woman with a good heart. She had absolutely no one to turn to, however, and Addax had been kind to her, so it was natural she'd grown dependent on him. So very natural.

And it was natural that he should like it.

Things were stirring in him that shouldn't be stirring.

Suddenly, Maximilian bolted past him. Startled from his thoughts, Addax watched as Maximilian thundered up to Emmeline where she was walking and cut her off. His horse kicked up some of the mud from the road, hitting her traveling dress with it, and she was forced to come to a stop as Maximilian demanded to know where she was going and how close they were to Alston Castle. As Emmeline and Maximilian discussed the end of their journey, Addax mounted his horse and moved it aside as the carriage pulled up. He took up pace beside it as it continued down the road, but Claudius opened the door, standing in the opening and looking at the landscape.

"I shall be staying the night at Alston Castle, but returning to Raisbeck on the morrow," he said. "I've been away from home long enough. May I have your brother escort me home?"

Addax looked over his shoulder at Essien at the rear of the group. "Aye, my lord," he said. "The Earl of Bretherdale should be afforded all due consideration."

Claudius was satisfied. "Thank you," he said. "I did not bring any knights with me, you know. Simply soldiers. But Alston has knights and a larger army because of the mines. De Witt had hundreds of men assigned to protect the mines."

Addax looked at him. "Thieves?"

Claudius nodded. "Thieves and jealous neighbors," he said. "I knew Ernest de Witt. I think the man was the suspicious type but I suppose that it is better to be safe."

Addax considered that. "But this area is remote," he said, looking around. "I should not think thieves or jealous neighbors would take the trouble to come all the way to the Pennines to rob mines. There must be easier ways of collecting ill-gotten gains."

Claudius conceded the point. "True," he said. "But the de

Witt mines are very rich. It must be worth the risk."

"Your lands border the de Witt lands, don't they?" Addax said. "And you have no ore on your property?"

Claudius shook his head. "We border the southwest portion," he said. "Unfortunately, no valuable deposits to the south. Which is why it was vital that I brokered the marriage contract between de Witt's widow and Max. Now, Bretherdale will be an enormous empire that can support itself easily. It will be important to find new buyers who will be willing to pay more for the raw ore."

Like Scots aiming for Berwick, Addax thought. They'd veered back on the subject that was at the heart of Addax's trip to the Pennines, so he chose his words carefully.

"Then you intend to help him expand the mining operation, my lord?" he said.

Claudius was looking at the small village up ahead and also the fact that Maximilian was riding back in their direction without his wife. She seemed to be far up ahead, still walking.

"Max is many things, but he does not have a head for making money," Claudius said. "He needs my help."

Addax, too, couldn't help but notice that Maximilian was returning alone. "He earns money on the tournament circuit," he said. "When I allow him to win, that is."

Claudius chuckled. "You are good to him, Addax," he said. "But to answer your question, I do intend to help him expand the operation. There are many who will pay a good price for the ore, probably better than what they already get for it."

Addax looked at him. "You mentioned that on the day Max and Emmeline married," he said. "You sounded as if you already had men lined up to purchase the ore, and when I said that Max would be pleased, you said it was not for Max. That tells me that you have big plans for the mining operation, bigger than anything de Witt did with it. Whatever it is, I still think Max will be grateful for your help."

It was a very leading thing to say, but Addax had planned it that way. He wanted to see if Bretherdale would explain his comment from the night of the wedding feast. Before he had a chance, however, Maximilian joined them, reining his excitable horse to a halt next to the carriage.

"That woman is by far the most impertinent, frustrating female I've ever had the misfortune to know," he said angrily.

Addax could feel trouble brewing again. "Where is she going?"

Maximilian threw his thumb in the direction he'd come from. "Evidently, Alston is over the rise," he said. "She wants to announce my arrival to the village we are about to pass through so the villagers can have the opportunity to see me. What do I care about a bunch of filthy peasants?"

"They are your vassals now," Addax reminded him. "It would be good for them to know their new liege."

Maximilian scratched his neck irritably. "I do not care," he said flatly. "In fact, I already hate this place. These towns, the castle—I haven't even seen the castle yet and I cannot stand it. I'm going to leave that woman at Alston and go about my business. I have no intention of spending any time here."

Addax looked to Claudius to address that comment, because he didn't really have the right to. Claudius was clearly unhappy with his son's attitude, but given he'd forced him into the marriage, it wasn't as if he could condemn him. He had every right to be upset.

"I would suggest you at least pretend to be a benevolent lord," Claudius said. "Most of these people work in the mines, I would imagine. Ernest told me some time ago that nearly everyone in his lands has something to do with the mines. If those working your mines do not like you, as your liege, bad things can happen."

Maximilian frowned. "Like what?"

Claudius was frank. "Production can suffer," he said. "They may not want to work hard for you. They may also steal from you. Max, I know you are only seeing the money in this marriage, but if your vassals decide not to work the mines because they do not like you, and production of the ore suffers, your wealth will be limited. You will spend it faster than you make it, and, eventually, you will be destitute. If that happens, I will not lift a finger to help you."

Maximilian shrugged. "What do I care?" he said. "I will simply go back on the tournament circuit. I do not need the de Witt money."

Claudius had to rethink his strategy, because listening to his son talk, he couldn't be sure that the man wasn't going to deliberately run the operation into the ground.

"Then if you do not care, as you put it, turn the mining over to me," he said. "I will manage it. I will handle your workers and vassals. But I will also take a percentage of it."

"But it is my money."

"Money you'll not have if you destroy everything de Witt has built," Claudius said. "Are you truly that foolish, boy? I never thought I raised an idiot, but your behavior since your marriage has indicated otherwise. It has disgusted your friends. It has disgusted me. There are men who would give everything they have for a marriage like this, yet you treat it like a disease. Wise up before it is too late, Maximilian."

The fatherly scolding had Maximilian reconsidering some-what, mostly because he knew his father was right. He'd been handed an advantageous marriage, and he knew it.

But he still wasn't happy with it.

Frustrated, he rolled his eyes.

"Very well," he said. "You take charge of the mines. Do what you will with them. But most of the money coming from them is mine."

"We will work out something agreeable to us both."

"Good," Maximilian said. They were drawing closer to the village now, and they could see people gathering in the street, greeting Emmeline as she came through. Maximilian could see her, and he sighed sharply. "Whatever happens, I do not plan to be here for long. Long enough to take whatever money I can and visit every tavern from here to Carlisle. In fact... as I recall, there is a lady I met at a tournament in Kendal who resides in Penrith. That is not far from here, is it?"

"Nay, it is not far," Claudius said. "About a day's ride to the west."

Maximilian nodded. "Then that is where I shall go," he said. "I'll spend my wife's money on a certain young lady, and my wife will have nothing to say about it. Papa, the mining operation is yours. Administer it in good health!"

With that, he spurred his horse forward, riding into the village just ahead of the escort as Emmeline announced him to the villagers who were standing around. Addax could hear her voice in the distance. But he turned to Claudius, still inside the carriage, noting that Claudius didn't seem too thrilled.

"Did you think he was going to react like this to a marriage?" Addax asked quietly. "Because I did not know this side of him. I am not entirely sure I like it."

Claudius didn't have an answer for him, mostly because he agreed.

He wasn't entirely sure he liked it, either.

CHAPTER ELEVEN

Alston Castle

*D*OES MAX HAVE *any idea how rich he is?*

That was what Addax was thinking as he listened to the scale of the de Witt mines as it was explained to him.

"With eleven lead mines, you can imagine that there are many men needed to cover that ground," the knight said. "We have nearly a thousand soldiers, but that is needed to protect everything."

"And you coordinate it all?" Addax asked incredulously.

"I do, my lord."

Addax was astonished. He was in conversation with a knight by the name of Adonis de Mora who had served Ernest de Witt for several years until the man's death. Adonis and his father, Pierre, who was also a knight, had been in charge of the security for the mines and the transportation of the goods. Ever since his arrival to Alston Castle two days ago, Addax had spent most of his time in the company of Adonis, while Maximilian had spent both of those days—and nights—at a nearby tavern called the Saddle and Swine.

No one tried to bring him back.

A few things had been clear to Addax from the start. The first was that Maximilian genuinely had no interest in Alston, its people, its mistress, or its operation. Addax had tried to convince him to stay at first, considering this was now his property, but Maximilian truly had no interest in remaining. He'd spent all of an hour walking through the bailey, looking at the stock inside the stables, inspecting the keep and anything of value, and then he promptly demanded whatever money was available.

Emmeline, who was very glad to be home, proceeded to give Maximilian a sack of coins that had been inside a pewter pitcher on the mantel of the solar. It was a rather large sack of coins, which pleased Maximilian, and he promptly rode out of Alston with his bag of money. That was all he cared about. Addax had watched him go and then proceeded to apologize to Emmeline for the man's behavior, which was unnecessary. She was glad to see him go. Furthermore, she admitted to Addax that she hadn't given Maximilian all of the coinage that he was entitled to. Knowing that he was simply going to waste it on drink, and God only knew what else, she was disinclined to give him everything.

Addax heartily agreed.

Her secret was safe with him.

The first night back at Alston Castle had been a quiet affair. Everyone was weary after the trip from Berwick, so there was no great feast or celebration. Alston populated by an enormous army and a fleet of servants, and everyone knew that Emmeline had been married, so it seemed strange to them that there was to be no celebration. But not so strange considering the groom had left for parts unknown and his father had already retired for the evening. That left Addax, Essien, and

Emmeline to keep one another company over a simple meal, and that was when Addax was introduced to Adonis and Pierre de Mora.

Spending the vast majority of his time with the two Alston knights had been Addax's routine since his arrival. Today, he was with Adonis as they walked the walls of Alston, which were so tall that they were vertiginous in some places. Addax never thought he was fearful of heights until Adonis took him to a tower that was at least seven stories tall, high enough that a huge swath of Alston lands could be seen from the top, including four of the mines. The steps leading up to the top were narrow, barely big enough for a man's foot, and quite steep. It was a great view, but Addax couldn't wait to get down.

But down they came, eventually, and now they found themselves near the gatehouse, where Addax was much more comfortable, discussing the security of the mines. Addax had to admit that it was quite an elaborate operation.

"I must say that everything you've discussed is quite impressive," he said. "You and your father are to be commended."

Adonis smiled, displaying his crooked teeth. In spite of his name, he was not a handsome man, but he was big and strong and able. "My father and Lord Ernest were friends as children," he said. "When Lord Ernest's father died, he asked my father to come and help him. He knew this was a large and important operation with the mines, but what makes the situation strange was that Lord Ernest's father actually kept him from the business of the mines, so when Lord Ernest took control, he knew nothing. He and my father had to figure out how everything worked. My father knows these lands better than Lord Ernest did."

Addax looked out over the large green hills. "It was generous of your father to help," he said. "It sounds as if de Witt owes him a great deal."

Adonis leaned against the wall, looking over the landscape as well. "He compensated my father quite well," he said. Then he looked at Addax. "Lady de Grey assured my father that the compensation would continue with the new lord."

Addax suspected the man was looking for some inside information. A new lord could mean new ways of doing things—and a new pay scale. "If Lady de Grey promised your father that nothing would change, then I would take her at her word," he said. "Nothing has been said to me that would indicate otherwise."

Adonis looked at him a moment before averting his gaze, shaking his head as he did so. "Forgive me," he said. "It is only that the new Lord Rheged—"

Addax interrupted. "*Who* is Lord Rheged?"

"That is the hereditary title of the lords of Alston Castle," Adonis said. "It is only that Lord Rheged left as soon as he arrived, and he made no effort to greet either my father or myself, and find out anything about Alston Castle and its workings. Is he displeased somehow, my lord?"

Addax knew the man was uncertain about his future. He had suffered from that fear at various times in his life, so he understood it. He sought to give the man some assurance without saying too much.

"He had pressing business elsewhere," he said, though it was a lie. "He will return, and I am sure you will find that nothing will change. I would not worry."

That seemed to give Adonis some comfort. "Then I will not," he said. "Thank you for your candor. Now, would you like to ride out to the nearest mine? I would be pleased to show it to you."

Addax shook his head. "Later, if possible," he said. "For now, I'd like to know how the ore is sold. Who your customers are. What can you tell me?"

Adonis shrugged. "Not much," he said. "That was always Lady de Witt... I mean, Lady de Gray's responsibility. She can tell you much more than I can."

"Then I shall ask her," Addax said. "Thank you for taking the time to explain the mines to me. I appreciate it."

Adonis smiled politely. "I am glad to do it," he said. Then his smile faded. "And... and you serve the new Lord Rheged, my lord? Will you be staying?"

Addax hadn't actually introduced himself beyond his name to de Mora, who was more than willing to tell him anything he wanted to know. The man was trying very hard to be helpful, perhaps to keep his position. The introduction of a new knight possibly meant he wouldn't be needed any longer, but Addax shook his head.

"I do not serve Rheged, and I am not staying," he said. "My liege is the Earl of Hereford and Worcester. I have also served William Marshal and Baron Blackadder, Ajax de Velt, at various times. I am simply a friend of Lord Rheged and was asked to accompany him to his new property."

Those names meant something to Adonis, who seemed to stand up a little straighter when he realized he was facing an elite knight. To have served such masters surely meant he was one of the very best.

"I see," he said. "To serve Hereford... He is an important man."

Addax nodded. "He is, indeed," he said. "De Mora, I will be sure to let Lord Rheged know just how helpful you have been. I will also tell the Earl of Bretherdale. You are aware that he is Lord Rheged's father."

Adonis nodded. "I was informed."

"Bretherdale, at the very least, will want to know. He will be comforted to know that his son has good knights to serve him."

"Your kind words are appreciated."

Addax smiled, seeing that the man was more nervous about his position and the future than he let on. He wagged a finger at him.

"Don't worry so much," he said. "No one is going anywhere. Go about your duties with confidence."

With that, he turned for the break in the wall with the ladder that led down to the bailey below.

He had a lady to see.

⌘

SHE'D BEEN WATCHING him all morning.

In the solar of Alston's keep, a room situated on the entry level, right up front, and with a grand oriel window to overlook the gatehouse and the main part of the bailey, Emmeline had been watching Addax all morning.

It was a chamber that had belonged to her since Ernest's death and, truthfully, even before that. It had an enormous table that faced the window, and alongside that table, and underneath it, were wooden boxes that contained years of records of the de Witt mines. There was also a cabinet next to the table that contained neatly organized stacks of vellum that held the most recent production and sales records. Those were records that Emmeline had been keeping for almost ten years, ever since she married Ernest and he decided that he didn't want to do the clerical work any longer. He gave his young wife the burden, and, fortunately, she'd taken to it.

Along with the financial records, that also meant she was in charge of the money.

That was something she'd been very good at.

More than that, she was protective over it. She knew very well that her marriage to Maximilian entitled him to the wealth, and if she'd liked the man, that would have made it easier to surrender the coin.

But she didn't like him.

Furthermore, it seemed to her that Maximilian was going to behave exactly the way Ernest had—he wanted money, sacks of it, for his spending habits, which in Ernest's case meant gambling, and Emmeline had learned quickly early in their marriage to hide money from him. If he knew where the money was, he would take it, so she hid it all over the keep in small increments. The larger coffers—and they were literally chests filled with coin—were strategically hidden away in the stores in the lower level of the keep. Thousands of pounds were camouflaged alongside barrels of turnips, sacks of carrots, and other stores. There was no way to get to them without weeding through a thousand boxes, barrels, and sacks.

Only a few people in the keep knew they were there. The cook and the kitchen servants knew. Adonis and Pierre knew. Emmeline's maid knew, but the woman was old and hard of hearing, and when Ernest had demanded money, she'd pretended she didn't hear him. Ernest would find the sacks of money around the keep, and that kept him from searching for the larger stores of it. Like a child, in a sense, he'd been baited away.

Emmeline hoped that Maximilian was just as easily satisfied.

She had hinted to Addax that the sack of coins Maximilian took from the solar on the day he arrived wasn't all there was. Even if Addax was Maximilian's friend—and he'd made it clear that their friendship superseded anything Emmeline and he had built—she trusted him not to tell Maximilian. She knew that Addax was well aware of Maximilian's frivolous nature. She'd gotten that sense from him quickly. Another person to hide the money from was the Earl of Bretherdale himself, a man who had asked about it before leaving that morning to go home with Essien as his escort. With both Maximilian and his father gone, Emmeline felt as if she could breathe again. She was home, her new husband and his father had departed, and she was free once again.

Sort of.

There *was* Addax.

He was, perhaps, the biggest factor of all. A man who had been by her side since the moment she was introduced to Maximilian. He was the one who had stepped in to talk to her, to get to know her, but that was purely out of necessity, considering how Maximilian had behaved. He'd been easy to get along with, and he got on very well with Maximilian, which hadn't gone unnoticed by Emmeline. In fact, on the day of their arrival back to Alston Castle, Emmeline had spent nearly the entire day wondering if the situation between her and Maximilian wasn't somehow her fault. Perhaps she had done something that had caused Maximilian to ignore her. Perhaps she had given off a mood that was a deterrent to her new husband, so perhaps all of this had been her fault from the beginning. He'd told her he'd liked blondes and not brunettes, and he'd told her that he liked his women younger.

That had immediately put her on her guard.

Perhaps she could have tried to change his mind, but the effort didn't seem worth it. If she had to pretend to be something she wasn't, or lure a man in as if she was second best against what he wanted, then he wasn't worth it at all. She hadn't done anything wrong.

Maximilian had been the cause of it all.

Ever since she had married the man, all she had done was analyze the situation and rationalize it. She'd wept over it and, in a fit of momentary madness, even tried to kill herself. But that wasn't who she was—that didn't define her character—and she finally came to the conclusion that she was going to treat her new husband exactly the same way he was treating her. With indifference and a lack of respect. They were married, and she could do nothing about that, but that didn't mean she had to like it. Or him. She simply could not believe that a man like Addax, who was kind and thoughtful and insightful, could be friends with someone like Maximilian.

It was a mystery.

But one thing that wasn't a mystery was Addax himself. She'd come to the conclusion over the past couple of days that she would have given up all of Alston's treasure if it had been Addax she married and not Maximilian. In her view, Addax was perfect. He listened to her when she spoke, he respected her opinion, he was thoughtful to her wishes, and he was kind when she needed it. She thought perhaps that she felt an attachment to him because he'd fished her out of the river on that dark and icy night, but she realized that she would have felt attached to him regardless of his heroic actions. Not only was he handsome and beautifully built, but he had dark eyes that glittered at her in a way that made her feel giddy and warm. Those dark eyes reached into her soul and touched places that no man had ever touched. Was she infatuated with him? Without a doubt.

... But was she feeling more?

She was terrified to face that answer.

So, Emmeline went back to her usual duties now that they had returned to Alston and ignored what she might, or might not, be feeling for a man who was not her husband. Addax spent his time with Adonis, learning about the castle's function and the mining operations, something that he could explain to Maximilian, because Emmeline certainly didn't want to. She managed the records of sales and production, and she handled the money, and she knew that at some point she was going to have to explain it to her husband, but she'd made a decision early on that she wasn't going to tell him everything. She was only going to tell him what he needed to know. If he was anything like Ernest, he would only be concerned with the end result—the money. Ernest had left her alone to do what she needed to do, and she wanted Maximilian to do the same thing.

What she wanted was control.

And she was going to have it.

Seated at the enormous table that had been shipped all the way from Spain by Ernest's father, she could see the bailey from where she was seated. That meant she could also see the northeast tower that soared seven stories above the land. She saw when Adonis and Addax went into the tower, no doubt to survey the landscape, and she clearly saw when Addax came shooting out of the tower as if the devil was chasing him. She had to grin because she knew the stairs up to the top level were narrow and treacherous, only for the strong of heart. Addax could win a tournament and defeat men like William de Wolfe, but perhaps those treacherous stairs were more than his bravery was willing to bear.

That brought a giggle.

Emmeline had been working on the production quotas for the coming month, but she set her quill down to watch Addax and Adonis on the wall walk in conversation. Emmeline liked Adonis, but she looked upon him more like a brother, and in years past, he had hoped that she might look upon him more as a lover. Ernest certainly had no interest in her, as young and beautiful as she was, but that didn't stop Adonis from pining after her for a few years. When he realized that his attention was unrequited, he simply resigned himself to working alongside the beautiful woman that he greatly admired.

Emmeline's smile faded as she thought on Adonis and Pierre and how their lives might change if Maximilian decided he no longer wanted the father and the son to serve Alston. The two had, of course, sworn fealty to the House of de Witt, and that meant staying with Lady de Witt after her husband passed away, so the truth was that they were sworn to the family and not to the castle itself. They handled so much of the mining operations between the two of them that Emmeline sincerely hoped Maximilian would not send them away. She was determined to do her best to make sure he did not. Even if she did not want Adonis for a lover, that didn't mean she wanted to see the man cast aside.

He'd earned his right to stay.

Emmeline watched Adonis and Addax for quite some time as they conversed upon the wall walk before she finally picked up her quill again and went back to her figures. There was a silversmith guild in Manchester who made a large purchase of ore every year, and they were coming upon that purchase again. Ernest had insisted on negotiating the price, even if he didn't have any other inclination to administer the business, and

Emmeline knew that the past three years had seen the prices increasingly raised. Their mines produced good ore, and she didn't want to see the silversmiths go anywhere else to purchase their raw material because she was afraid their displeasure in the Alston ore would get around, and it might make it difficult for her to sell to other guilds. Just as she pondered sending the silversmith guild a missive telling them that she was going to be reducing the price per ton, someone knocked softly on the solar door.

"Come," she said.

The panel, carved from a dark slab of oak, swung open on brass hinges to reveal Addax standing in the doorway. When Emmeline looked up and saw him, her heart leapt with joy. With a smile on her face, she set the quill down.

"Tell me something," she said.

He came into the chamber, those dark eyes glittering at her. "Anything you wish."

"Did you not enjoy the view from our tallest tower?"

He looked at her frowning, before turning to the oriel window and realizing she had a perfect view of the tower. Knowing his fear of heights had been discovered, he shook his head vehemently.

"I did *not*," he said, seeking out the nearest chair and planting himself firmly. "That tower ought to be burned to the ground. It is terrifying and meant for fools. I never want to see it again."

Emmeline laughed heartily. "I do not blame you," she said. "Adonis and Pierre do not seem to be bothered by it, but it frightens me to death. I will not go near it."

Addax was grinning at her, flashing his big white teeth. "Nor I, anymore," he said. "Might I suggest we form an army of our own and tear it down one night when no one is watching?"

He was jesting with her, and she liked that. She had come to see that he had a sense of humor she found utterly charming.

"I am listening," she said, in on the joke. "What did you have in mind?"

"Do you have any siege engines?"

"What are those?"

He made flinging motions. "Trebuchets," he said. "They are attached to a frame and have an arm that sticks up. You lower the arm, load it with rocks, and launch it at the enemy."

Realization dawned. "A catapult!" she said.

He nodded. "Aye," he said. "Do you have one?"

She shook her head. "Alas, we do not," she said. "I do not think the de Witt family has gone to war in forty years. Ernest's father never did as far as I know, and Ernest never did."

"A pity."

"Mayhap we can borrow one!"

His grin was back. "Aye," he said. "Mayhap we can. Northwood has them, but they are too far to the north. Moreover, they need them against the Scots. I would not take away their siege engines."

"Can we simply not build a fire in the base of the tower and hope it burns it down?"

He shrugged. "Possibly," he said. "But you risk the chance of the fire spreading."

"I would not wish to burn the entire castle down."

Addax sighed dramatically. "Then I suppose we shall simply have to look at that horror every day until I can think of a way to topple it."

Emmeline laughed softly. "Mayhap we will get lucky and lightning will strike it and knock it down," she said. "One can hope."

He snorted. "One can," he said. "But I will say that the view was spectacular from the top."

Emmeline nodded. "It truly is," she said. "Is that what Adonis was doing? Showing you the view?"

Addax nodded. "He was showing me the land and the mines within range," he said. "I asked him some questions that he could not answer. He said you would know more."

"What would you like to know?"

"It was only curiosity, really," he said. "I wondered how the ore was sold and to whom. Do you ship it over the sea or only to local customers? That kind of thing."

Emmeline had her quill in her hand. She pointed to the cabinet with the stacked records. "See all of that?" she said. "Every one of those sheets has records of sales. When, where, and to whom."

"I'm told there are ten mines."

"Eleven," Emmeline corrected him. "Silver can be extracted from lead, only we do not have the capability here to do that. We simply sell the ore, to the silversmith guilds mostly, but also to bankers. They use their own process to extract the silver for coin or jewelry or whatever they want."

"Your prices must be reasonable, or you would not be so successful."

She shrugged, looking down at the vellum she'd been writing on. "Ironic that you should say that," she said. "Ernest raised prices on the ore over the past three years, and I was just considering lowering the price and sending word to the silversmith guilds who have purchased from us. Last year, not everyone who usually purchased from us did so, which leads me to believe they were buying elsewhere."

"May I ask what the price was?"

She leaned over and pulled a rolled vellum from the cabinet, carefully done so as not to disturb the other rolls next to it. She unrolled it, reading the contents.

"When I first began keeping records, a wagonload of ore sold for around three hundred pounds," she said. "Ernest raised it to almost six hundred pounds."

"And people were still paying it?"

She nodded. "The quality of our ore is pure," she said. "You cannot find it as pure anywhere in England."

Addax was interested. "De Mora was telling me that he and his father create the schedules for the mines," he said. "They oversee the mine commanders, who manage the workers."

Emmeline nodded. "They do," she said. "They have always done a remarkable job."

"I think Adonis is afraid they might lose their position with the new Lord Rheged."

Emmeline seemed to lose her good mood. "I hope he will not send them away," she said. "I do not know why he would, but he seems to be contrary in everything he does."

Addax thought on her statement for a moment. "I do not know if this helps, but I have known Max for a few years," he said. "I have refrained from telling you what I know of him because I wanted you to form your own opinions, and, quite honestly, it is none of my affair. The Max I know was humorous, a little reckless, a little selfish, but always loyal. But his father forcing him into marriage has caused him to revolt. I believe that is what you are seeing—a revolt."

Emmeline sat back in her chair. "Aye, but the revolt is against me," she said with some passion. "I have not done anything to deserve his resentment, yet I bear the brunt of it."

Addax lowered his gaze. "I know," he said. "I think that all he needs is time. I *hope* that is all he needs, because I cannot stay here forever to mediate. I have my own life to live."

Emmeline watched his lowered head. He was looking at the way his black hair draped over one side of his face, long past his shoulders, but with a hint of a curl to it. He had the most miraculous hair. It made him look wild and free, like an untamed stallion.

But his words cut her like a knife.

"Of course you do," she murmured. "You should not even have to be here now. I do not know why Maximilian asked you to come."

Addax shrugged. "To take a rest from the tournament circuit," he said. "I will only be here through the summer, and then I shall return."

"Return to being a champion."

"Aye."

"But is that all?"

He lifted his gaze. "Is what all?"

She shrugged, setting her quill down and standing up from the chair. "Is that all you ever want to be?" she asked. "A tournament champion? Surely there is more you want."

"Like what?"

She came around the table, leaning on the end of it as she stood in front of him. "Like… well, like marriage and children," she said. "Look at your friend Max. Even he married well, though I cannot imagine why a man like him should have such good fortune in a wife. Surely you want to marry and live well?"

He was gazing up at her. "Of course I do," he said softly. "I want to marry a woman who knows her own mind, stands up to the unrighteous, mayhap manages a great empire that, shall we say, mines lead, and is terrified of tall towers."

Emmeline stared at him. His answer made her heart race so much that he surely must have heard it bashing against her ribcage. God, if it were only possible. To hear him voice what she'd been thinking nearly drove her to tears, but instead, she forced a smile.

It was only a dream, after all.

A silly, impossible dream.

"A woman like that would exhaust you," she said. "She would argue every little command you gave and question every decision. She would not be content to be submissive by your side, and you, my great king, would not tolerate that. You need a submissive queen."

"I would be bored out of my mind with a submissive queen."

Emmeline sank to her knees a few feet in front of him, sitting back on her heels. "Do you ever think you'll go back?" she asked sincerely. "To Kitara, I mean. So much could have happened since you left. Mayhap... mayhap your father has regained control and has spent all of these years looking for you. Is such a thing possible?"

Addax was having difficulty with the fact that she was on her knees in front of him. He knew she hadn't done it on purpose. Instead of sitting on a chair, she was sitting on the floor, and he had never in his life wanted to grab someone as much as he wanted to grab her. He wanted to wrap his hands around her face and pull her lips to his, tasting her in a way she'd never been tasted before. Her skin, so smooth and flawless, needed to be tasted as well. Touched and tasted. This woman who belonged to another.

This woman who was getting under his skin.

"I suppose anything is possible," he finally managed to say. "I was very young when I fled the Larkana Palace, so I do not remember much. Just flashes of memories, really. More like dreams. I do know that something very bad was approaching, and my father was burning the city rather than let his brother have it."

"What was your father's name?"

"Amare."

"Amare," she repeated softly, rolling it off her tongue. *A-mar-ay*. "That is a very strong name. What was he like?"

Addax sat forward in the chair, his elbows resting on his knees, his face about a foot from hers. "He played with his children a great deal," he said as visions of his father rolled forth from the cobwebs of his memory. "He had a deep laugh—a very deep laugh. And he liked to tickle. I remember him tickling Es and Adanya until they cried, and then my mother would scold him. But he would just laugh."

"Who is Adanya?"

"My sister."

She nodded in understanding. "The one you lost sight of along with your mother."

"Aye."

"She was younger than you?"

He nodded. "I was the oldest."

"And what do you remember about your homeland?" Emmeline asked, but then she suddenly stopped herself. "Forgive me. If it is too painful to speak of, you do not have to answer. I was simply curious."

He shook his head. "It is not too painful to speak of, but the truth is that I remember very little," he said. "I remember golden deserts, great mountains, and an enormous river running next to the city. The Larkana Palace had been the home of my ancestors. It was not built like an English castle."

"How do you mean?"

He looked at the stone walls around him. "My homeland was very hot and very dry," he said. "These walls are built to keep out the cold, but if there is no cold and only heat, you must build a different way. You must build a castle so that the breezes blow through it and keep it cool, but you must also have the ability to close up those walls to keep out the monsoons."

"What are those?"

"Terrible storms with rain and wind."

Emmeline smiled faintly. "It sounds fascinating," she said. "And these open palaces—what do they look like?"

He looked to the north wall, the one with the oriel window, and gestured. "Imagine that wall was only pillars to hold up the roof," he said. "Usually, the pillars had great curtains that hung between them, keeping out the insects and vermin, but still allowing the breezes to flow. When the weather turned bad, the servants would bring out great panels of wood and secure them across the openings. It was enough to keep out the storm and winds, but sometimes, my father liked to leave the pillars in his *istabalja* chamber open and watch the storm. My father thought that he was honoring Allah by doing so. If He was kind enough to send a storm, then he should enjoy it."

She grinned. "Who is Allah? A god?"

He nodded with great certainty. "It is another name for God."

"And *istablaja*? What does that mean?"

"It's a formal type of chamber. A receiving chamber for the king."

Emmeline nodded in understanding, but she was staring at

him openly. Studying him. Addax could see that there was more on her mind. "What is it?" he said. "Why do you look at me so?"

Emmeline shrugged faintly. "Because I was thinking that you should be ruling a million people," she said, almost wistfully. "You are a king. You should have a queen and a dozen sons, and your legacy should be secure. I have seen over the short time I have known you that you have strength of character and that you are quite diplomatic. You are wise and curious. You are kind. You are everything a king should be but seldom is. Yet... here you are. Because of greed, here you are. You ride in tournaments. You have no property, no family. I have been feeling sorry for myself since the introduction of that man I was forced to marry, but I realize that you... Fate has treated you most unfairly, Addax. You deserve so much more."

He chuckled softly, reaching out to stroke her cheek in gratitude, perhaps even affection, before sitting back in his chair. "Do not feel any pity for me," he said. "It could have been much worse. As it is, I am wealthy and I have friends and I am happy. Truly, there is nothing to be sorry for."

"That you can even say such a thing speaks well for you. Most men would be bitter."

"I am not most men."

"I am finding that out for myself."

The way she said it was quite leading. At least, Addax thought so. Was she intimating that she was finding him as attractive as he was finding her? Or were they simply words from one friend to another? He wasn't certain, and, to be honest, he probably should have excused himself before things were said that couldn't be taken back.

But he couldn't seem to manage it.

"I hope that is a good thing," he said, then immediately thought, *Why did I say that?* It sounded so... seductive. Alluring. He hadn't meant it to sound the way it had, so he quickly tried to recover. "I do not think you've come to know my brother. Essien is a man of character, also, though he's a bit more emotional than I am. He's a passionate man."

Oh, God, why did I say passionate? I didn't mean passionate! he thought, but Emmeline didn't react to what could have been very suggestive comments.

"He's fairer than you are," she said. "And I do not think he looks much like you."

"He looks like our mother."

"What was her name?"

"Kiya."

Emmeline smiled. "That is a lovely name," she said. "She must have been a beautiful woman."

Addax nodded. "She was fair-skinned, with eyes that were green and gold. Very beautiful."

"Did your parents have a happy marriage?"

"Very much."

Emmeline thought on that before standing up. "That is lovely," she said. "I am glad they knew happiness, even if it was short-lived. Some people marry and never know happiness at all, so they were fortunate."

"I think so," Addax said as he watched her go back to the table and sit down. "Take heart, my lady. You may be happy yet. Give Max time. He may come to his senses. He would be a fool not to."

Emmeline sighed as she looked at the table in front of her. "It does not matter," she said. "We are married, but I will never be his wife, not really."

"You do not know that for certain."

She snorted rudely. "And what do I know for certain?" she said. "That is he is using the money I gave him to pay for drink and for a woman to fuck? Money *I* gave him? I am not stupid, my lord. I know exactly what he is doing, and I will tell you this now—if he ever tries to climb into my bed again, I will fight him to the death. I would rather die than let him touch me. So, nay—there will be no happiness in this marriage. That has already been established. And I shall go to my grave having never known a loving touch or the kiss of a man I love beyond all reason. That is why I envy your parents—at least they knew what love was. Mayhap it was not for long, but at least they knew it."

"Emmeline, you cannot—"

She cut him off, though not rudely. "Just... leave me alone now, Addax," she said. "Please. I have work to do."

Addax's gaze lingered on her a moment before he stood up, quite sadly, so very sad that he'd upset her. He could feel her pain, her angst, with every word, and what was more troubling was that he wanted to do something about it. He'd never wanted to be Maximilian, ever, but at this moment, he wished he was. He would have taken Emmeline in his arms, looked her in the eyes, and then kissed her with passion beyond all reason. He felt a kindred spirit with her as he'd never felt with anyone, this beautiful woman he would have been so very proud to have on his arm.

This is my wife, Emmy, he would have introduced her.

And he would have been the envy of all men.

But instead, Maximilian was married to her. And abusing every second of that marriage.

Without another word, he left the solar, shutting the panel

behind him and heading for the keep entry. But he paused before he headed out, thinking that he should at least say something comforting to her. Something that might help her at least deal with the bone-crushing sorrow she was feeling. He'd managed to do that several times before, but perhaps it was needed now more than ever. Retracing his steps to the panel, he lifted his hand to knock but was stopped by what he heard on the other side of the door.

Bone-crushing, agonizing weeping.

Her sobs broke his heart.

CHAPTER TWELVE

Six months later

*D*ID I HEAR *that correctly?*
"What do you mean, there is no more money?"

Maximilian was facing off against his wife in the solar of Alston's great keep. He'd come looking for coin, and Emmeline told him that there wasn't any more. Enraged, he looked at the woman as if she'd just committed some horrible crime, but Emmeline wasn't backing down.

She stood her ground.

"Just what I told you," she said steadily. "You have managed to spend all of the coin we had. I'm expecting payment for an ore shipment any day now, but I do not know when that is coming, so if you want money, you'll have to ask your father for it or you'll have to wait."

Maximilian was furious. In the past six months, with drinking and whoring and eating like a king, he'd managed to put on a good deal of weight. No tournament riding meant he wasn't working off what he ate or drank. Additionally, his right arm hadn't healed correctly, and it was painful to hold the lance, or anything else, with that wrist, so he was facing the end of his tournament career and grossly unhappy for it.

He blamed Emmeline entirely.

Lady de Witt, he called her. He couldn't even bring himself to call her Lady de Grey, not even when she discovered that the one time he'd bedded her in the storeroom of St. Andrews Cathedral had produced a pregnancy. She was six months pregnant with his child, and more stubborn and argumentative, in Maximilian's view, than she'd ever been. He didn't even believe that the child was his, because they'd only been together once, but she assured him that it was, as loath as she was to acknowledge that he was the father. Their marriage over the past six months hadn't just deteriorated.

It had descended into hell.

"What is the shouting about?"

Addax stood in the doorway. Because of her pregnancy, and Maximilian's increasing alcohol consumption and hostility, he'd chosen not to leave when the summer transitioned into autumn. Maximilian hated having him around these days because he always took Emmeline's side. Everyone took Emmeline's side.

Maximilian was so angry about it that he could spit.

"God," he groaned when he saw Addax. "Not you. What do you want?"

Addax came into the chamber. "I could hear the shouting outside," he said. "What is the argument about this time?"

Maximilian couldn't even look at Emmeline. "She tells me there is no more money," he said. "I know she is hiding it from me!"

"I am not hiding it from you," Emmeline said, though it was a lie. She very much was. "You've spent it all on drink and women. Why don't you go spend some of your own money?

You've made enough on the tournament circuit. Go spend that for a change."

Maximilian whirled on her, teeth bared. "You'll not tell me what to do," he growled. "I'll break your bloody neck."

Addax was there, pushing Maximilian away from Emmeline, who had picked up the fire poker. That had happened a few times, too, when Addax wasn't around. Maximilian had moved in to hurt her, and she'd brained him with the poker. Once she very nearly put his eye out.

"Put the poker down, Emmy," Addax said quietly, holding out a hand to her in a gesture to lower the rod. "Put it down, my lady. Thank you. Now, Max, you cannot attack your wife. We have talked about this. She carries your son. Would you truly injure your son?"

Maximilian was furious. He kicked a table over and tossed a chair into the wall. "This is *my* property," he shouted. "The money is mine. Where is it?"

"You've spent it all," Emmeline shouted in return. "You've spent almost one hundred pounds in six months. There is no more!"

Maximilian kicked another chair. Addax was about to bodily remove him from the solar when he heard the gate sentries take up the cry. Someone was arriving. He dared to move out from between Emmeline and Maximilian to look out of the window, spying his brother as the man went to greet Claudius. Addax hadn't seen Claudius in about three months. Quickly, he turned back to Maximilian.

"Your father is here," he said, putting his hands on the man and steering him toward the door. "Go and greet him."

Maximilian quit the solar, grumbling all the way. Addax watched the man go to the keep entry, throw the door open, and stomp out to the bailey before turning to Emmeline.

"Are you well?" he asked softly. "He did not hurt you, did he?"

Emmeline shook her head. "Of course not," she said. Then she smiled weakly. "How could he with my champion nearby?"

Addax put his finger to his lips in a silencing gesture. "What did I tell you about that?"

Eyes twinkling, Emmeline went over to him, stood on tip-toe, and kissed him on the cheek. "There," she said. "You have my gratitude."

Addax lost his humor and very nearly his self-control. She'd done that before—kissed his cheek in gratitude—and nothing on earth had ever inflamed him more. Not in a rage-inducing sense, but in the sense that he was completely, and utterly, in love with Emmeline, and he wanted nothing more than to tell her. To touch her. The past six months at Alston had been some of the most wonderful of his life, but also the most distressing. He'd hinted to her about his feelings, once, but only once. There had never been another instance. Moreover, his behavior had always been polite. Polite bordering on perhaps a little too friendly. He'd been a paradox and had struggled not to be.

In turn, Emmeline had behaved in much the same fashion. They laughed together, had conversations that lasted hours, and there was a particular board game that they would play and play again. When Addax didn't win, he would lie down on the floor, facedown, and refuse to move until she agreed to play him again so that he might triumph. It was a little routine they had, something hilarious and sweet and warm. He lived for those moments.

He lived for her.

But he couldn't tell her that.

Unfortunately, his relationship with Maximilian had also deteriorated. The loss of complete use of his right arm had reduced Maximilian to a sullen, bitter, unhappy man. Addax didn't want to behave in any way toward Emmeline that would draw Maximilian's ire to her even more, because the last thing he wanted was for Maximilian to suspect that anything was happening between him and Emmeline.

God only knew what would happen if that occurred.

So Addax played it safe. Or, at least, he tried to, but when Emmeline kissed him on the cheek to show her thanks, all of that careful composure threatened to shatter.

And he couldn't let it.

"What have I told you about doing that?" he said, jaw twitching. Then he jabbed a finger at her. "You will not do that again."

Emmeline didn't take him as seriously as he did. "It is the most genuine display I can give you," she said. "It is only a kiss, Addax. Parents kiss children. Children kiss mothers. Friends kiss friends. There is nothing wrong with it."

"You do not see me kissing Max, do you?" he pointed out. "Next time, simply shake my hand. That is enough."

She waved him off, irritably, and he quit the solar, following Maximilian's tracks outside and trying to steady his breathing.

She always made his breathing come hard when she kissed him.

The vixen!

Claudius was dismounting his horse just as Addax headed toward the gatehouse. He could see Maximilian up ahead, talking to his father before the man was even off his horse, and he knew what it was about. He was complaining about Emmeline again. But Claudius did what Claudius always did, and that was wave his son off.

He didn't have time for his nonsense.

"If the money is gone, whose fault is that?" Claudius said as Addax walked up to him. "I've told you to curb your spending, but you have ignored me. I have also told you that if you lose all of your money, I will not lift a finger to help you. Greetings, Addax."

Addax dipped his head respectfully to the Earl of Bretherdale as Maximilian stood there with steam coming out of his ears. But Addax couldn't help but notice that the earl had arrived with three men Addax didn't recognize. One was well dressed, while the other two weren't particularly tidy. Claudius saw that Addax was observing his traveling companions, so he waved his hand at the men in a silent gesture to dismount their horses.

"I've brought customers," he said simply. "May we go into the solar and discuss the purchase of ore?"

He was looking at Maximilian, who suddenly wasn't entirely upset at the mention of money coming in. Customers, his father had said.

He was all smiles.

"Of course," he said, moving swiftly to the man in the finery. "Let us go into the solar and discuss. I am Maximilian de Grey. Claudius is my father."

He was already moving the man toward the keep, and Claudius had to intercept him. "This is Lord Gavinton," he said. "He's an important advisor to King Alexander, and we must show him all due respect."

Lord Gavinton.

Addas realized that the very Scots that Cole had been concerned with had finally arrived. Truth be told, Addax had nearly forgotten about them over the months he'd been at Alston, because his focus had been on Emmeline and Maximilian. Claudius had visited Alston two or three times since their initial arrival, but there had never been any mention of buyers or customers or even Scots. In fact, Claudius had shown little to no interest in the mine operations other than the money that they produced, much like his son.

But that all may have been a ruse.

The Scots in front of Addax were a testament to that.

Therefore, he showed little interest in the visitors as Claudius and Maximilian led them to the keep. Addax and Essien eyed one another, as they both understood the significance of the arrival. In fact, Essien had spent the past six months at Raisbeck Castle with Claudius because Claudius had invited him to remain, given he had no knights, and it was exactly where Cole wanted him. Addax could tell by his brother's expression that there was more going on with the situation than met the eye. As Claudius and Maximilian neared the keep with their guests, Addax casually joined his brother, bringing up the rear.

"It has been a while since I last saw you," he said. "What is new and exciting at Raisbeck these days?"

Essien shook his head. "Only that which you see," he said. They were far enough back that he could speak without being heard. "I've not told you that the Scots have been in almost constant contact with Claudius. This visit has been planned for months."

Addax kept his attention on the men ahead of him. "Why did you not send word so I would not be surprised by it?"

"Because Claudius is not like his son," Essien said. "The man has a suspicious streak. He watches. He is watching me even now."

Addax looked at him. "He does not trust you?"

"He trusts me," Essien said. "But he is still suspicious of everyone around him. That is why he does not have any knights. He does not want anyone at Raisbeck to have power but him."

It was an interesting situation. Addax simply nodded and headed for the keep himself, ahead of Claudius and Maximilian and the Scots, making sure the entry door was open for them, but he headed straight to the solar to see if Emmeline was still there.

She was.

She had been writing something on a large piece of vellum with her quill. An abacus sat next to her, and she glanced up, quickly, when the solar door opened. She smiled at Addax right away, but she heard voices in the entry.

Her smile faded.

"Claudius?" she asked.

Addax nodded. "He has brought some buyers for the ore," he said quietly, quickly. "Whatever you do, you must not agree to a deal today. I will explain later, but you must trust me."

She frowned. "Not agree—?"

"Tell them you're not sure about the inventory. Tell them it's already sold. Just think of something and do not sell. It is important."

She went to question him again, but Claudius appeared behind him, and Addax held open the door so he and Maximilian and the Scots could enter. Maximilian went straight to the pitcher of wine, and when he saw there were not enough cups, he demanded that Emmeline go fetch some, but Addax volunteered. Emmeline was introduced by Claudius to men named Lord Gavinton, Holmes, and Wendall. He introduced them as friends, but also as men who wished to do business with the de Witt mines, as they were still known. The name de Witt meant something when it came to lead ore, so neither Maximilian nor Claudius had seen any reason to change the name of the mines.

After what Addax had just told her, Emmeline was on her guard. She knew he wouldn't have said such a thing had he not had good reason. The problem was that she wasn't technically in charge of the mine or the sales, meaning any deal struck by Maximilian would have to stand no matter how she felt about it. She was sure that Addax understood that, which was why she knew that his request must have been crucial.

She settled back down to her books and kept her mouth shut, watching.

Waiting.

Maximilian's move wasn't long in coming.

"Now," he said. "My father says you wish to purchase ore."

Lord Gavinton, the man at the lead of the delegation, nodded his silver-haired head. "Aye," he said in a thick Scots accent. "There's been a sickness in the north, and the priests are asking for lead coffins and crypts. They want something tae keep whatever sickness killed them from spreading, and they believe the lead will do that."

It sounded plausible enough, but Emmeline spoke before Maximilian could. "I am so terribly sorry to hear of such a thing," she said. "How many people have died?"

"Hundreds, m'lady," Gavinton said, looking her squarely in the eye. "I know Claudius, and I heard about the marriage tae the de Witt lead mines. We need the lead badly, m'lady."

Emmeline thought he sounded a bit dramatic. "It sounds as if you do," she said. She could see Addax in her peripheral vision, over by the open solar door, and his words were rolling around in her mind. *You must not agree to a deal today.* "Unfortunately, we may have a problem providing you with what you need. How soon do you need it?"

Everyone looked at her immediately. Maximilian's features were full of disbelief, while Gavinton and Claudius seemed to only show concern.

"Problem?" Maximilian spat at her. "What problem?"

Emmeline's gaze moved to him. "If you ever stopped spending money long enough to show any interest in the mines that make you your money, then you would know that we've had six of them flood over the past week," she said. "The heavy rains we've been having have wreaked havoc with them. Only five of them are producing right now, and one of those is almost completely flooded, too. I have other orders to fill, so I cannot supply ore to Lord Gavinton right away."

She'd fired a shot right across Maximilian's bow, and he was embarrassed and furious over it. But what she said was the truth, in fact—several of the mines had indeed flooded, though they were still working. They simply weren't producing as well as they should have been. But Maximilian was having difficulty controlling his temper.

"I permit you to tend to business matters because you are much better at it than I am," he said through clenched teeth. "When would we be able to provide Lord Gavinton with his ore?"

Emmeline looked at the vellum in front of her. "I am not entirely sure," she said. Then she looked to Gavinton again. "How much would you need, my lord?"

Gavinton looked to his comrades. One whispered in his ear. He listened before speaking.

"Fifteen tons or more," he said. "We require a great deal, m'lady."

Maximilian stepped in. "That *is* a great deal," he said, little gold coins dancing in his eyes at the prospect of such a huge sale. "What are you willing to pay?"

Gavinton looked between Claudius and Maximilian. "I was hoping you could see your way tae providing us with the ore for a good price," he said. "It is for the dead, after all. It would be charitable if ye were tae sell it tae us for fifty pounds a ton."

Emmeline gasped. "Fifty pounds a ton?" she repeated, shocked. "Forgive me, my lord, but it cannot be done. It cannot—"

Maximilian cut her off. "Would you be able to pay in advance?"

"I would, m'laird," Gavinton said. "But when would I get it?"

"Wait," Emmeline said, standing up. "Wait, please. My lord, I am sorry, but our ore sells for four hundred pounds a ton. I have hundreds of mine workers, and fifty pounds a ton would not even pay for their labor. It cannot be done."

Maximilian whirled on her, slamming his fist on the table. "I will say if it can or cannot be done!" he boomed at her. "Sit down and shut your lips!"

Emmeline wasn't afraid of him, especially not with Addax still standing near the door. "Forgive me, but I cannot," she said, looking to Gavinton. "Surely you understand, my lord, that we cannot sell it for anything less than three hundred pounds a ton. I will go that low for you, and at that, it is substantially less than what we sell it for to others. We must be able to pay our workers a fair wage. I hope you understand."

She made the mistake of getting too close to Maximilian,

who reached out and grabbed her by the back of the neck.

"Excuse me," he said, shoving Emmeline toward the solar door. "I must discuss this with my wife in private."

He was hurting her, but she couldn't do much more than walk to the door, because he was shoving her in that direction.

"Max," Claudius said, standing up and shaking his head at his son. "Take your hand off her. She carries your son. You must be gentle."

Gavinton stood up also. "I canna pay ye three hundred pounds a ton," he said. "But I can pay ye one hundred. I'm sorry, but I must have it."

"It is yours," Maximilian said as he let go of Emmeline, but he gave her a shove at the same time he let her go, and she stumbled into the doorjamb. "You shall have your ore, Lord Gavinton, but I want the money now. Do you have it?"

Gavinton started to nod, but Emmeline pushed herself away from the doorjamb, back in their direction.

"Nay," she said. "My lord, you may as well steal it from us for that price. The mines are the only way Alston has survived all these years, and if you take the ore for that price, people will starve. I will not be able to pay our workers. You must under-stand that—"

Maximilian took a step back and smacked her right in the mouth. She yelped, her hands flying to her mouth, as he turned to Gavinton with a forced smile.

"You will have your ore," he said firmly. "But I want the money now. If you want fifteen tons of ore, I want fifteen hundred pounds."

Gavinton was looking at Maximilian with a horrified ex-pression. He then looked at Claudius, who seemed to have the same horrified look on his face, only he was controlling it a little better. Gavinton was about to say something, but he caught the swift movement of something out of the corner of his eye, and the next thing he realized, Maximilian was being clobbered with an ash shovel from the hearth. Emmeline smashed it right over his head as the chamber deteriorated into chaos.

Addax and Essien rushed in as Claudius, pulling Gavinton and his colleagues with him, rushed out. The blow had stunned Maximilian, and Emmeline managed to strike him again before Addax pulled the shovel out of her hand.

"Tend to him," he barked at Essien. "I will tend to the lady."

With that, he pulled Emmeline out of the solar and rushed her to the steep mural stairs that led to the upper floors of the keep. He wanted to get her away from Maximilian, who would have every right to beat her for doing what she did, and there wouldn't be a damn thing Addax could do to stop him. He'd already interfered in their marriage far too much, and he didn't want to have to show his true loyalty if Maximilian pushed him into it, so the best thing to do was remove Emmeline.

He didn't take her back to her bedchamber, however. He knew Maximilian would go looking for her, and he didn't want the man to find her, so he pulled her into the section of the keep that he'd been sleeping in. His chamber was on the top floor, up two more flights of angled stone stairs. When they reached it, he shoved her inside, pulling the door shut behind them and bolting it. Only then did he let her go.

Addax was more rattled than he'd realized. He was standing about five feet away from Emmeline, looking her in the face and realizing Maximilian's slap had cut her lip. He could see blood on the corner of her mouth. With a heavy sigh, he went to her and lifted a hand to her mouth to see how bad the wound was.

But Emmeline batted him away.

"Leave me alone," she said, putting her hand over her mouth. "I'm well enough. He didn't hurt me."

Addax watched her back away from him. "You are bleeding," he said.

She wiped the hand over her lips, looking at the faint smudges of blood on her skin. "It does not matter," she said. Then she lifted her eyes to him. "I will not let him humiliate me and strike me, Addax. He has been doing it since the beginning of our marriage, and I made the decision a long time ago to treat him as he treats me."

Addax knew that. He sighed heavily. "I do not like it any better than you do," he said. "But there will come a day when I am not around to protect you, Emmy. You know this. I cannot remain at Alston for the rest of my life. I was due back on the tournament circuit three months ago, but still, here I am."

She lowered her bloodied fingers from her mouth. "I did not ask you to remain here," she said. "Nothing is forcing you to remain. You can leave any time you wish."

He snorted, without humor. "And wonder when Max will finally kill you?" he said, shaking his head. "Nay. I could not live with that on my conscience."

Emmeline didn't know what to say to that. He'd hinted before at hidden feelings, but only once. He had too much honor to do anything else. But now, it seemed that he was hinting at it again. As if he cared for her, personally. Why else would she weigh on his conscience? Since nearly the day she'd met him, Addax had been on her side in anything to do with Maximilian. A man who was his friend.

Yet… Addax always sided with his friend's wife.

But it was more than that. It was their conversations, the games they played, the way he behaved toward her. Never anything inappropriate, but he was always friendly and kind and gentle. There was warmth in his eyes when he looked at her. How could a man show a woman such attention and not feel something for her?

Aye... she had indeed suspected all along that there was more to it.

Emmeline moved over toward the bed, sitting heavily, facing the lancet window as a cool breeze blew in. It lifted her hair as she thought on Addax and the fact that he *was* due back on the tournament circuit. But the Black Dragon had remained at an unimportant castle mediating the marriage of unimportant people. Perhaps it was fear, as he'd said.

Or perhaps it was something more he wasn't willing to admit.

God knew, she longed to hear those words.

"So you remain because of me," she said after a moment. "You remain because you are afraid that Maximilian will kill me."

"Aye."

"Is that all?"

"Is what all?"

"That you only remain because you fear for my safety?"

"What else could there be?"

"Because you love me?"

Even as it came out of her mouth, Emmeline regretted it. She had no idea why she said that, only that it came out before she could stop it. She longed to hear the words, but she didn't want to force them out of him. Immediately remorseful, she bolted off the bed and looked at him, wide-eyed.

"Forgive me," she whispered quickly. "I did not mean it. I should not have said that. I do not know why I did."

KATHRYN LE VEQUE

He just looked at her. She could see his jaw working, those dark eyes glittering with unspoken words, unspoken thoughts. A thousand different emotions rippled across his face, but still, he didn't say a word. He just looked at her. After a moment, he simply shook his head.

"I do not love you."

Those five words made Emmeline suck in her breath as if he'd just done something horribly painful to her. As if he'd shoved a dagger between her ribs, straight into her heart, because even now, that heart was broken into a thousand pieces of pain. She was having trouble catching her breath, trying not to seem as if those five words had shattered every hope, every bit of light, she'd ever had.

I do not love you.

"Of course you do not," she said, her voice trembling. "I do not know why I said it. We are friends, and your actions toward me have only, and always, been chivalrous. It was arrogant of me to even think it was anything else."

Quickly, she moved toward the door. He was standing next to it, but she wouldn't look at him. The moment she put her hand on the latch, he put his big hand on the door, preventing her from opening it. He was looking at the side of her head as she looked down at her hand on the latch.

But he wouldn't let her open it.

"I do not love you," he repeated in a husky whisper. "A word has not yet been created in your language for what I feel for you. It is more than love. It is as ageless as the stars, as powerful as the heavens. In the language of my land, it is called *zahid*. It means worship, devotion, adoration, fondness, passion, and reverence. Love is a limited word, Emmy. What I feel for you is more than love."

There. He'd said it. Addax couldn't believe that he'd said it, but it had all come out so easily. Terrifyingly easy. He could see that she had begun to tremble, and as he watched, she closed her eyes and tears streamed down her cheeks.

A river of tears for a river of longing.

"That is everything I feel for you and more, also," she murmured. "But I told you when I married Maximilian that I would not take a lover even if he did. He may be unfaithful to his vows, bodily, but I will not. I cannot."

"Nor can I," he muttered. "I will not cross that boundary. But I cannot help what I feel."

"I cannot help what I feel either," she said. "Surely... surely you have known this."

"I have suspected."

Emmeline took a step back, away from him, before turning her tear-stained face to his. "I would give everything I owned if this child I bear was yours," she whispered. "I hate that it is not. I hate that I shall bear the child of a man I hate with all my soul. A man who has only shown me loathing and fear."

"I know."

"It is not fair."

"Nay, it is not."

She broke down into soft sobs, hanging her head, but Addax would not comfort her. At least, not physically. He was afraid of what would happen if he put his arms around her, and terrified he wouldn't be strong enough to let her go. Her soft body against his was all he dreamed of these days. Strange how a confession of love didn't devastate him like he'd thought it would. The fact that she felt the same way wasn't a surprise, either. Somehow, he'd known.

"Will you do something for me?" he asked softly.

She nodded, wiping her eyes with the back of her hands. "Anything."

He pointed at the bed. "I want you to lie down and rest," he said gently. "I will go and see how Max is faring and try to talk him out of any reprisals. You must know that it is becoming increasingly difficult for me not to punish him when he attacks you."

She stopped weeping, her eyes widening. "You must not do anything," she said. "Addax, he would turn against you. He would turn your friends against you. He is a petty, devious man, and although I do not think you see those qualities in him, I do. You have achieved too much to let him ruin things for you. Please... you must never act against him, no matter what he does."

Addax sighed heavily and averted his gaze. "I know."

"Promise me."

He tipped his head up, eyeing her. "I will," he said. "But the longer I remain here, the more it is likely to happen."

"Will you leave me, then?"

"I do not know," he said honestly. "I could not leave, knowing how he is with you... and I could not leave you alone with him. I could not leave you in any case because of what I feel. I am in a difficult position."

"Then what are you going to do?"

He shook his head. "I suppose there is nothing to be done, not now," he said. "I must think on it, but until I can come up with a solution, I'm not going anywhere. Until then, just remember what I said... *zahid*."

She wiped at her eyes. "*Zahid*," she whispered in return.

He simply nodded, keeping his gaze averted, and Emmeline took a few steps toward him. She was standing close to him, but he still wouldn't look at her. He was looking at the floor, the bed, the door—anything so he didn't have to look her in the face. As gentle as butterfly wings, she touched his face and kissed him on the right cheek.

"I am so very sorry," she whispered. "But thank you."

His hand, once on the door panel, drifted down until it came into contact with her arm. Emmeline could feel it moving down her forearm, to her wrist, until he came to her hand. Their flesh touching sent bolts of excitement through her, lightning strikes of pain that made her gasp and turn her head away from him.

But she didn't pull away.

She stood there and took it, feeling the pain shoot up her arm, feeling her heart race and her stomach tremble. He gripped her fingers tenderly, and she latched on to him, holding his hand tightly enough to break his bones. Gently, ever so gently, he lifted her hand to his lips and kissed her fingers. She could feel the scratch of his beard and his hot breath against her flesh.

She gasped again, only louder.

It was a moan.

Emmeline turned in his direction as he still held her hand, putting her free hand on the back of his head, the tears rolling down her cheeks as she touched his beautiful black hair. She ran her fingers through it, oh so softly, feeling the texture as his lips remained on her hand. He just held it against his mouth, breathing on her, as she stroked his hair, and when she finally looked at his face, she could see that his eyes were tightly closed. He had a look of such agony in his expression.

He was a man in torment.

Emmeline could see it. She hated that he was in such pain.

Gently, she tried to remove her hand from his, but he wouldn't let go. She finally had to yank it free and then put her hands on his broad shoulders to turn him for the door, because he seemed incapable of breaking out of whatever trance held him.

"Go," she whispered, unbolting the door and pulling it open even as she tried to push him through. "I will stay here and rest. You must tend to Maximilian."

Like a man waking from a deep and turbulent sleep, Addax drew in a long and unsteady breath before opening his eyes. He was staring out into the corridor, feeling Emmeline's hands on his shoulders as she tried to guide him out of the chamber. He blinked, trying to orient himself, realizing that holding Emmeline's hand had very nearly thrown him over the edge. He had her hand and he wouldn't let it go. He didn't know how he was supposed to function now, but he was going to have to try.

Try to act as if the woman he loved wasn't married to another.

"Go," Emmeline said again, giving him a little shove. "I will see you later."

He nodded as he stepped, stiffly, out into the corridor. "I will return once I've seen Max."

"Addax?"

"Aye?"

"*Zahid*, my darling."

He couldn't look at her. All he could feel was glory in his heart and a lump in his throat. Taking another deep breath, he turned his head, seeing her in his periphery over his right shoulder.

"*Zahid*," he whispered.

And then he was gone.

CHAPTER THIRTEEN

*B*REATHE, MAN, BREATHE... *and do not let Essien see how rattled you are!*

"Where have you been?" Essien asked. "How is Lady de Grey?"

Addax ran into this brother in the foyer of the keep. He gestured back up the stairs in answer to his question.

"She is resting," he said, still not recovered from his confession with Emmeline but trying to pretend everything was normal. "She is upset, naturally. Where are Max and the Scots?"

Essien pointed out to the bailey. "Talking to Adonis and his father," he said. "I could not get to them in time to tell them what had been said, Ad. They confirmed that some of the mines are flooded but have assured both Max and his father that production will continue. Max and Claudius are calling the lady hysterical in her reaction to the flooding, but have stopped short of calling her a liar. However, Max is furious with her. He thinks she is trying to keep him from the money he has a right to."

Addax shook his head with regret. "It is my fault," he said. "I told her not to sell to the Scots, so any untruth has come from me. I have put her in this position."

Essien lifted an eyebrow. "Then you had better think of a way to smooth this over, because Max is speaking of punishment," he said. "He has agreed to sell to the Scots for one hundred pounds a ton, and the Scots are prepared to pay him now for the ore."

Addax couldn't stop shaking his head at the irony of the situation. "Damnation," he muttered. "So the Scots get their ore and Alston loses money that would have kept their people going for God knows how long. Max is only seeing the immediate need—*his*—and he's not thinking of the future of Alston. The lady tried to tell him."

"What do we do?" Essien asked.

Addax thought a moment. "First and foremost, Cole needs to know that the sale of the ore will happen," he said. "I do not dare send a missive to him, but you can. If I recall correctly, Fourstones Castle is about twenty miles to the north. That is a Burleson property."

"And?"

"And he is an ally of de Velt," he said. "If you can deliver a missive to Burleson and ask him to send it by messenger to Berwick, you can send that information to Cole. He needs it."

"How can I do that if Bretherdale expects me to return to Raisbeck with him?" Essien asked. "The man thinks I am sworn to him now."

"But he is not leaving for Raisbeck today or tonight," Addax pointed out. "Leave now for Fourstones. You'll be back by morning."

Essien cast him a long look. "Very well," he said. "That is a long ride in a short period of time."

"You are young and strong. You can make it."

Essien shook his head. "I am not young any longer," he said. "I'm getting old, like you."

Addax rolled his eyes at his complaining brother. "Go," he said. "I will hold Claudius and the Scots here as long as I can."

Essien nodded, but he again threw a thumb in the general direction of the bailey. "And you had better try to ease the situation, or Max will have the lady drawn and quartered."

Not literally, but figuratively. Still, Addax knew that Maximilian was capable of cruelty when the situation called for it. He'd seen it quite a bit over the past six months. That man wasn't someone he'd known all these years.

The man Maximilian had become was a stranger.

As Essien slipped out toward the stables, Addax headed out to the bailey, where he found Maximilian and Claudius and the Scots still in conversation with Adonis and Pierre. As he walked up on the group, Claudius caught sight of him and extended an arm to welcome him into their huddle.

"Ah," he said. "Addax. I am glad you have returned."

Addax dipped his head politely. "How may I serve you, my lord?"

Claudius gestured to Adonis and Pierre. "We were just speaking with the de Moras, and they tell us that although the mines are indeed flooded, they are still producing," he said. "Surely Lady de Grey was simply being overly cautious?"

Addax shrugged. "I would not know, my lord," he said. "I am not involved in the business. But I would agree that Lady de Grey was simply being overly cautious. She has also mentioned that there are customers who are expecting ore shipments soon, so anything produced now must go to fill the existing requests."

Maximilian was looking at Addax with a decidedly unhappy expression. "But those customers have not yet paid," he said. He gestured to the Scots. "Lord Gavinton has brought money with him. It seems to me that we should take the money and give them the ore."

Addax looked at Bretherdale, who seemed to be siding with his son. The Scots were ready to pay, and pay now.

Money talked.

The problem was that Addax shouldn't be involved more than he already was. He had no right to give his opinion about anything, so he simply forced a smile as he looked at Bretherdale.

"You must do what you feel is right, of course," he said. "I am simply a servant, my lord. This is Max's decision, not mine."

That had Maximilian smiling. "You see?" he said, looking to his father, to the Scots. "Addax agrees we must do what is right. That means the men with money can have their ore. Others who have not yet paid for it will have to wait."

Addax didn't correct him. More and more, he was starting to see what a petty fool Maximilian was. He couldn't believe he'd never seen it before. With every day that passed, he was questioning how he'd ever become friends with a man like that in the first place, but the fact remained that he had. And here he was, more entrenched in the situation than he wanted to be. But linked to the situation by a beautiful young woman he couldn't get out of his mind—or out of his heart.

He was in deep.

"Then it is done," Bretherdale said. "Come; let us retire to the solar and discuss the details of the ore delivery. Adonis, can they use the wagons from the mines to bring their ore north?"

Adonis nodded. "Aye, my lord," he said. "They may use the wagons. We have men who will transport the ore north, but the wagons must be returned."

"Agreed," Gavinton said. "We will be moving it tae Dumfries. It should only take a few weeks. May we discuss how ye usually deliver the ore?"

Adonis and Pierre, his white-haired father, went to speak with Gavinton and the Scots while Bretherdale stood aside and simply listened. The deal was done. Everything had fallen into place in a situation that, early on, might have gone badly for him. But it hadn't. The Scots had only offered one hundred pounds per ton because another one hundred pounds, per ton, was going to Bretherdale as the broker of the deal. That was all the money the Scots were willing to pay, but the lands that were to be given to Bretherdale were just west of Gretna Green. The Douglas Clan had donated them for the cause, and Gavinton had brought a signed deed from the Lord of Douglas himself, William.

Everything had fallen into place.

Even if the deal would produce a war against England.

As Claudius contemplated his good fortune at England's expense, Maximilian was contemplating quite another good fortune. He was to receive fifteen hundred pounds for the ore, and receive it today, which solved his money problem. He didn't care what that bitch he'd married said. In the end, he would have what he wanted, and there was nothing she could do about it. But the fact that she had challenged him in front of his father and the Scots wouldn't go unanswered. She'd done things like that before, and fought with him every chance she got, but pregnant or not, he wasn't going to tolerate it any longer.

She carries your son.

That was what his father had said to him, reminding him not to injure her in his anger. Frankly, he didn't care. The woman he'd been seeing in Penrith for the past six months was also pregnant with his child, and he liked her much better than his own wife. She didn't fight with him. She catered to his every whim. She stole money from her own father to give to him. That was exactly what he wanted in a wife. Not a shrew who tried to hit him with shovels.

Maximilian could see, without a doubt, that Emmeline was the obstacle between him and the de Witt money. She was the obstacle between him and his mistress in Penrith. She was the obstacle between him and a very happy life.

And obstacles had to be removed.

The time had come.

CHAPTER FOURTEEN

ZAHID...

Emmeline couldn't have known that when Addax returned to her later in the day, he'd found her sleeping and simply left her alone.

She'd awoken to the colors of sunset on the walls.

For a moment, she was still half-asleep, watching the sky beyond the window. She didn't exactly know where she was, and it took her a minute to realize she was in Addax's chamber.

That brought a smile to her face.

It also took her a moment to realize that the conversation with him earlier had not been a dream. *Zahid,* he'd told her. Something more than love. To know that he loved her left her feeling as if she could face the rest of her life with courage, as if her marriage to Maximilian didn't matter. She had Addax's love, and that was her only concern.

But that was also the problem.

He gave her a false sense of hope.

Rolling onto her back, Emmeline found herself staring up at the ceiling and pondering the situation. Perhaps she always knew Addax felt for her the way she felt for him, but to hear it verbalized was something completely different. She still didn't know why she'd asked him if he loved her, but she had. And he had responded the way she thought he would. There was no surprise there, but there was a sense of euphoria.

But it was a selfish feeling.

She was being selfish.

That was something she didn't want to acknowledge, yet something she knew was true. She had even asked him if he intended to leave her, but he said that he didn't know. Addax was a great man, admired by many, and a man who should have been ruling his own kingdom. He was far beyond her grasp, and she knew it. The truth, as brutal as it was, was that he was wasting his life at Alston. The role he found himself in was as mediator between two people who hated one another, and unless she took a stand and did something about it, he would be doing it for the rest of his life because he thought that was what she wanted.

It *was* what she wanted.

But she couldn't let him do it any longer.

For his own sake, she was going to have to tell him to go.

The realization of what she had to do left her feeling sick in the pit of her stomach. Emmeline put her hand on her belly, feeling the gentle rise of the baby that was growing inside of her. A child put there by a monster. As she had told Addax, it simply wasn't fair what had happened to the both of them, but the difference was that he had a way out. She didn't.

Emmeline knew she was going to have to show him the way out.

Perhaps his admission of love for her was enough to get her through the rest of her life. She was a reasonable woman, and a strong woman, and she knew that she couldn't use Addax as a crutch for the rest of her life. She was going to have to ask him to leave so he could at least get on with his, as painful as that was for her.

She had to love him enough to do what was right for him.

Emmeline didn't realize that tears had made their way down her temples, not until she felt them running on her ears. Sitting up, she wiped her ears and her face, knowing that she should be grateful that she had experienced love at all. She'd had two husbands and never felt that emotion. The fact that she felt it for a man she was not worthy of was ironic, but she was grateful to have experienced it just the same.

It was going to have to be enough.

Rising from the bed, she straightened her garment and walked over to the window, looking out over the land as evening approached. Down below in the bailey, she could see part of the kitchen yard, and it reminded her that there were four newborn goats. Thoughts of Addax turned to thoughts of goats. Alston kept a small herd of them because Emmeline liked to make cheese from the milk. Baby goats meant more milk, but it also meant she had a sweet little pet until they grew up big enough to nibble on her skirt and tug ribbons from her hair. There were a few bully juvenile goats in the yard that did just that.

Even so, the thought of them still made her smile.

As she turned away from the window, she could feel the baby kicking in her belly, and she put her hand against the firmness of her stomach to feel more butterfly kicks. Even if she hated the baby's father, she certainly didn't hate the baby, and she smiled as she felt a few little punches and rolls. The baby was growing more active now, and above the turmoil at Alston Castle, Emmeline was deeply grateful for the chance to carry a child, something she'd never thought she would do. It only proved that Ernest had been the problem, and not her. She felt vindicated in a way, but more than anything, she simply felt happy that in a few months, she would be holding her baby in her arms. She was positive that it was a girl, and the girl already had a name.

Elizabetha.

She'd had a friend many years ago by the name of Elizabetha, back when she was fostering, and Elizabetha de Burnley had been sweet and pretty and thoughtful. Unfortunately, she had died of a fever, and Emmeline always swore that she would name a daughter after her dear friend. Therefore, when Elizabetha rolled around in her belly, she would talk to her gently and tell her how eager she was to meet her. It was, perhaps, the only real joy she had in her situation.

She endeavored to focus on it.

Exiting the chamber, Emmeline found herself on the stair landing. This floor had three small chambers on it, and on the next level below there were three larger chambers. Mostly visitors, and in particular male visitors, slept on this side of the keep, so the chambers weren't elaborate. Simply functional. She made her way down the staircase to the floor below, which was quiet at this hour, and found her way to the mural stairs. There was a landing at the top of the stairs, and one could either go to the visitor side of the keep or to the family apartments.

She headed to the family apartments.

The keep was quiet at this hour, and she could only imagine that Maximilian and his father and the Scots were in the great hall, drinking all of the fine wine and demanding copious amounts of food. It seemed that was all Maximilian ever did when he was in residence. The man had developed a love for gluttonous eating. That also meant that if the men were in the hall, she would not be. She would take her meal in her chamber. She was too tired to deal with Maximilian and the deals he wanted to make with the Scots, but come the morrow, she would be forced to assess the damage. She had a feeling that regardless of what she said, Maximilian would do exactly as he pleased.

He usually did.

But at least the money was safe.

Even if Maximilian decided to defy her and sell the ore for the paltry sum of one hundred pounds per ton, there was enough money in the coffers hidden in the sub-levels that she could still pay the miners a fair wage and not lose a great deal. Emmeline always saved for those times that would not be so prosperous, so Maximilian's deal with the Scots wasn't going to destroy them. However, she was coming to understand why Addax had told her not to make the deal. Clearly the Scots wanted to cheat them.

And Maximilian, the fool, was letting them.

The family apartments were softly lit at this hour. She went into her chamber, which was warm from a fire in the hearth that her maid had started. The maid, an old woman who had been at Alston long before she arrived, had been a godsend all those years Emmeline had been married to Ernest. The woman had taken care of her like a mother. But the maid was nowhere to be found as she went to her dressing alcove to change out of the day dress. The night was coming, and the temperature was dropping, so she hunted down a heavy shift and an equally heavy robe that was made from red brocade with rabbit trim. It would be soft and warm for the evening to come. As she finished dressing, she heard the chamber door open.

"M'lady?"

It was old Aline, the maid, and Emmeline called to her. "In here," she said. "I was just preparing for bed."

"You're not joining the men in the hall?"

"Is that where they are?"

"Aye," Aline said, hobbling over to the alcove and looking her over. "There they are. No one has seen you since this morning."

Emmeline sat down at her dressing table, examining her face in the fine mirror. She'd all but stopped using the cosmetics that Ernest had liked her to wear, mostly because none of the men around her these days seemed to care.

"No one has seen me because I do not wish to see Maximilian," she said. "We had angry words again this morning, and Sir Addax took me up to his chamber and told me to stay there while he straightened out Maximilian. I took a nap."

Aline had linens in her arms, having just come up from the laundry. She frowned at Emmeline as she entered the alcove to put the linens in the wardrobe that held them.

"Angry words," she grumbled. "More like shouting and yelling. All he does is shout and yell."

Emmeline continued to look at her face in the mirror, picking up some iron tweezers to tweeze away some errant hair around her eyebrows.

"As long as he is in the great hall and away from me, he can shout and yell to his heart's content," she said. "It is of no concern to me."

Aline glanced at her. "But he is not in the great hall, my lady."

Emmeline paused to look at her. "Where is he?"

"I saw him in the solar."

"Now?"

"As I was coming up here."

So Maximilian was in the keep, nosing around in the solar. *Her* solar. She hadn't seen him when she crossed the mural stair landing, which had a clear view to the entry below. His presence in the keep simply meant she would bolt her door to her chamber, the same thing she'd done too many times to count. She returned to her eyebrows.

"I am rather hungry," she said. "Will you please bring me some food?"

Aline put the last of the linen away. "With pleasure, my lady," she said, moving out of the alcove. "Cook has made boiled beef with gravy, carrots, pea pottage, and your favorite—candied apples."

Emmeline stopped tweezing again and looked at her. "If she gives the candied apples to anyone but me, I shall be greatly disappointed."

Aline chuckled. "She knows," she said. "But we could smell them all afternoon as she made them. I'm surprised you did not smell them, too. Honey and butter and cinnamon covering slices of apple. Delicious!"

Emmeline sniffed the air just in case there were remnants of the smell of cinnamon, which was her favorite. "I think I can smell them after all," she said, grinning as she set her tweezers down. "Bring me a good deal of food. The babe is hungry this night."

Aline looked at her mistress's rounded belly, made little happy sounds, and rushed out of the chamber as fast as she could go. Emmeline had to chuckle because she was certain that Aline was more excited about the child than she was. The woman had already fashioned little clothes for the infant, and several of the servants had made things like blankets and caps. It seemed that an impending child was reason for everyone to be happy.

Especially when Alston had historically been a place with little happiness.

Feeling lighter of spirit than she had in a very long time, Emmeline went to the door and bolted it, leaning against it as she thought of the baby and of Addax. Two things that, indeed, made her very happy. But her smile faded as she thought of Maximilian down in her solar, undoubtedly poking around and ruining her organization. Making a nuisance of himself.

He was good at that.

With a sigh, she came away from the door and went over to the hearth, where a chair and a footstool sat, warmed by the flames. She sat down in the chair, putting her feet up on the stool and wondering where Addax was. If Maximilian was in the solar, then Addax must be nearby, because he rarely let Maximilian out of his sight when he was at Alston. Maximilian prowled and Addax prowled after him. But they also had guests on this night, so Emmeline's guess was that Addax might be in the great hall with Bretherdale and the Scots, perhaps trying to be a good host, since Maximilian clearly wasn't present. It did puzzle her as to why Maximilian would be in the solar, however. Perhaps, after she'd eaten, she'd go downstairs to see what trouble he'd caused.

And she'd take her fire poker with her.

☙

HE'D FOUND AN extra stash of coins.

Maximilian knew that Emmeline kept little sacks of coins all over the solar, and in digging around, he'd found a small bag tucked behind a book on the shelf. There were, perhaps, two hundred pence in the bag, but it was enough for him. Enough for him to leave this night and come back later. He had to leave because he was about to do something, and he needed to establish an alibi somewhere else. Anywhere but Alston.

His wife was going to have an accident.

Wife. He snorted at the word as it rolled through his mind. Overlord was more like it. Jailor, governess... She controlled the purse strings and therefore controlled him. Well, no more. He'd made that decision earlier in the day. She'd challenged him one too many times.

It was time to do something about it.

He spent another half-hour poking around in the solar looking for another sack of money, but found nothing. Through the open door, he'd seen Lady de Grey's maid go up to her chamber and then come back down again. He didn't know where Emmeline was, but logic told him that she was more than likely in her chamber, because that was where she usually was at this time of night. She didn't oversee the meals like some women did, but rather left that up to the cook, who was quite adept at her job. Maximilian could smell the savory scent of roasting beef on the air, but he wasn't hungry. His father, the Scots, and, most importantly, Addax were in the great hall as the meal was being prepared, and that was where Maximilian wanted them.

Most especially, he wanted Addax there.

A man who had once been his friend.

Perhaps that was one of the most difficult things of all about his marriage to Emmeline. Addax had been there from the beginning, first as an advisor and support to him, but that gradually transitioned into him being support and advisor to

Emmeline. That all started back in Berwick, and it only got worse once they reached Alston. The more difficult Emmeline would become, and the more Maximilian would fight against her, the more Addax would try to be neutral about it and salvage the situation, but he always ended up siding with Emmeline.

It had taken Maximilian six months to realize that he was mourning the loss of a friendship.

Addax hadn't taken his side in anything since the day he married Emmeline. Perhaps in little things he did, but never in anything that really mattered. Maximilian couldn't honestly say that he thought Addax was in love with Emmeline, because he truly didn't think so. The man was simply being chivalrous. The Addax he knew liked women but wasn't a womanizer. He had respect for the fairer sex, which was something Maximilian had never had. There wasn't anything that had come between them in the years they'd known one another, but the introduction of Emmeline was the start of the great divide.

Maximilian felt as if he'd lost a brother.

And that was why he needed Addax in the great hall, away from the keep, so Maximilian could do what he needed to do. Emmeline was the beginning of all the trouble, and with her, it would end. Maximilian had to take the initiative.

And it would be tonight.

So he busied himself in the solar. He pawed through Emmeline's carefully organized boxes of vellum. She was a meticulous record keeper, and Maximilian looked over a few of them to see how prosperous Alston really was. He'd never paid any attention to it because he didn't care. As long as he had his money, he didn't care how it was earned, but he could see that Emmeline controlled a very detailed operation. She was helped by the two de Mora knights, men that Maximilian hadn't bothered to get to know, and maybe the truth was that he felt like an outsider in his own empire. He refused to admit that that was his own doing, so it was just easier to blame Emmeline for everything.

That helped him justify what he needed to do.

When Emmeline's maid came back down the mural stairs, he called to the woman as she walked past the door and asked where Lady de Grey was. The old maid told him that she was in her chamber and that the maid was going to fetch her supper, so Maximilian told her to bring him some food also. When the old woman scurried away, that gave him time to think about how he needed to accomplish his task. That old woman was always around his wife, so it was quite possible she would be caught up in what he intended should happen. He couldn't have a witness.

And that gave him an idea.

When the old maid returned about twenty minutes later, she brought food into him, but he told her that he was going to eat his meal with his wife. That brought a look of horror from the old maid, but she didn't say anything. She simply picked up the food and headed for the stairs with Maximilian behind her.

That was to be her fatal mistake.

The mural stairs of Alston were made of stone, wide but steep. They led up to a landing on the level above that branched into two different directions. The old maid was carrying a heavy tray at this point, with food for both her mistress and her mistress's husband, and she was focused on not spilling anything as she came to the top of the stairs. She wasn't paying attention to Maximilian as he came up behind her, and just as she reached the top, he yanked on her hair. Then he simply stood aside as she went tumbling back down the stairs, breaking her neck about halfway down.

She was dead before she hit the bottom.

There was no one in that part of the keep to hear or see anything at that time of night because even the house servants were helping in the kitchens, so Maximilian slipped into the entry to the visitors' section of the keep, just enough so that Emmeline wouldn't see him.

Then he started to shout.

"Help! My lady, hurry! There has been an accident!"

He called out several times until he heard movement up the flight of stairs to the family apartments. He heard a door open, and possibly hit the wall, and then he heard footsteps.

"What happened?" Emmeline called down the stairwell. "What is it?"

Maximilian didn't want her to recognize his voice, so he screamed a high-pitched sort of wail. Not enough for her to distinguish him. He heard her footsteps as she came down the stairs, and he sank back into the shadows, watching her as she came to the top of the mural stairs. She'd only been puzzled until she looked at the bottom of those steeps stairs and saw her maid there, twisted oddly from the fall, with food scattered everywhere.

She screamed.

"My God!" she gasped. "Aline!"

She started to take the first step, heading down to help her maid, and that was when Maximilian came out of the shadows. Emmeline caught movement out of the corner of her eye, turning to see him bearing down on her. Unfortunately, she was two steps down already, with nothing to grab on to as he lashed out a boot and caught her in the hip.

"You have vexed me for the last time, you bitch," he growled. "Die, and good riddance!"

Unable to stop her fall, Emmeline went down, face-first, screaming as she hit the stairs and began to tumble. But by the time she hit the bottom step, she wasn't screaming anymore.

There was only silence.

Maximilian ran out of the keep through the servants' entrance near the kitchen yard, out to the stable, and never looked back.

CHAPTER FIFTEEN

*G*OD HAVE MERCY…

It was a girl.

Unconscious, and badly injured from her fall down the stairs, Emmeline delivered a baby girl who didn't live more than a few minutes shortly before dawn. Aline was dead, and the physic that had been summoned from Penrith hadn't arrived yet, so the cook and two female servants delivered the tiny infant that looked more like a hairless puppy than a human child. Addax was present at the birth, and he'd taken the baby, holding her until she no longer moved. She was far too small to survive, and he wanted to make sure the child, Emmeline's longed-for child, did not die alone. As the infant squirmed and struggled, he prayed to God for mercy, told her how beautiful she was, and then told her of a pet cat he'd had as a child. He told her anything he could think of so she was comforted during her transition to the next world.

And then he wept.

God's mercy hadn't been meant for the infant.

Through it all, Maximilian was nowhere to be found. They'd hunted for an hour until someone had the idea to ask the gate guards, who told them that Lord Rheged had ridden from the gates earlier than evening. Right about the time a kitchen servant came in to bring Lady de Grey the boiled fruit juice that Aline had forgotten. The gate guards hadn't thought to stop Maximilian, of course, because he was in and out of Alston all of the time. There was no reason to even mention his departure until they were asked. Addax, who hadn't left Emmeline's side since she was found at the bottom of the stairs, had no doubt in his mind that Maximilian was responsible for what happened.

And he was going to kill him.

Meanwhile, Claudius was beside himself. His son was gone, his son's wife had been injured in a brutal fall, and the child she was carrying had died. Addax sent Adonis out to find Maximilian, telling him to bring him back by force if necessary, while Addax tore himself away from Emmeline's side long enough to tightly wrap her tiny baby and tuck the child away in the cold vault of Alston until they could make a decision what to do with her. But he quickly returned to Emmeline's side, tending the enormous bump on her head carefully, until the physic finally arrived.

Pierre had gone for the physic personally because he knew the man—the same man who had been present when Ernest passed away. The physic was surprisingly young, a former priest, with oily skin and messy hair, and smelled like a compost heap. Addax smelled the man before he even saw him and was reluctant to let him near Emmeline, but Pierre assured him that the young physic was competent. Only then did Addax step back and let the man work.

What he saw impressed him.

Addax had been around enough wounded men to know

how things worked. Truth be told, he probably would have made an excellent physic himself had he wanted to, so he stood over the young man as he inspected every inch of Emmeline's limbs for signs of fracture. He inspected her head and the enormous bump, seeing that they had already been treating it with arnica and cold water.

There was a bowl next to the bed with the crushed leaves and water, and he added white willow powder to it and instructed one of the kitchen servants, standing in the corner with the cook, to wring a rag out in it and keep it pressed to the bump. Even if the man was smelly and young, he knew what he was doing.

That gave Addax some confidence.

"The lady was carrying a child when she fell," he told the physic. "The child has since been born and has died."

The physic looked up from inspecting a cut on her ear. "Where is the child?"

"I put her in the vault."

The physic looked concerned. "I must inspect the child," he said. "I also must see the nourishment sack that was born with it. Did you deliver this child?"

Addax motioned to the cook, who came forward. "I delivered the child, m'lord," she said. "Everything came out that was supposed to."

The physic frowned. "And how would you know that?" he said. "What do you know at all?"

The cook was an older woman with a big nose, red hair that she kept tied up on the top of her head, and a no-nonsense manner. She wasn't going to take any accusations from a man who was young enough to be her son and probably knew only half the things she did. When it came to children and childbirth, she was an expert.

"Because I've given birth to twelve children myself," she said as if he were in need of a lesson. "You cannot gain more experience than that. I know what it looks like to have a child, and if something was wrong, I'd tell you."

The physic backed down a little in the face of a big, angry woman. "I see," he said. "Then everything passed well with the mother?"

The cook's name was Elza. She nodded, her gaze moving to Emmeline and her eyes tearing up. "Aye," she said. "It was a little girl. She was so happy to bear a child, and now... now her little girl is gone."

She wiped at her eyes, her nose, as the physic ignored the emotion and motioned to the coverlet. "Pull it back," he said. "I want to inspect her belly."

Addax stepped back to give them some privacy as Elza pulled back the coverlet, holding it up a little to block the view from the men in the room. There was still blood on the mattress, on the shift Emmeline was wearing, all evidence of the trauma she had suffered. The physic poked at her stomach through her shift, feeling for symptoms that might suggest there was a problem, but he seemed satisfied. Elza covered Emmeline back up, and the physic looked her over as he scratched his head.

"Her hands are very bruised," he said. "But, surprisingly, I cannot find any broken bones. I do not think anything else was terribly damaged, but she's battered. It will take time for her to heal."

Claudius came out of the shadows. He'd been watching everything very closely, quite upset by what had happened. His Scots had departed, heading home quickly after such a disastrous day at Alston, but they'd left their money behind. He'd been paid. That meant that he could focus his attention on Emmeline. Perhaps the marriage he'd arranged wasn't a great one, but he'd come to know his son's wife a little over the months, and he'd discovered a bright young woman. She was a good match for Maximilian, if only his son would see reason. But Maximilian thought she was stubborn, whereas Claudius thought she had fire. She wouldn't let Maximilian abuse her, and Claudius respected that. It wasn't as if he could do anything with Maximilian anyway. He never could.

But, much like Addax, he thought the man's absence in the face of this accident was clearly suspect.

He prayed he was wrong.

"Will there be more children?" he asked the physic. "Will she be able to bear a son?"

It was a tasteless question. Addax looked at Claudius and tried to hide his disgust, but he couldn't quite manage it. The physic merely shrugged.

"I am not entirely sure she will even awaken, so I cannot speculate about another child," he said. "Give her time, is all I can tell you. She needs time."

"She has awakened."

The words were mumbled, barely audible, but those around the bed heard them. That included Addax. Shocked, he looked down at Emmeline to see that her eyes were open. The left one was swollen where she'd fallen, but they were open and staring at the ceiling. Addax shifted closer to her.

"My lady?" he said softly. "You have had an accident. You fell down the stairs. Do you remember?"

Emmeline stared at the ceiling for the longest time. She was trying to process what Addax had calmly told her, and he'd done that so she wouldn't be frightened or confused about why she was in bed with people standing over her. It worked—Emmeline wasn't confused, but it was clear that she was muddled. Slowly, her eyes moved in Addax's direction. Her head started to move, too, but the movement made her wince in pain.

"God," she whispered.

The physic was on the other side of her. "Where does it hurt, my lady?" he asked. "Can you tell me?"

Her breathing had quickened, evidence of great pain. "My... my neck," she said, fighting off tears. "My shoulder."

The physic was trying to visually inspect the area, but he knew that wasn't sufficient. "May I examine your neck, my lady?" he asked.

Emmeline looked at him, recognizing him as the same physic who had tended Ernest—so she whispered her consent, and he immediately ran his fingers along her neck and her left shoulder. When he came to her collarbone, he paused.

"Ah," he said with certainty. "Her shoulder is cracked. I can feel it. My lady, you must not move your left arm or shoulder. I will have to wrap it."

Emmeline drew in a deep, steadying breath. "I won't," she said. "My hands hurt also."

"I suspect you may have broken a bone or two in your hands," the physic said. "Can you move them sufficiently?"

Slowly, Emmeline moved her right hand, open and closed. "Mostly," she said. "But it hurts."

"Stabbing pain?"

"Not really. Just pain."

"Then mayhap nothing is broken," the physic replied. "But be careful with them. They will heal in time."

Emmeline closed her eyes because, now that she was conscious, the pain in her shoulder and hands was beginning to take its toll. There was also an aching pain in her belly, and she remembered what she'd heard as she was coming out of unconsciousness. Claudius was asking about other children. She was terrified to ask about her baby, but she knew she had to. It took all of the strength she had in her to summon the courage.

"Addax?" she said softly.

He was right beside her. "My lady?"

"Is my child well? Please tell me the truth."

He didn't hesitate, but he was gentle. "I am afraid she did not survive the fall," he said. "She was born about an hour ago, and I held her so she was not alone. I told her that she was beautiful, and I told her that she would go to heaven, where she could play in the sun all day long. I told her about a cat I used to have as a child and assured her that she could play with my cat in heaven. He will keep her company. She was at peace, my lady."

That was possibly the most beautiful thing he could have said to her, delivering tragic news in the kindest way possible. Emmeline burst into tears, weeping softly as Addax wiped away the tears that were falling down her face and onto her hair. She lifted one of her battered hands, grasping at his fingers, and he held it as tightly as he could without hurting her.

"It was a girl," she sobbed. "I knew it was. I named her Elizabetha. Will you tell the priests when they bury her so they know she has a name?"

Addax continued to hold her head, wiping at her tears and struggling not to cry himself. "Of course I will," he said. "That is a beautiful name."

"I named her for a dear friend," she said. "My friend who

died as a young girl. Mayhap I should not have given her a cursed name. Two girls named Elizabetha, and both have died."

Addax shook his head. "It is not a cursed name," he assured her. "What happened was simply an accident."

Emmeline suddenly came alive. Her eyes flew open and her features were taut with rage. "It was *not* an accident," she declared. "It was Maximilian!"

Addax felt a wave of horror wash over him. "What did he do?"

Emmeline was trying to sit up even as Addax and the physician were trying to force her to stay down. "I was in my chamber, and I heard someone crying that there had been an accident," she said, still sobbing, but now with anger to it. "When I went to see what had happened, I saw Aline at the bottom of the stairs in the entry. Maximilian came up behind me and kicked me. I fell down the stairs, but I do not remember hitting the bottom. Only… falling. It seemed like forever."

"And you are positive of this? He kicked you?"

Emmeline looked at him with an expression he'd never seen before. So… devastated. "He told me that he hoped I died," she said, her voice quivering. "It was him, Addax. He tried to kill me."

Addax had never in his life been forced to employ more restraint than he had at that very moment. His accusing gaze moved to Claudius, who simply closed his eyes in agony and turned away. The man was shaking his head, unwilling to respond to Addax's expression because he knew there was nothing he could say. He'd known all along—and Addax had too—that Maximilian was at the bottom of this. Adonis had ridden off, looking for him, more than an hour ago. It took less than an hour to reach Penrith, which was where Addax told

Adonis to look, because that was where Maximilian usually went. To the woman who was pregnant with his child, so the rumors said.

Maybe they were true.

The one thing for certain was that Maximilian had tried to kill his wife.

With Claudius unable to face him, Addax returned his attention to Emmeline, who forced a smile onto her pale, bruised face.

"I believe you," he said quietly. "Trust me when I tell you that this will not go unpunished."

Emmeline's eyes were wide. "But what are you going to do?"

Addax shook his head, as if she shouldn't be troubled by such a thing. "I must speak with Bretherdale, so I want you to let the physic wrap your shoulder so it will heal," he said. "You must let him tend to your wounds."

Emmeline was agreeable, but she wouldn't let him go. She was frightened, terrified that Maximilian was going to bust into that room and finish the job. She knew that Addax would protect her, but still, she was in a haze of panic. Addax patted her hand gently, finally peeling her fingers off him so the physic could wrap her left shoulder. He needed to bind her arm to her chest to help the shoulder fracture heal. As the physic and the cook propped Emmeline up so the physic could get to work, Addax went over to Claudius.

"My lord," he said through clenched teeth. "If you know where your son is, now would be the time to tell me."

Claudius was pale with distress. "I do not know," he said honestly. "If I knew, don't you think I would have told de Mora? He's out looking for him now. I can only assume he is in

Penrith with that wo—"

He didn't finish, unable to look at Addax, but Addax finished for him. "You mean the woman he's been spending all of his money on?" he said. "I know about it. The one who carries his child."

Claudius did look at him then. "I heard," he said. "Addax... I do not know why Max did what he did to Emmeline, but mayhap it was a mistake. Or an accident. You should hear his side of the situation before you judge him."

Addax looked at Claudius as if the man had gone mad. "*Judge* him?" he repeated. "I do not need to judge him. It is not my place to judge him. But I can tell you that the man who married Lady Emmeline is not the same man who has been my friend all of these years. That man is a despicable, vile excuse for a mortal being. To do that to Lady Emmeline is unforgiveable."

Claudius was put in the position of defending a son who was indefensible. "You only say that because you are in love with her," he said. "It is clouding your judgment."

Addax was preparing to argue with whatever excuse was about to come out of Claudius' mouth, but that statement had his blood running cold. In fact, it enraged him, and that control he held so carefully began to slip. Everything began to slip, including the respect of knight to lord. Now, it was simply man against man. With Claudius' statement, the respect was gone.

"Still your tongue, man," Addax hissed. "Are you trying to deflect blame for your son's heinous actions by accusing me of immoral behavior? If you had raised your son with the slightest bit of moral character, we would not be having this conversation. You have created a monster, de Grey. That monster is now trying to kill people, and you want to make it seem like I am at fault here? If that is true, then you're as despicable as he is."

Addax was a very big man with big hands, big muscles, and a menacing disposition when the mood struck him, so Claudius had to back away from a genuinely furious man.

"Addax, I realize you are distressed," he said, holding up a hand as if to prevent Addax from charging him. "I realize this is a difficult situation. All I am saying is that things are not always the way they seem. There may be other—"

"I have returned," came a voice from the chamber door. "God's Blood, what's all of this? What happened to Lady de Grey?"

Addax and Claudius were interrupted by Maximilian making a sudden appearance in the doorway. He had the look of a man who had no idea what was going on, or what had happened, and he even marginally projected the sense that he might actually be concerned. He was looking at Emmeline, but his focus soon turned to Addax and his father, who were looking at him in various degrees of surprise.

"Well?" Maximilian said to Addax. "What happened? De Mora tells me she had an accident."

No one saw Addax move. One moment, he was standing with Claudius, and in the next, he was on top of Maximilian.

And Maximilian never stood a chance.

C3

STARS BURST BEFORE his eyes, followed by incredible pain.

The next thing Maximilian realized, he was out in the corridor, sitting on his arse, and Addax was bearing down on him. Another blow and he lost two teeth on the left-hand side of his mouth.

Maximilian couldn't even get his hands up to fight back fast enough, because Addax was pounding him in the face and on his head and neck, and he was quickly starting to fade. No one long survived the fists of the mighty Black Dragon, who was in full force at the moment.

Maximilian could hear his father screaming.

"Addax!" Claudius was shouting. "Stop, Addax, *stop!*"

But Addax wouldn't stop. He was in a rage—a blinding rage—and there was no seeing reason. He was out to kill Maximilian, and beating down his opponent with blows that were devastating. Maximilian was only half-conscious when he felt himself being lifted up and tossed.

He fell down some stairs, landing on his recently healed right arm.

The bones broke again.

But Addax came flying down the stairs, too, landing on top of him. The body blows were coming, and when Maximilian didn't respond fast enough, Addax grabbed him by the hair and dragged him down the stairs that he'd kicked Emmeline down. When they reached the bottom, Addax half threw him, half slung him toward the entry door. As he swooped down on him yet again, the entry door opened and Essien appeared.

Having just returned from Fourstones Castle, Essien had heard about the lady's accident and was coming in to see if he could be of assistance when he walked into a bloodbath. Maximilian was covered with blood, and Addax seemed to be the one spreading it around. Claudius, Adonis, and Pierre were following at a distance, but Claudius was in a panic. He was screaming at Addax to stop, and when he saw Essien, he called to the man.

"Stop your brother!" he cried. "He has gone mad!"

Startled, Essien threw down his saddlebags and went after Addax, grabbing him from behind. But Addax didn't want to be grabbed. He had Maximilian around the neck even as he shoved Essien back by the chest, but Essien came back stronger and grabbed him again, locking up his left arm and pulling him away from Maximilian.

"Addax, *stop*," Essien demanded, trying to pull his brother away. "What in the hell are you doing?"

Addax was straining against him, more enraged than he'd ever been in his life. "He tried to kill Emmeline by kicking her down the stairs," he snarled. "He killed the child she was carrying, and now, I am going to kill *him*."

It was a shocking answer, once that nearly had Essien so startled that he almost let his guard down. In fact, he started to, but Addax felt him slacken, and he pulled away in an attempt to get back to Maximilian. Realizing this, Essien did what he normally wouldn't do—he grabbed his brother by the hair, holding the back of his head, as he whispered in his ear.

"You need to stop this *now*," he hissed. "Have you gone mad? You are only going to make this situation much, much worse!"

Addax was still struggling against his brother. "Not if I kill him first."

Essien yanked on him, trying to pull him further away as Claudius ran to his son's side to help him. "Addax, listen to me," he said. "If you kill him in front of Bretherdale, the earl can have you brought before a magistrate. They may even execute you for murder. Is that what you want? Hereford might not be able to get you out of it. *Think!*"

Addax was trying to think. He truly was. But he was so crazed with anger and hatred that he simply wasn't thinking straight. But that all stopped when a feeble voice called to him from the top of the mural stairs.

"Addax?"

It was Emmeline. Her left arm was bandaged to her chest, and she had blood all over the bottom of her shift, but she was on her feet. With the help of the cook and the physic, she was on her feet. God only knew what strength it took to get her there, but she had forced herself out of her sickbed because of the chaos Addax had created. He stopped struggling against Essien when he saw her.

"Get back to bed," he told her. "You should not be up."

Emmeline's gaze was on him, but only for a moment. It soon moved to Maximilian, who was sitting up with his father's assistance. The man was bloodied and battered, and still only half-conscious, but he was alive.

That was all Emmeline needed to see.

"Addax," she said again. "Come here, please."

Addax didn't hesitate. He pulled free of his brother and took the stairs two at a time to her. She ordered the physic and the cook away so she could speak to Addax privately, but she could hardly stand on her own, so she had to grab on to him with her one good arm. He held her tightly, trying to turn her around to get her back to bed, but she balked.

"Stop pushing me around," she said. "I want you to listen to me."

He did as she asked and stopped trying to move her. "What is it?" he asked. "Truly, Emmy, you should not be—"

She cut him off, quietly done, but unmistakably. "Listen to me, and listen closely," she said, barely above a whisper. "I want you to leave. Take your things and leave this instance. Do you understand me?"

He looked at her, puzzled. "Why?" he demanded. "I cannot—"

She cut him off again. "If you think this is a simple thing for me to ask you, then you would be wrong," she said hoarsely. "You have attacked the man I am married to. His father is an earl. You are in a good deal of trouble now, and I could not stand it if those two tried to prosecute you for your crimes. They can, you know. And they will ruin you."

He was starting to calm down a little. She was saying essentially the same thing Essien had said, so the control that had eluded him so far was starting to come together again. He understood what they were saying, completely, but he couldn't agree with it.

He wouldn't.

"No one is going to ruin me," he said quietly. "But I could not let what he did to you go unpunished."

Emmeline knew that. She knew exactly why he'd done what he'd done, but that didn't stop her from the utter terror she was feeling at the moment. She'd already decided to ask him to leave earlier in the day, but this incident had set that decision in stone. He had to leave, or very bad things were going to happen.

Tears were swimming in her eyes as she looked at him.

"There were times in my life that I prayed for a guardian angel, but God had other plans for me," she murmured. "He sent me a dragon to watch over me, and I love that dragon more than words can express. But you have given away our secret by attacking Maximilian. They will know of your feelings for me, and that means you cannot stay. You *know* you cannot stay."

That was true. All of it. He hadn't considered the fact that he'd betrayed their secret with his actions, but he could see now that he had. Still, it didn't matter. If he had it to do all over again, he would do the same thing.

Again and again.

"I could not let his deed go unpunished," he said simply.

"I know," she said softly. "Addax, I am not asking you to go. I am telling you. You *must* leave. You must take your things and leave at this moment. Get out before they try to ruin you. Get out before they turn what we feel for one another into torment. Please, my love. I want you to go."

Addax was starting to become emotional as the reality of the situation began to bear down on him. "But... how will I know what I leave behind?" he said, his voice tight. "How will I know how you are? If you are well? If Max is behaving himself?"

She sighed faintly. "You know the answer to that," she said. "You must not think of me at all. I am another man's wife, and I cannot have you wasting your life pining for me. You know I am right."

"But—"

"*Zahid*, Addax," she whispered, interrupting him. "You will always have everything of me. But you must go, and you must leave me behind."

"You ask too much."

"I know. But it is all we can do."

Addax felt as if he'd been hit in the chest. He audibly exhaled as if there had been an actual blow. Emmeline watched his face for a moment, holding back the explosive grief she was feeling, but knowing it was the right thing to do. Addax had to save himself. After attacking Maximilian, there was nothing else he could do.

"Essien?" Emmeline called. "Please come to me."

Essien, who had been watching the situation from afar, quickly made his way up the stairs. He stood a step below Emmeline and Addax, watching the two of them, seeing the naked agony in his brother's face, and he knew why. He'd always known. Addax was in love with Emmeline, and that love had overtaken him. He could no longer hide it.

Emmeline, this time, was the strong one.

"Essien, you must take your brother and get out of here," she said quietly. "Gather your things and go now. Go back to the tournament circuit, and do not let your brother come back here. If he does, they will ruin him. And that must not happen."

Essien could see that she meant it. Every word of it. But Addax was about to crumble before his eyes. The strongest man he'd ever known was having the weakest moment of his life. But the lady was right—he had to leave before Bretherdale and Maximilian did something terrible to him, and Essien appreciated that the lady was trying to save him. Even in her injured state, she was only thinking of Addax. But God... It was painful to watch.

After a moment, Essien nodded.

"We will go," he said quietly, reaching out to peel his brother off Emmeline. "Ad, let her go. We must leave."

Addax refused. He had her good hand, and he also had an arm around her waist, supporting her, but he wouldn't let go.

"Oh, God," he breathed. "I am not sure I can."

Emmeline pried his fingers off her hand and tried to step back, weak as she was. "Addax, let go of me," she said. "Please. I must go back to bed."

That caused her to loosen his grip, and she staggered back so the cook could catch her. Old Elza had her tightly, tears in her eyes because she'd heard what had been said. The physic, however, hadn't heard anything because he'd been further away, but he stepped forward to take Emmeline. As the cook and the physic turned her toward the stairs that led up to her chamber, Addax spoke softly.

"*Zahid*, Emmeline," he said. "For always."

Emmeline couldn't hide the tears. As the cook and the physic helped her take one stair at a time, Essien pulled Addax down the flight of stairs with him.

"Come," Essien said. "We must go."

Addax nodded dumbly, but he also gestured back toward the mural stairs. "My things are in my chamber," he said weakly. "I must go get them."

"Nay," Essien said. "Go prepare your horse. I will get your things."

"I can get them."

"That was not a suggestion. *Go* prepare your horse."

It was Essien giving the commands for a change, because Addax was incapable of thinking clearly. After a moment's hesitation, Addax headed out of the keep, into the night beyond. Essien watched him go, making sure he wouldn't try to double back. When Addax was far enough away, Essien turned to Claudius and Maximilian.

"I am taking him out tonight," he said quietly. "He will not come back."

Claudius was quivering with fear, with rage. "See that he does not," he said. "But he may yet feel my wrath for what he has done."

Essien fixed on the earl. "If I were you, I would not start any trouble," he said. "Addax has the backing of de Velt and de Lohr. One word from him and they will march on Raisbeck and Alston and raze them both. If you do not wish to lose every-thing you have, then take heed—keep your lips shut and ensure that Lady Emmeline remains safe and sound for the rest of her life, for any word that she has been injured again, or worse, and there is nothing I can do to hold my brother back. He will come back, and he will kill you both. Is this in any way unclear?"

It was a heavy threat, but one that Claudius believed implicitly. There was no way he could defend himself against de Velt or de Lohr, and they both knew it. Therefore, there would be no retaliation for what Addax had done to Maximilian.

They were fortunate it hadn't been worse.

With a brief nod, Claudius turned his attention back to Maximilian, who was in a bad way. But Essien didn't care. He headed back up to his brother's chamber, gathering all of his things, before returning to the stable where Addax was already on his horse, mounted. He was just sitting there, waiting. Waiting to start the rest of his life without the woman he'd been foolish enough to fall in love with.

Something went out of Addax al-Kort that night.

Something he would never find again.

CHAPTER SIXTEEN

Six months later

*T*HE BABY GOATS *are in fine form today!*

Emmeline had already been hopped on and nibbled on. The servant who usually brought in the milk was ill on this day, so Emmeline had stepped in to milk the mother goats, something the baby goats took exception to. Not so much exception, really, as they simply wanted to play. The moment she sat down on the three-legged stool with her bucket was the moment the little goats decided she was a mountain to climb.

And they tried.

So the baby goats jumped and stepped on her and tried to climb her as she milked their mothers. They really were awfully cute, and she would pat their little heads in between milking teats. There was also a big goose in the kitchen yard, one the cook was trying to fatten up for a coming feast, and he seemed very interested in what she was doing, too. Between the goats and the goose, it took Emmeline twice as long as usual to finish her task.

But she didn't really mind.

They were sweet distractions.

It was a mild summer's day in a string of several mild days. The rainy season was just on the horizon, so Emmeline enjoyed the sun while she could. These were days of normalcy, or as normal as they could get, though from time to time she thought about the child she should have had in her arms by this time. A baby that would have been three months old, probably with her hair and eye color, and her smile. Instead, that baby was buried in a small crypt in the nave of St. Catherine's Church in Penrith.

Elizabetha, the crypt said.

She thought about her every day.

There was someone else she thought of every day, too. Addax had never left her mind, not for a moment. He was the last thing she thought of at night and the first thing she thought of in the morning. She'd never heard from him again after his departure from Alston six months ago, but it was better that way, even if it was painful. She imagined he was back on the tournament circuit as the Black Dragon won purses and made a name for himself. She hoped he was happy, or at least trying to be happy. She hoped he was safe and warm and healthy. She hoped and prayed for all of those things for the man she still loved with all her heart, and always would.

Zahid.

More than love.

Since his departure, however, things at Alston had changed. Quite honestly, Maximilian had changed. He wasn't suddenly a wonderful husband, but his behavior had changed. He didn't fight with her as they had the first six months of her marriage, and she, in turn, didn't fight with him. He tried to understand a little more about how the money was made and how the mines worked, which made him less demanding when it came to coinage. He still asked for it, and she still gave him what she could whenever he asked, but she'd heard that the woman in Penrith that he was fond of had given birth to his son, and she suspected he was spending the money on the boy.

Not that she could stop him.

But something had shocked both Maximilian and Claudius into better behavior toward her since the night she was pushed down the stairs. Claudius especially. He came to visit quite frequently these days, and she further suspected that Bretherdale's presence had something to do with Maximilian's change in demeanor. Sometimes, Maximilian could actually be pleasant when his father was around. When he wasn't around, Maximilian was civil and little more. He'd asked her once, about three months ago, if she wanted another child, and she had declined, knowing what that involved with him. He'd never asked again, but she supposed she should give the man credit for at least asking. They'd come to a stable coexistence, the two of them. It wasn't ideal, but it was better than it had been.

She was grateful for small mercies.

The stable coexistence also meant he spent more time at Alston, strangely enough. Like today—Pierre had taken him to inspect one of the mines, something Maximilian had been reluctant to do, and learn about, but he was becoming more accustomed to it. His right arm, broken twice now, hadn't healed correctly the second time, either, so returning to the tournament circuit was out of the question. The King of Chaos had hung up his lance for good, so he'd resigned himself to learning about mines and things.

At least it kept him busy and out of her hair.

Finished with the milking, Emmeline hauled two full pails into the kitchen for the cook. Because of the ill servant, the chickens hadn't been fed either, so Emmeline volunteered.

Usually, the fowl were left to their own devices when it came to feeding, but the cook liked to feed them the wheat grain that wasn't good enough to be ground into flour because she thought it made their meat sweeter, so Emmeline walked the yard and tossed the grain to the chickens. The goose gobbled it up, too, and the little goats wanted to play again. Emmeline kept having to pull the hem of her dress away from little teeth.

"Do you know how to talk to the animals?"

Looking up, she saw Maximilian standing several feet away. She hadn't even heard him enter the yard. "Not that I'm aware of," she said, tossing more wheat to the chickens. "Why do you ask?"

Maximilian pointed to all of the animals milling around her feet. "Because they follow you around like you have given them orders," he said. "You must speak their language."

She held up a handful of grain. "I speak the language of food," she said. "Every creature understands that."

Maximilian shrugged. "True," he said. He watched her for a moment before continuing. "I came to tell you that I just received a missive from Raisbeck."

She glanced up at him. "Oh? And how is your father?"

"Dead."

Emmeline stopped spreading the grain, looking at him in shock. "Sweet Mary," she said softly. "He is?"

"Aye."

It took her a moment to digest the news. "I am so very sorry to hear that," she said. "When?"

Maximilian was still looking at the chickens. He didn't seem particularly distressed, but he did seem stunned.

"This morning, evidently," he said. "His servant went to wake him and saw that he was dead."

"Are you going to Raisbeck immediately?"

Maximilian nodded. "Aye," he said. Then he eyed her. "That means I am the new Earl of Bretherdale, and you are the new countess."

Emmeline waved him off. "That does not matter to me," she said. "It never has. Your father was a kind man in the end, Maximilian. Is there anything I can do to help?"

Maximilian shook his head. "I do not think so," he said. "I will go to Raisbeck and make arrangements for the funeral. You should probably attend, as the new countess."

"Of course I will attend," she said. "Would you like me to go with you?"

"Not now. I'd rather go alone."

"I understand."

He continued to look at her. "My father liked you, you know," he said. "I think he felt guilty for forcing marriage upon us, but he grew to like you."

"I liked him."

"He thought you would make a fine countess."

"I hope I can do good for the people of the earldom."

Maximilian shrugged and turned away. "I am certain you can," he said. "But let us deal with the burial first. I do not know when I will return, but I will send word about his mass once I make arrangements with the priests in Penrith."

"Very well," Emmeline said. "I will wait to hear from you."

With that, Maximilian turned away, heading off to the stables to collect his horse. Truth be told, he wasn't sure how he felt.

Numb, possibly.

He thought it rather ironic that, for all the times his father told him he was sick or dying, his actual death should come so quickly and unexpectedly. He wasn't sure he was prepared for it. Even though he and his father had had a contentious relationship, the man was still his father. The future had changed for him now. So much had happened within the past six months that it was difficult to know how to chart the path he wanted to chart.

The perfect example was Emmeline.

Once, he'd tried to kill her. That had been his intention, but Emmeline was strong. She survived the fall down the stairs, even if the child hadn't, and he had been rewarded for his treachery by taking a beating from Addax that left him crippled and wounded for several weeks afterward. Once he regained his wits and his strength, he wanted vengeance against Addax for doing that to him, for challenging him in his own home and punishing him for his actions, but his father had convinced him that revenge against Addax al-Kort would only cause him harm in the long run.

Claudius had explained, but Maximilian already knew, that Addax was beyond reproach. He was supported by not only the Earl of Hereford, but also the House of de Velt. Addax and his brother were thick as thieves with some of the most powerful men in the country, and Claudius had convinced Maximilian that if he tried to seek vengeance against Addax in any way, armies would descend on Alston and wipe it from the earth. Given that Maximilian knew the strength of both the House of de Lohr and the House of de Velt, he believed that implicitly.

His vengeance was forgotten.

But his emotional wounds from a former friend turning on him hadn't.

He still wasn't over the fact that Addax had beaten him badly when he discovered Maximilian's role in Emmeline's accident. It had never even crossed his mind that Addax would turn on him like that. Maximilian had operated his entire life with so much impunity that it never occurred to him that he would be punished for doing something that in his mind was necessary, but most people would view as heinous. But a few simple words from his father explained it all—*He's in love with Emmeline*. So much made sense when he understood that, but there was no sense of jealousy because he had no feelings for Emmeline. There was simply a sense of regret.

He regretted everything.

Still, he was married to Emmeline, and the marriage wasn't going to go away. Emmeline wasn't going to go away. Maximilian would have gladly given her over to Addax as a mistress, but he knew that wasn't what Addax would want. He had too much integrity. But that accident, and that beating, had changed the tides of Maximilian and Claudius. After Emmeline's accident, Claudius started visiting nearly every week to make sure she was still in one piece. He feared Addax so much that he had to make sure personally that she was alive and healthy. But also during that time, a strange thing happened.

The lady showed what she was made of in a way Maximilian could understand.

She'd changed, too.

It all started a couple of weeks after Maximilian had been beaten. He had broken arms, broken bones in his face, and somewhere along the way he had managed to break an ankle, so he wasn't able to walk. Servants mostly saw to his needs, and his father did for the first couple of weeks, but after that he started seeing Emmeline in his chamber, making sure his meals were delivered hot and his bandages were regularly changed.

The very woman he'd tried to kill was taking charge of his

care.

Given that she was the chatelaine, that wasn't unusual, but it would have been completely understandable had she remained far removed from him. Quite honestly, he had expected her to. She had lost their child because of him, and he was quite sure her aversion to him had become part of her very fabric. But he watched the woman make sure he was taken care of even though she was still recovering from his attempt on her life, and that understanding of her character did something to him.

He started to rethink everything.

Maximilian had once been a man of reason, or reasonably reasonable, but the forced marriage had done something to his spirit. His rebellion against it had gone beyond even what he thought he was capable of. It had all been rebellion against his father's wishes, but it had taken a near-death beating to realize there was nothing he could do about it. He had a wife that he didn't want, a wife who was showing her true character by tending to a husband that had tried to kill her.

From that moment forward, things changed.

He still didn't want a wife, but he could see that she was a good woman. The woman in Penrith who had given birth to his son was a merchant's daughter who was selfish and vain, and quite pretty, but she was petty. He had seen it. He was still fond of her, however, so his opinion of her had never changed, but in seeing Emmeline go about her duties even as she healed from her own wounds made him think that maybe she wasn't as bad as he'd thought she was.

Maybe there was something redeemable in her after all.

Therefore, a fragile peace settled at Alston. There were no more screaming matches or battles with fireplace pokers.

Maximilian became aware that when he spoke civilly to her, she would be civil in return. He couldn't quite bring himself to be kind or even interested in her, but he could be marginally amiable. It made his life much easier if he was.

Maximilian had to admit that living this way was much more pleasant than living the way they had before. He wasn't a man prone to chaos, in spite of his nickname on the tournament circuit, so the peace at Alston Castle was to his liking these days. Even his father had commented on it.

He was glad his father had lived long enough to see it.

Frankly, *he* was surprised he had lived long enough to see it.

But the fact remained that he had a mistress in Penrith who had just delivered his son. He figured that if Emmeline didn't make a fuss over it, then he wouldn't either. He once thought to marry this woman, this daughter of the merchant, but the more time passed and the more he saw how Emmeline was truly suited to the life of a countess, the more he didn't want to get rid of her. Besides, she was well loved at Alston Castle and in the villages within the property boundaries, so he knew her absence would be felt. He saw value in her management skills, and with her he knew that Alston would remain prosperous. With his father's death, he would also inherit Raisbeck Castle, which wasn't quite so prosperous, but it was quite large, and there were a few things he thought that Emmeline would be able to help with.

The merchant's daughter would have been useless.

Odd how his thinking had changed these days. There had been a time when he would have been very happy to see Emmeline go, but he had finally come to terms with her value. Now that his father was gone, it was oddly comforting to know that she would be there to help him manage the estate. He really had no head for management, so the future of the Bretherdale earldom would fall to the new Lady Bretherdale.

And he was content with that.

As Maximilian took the road southwest, heading toward Raisbeck Castle, he could see the smaller road that led to Penrith branching off to the west. That was the path he always took to go into town, and after a moment's deliberation, he decided to go to Penrith and inform his mistress of his father's passing. It wasn't that far out of his way, and he wasn't in any hurry to get to Raisbeck, so he directed his horse onto the smaller road and headed into Penrith.

The closer he drew to the village, the more he thought about visiting his mistress. Anna was her name—or Anna Maria, as her father called her, because the man had been born in Navarre. Her father knew that she had given herself over to the son of the Earl of Bretherdale, and because he hadn't been born in England, he didn't want to create problems for the earl by protesting the behavior of his son. He might find himself thrown out of the country altogether. He was a merchant, his business selling imported items, and he didn't want to offend any potential customers, because his business was dependent upon word of mouth. That meant he'd looked the other way when his daughter delivered a bastard.

As difficult as it was.

By the time Maximilian reached the village, he had thoughts of Anna Maria's body on his mind. There would be no better comfort for a grieving son than her soft flesh and talented mouth. Her father's merchant stall was toward the center of town, which had a narrow street and buildings crowding right up to the edge of it. The merchant had a yellow and red flag painted over the doorway, indicating his store sold goods from the Continent, and Maximilian reined his horse into the alley behind the stall. Taking his purse and his broadsword with him, he went inside.

Usually, Anna Maria worked the front of her father's stall, and this day was no different. She was helping a woman select silk from across the sea when she caught sight of Maximilian entering. She smiled at him, leaving the woman to fend for herself as she joined Maximilian by the entry door.

"Greetings, my lord," she said in her seductive voice. "I did not expect you today, but it is all the more pleasurable to see you."

Maximilian smiled weakly. Anna Maria was a small woman with big breasts and big, round hips, made rounder after childbirth, but she had a pretty enough face. Emmeline was prettier, but that was of little matter to him. Anna Maria was what he needed.

He needed her now.

"Can we speak somewhere privately?" he asked.

She nodded quickly, leading him to the rear of the stall, where the stairs to the living quarters above were. She took him up a rickety flight of stairs, into the rooms that she shared with her father and brother and grandmother. The old woman was watching the baby as he slept peacefully in his cradle, and Anna Maria stood over him proudly, indicating for Maximilian to admire what they had created together.

"Look at him," she said dreamily. "Is he not perfect?"

Maximilian nodded to the dark-haired infant. "Young Claudius is quite perfect," he said, but he was distracted. "Speaking of Claudius, I came to tell you that my father passed away this morning. I was on my way to Raisbeck, but I wanted to detour to Penrith to tell you."

Anna Maria's features softened with sympathy. "I am sorry to hear that," she said. "How do you feel? Are you terribly sad? I know you and your father did not always get on."

He shrugged. "I am saddened, of course," he said. "He was still my father."

"But now he can no longer tell you how you can live your life. Now you can live it as you choose."

He eyed her. "I always live it as I choose. Why would you say that?"

Anna Maria shook her head. "Because you have told me he controlled your life," she said. "He forced you to marry a woman you hate. He was only thinking of himself when he did that. He was not thinking of what you wanted."

Maximilian heard his own words regurgitated from her mouth. "I suppose he was thinking of what was best for Bretherdale," he said, his gaze drifting to the baby. "I have a son now. Who is to say that he will not do what I tell him to do and marry whoever I choose for him?"

Anna Maria looked at the baby too. "My father already has plans for him," she said. "He says he will marry a princess from Navarre."

Maximilian cocked an eyebrow at her. "He is the son of the Earl of Bretherdale," he said, using his new title. "I will decide who my son will marry."

Anna Maria, usually so compliant, shrugged. "You will have to discuss that with my father."

Maximilian frowned. "Then where is he?" he said. "We will discuss it now."

He was raising his voice, and Anna Maria held up her hands to quiet him. "Shh," she said, looking at the baby with concern. "Do not wake him."

Maximilian couldn't believe the woman was actually telling him what to do, no matter how small it was. The shock of his father's passing was contributing to an unhappy mood.

"I did not come here to have you dictate my son's life, nor my own," he said. "I came to tell you that I may not be able to come by for a time. I must make arrangements for my father's burial and assume the mantle of the Earl of Bretherdale."

Anna Maria was watching him with her big brown eyes. "You are an earl now," she said. "That is a proud thing. Mayhap… mayhap you should acknowledge your son so that people will know he is the child of nobility. He deserves everything your name can bring to him."

"You know I cannot do that."

"Why not?"

Maximilian didn't want to argue with her. He threw up his hands and turned for the door. "I am leaving now," he said. "I will be back… sometime. I do not know when."

She was trailing after him. "But why can you not acknowledge that you have a son?" she said. "You said you would."

He rolled his eyes. "I said nothing of the sort."

Anna Maria was on his heels as he put his hand on the door latch. "Before he was born, you told me that you would take care of him and of me," she said. "Your father is dead. You are now the Earl of Bretherdale. Why would you deny your only son?"

"Because he is a bastard. Must I really explain this to you?"

"But he should not be," she insisted, grabbing his arm. "You told me months ago that you would marry me. Do you remember?"

He *had* told her that in the weeks leading up to Emmeline's accident, but he hadn't really meant it. He'd only told her that so she'd stop crying, because she'd wept through her entire pregnancy. She wept because her child would be a bastard, wept because all of Penrith was gossiping about it. It was no secret who the father was, and she wept about that, too. So he'd told her things he didn't mean simply to quiet her. Or mayhap he did mean them at the time. He wasn't sure.

But he surely didn't mean it now. Becoming the Earl of Bretherdale changed things.

He'd changed.

"I am already married," he said quietly, with annoyance. "You *know* this."

"But you said—"

"I only said it so you would stop weeping," he snapped. "I said it so you would quiet down, so I could bed you without having to listen to your constant sobbing and complaining. The truth is that I cannot marry you, and you know it."

Anna Maria was grossly unhappy and growing more unhappy by the moment. "Then I will marry someone else," she declared. "I will tell them that my husband has died. They will raise your son as their own, and you shall never see him again!"

Maximilian had the door open at that point, with the staircase leading down to the stall behind him. But he paused on the top step, eyeing her dangerously.

"You'll do nothing of the sort," he said. "I will take care of you and the boy, but I cannot marry you. You have always known this, so I do not know why you are having a tantrum about it."

New mothers were unpredictable creatures. Maximilian had learned that. Anna Maria had been unstable since the day she realized she was pregnant, and the birth of the child had done nothing to ease those symptoms. She was quite angry with him now.

"Mayhap I do not want to be your mistress any longer," she said. "I have been speaking to my father, and he is certain that if he sends me back to Navarre, I can find a decent husband who will accept my child as his own."

"If you go back to Navarre, the child stays with me."

Anna Maria's mouth flew open in outrage. "He is *my* child!" she cried. "I'll not leave him to your shrew of a wife! *Never!*"

"He is my son. If I want to take him, I will."

"I would have to be dead before I would let you do such a thing!"

"Dead or alive, he is my son. And you will never take him away from me."

"I gave birth to him. He's mine!"

"He is the son of the Earl of Bretherdale and a whore. What do you think being a mistress is, you little fool? The child does *not* belong to you!"

That threw her over the edge. With a shriek, Anna Maria charged Maximilian, who was at a disadvantage standing on the top step. Before he could protect himself, Anna Maria rammed straight into his chest, shoving him back as hard as she could. Maximilian stumbled down a few steps but caught himself on the railing. The railing, however, was wooden and weak and unable to support his weight when he hit it with the force of Anna Maria's shove. It cracked and broke, and he went over.

Headfirst to the ground below.

Anna Maria's brother, Alejandro, had been working in a small shed when he heard the commotion. He rushed out in time to see Maximilian lying in the dirt, bleeding from the head, and his hysterical sister. Their father, who had been in the shop, came running out to see what had happened, and when he saw the crumpled figure of his daughter's lover, he shut the door into the shop so his customers couldn't see what had happened.

Very quickly, he realized they had a catastrophe on their hands.

Alejandro didn't think Maximilian was breathing. Anna Maria was distraught. She swore that she hadn't pushed him off the stairs, but her father knew that they would be blamed regardless. The Earl of Bretherdale would come down on them for killing his only son, and they would not survive.

Fear fed his decisions that day.

Benecio Agoretta y Zubiri, a name he'd changed to the Norman fashion of Benedict de Agoretta, knew what this meant. Customers would turn away, and his business would not survive. His daughter might even end up imprisoned. They would *all* end up imprisoned. He'd always known the earl's son would cause them trouble, but he hadn't imagined this was the kind of trouble the man would cause.

They had to move quickly.

He ordered Alejandro to find Maximilian's horse and send the animal away. Then he brought around a handcart while he ordered his daughter and mother to pack up everything they could in the apartment. While that was going on, he loaded up straw from the small livery in the back of his property into the handcart, and when Alejandro returned from having set the horse free, Benecio and his son picked up Maximilian and carried him, still bleeding, to the handcart. They covered him up with more straw, and Alejandro took the handcart through the back alleyways and small paths of Penrith until he reached the River Eamont.

The body went in.

After that, it was a mad scramble to pack up what they could, as fast as they could. Benecio closed the shop early so they could load as much merchandise into two wagons as possible. Once that was done, and the family apartments were cleaned out, he set fire to the stall, and, under the cover of darkness, his family headed out of town. While everyone ran to fight the fire, no one noticed the de Agoretta family departing from a smaller road.

Back to Navarre, from where they'd come.

Never to be seen again.

CHAPTER SEVENTEEN

Alnwick Tournament

V*ICTORY IS ONCE again mine!*
    The Black Dragon was in fine form today.

The dagger given to Addax by his father, the one that had belonged to generations of his forefathers, was front and center yet again as he made his run down the guides toward his opponent, a de Royans knight. Given that the tournament was closed to Netherghyll, seat of the House of de Royans, men either related to the family or working for the family had competed in nearly every event. The dagger with the onyx eyes was once again watching him ride to victory, but so was something else.

The "worthy" pin was in full view next to it.

The favor had been his charm.

For nine long months, the pin had gone everywhere with him. It had competed in every event, attended every meal. In Catterick last month, the daughter of the Earl of Brompton had asked him about it, and he explained that it was from the woman he loved. That had deterred her, because she'd been actively pursuing him through the entire tournament, but knowing he had a love somewhere had cooled her down somewhat.

It hadn't been the first time, and it wouldn't be the last.

After they left Alston Castle on that horrific night he refused to remember, Essien had taken him straight back to Berwick and to Cole, where the entire sordid affair came out. Cole had been sympathetic, and Corisande had been even more so because she adored Emmeline, but Cole also knew that Addax had to get back to work and focus that grief on something else. That something else had been the tournament circuit.

He was back.

It was still the northern circuit this time, because he liked the venues and knew the crowds. The squires and men that Cole had given positions when Addax and Essien went off to Alston were returned to him, and they'd added even more men because Addax was raking in a fortune with every tournament. Catterick, York, and Manchester had been particularly profitable, so profitable that Addax and Cole were in discussion about Cole selling him the de Velt property of Cloryn Castle on the Welsh marches. Addax had the money, and, as he'd told Cole, he couldn't continue wandering for the rest of his life, so Cloryn, which was small but strategic, would be perfect for him and an eventual family.

But that was something Addax wasn't ready to talk about yet.

These days, he was focused on winning, drinking, and reaffirming bonds with men he'd known a very long time, men he trusted not to change into something he didn't recognize. Beau de Russe was one of them, as were three knights he hadn't seen in a while, even though he'd known them since his first days in

England. Ares, Atlas, and Anteaus de Bourne were descendants of the kings of Northumbria, and were Corisande's brothers.

Ares, in fact, was the Sheriff of Westmorland, a prestigious post given to him by the king. But in the Catterick tournament, and this tournament, he was simply Ares de Bourne, Hades' Wrath—or simply *the Wrath*. Every competitor had a nickname, and that happened to be his. His brother, Atlas, went by *the Kraken*, while the youngest brother labeled himself *God's Favorite Child*. That brought laughter from most until Anteaus completed in the joust, and then men began to realize that he might very well *be* God's Favorite Child.

The man had quality skills.

Whatever he was called, Addax liked him. Anteaus and Essien were the same age, and close friends. Even if Addax had been ripped from the woman he'd fallen in love with, he was surrounded by men who loved him, and whom he loved in return, so it had been a salve to his soul. Knocking Atlas de Bourne from his horse earlier that day had done wonders for his spirit, even if Atlas didn't think so. But it didn't matter.

Addax was back where he belonged.

It was the midday break in the tournament while the arena was cleaned of debris, before the afternoon rounds began, and Addax was with Beau, Ares, Atlas, Anteaus, Cole, and Corisande beneath a big oak tree near the edge of the tournament village. Corisande and a few servants had come down from Berwick with Cole for the festivities, bringing an enormous amount of food with them, and the men were eating with gusto. There was chicken that had been rolled in egg, then flour, and fried in suet, along with stuffed eggs, onion tarts, sausages, apples, and more.

Blackadder's household never traveled lightly.

Addax ate until he could hold no more, sitting with Ares and Anteaus on the ground by the trunk of the tree. Anteaus had eaten so much that he lay on the grass in misery as Addax and Ares talked about the gathering of some lowland clans south of Edinburgh. That was the latest news coming out of Scotland these days, and Addax was fairly certain the ore purchase those months ago was being put to use in those gatherings—coinage and weapons. Since that was an Executioner Knights issue, he didn't mention it to Ares, who was not part of the guild.

But Addax was positive he knew all about it anyway. He and Cole were close, and Cole was deeply invested in the Executioner Knights, so it was probably just a matter of time before the de Bourne brothers became part of it as well.

They would make welcome additions.

"Where is Essien these days, Addax?" Anteaus asked, his hands over his eyes as he lay there in gluttonous misery. "Cole said he was in the north, somewhere."

The truth was that Essien was on a mission for the Executioner Knights these days. He was the one collecting all of the information on the clan gathering and feeding it back to the northern warlords through channels. But Addax seemed casual about his brother's absence.

"He is conducting some business for Cole," he said. "You know Es—everyone likes him, so he makes even the most difficult task simple. He knows I am in with the circuit in Alnwick this week, however, so I expect to see him soon."

"Sooner than you think."

The statement came from a man approaching the group, and they all looked over to see none other than Essien himself approaching. Anteaus managed to push himself off the ground to embrace a friend he'd not seen in months, and Essien laughed softly as Anteaus not only embraced him, but slapped him on the shoulder in a show of brotherhood. As the two of them greeted one another, Addax still sat against the trunk of the tree, smiling as he observed the return of his younger brother. Even though he'd known Essien would return to him, because Essien was skilled and careful, there was always that chance of danger. Seeing Essien returned filled Addax with relief.

His little brother was with him once again.

"Welcome back, Es," he said as Essien approached him. "Have some food. Cori has brought more than we can eat."

Essien was exhausted. That was clear. He picked up a couple of stuffed eggs and shoved them in his mouth, washing them down with watered wine that Anteaus handed him. Once that was all down in his stomach, he burped and looked around for more, finding a piece of chicken to wolf down. Chewing, he turned to his brother.

"I brought some things back for you," he said. "Come back to the encampment with me and I'll show you."

Addax rose wearily from his seated position, stretching out his left shoulder because he'd taken a hard hit earlier in the day, and it bothered him. But he and Essien began heading over to the encampment as Essien continued to chew on the piece of chicken.

"How was the weather?" Addax asked as they moved through the village crowd. "I heard there were terrible rains up north."

Essien took the last bite of chicken and tossed the bone away. "Bad enough," he said. "It seems dry down here."

"It is."

"And warm."

"Nicely warm."

"How did your bout go this morning?"

"I won. I face a de Royans this afternoon."

"Oh?" Essien looked at him. "Which one?"

"Marston," Addax said. "Son of the lord of Netherghyll. He's very young, however, so it could go either way. I will either trounce him or he will destroy me. I do not see it going any other way."

Essien grinned. "Have you been watching him?"

Addax nodded. "I have," he said. "The lad is incredibly talented. His father is so proud that he could burst."

"And taking down the Black Dragon would make him arrogant for the rest of his life."

Addax snorted. "Probably," he said. "But young men like that must know that they cannot conquer everything at such a young age. It takes time and skill. Not everything is so easy."

"Then you intend to trounce him."

"I do. Sorry to say, but I do."

"It will be better for him that way."

The two of them chuckled as Addax was suddenly mobbed by a group of children who had seen him compete. They clamored around him, demanding stories and money. Addax had to politely beg off, finally using Essien to run interference while he slipped away and into the competitors' encampment, where the children were not allowed.

"Well done, Es," Addax said as Essien caught up to him. "You are officially a terrorizer of children."

Essien started to laugh. "At least I terrorize someone."

Addax was grinning as he looked casually around the encampment. "Now," he said, "what is so important that you had to separate me from the others?"

"The usual business," Essien said, mirroring his brother's casual demeanor so they didn't look as if they were discussing critical issues that some may want to listen in on. "I've already given Cole my report, but it seems that any building rebellion the Scots might have toward Berwick is slowing."

"Truly?" Addax said. "That is good news."

"It is," Essien said. "The men I spoke with, men I trust, said that there is some turmoil in Alexander's court right now. No one knows what, exactly, it is, but Lord Gavinton has disappeared. The rumor is that the man has been murdered."

Addax's eyebrows lifted as he looked at his brother. "Interesting," he said. "I wonder why?"

"I do not know," Essien said. "But he fell out of favor somehow. Some say he told an English ally of the plans for Berwick, and the ally has sent word to Henry."

That brought Addax to a halt. "Bretherdale?"

Essien shrugged. "Bretherdale has no connection with the king," he said. "The man was eager to do business with Gavinton. We all saw it. Ad, there is something else you should know."

"What?"

"Addax!" Someone was calling his name, and both Addax and Essien turned to see Ares heading in their direction. He was waving an arm. "Addax, wait!"

Essien tried to conceal his frustration at being interrupted when he was about to tell Addax something he knew his brother would want to hear, but he stood back as patiently as he could as Ares caught up to them.

"The field marshals are looking for you," Ares said to Addax. "Evidently, young Marston de Royans has drawn the first bout, and that is against you. They want you on the field now."

Addax grunted unhappily. "But I had the last bout of the morning," he pointed out. "I've hardly had any rest. Do they know that?"

"They do."

"And they still want me to go now?"

"You'd better go back to the field and talk to them."

Addax frowned, but there was little he could do, so he turned to his brother. "Do you mind having the men bring my equipment and horse to the field?" he said. "Not Kartikeya. He just went in the last round, and I think he has a strained tendon. Bring forth Indra. He's not quite as experienced as Karti, but he's strong. He needs the experience."

Essien simply nodded. He gave up on trying to tell his brother what he'd come to tell him, at least for the moment, and headed back to the encampment to get the men moving. The squires grabbed the joust poles, including the one that had just been repaired, while the man who tended the horses singled out Indra, the heavy-boned Belgian stallion the color of storm clouds. That was why Addax had named him after the Hindu god of weather.

With Essien leading the way, the Black Dragon's entourage headed for the arena.

The first bout of the afternoon went off about an hour later. Marston de Royans was a big lad with shiny blond hair and a winning smile, and he had an entire group of young ladies fawning over his every move. Addax simply sat on horseback on the other side of the arena, watching how distracted Marston was because he would rather soak up the adoration of his worshippers than focus on a very dangerous opponent.

That meant he was going to pay in a big way.

On the very first run, Marston was coming on too fast. He lowered his lance too early, pointing it right at Addax's head. That gave Addax time to position his lance lower, because Marston's center of gravity was too high, so when he ducked Marston's lance and planted his own right into Marston's abdomen, young de Royans went flying off the horse and landed right on his back. His herd of females screamed at the sight, and Addax won himself Marston's extremely expensive Flemish charger. A more glorious horse had yet to be created, as the beast's coat was an iridescent gray with flecks of silver in it, and his mane and tail were as black as coal. As Marston's father raged, Addax collected his new horse and promptly gave it over to Essien, who mounted it gleefully and rode off with it.

Addax could hear Marston's father screaming all the way across the arena.

Snorting at the young knight he'd just taken down a few pegs, Addax rode from the arena to the cheers of the crowd. Beau, Ares, Atlas, and Anteaus met him just outside of the arena to congratulate him. Addax dismounted Indra, who had hardly worked up a good sweat, and handed him over to one of his men. He stood and chatted with his friends for a few minutes until Ares was called away because his bout was coming up. Atlas and Anteaus left with him, and Cole escorted Corisande back to the village because there was something she wanted to purchase. That left Addax heading back to the encampment on his own.

As soon as he walked into his cluster of tents, he could see Essien over by the de Royans horse he'd just been given. With a smile, Addax headed over to him.

"How do you like your new horse?" he asked.

Essien was already in love with the animal. "He's magnificent," he said. "Are you sure you want to part with him?"

"If you do not wish to keep him, I will gladly take him back."

Essien shook his head quickly. "Nay," he said. "I will happily keep him. He's an incredible animal. I wonder what his name is?"

Addax shook his head. "What does it matter?" he said. "You would rename him anyway, and make him your own."

"True," Essien said, patting the horse as it munched grain from a bucket. "Any ideas?"

Addax nodded. "This one is young, just like his former master," he said. "But when he reaches full maturity, he will be a terror. I would call him Shiva the Destroyer. Nothing else is worthy of him."

Essien grinned, slapping the horse on the neck. "Shiva," he said. "It is perfect."

"Of course it is," he said. Then he faced his brother. "Now, what were you going to tell me when I was called away to my bout?"

That question changed the mood considerably. Essien's smile faded as he looked at his brother.

"Nothing good, I am afraid," he said. "Bretherdale is dead. And so is his son."

Addax wasn't expecting that. For a moment, he simply stared at his brother as he processed what he'd been told, but very quickly, his eyes widened and he reached out, grabbing Essien's arm because had to steady himself.

The world was rocking beneath him.

"Max is *dead*?" he managed to spit out.

Essien nodded. "Aye," he said, noticing that his brother looked exceptionally pale. "Come with me. Let us find you a place to sit."

Addax let Essien lead him back to his tent, where Essien promptly poured his brother a full cup of wine. Addax downed it in two big gulps, sitting for a moment and struggling to pull himself together.

"I think you'd better tell me everything, Es," he said hoarsely. "How do you know this?"

Essien sat on a cushioned stool and faced him. "I knew you would be angry with me if I poked around Penrith and Raisbeck Castle, but I had to go," he said quietly. "I wanted to see how Lady Emmeline was faring. My intention was to stay the night at Raisbeck and speak with Claudius. He liked me, and I felt that he would not refuse me."

Addax hung his head. "Why?" he finally asked. "*Why* would you go there?"

"Because I know you have been agonizing about Emmeline since we left Alston," Essien said, hoping his brother wasn't about to explode on him. "I thought I could give you some comfort about her. That she was well. Addax, I was only trying to help you. You know this."

Addax did. But he was still in great turmoil. He wanted to hear, but he didn't want to hear. He'd tried so hard to at least come to terms with the situation, but now, he felt as if he'd been thrown back into the fire again. Finally, he wiped a weary hand over his face.

"So you went to Raisbeck," he muttered. "What happened?"

"I was met by Pierre de Mora," Essien said.

That caused Addax to lift his head, looking at him with surprise. "At Raisbeck?"

"Aye."

"Why was he there?"

Essien held up a hand for patience. "I will tell you what he told me," he said. "He was there at Lady de Grey's request because there was no one else to man the castle. Claudius didn't keep knights, if you recall, so she sent Pierre there to oversee things."

"But *what* happened?"

Essien shook his head as if the situation baffled him. "It was the strangest thing," he said. "Claudius and Max died on the same day. Claudius passed away in the morning, and word was sent to Alston. Max departed to go to Raisbeck and was never seen again. No trace of him has ever been found. It's as if the man never existed."

Addax was growing more puzzled by the moment. "But that does not mean he is dead," he said. "Knowing Max, he could be a hundred different places. You know he wanders."

"His horse was found, Ad," Essien stressed softly. "His horse was found with his money and weapon missing. The local magistrate believes he was robbed and murdered and thrown into any number of rivers in the area. He has declared him dead."

Addax stared at him a moment before lowering his head, rubbing his forehead as if it would help him understand the situation better.

"My God," he muttered. "Claudius is dead. Max is dead. That means... that means Emmy is the dowager Countess of Bretherdale."

Essien shook his head. "Nothing was ever official," he said. "De Mora told me that Claudius and Max died on the same day, so Emmeline never assumed the title because Max didn't really inherit it. That's what the magistrate said, anyway. Emmeline only sent de Mora to Raisbeck because it belonged to the de

Grey family, and she is a de Grey."

Addax was sitting down, his elbows resting on his knees and his hands hanging as he looked at his feet. Claudius and Max dying on the same day put the inheritance of Bretherdale into confusion. He could see that. But that also meant Emmeline was without a husband.

The woman was, at the very least, a wealthy widow.

"How long ago did this all happen?" he finally asked.

"About three months ago, from what I was told," Essien said. He lowered his head, trying to look at his brother's face. "Ad, you realize that Emmeline is now a widow. Unmarried."

Addax nodded slowly. "That was just crossing my mind."

"What are you going to do?"

"I… I do not know. It's been nine months, Es. I cannot go running back there."

"Why not?"

Addax's head came up. "Because she has had nine months to forget me."

"Have you forgotten her?"

That brought Addax pause. "Nay," he whispered. "Of course not."

Essien's eyebrows lifted. "I am telling you this because you must go to Alston," he said. "Henry has been notified of the deaths of Claudius and Max, and if his law advisors tell him that she is, by definition, the dowager Countess of Bretherdale, that makes her a valuable commodity."

"I realize that."

"Are you just going to sit here and let her marry for a third time? Someone who is *not* you?"

Addax's jaw was twitching. "If she marries me, she loses the title."

"You think the title means more to her than you do? Do you really think she's that shallow?"

The twitching in Addax's jaw grew worse. He stood up, pacing the tent, raking his fingers through his hair, and generally fidgeting as he pondered the unexpected turn his life had taken on this day.

Emmeline was a widow.

Emmeline was a widow!

He could hardly get it through his head. The woman he dreamt of morning and night was without a husband. Essien was correct—was he truly going to stand by and watch her marry for a third time, someone who might be of a higher station than him, someone who could elevate her in the eyes of England?

But the truth was that *he* was a king.

There was no one higher than him.

He was *Qara Ejder*—the Black Dragon, the thirty-second King of Kitara, heir to the Jasmine Throne. That was his right, and his bloodlines went back further than any king that England had to offer. He was more of a king than Henry or Alexander could ever hope to be.

And this king wanted to take a wife.

"Nay," he said after a moment. "She is not that shallow. Not Emmeline."

Essien stood up. "Then go to her," he begged softly. "Go to her and ask her if she will have you. Sweet Christ, Addax, this is the woman you love. I know you better than anyone, and you will never love another. You have lost so much in life. We both have. You must not let this chance slip away. Our father would not want you to."

Our father would not want you to. That was like a shot to his heart. Addax realized that his brother was right. He had lost everything—his family, his throne, the very things that made him who he was. His entire life he had worked hard to make something of himself, and, as he saw it, perhaps God had a hand in Maximilian's death. Perhaps God, for once, had shown Addax mercy, knowing how he felt. Knowing that for once in his life he deserved something good to go his way.

This was his chance.

"I've often wondered what Abba would think of what we've done with our lives," he said softly. "If he could see us now, what would he think? Would he think we've become too selfish with our collection of horses and the money we've won on the tournament circuit? Or would he think we've accomplished something important?"

Essien shrugged. "I think he would want us to be happy, no matter what we did."

"Do you?" Addax said. "Because I am not sure. If we were still living in Kitara, I would be the crown prince, and you would be the next in line for the throne. If Abba was dead, then I would be king and you would be the crown prince. We would be ruling a kingdom, Essien, but instead, we are sworn knights in a country we were not born in. Our friends do not have the same heritage that we do. They do not share the same background or even the same language. We ride in their tournaments, we win their money, but when de Lohr calls, we rush to do his bidding. We kill, we spy, and we change the fate of a nation with what we do. Do you really think Abba would be proud of his sons?"

Essien nodded. "I think he would be very proud," he said. "Addax, we escaped death. We ran from it in Kitara, we ran from it in the Levant, and we have found our place in the world.

Mayhap we were never meant to stay in Kitara."

"Why do you say that?"

Essien cocked his head seriously. "Do you think you could have held the throne with Ekon so desperate to have it?" he said. "We would have been in a battle every day of our lives. Even if we killed Ekon, the man had supporters. He was a bad seed that infected many. I do not think I would want to be in a battle every day of my life. Do you?"

Addax sighed faintly. "Nay," he said. "I would not."

"Then mayhap your destiny was not as the King of Kitara. Mayhap it is as the husband of Emmeline de Grey, and mayhap you are in England for a reason."

"What reason?"

Essien smiled faintly. "Because you will have many children, who will in turn have many children," he said. "Your children will become knights and lords and great men who will guide England. And mayhap one of your children will do something so important that it changes the world for everyone. You never know."

Addax chuckled. "Nay, you never do," he said. But he soon sobered. "All I want is to make Abba proud. That is all I've ever wanted."

"He was proud of you the moment you were born."

Addax was grateful for the vote of confidence. Usually, it was him bestowing wisdom on Essien, not the other way around. Reaching out, he patted his younger brother on the cheek.

"Many thanks, Es," he said softly. "And now, I am going to find my destiny. At least, I hope she is my destiny. Will you send word to Henry about the situation? You can tell Cole about it, but do not delay sending word to Henry. If he knows

Emmy is a widow, I do not want him betrothing her to another. Tell him… tell him the King of Kitara has chosen his wife, and it is Lady Emmeline de Witt de Grey. Tell him I do not care about the earldom or the lands. I only care about her. Will you do this for me, Essien? Will you help me?"

Essien smiled broadly, grabbing his brother by the hand. "I will do better than that," he said. "I will ride to Henry myself and tell him."

Addax was slowly being consumed by joy. There was apprehension there also, but the joy was overwhelming. Emmeline was within his grasp.

He'd never thought that he would see the day when that was possible.

"Thank you," he whispered sincerely. "But we must once again ask Cole to take care of the men we have acquired. I will take what I can carry on Indra, but turn the other horses over to Cole for safekeeping. I'll return for them someday, but right now… right now, I have business elsewhere."

Essien nodded, feeling his brother's excitement. He'd hoped this would be his reaction when he returned with the news about Emmeline, but he couldn't be sure. Addax had done all he could to purge thoughts of her from his mind, so he was glad to see those efforts had been fruitless.

If anything, he loved her more than he ever had.

As Addax rode out about an hour later, Essien went to Cole to tell him the tale. Cole not only agreed that Essien should go to Henry, but Cole was going to go, too. As Addax headed as fast as he could for Alston Castle, Essien and Cole headed south to London.

They were to convince one king to let another king have that which he so desperately wanted.

A future.

CHAPTER EIGHTEEN

Alston Castle

*M*ORE GOAT TEETH!

The little goats weren't behaving.

Emmeline found herself in the kitchen yard on this robust morning, preparing to turn the goats out into the field to the east of the castle because it was full of soft green grass and the last of the summer flowers. The goats had been grazing to the west, along the banks of the River Tyne, but they'd eaten up almost everything, so it was time to turn them out into a fresh meadow. Emmeline opened the postern gate and walked out with her goat army behind her.

It was a glorious day, warm and sunny, and she lifted her hand to shield her eyes from the sun as she watched the goats rush out in front of her. The lure of buttercups and other tasty treats were calling to them, and the little goats were looking for stumps and rocks to jump on. Also following her out to the meadow were two big dogs belonging to Adonis, Cane and Able, and they were good protection for the goats as they grazed, so the dogs wandered out into the meadow to find a place to lie in the sun.

Emmeline was dressed simply, in a broadcloth dress that was too big for her because ever since Addax left, she'd not had much of an appetite. That was the truth of it. She'd lost weight to the point where all of her clothing was too large for her, but that wasn't anything she thought much about these days. Other than Adonis, there wasn't anyone to see her, and she didn't care what he thought, so she cinched or tied up the dresses as best she could while one of Elza's kitchen servants, who had become her new maid, used needle and thread to alter the dresses.

Life at Alston had changed these days.

It was truly astonishing to realize just how the situation had transitioned from one of daily angst and apprehension to one of peace and calm. Emmeline had only been existing in the ten years she'd been married to Ernest, and then for the short time she'd been married to Maximilian, everything was in upheaval. But the last few months of their marriage had seen the situation calm enough that she'd had hopes that they might peacefully coexist for the rest of their lives. Emmeline had never wished for the moon when it came to Maximilian. She would take the small victories most gratefully. But he'd left for Raisbeck on the day he received word about his father's passing, and that was the last time she ever saw him. When she hadn't heard from him a month later, she sent word to Raisbeck, and that had started the chain of events that now saw her a widow again.

Once again, she was free.

She had long stopped wondering what had become of Maximilian. It wasn't that she was trying to be cruel, but simply realistic.

He was an episode in her life that she would much rather forget. Nothing good had come out of that marriage, and she simply didn't want to remember it. Other than Maximilian's horse, no trace of him had ever been found, and the local magistrate had concluded that his body must have been thrown into the River Tyne. In fact, Penrith had seen two local murders over the past year, and both victims had been tossed into the river. It was no coincidence that Maximilian turned up missing, or so the magistrate thought. He was convinced that it was the same murderer.

And life moved on.

Therefore, Emmeline had to take charge of not only Alston Castle, but of Raisbeck, and that meant finding out what had been done with Claudius' body. Pierre helped her with her fact finding, and they had discovered that Maximilian had never made it to Raisbeck Castle, meaning whatever happened to him happened between Alston and Raisbeck, because that was the road the horse had been found wandering on.

The servants and soldiers of Raisbeck Castle, having no direction on what to do with their lord, had simply put Claudius in a wooden box and stored him in the vaults below. They hadn't even buried him because they didn't know if they should, so Emmeline made sure that Claudius had a proper burial at St. Catherine's Church in Penrith. That was where all of the de Greys were buried, and she was the only one at his funeral mass, watching as the man was buried next to his wife, sleeping for eternity at the feet of his parents.

After that, there wasn't much more to do other than station Pierre at Raisbeck to make sure it was properly managed while she and Adonis remained at Alston Castle. The mining operations still continued, customers still received their orders, and everything continued on as it should. It all would have been perfect except for one thing...

Addax.

There wasn't a day that went by that she didn't think of him. There wasn't a night that passed that he wasn't on her mind. He was with her so strongly even now that even if he wasn't with her bodily, he was most definitely with her in spirit. It was strange how a man she'd never even kissed, not really, was part of her as indelibly as the stars were part of the sky.

When Emmeline had been younger and was forced to read the books of love and romance that all young women were expected to read, she experienced through the written word the longing of one lover for another. The longing of Tristan for Isolde, of Cleopatra for Antony, and it was never anything that made a mark upon her—until she met Addax. Now, she understood the kind of longing that tore at one's belly or crushed one's spirit. When Maximilian had been declared dead, her first thought was to send word to Addax, but she quickly decided against it. As a widow, she would be expected to mourn her husband for a certain amount of time, and sending word to the man she loved that their troubles were finally over after the death of her husband wouldn't exactly reflect well on her. More than that, she didn't want to make Addax look bad, rushing to her side like an opportunist as soon as Maximilian was out of the way.

She was worried about perception for him.

Perhaps that perception didn't matter too much with her because she wasn't part of England's elite social circles, but Addax was. She didn't want his friends and comrades losing respect for a man who wouldn't even give the wife of a so-called good friend time to grieve his loss. Once, she'd had to send him away for his own good, and now, she would keep him away for the same.

But it didn't stop her from anticipating the day when she

could send word to him.

If he would even come.

And that had been her life until this moment. Days of darkness, days of sunshine, days of hoping for something that would probably never happen. She was still childless, and a widow, but at least she wasn't fighting with Maximilian on a daily basis or trying to avoid Ernest because he was so depressing. There was no Addax to talk to or play board games with—or laugh with—but she could still dream.

And hope.

The goats had found a dandelion patch that was making them very happy, so she wandered over to Cane and Able. Cane was stretched out in the sun, but Able licked her hand as she sat down and patted his big haunches. A breeze was starting to pick up, rustling through the summer grass, creating waves across the meadow. Perhaps this was what her life was meant to be for always. Perhaps this was only, and ever, what it was meant to be—Alston, animals, and lonely days.

She would have to be content with that.

"The last day I spent with my father was a day much like this." A voice suddenly rose behind her. "It was a day that started out like any other, with blue skies and clouds high above. There was no rain because it was not the rainy season, so the air was hot and dry. Little did I know that it was a day that would change my life forever, but sometimes, that is what happens. There is a day in your life that changes it forever. A day that is so important that all days pale by comparison. The last day that changed my life forever was the day I first laid eyes on you in Berwick."

Emmeline knew the voice. God help her, she knew it. But he had to speak about ten words before she realized she wasn't dreaming, and then she turned around, nearly falling over in her haste.

Addax was standing behind her.

Emmeline could hardly believe it. In fact, she didn't trust her eyes for a moment. He spoke of the importance of days, but she hardly heard the words. She was shocked to the bone, struggling to her feet as if she'd never learned to stand up.

Everything was quivering.

"Addax," she breathed, a lump in her throat. "You... you're here."

He smiled faintly. "I am here."

"Truly?"

"Truly."

She blinked. Then her hand flew to her mouth as if to hold back the sobs that were threatening. Tears filled her eyes. All she wanted to do was run to him, but she knew she couldn't.

Uncertainty filled the air.

"You... you are most welcome, of course," she said, her voice trembling. "I did not hear you approach."

He glanced over his shoulder, at the castle behind him. "I saw you as I rode in," he said. Then he indicated the happy goats. "Are you a goatherd now?"

She chuckled, but that broke her composure and the giggles turned to sobs. Furiously, she wiped at her eyes to stop the tears, that didn't have the sense enough not to fall. She didn't want his first vision of her to be one of tears.

"These are my goats," she said. "I would not trust them to just anyone."

He nodded, smiling, but that smile soon faded. "I heard about Max and Claudius," he said. "I have come to give my condolences for Bretherdale."

I have come to give my condolences for Bretherdale. So he knew? That seemed like a strange statement to her, so Emmeline was careful in how she proceeded, because she couldn't assume anything. He wasn't running into her arms, and there weren't any indications that he wanted to be affectionate. Was it possible he'd really only come to show sympathy? And only for Claudius?

Was it possible he hadn't returned for her?

"It was kind of you to come and pay your respects," she said, wiping at the tears that were now under control. "Claudius is buried in Penrith, but Max was never found. I know he was your friend, Addax. I am sorry."

His brow furrowed. "Is that what you think?" he said. "I've come to pay my respects to a man I tried to kill the last time I saw him?"

"You didn't?"

He shook his head, very nearly scowling. "Nay," he said. "While I am sorry for Claudius' passing, I'm not sufficiently over my anger at Max yet. But I *have* come to see you. I... I have a question for you."

"What question?"

He paused. "You've been married to an old man and a man who was unpleasant to you at best," he said. "Would you now consider marrying a man who will love you, more than a man has ever loved a woman, until the day he dies?"

She blinked as if the question startled her. "Who?"

"Me, of course."

She knew that, but she had to hear it from him. She had to hear the words and not assume. Her mouth popped open, and it took her a moment to digest what he was saying. All of it. When she did, the tears returned with a vengeance.

"I wanted to send word to you about Max, but I did not know how you would receive it," she said, weeping. "I am expected to mourn my husband, and I was afraid of how cold it would appear if I was already asking you to return to me. I was afraid of what your friends would think."

Addax threw caution to the wind. He closed the gap between them in four long strides, taking Emmeline into his arms and holding her in an embrace that was as pure and warm as the first embrace that ever was. Her arms went around his neck, holding him tightly as she sobbed against him.

It was like music to his ears.

"Today is a day that will change my life forever," he whispered. "It is the day I held the woman I love and told her how much I loved her. How much I will always love her. How I will endeavor to be a good husband because she is more than I deserve. You will be my *mere jaan* forever, Emmy. I swear it."

Emmeline held on to him as if she were drowning and he was her savior. "As I will love you, and only you, in this life and beyond," she whispered. "Oh, Addax... is this really true? Is it really happening?"

He smiled, loosening his grip so that he could look her in the face. "It is true," he said, gazing into that face he'd seen for months in his dreams. A face devoid of the cosmetics she used to wear, but he thought she was more beautiful this way. "You are more magnificent than I remember. Truly, you grow more beautiful with each passing day."

He was stroking her cheek, and she leaned into his hand, relishing his touch. "I have missed you dreadfully," she murmured. "You were in my thoughts every day, from morning to night."

"Then why did you not send word to me? Why did I have to

hear it from others?"

Her smile faded. "I wanted to, I swear it," she said. "But it's as I said—I was afraid to. It has been eating me up, wanting to send word to you so badly yet knowing that I am expected to mourn a man I never loved. I did not even like him. How would it look if I took up with you so soon after Max's death? How would it look for *you*? The man was your friend."

She had a point. But it didn't change facts.

"I think Max ceased to become my friend the day he married you," he said. "The Max I knew for years would not do what your husband did. I do not know who that man you married was. He was a stranger to me."

"And to me," Emmeline said. "But I am sorry you lost a friend, Addax. I was always sorry for that."

Addax shrugged. "That was Max's choice," he said. "Who knows why men behave the way they do? I've seen the worst of that, since I was a small child when my uncle tried to overthrow my father. I've stopped trying to figure out what motivates men."

Emmeline couldn't disagree. She put a hand to his face, watching him close his eyes as she touched him. It was such a gentle touch, one full of promise and adoration. Now that the burst of joy at their reunion had faded, she took a good look at him.

"You must be weary," she said, looking at his dark-circled eyes. "I suspect you've been riding hard to get here."

He smiled weakly. "Day and night, practically."

"Where did you come from?"

"Alnwick."

"Then come inside," she said, releasing him from her embrace. "Rest and refresh yourself, and we will decide how best to plan what comes next for us."

He nodded. "An excellent suggestion," he said. "I fear there are many details we must discuss before I can marry you."

"Indeed," she said. "This is something we must navigate carefully, for I do not wish for you to look like a villain by marrying the widow of your friend so quickly."

"I do not care about me," he said. "But I do care about you. You were correct when you said that there was a mourning period. Mayhap Max had become someone I did not recognize, but that does not mean that, as my friend, he is not due respect. Truthfully, I am quite sad for the loss of my friend. Max and I knew some good times on the tournament circuit."

Emmeline smiled faintly. "Mayhap you will tell me of some?"

He grinned. "The ones that are proper for a lady, I will certainly tell you."

She chuckled, shaking her head at his cheekiness. "You mean there are some I cannot hear?"

"Several."

"How scandalous."

"You have no idea, lady."

She laughed as they began to walk toward the castle, leaving the dogs to watch over the goats. Addax wanted very much to take her hand, to physically express the joy he felt in his heart, but he didn't dare touch her. It was enough that he was back at Alston, and he was quite certain the tongues were wagging already. They knew why he'd come. But as they headed back, he also couldn't help but notice that Emmeline was much more slender than she used to be, which told him that perhaps she'd gone through more turmoil than she'd let on. He sincerely hoped those days of emotional havoc were over, for the both of them.

They entered Alston through the postern gate, into the kitchen yard. The sights and sounds were familiar to Addax, and he felt a sense of comfort. In spite of the situation with Emmeline during her marriage to Maximilian, he'd enjoyed some good times here. Playing board games with her came to mind, and how he reacted when he lost. That always brought laughter from her, something that was rare during that time.

He hoped to bring it back daily now.

Emmeline took him into the keep through the kitchens. Old Elza was there to greet him, promising she'd bring him some food and even slapping him on the arm because she was so happy he had returned. It was a stinging slap, and Addax chuckled as he rubbed his arm where she'd whacked him. He followed Emmeline up the narrow servant stairs to the entry level above, and she took him into the solar, shutting the door so they could have privacy. As Addax removed his gloves and some of his protection and weapons, Emmeline poured him a full measure of wine. It wasn't watered, and quite strong, but Addax drained the cup.

She poured him another.

"What did you call me out in the field?" she asked. "It sounded like mere… mere…"

"*Mere jaan*," he said. "It means 'my love.' My father used to call my mother that."

Emmeline smiled as she handed him the cup. "That's beautiful," she said. "You mentioned your mother was not from Kitara?"

"Nay," he said before taking another drink and smacking his lips. "She was Egyptian, a princess to her people. I have royal blood on both sides of my family."

"Do you know the language of her birth?"

"A little. Why?"

"I was wondering how to say 'my love' in your mother's language."

He smiled as he looked at her, reaching out to take her hand now that they were alone. "*Habibti*," he said softly. "I know this because she would say it to my brother and sister and I. For a male, it is *habibi*, but for a woman, it is *habibti*."

Emmeline considered that. "Then if I were to say it to you, it would be *habibi*."

"Exactly."

"Good," she smiled, squeezing his fingers. "You are my *habibi*."

He laughed softly and lifted her hand, kissing her fingers gently. But that wasn't good enough for him. They were quite alone, more alone than they'd ever been, and months and months of longing had built up inside of him. He'd never even kissed the woman properly. Realizing that he could brought him to his feet. Towering over her, he set the cup down before he took her in his arms again and slanted his lips, gently, over hers.

The magic commenced.

Emmeline responded instantly, engaging in a heated kiss as she wrapped her arms around his neck. She trapped him against her, opening her mouth to his seeking tongue, and when she suckled on it, Addax nearly went out of his mind. With a growl, he picked her up and set her on the table behind them.

Now they were running on instinct.

Emmeline was no shrinking maiden, but she was understandably inexperienced. She wanted to touch him very badly, but she had no idea how to initiate anything. She'd been bedded three times in both of her marriages, and the only one that had ever moderately aroused her was the second time, with Ernest, because he was willing to explore her at that point in his life. Therefore, she knew a little about foreplay. But very little.

What she didn't know, she could figure out.

She wanted all of him.

Emmeline took on the aggressor role. She wrapped her legs around Addax's waist, holding him tightly against her as they passionately kissed one another. Addax's hands were beginning to roam as he went from holding her tightly to stroking her back and arms. When she didn't stop him, he moved to her buttocks, squeezing them and pulling her body against his. Her legs were parted and his body was wedged in between them, even though they were fully clothed. Through his breeches, Emmeline could feel his hard arousal against her woman's center.

She'd never wanted anything so badly in her life.

Addax's mouth went to her neck, gently suckling her silken skin, and a hand began to gently pull back the neckline of her garment. Because she'd lost some weight, it moved easily, and he was able to pull it off her left shoulder, baring her skin. He could hear her soft grunts of pleasure as he kissed her cleavage, her shoulder, before moving lower. He pulled the bodice down her torso, exposing her left breast.

Emmeline cried out softly as his mouth clamped over a tender nipple. She began to pull at his tunic, trying to undress him, and Addax didn't stop her. In fact, he helped her. He wanted her as badly as she wanted him. In his fervor, he yanked the top of her garment down around her waist to expose both breasts.

And they were a beautiful sight.

He began to feast on them as his clothing came off in pieces until he was finally nude from the waist up. Mouth on her delicious breasts, he flipped up her skirts without any resistance whatsoever. In fact, she was working on his scabbard and his breeches, and he had her skirts up about the time she pulled loose his ties. His broadsword cluttered to the floor and his breeches slipped down to his mid-thigh.

He was between her legs, their bodies essentially naked from the waist down, and his big arousal pushed at her. Addax was a big man, and his male member was equal in size. Emmeline's eager hands moved to his enormous erection as she guided him into her. She'd never done that kind of thing before, but she knew where his manhood belonged. It belonged in her, deeply buried. When Addax felt her slick, wet heat, he thrust firmly into her.

Although it wasn't the first time she'd been bedded, it felt like it. The pleasure-pain of his entry was indescribable. Emmeline bit off her gasps of passion, sinking her teeth into his shoulder, as he thrust into her. Because she was so tight, he had to thrust three times before he was fully seated. But the feel of her was exquisite, everything he knew it would be, and he could feel her legs wrap around him and draw him in deeper. His arms went around her, holding her tightly as he began to move.

Addax's mouth was on hers, kissing her deeply as he made love to her on the oak table of the solar. Her quill ended up on the ground, and the ink almost spilled, but he had the presence of mind to grab it before it could topple. Addax felt things for Emmeline that he had never felt in his life, for anyone, an attraction that he couldn't control. It was more than the act of sex itself. It was a demonstration of the love he felt for her, feelings of worship and adoration that he'd built long before this moment.

It was simply the culmination of everything he'd dreamed of.

As he'd told her earlier—*There is a day in your life that changes it forever.*

For Addax, this was the day.

In his arms, Emmeline was nearly incoherent in her passion, feeling every move with the greatest of pleasure. He was thrusting himself so deeply that the intense pleasure of it was quickly driving her toward release. She'd never made love like this in her life—nothing had even come close. Addax was a magnificent form of a man, and he belonged to her. *Only* to her. This was their moment.

This was when they became one.

Addax's thrusts grew harder, firmer, and he ground his pelvis against her every time he plunged deep. It was moving and beautiful and powerful, and after one particularly deep thrust, he felt her release around him as pants of rapture escaped her lips. Still, he continued to make love to her, feeling another climax shortly after the first. Their lovemaking had reached such a frenzied proportion, and he could no longer stop his own release.

Addax tried to pull out of her, but her legs were wrapped around him and he couldn't remove them in time. He ended up spilling himself into her soft body, feeling every last twitch and spasm with more pleasure than he'd ever known to exist. But he still kept moving, loving the feel of what he'd put into her, marking this woman as he'd never marked anyone else. Emmeline was his, and would forever be his. God willing, he would marry her soon, and she would bear strong sons. Sons that were of Kitaran royalty, of Egyptian royalty, and of

Plantagenet royalty through their mother. No sons on this earth would have such powerful bloodlines, sons who would grow up to do great and noble things.

That was how he knew that this moment, this coupling, was meant to be.

That was how he knew this love was preordained.

Perhaps this was the reason he'd been forced to leave Kitara. Everything in his life had happened in a certain sequence from that point. Perhaps that was why de Lohr had found him, and why, eventually, he found his way to England and to the Executioner Knights and to the tournament circuit. He'd eventually met Maximilian and through Maximilian, he met Emmeline. Everything in his life had been building to this very moment, when he would find the woman he loved, a woman he had loved before time and would love after the earth was absorbed back into the cosmos.

This moment.

This time.

It was theirs.

With his body still joined to hers, Addax finally opened his eyes to look down at Emmeline. The top of her broadcloth dress was down around her waist and her skirts were hiked up over her pelvis, her legs open wide to receive him. The sight of it was enough to heat him up again. Lovingly, he bent over, kissing her shoulder, the tops of her breasts, before taking a nipple in his mouth again and suckling firmly.

In his arms, he could feel Emmeline shudder. She had her arms around his neck, but when he started suckling her again, she put one hand down to where their bodies joined, timidly touching his manroot as it remained embedded in her. Her warm, gentle fingers were wildly arousing, and Addax could feel himself growing hard again. Her touch set him on fire. His mouth captured hers again, and she responded feverishly.

When old Elza brought up some food to the solar some time later, she didn't dare knock on the closed door. She knew, as most others at Alston knew, that Sir Addax had returned because he loved Lady de Grey. Now they were behind closed doors, and Elza put her ear against it to see if she heard any bits of conversation. If she did, she would knock, but what she heard was most definitely not conversation.

With a grin, she took the food back to the kitchen.

CHAPTER NINETEEN

The town of Appleby

*H*OW CAN SHE *expect me to make a decision when I think everything is beautiful on her?*

That was what Addax was thinking as he faced Emmeline, who was holding up a piece of yellow silk. Shopping for silks wasn't exactly his idea of a good time.

"I am not going to tell you what to buy," he finally said. "You must make the decision. You are going to wear it, after all. Not me."

Three months after his return to Alston, a wedding was on the horizon, and Emmeline was shopping for bright, new fabric. Six months of mourning was all she could manage when it came to Maximilian, and in speaking with a priest at Our Lady of Grace in Appleby, it was agreed that six months was long enough due to the short nature of the marriage.

But there was another reason.

Emmeline was pregnant.

That was to be expected, given that Addax bedded her every day. Every single day. The more he had of her, the more he wanted, and they were evidently fertile together, because she was nearly two months along. Addax was over the moon about the impending child, and so was Emmeline. Happy, content, and in love—it was imperative that they marry soon.

The priest agreed.

But Addax wanted his brother present at the very least. He knew that Essien had gone to London to speak to Henry on his behalf, so it was a waiting game now. Essien knew where to find him, and every day, Addax watched the horizon for his brother, but he couldn't wait much longer. Meanwhile, he insisted that Emmeline purchase some new clothing because he didn't want her wearing anything she'd worn when she was married to Maximilian. Call it selfish on his part, but it really wasn't. When he looked at it, and when Emmeline wore it, it reminded them both of those unhappy days.

New wardrobe, new husband, new life.

That was what Addax wanted.

The largest town near them to shop for dry goods was Penrith, but Emmeline refused to go to that town, knowing Maximilian had spent so much time there. She also knew that his mistress was there, along with his bastard, so she refused to go anywhere near Penrith. That meant they traveled to Appleby, which was south of Penrith along the River Eden. It was a quaint little town with a decently sized merchant district, and it had a street dedicated to jewelers, some of which had purchased ore from Alston. Addax had taken a small escort into town, including Adonis, who was happy to get out and about.

As Adonis and the escort were given permission to walk about town for an hour or so, at least until Emmeline was ready to depart, Addax took her to the first of two larger merchants in town. The first one, in a narrow, skinny, three-storied building that leaned precariously, was stuffed to the rafters with goods including fabrics, furs, combs, and even perfume. Emmeline couldn't make up her mind about anything because she didn't shop very often, so she'd asked Addax to make up her mind for her.

But he was taking a stand.

"I realize you are not going to wear the fabric," she said, holding up a swath of yellow silk in front of her. "I am simply looking for some help in deciding if this is a good color or not. What do you think?"

"I think anything you wear will be beautiful because you're wearing it."

She grinned, lowering the fabric. "You are very kind," she said. "Do you like the yellow or not?"

"I like the yellow."

Chuckling, she handed the fabric off to the shopkeeper's wife for a dress length. Then she picked up a beautiful green brocade.

"Look at this one," she said, holding it up so he could see it. "Do you like green?"

"I like green."

Another fabric was given over to the shopkeeper's wife. Emmeline began poking around some more, touching fabric and holding it up to the light to see if it was something she would like.

"Ad?"

"Aye, love?"

"What was your mother wearing the last time you saw her?"

That brought him to a halt, and he looked at her curiously. "Why do you ask?"

She turned to him. "Because I should like to pay homage to her with a color you remember," she said quietly. "Do you recall anything special she wore?"

He had to think on that question, but it was a very sweet sentiment. That didn't surprise him when coming from Emmeline.

"I seem to remember her wearing a red dress once," he said. "It was for a festival called *Qurucu*, which means the Founding. There were all manner of games and contests, and she wore a red dress to match what my father was wearing."

"*Qurucu*," Emmeline repeated. "It sounds like a tournament."

He laughed softly. "Aye, it does," he said. "It was for the most part, only there weren't knights on horseback with big lances trying to smash one another. I remember having sweets there—milk boiled down so it was solid, made into balls, and then covered in flour and fried. They soaked them in honey and rosewater so it absorbed all the sweetness. Quite delicious, especially to a child who could not get enough of them."

"Sounds wonderful," Emmeline said, putting her hand on her still-flat belly. "I think I could use some sweets when we are finished with this."

"Are you hungry?"

"Surprisingly, I am," she said. "I feel well enough today."

"Good," he said, leaning over to kiss her on the ear when no one was looking, and then he placed his hand gently on her stomach. "It makes me very sad when you feel so poorly that you cannot eat anything."

She looked over her shoulder, smiling up at him. "I am grateful for every pain, every sick feeling," she said. "That means our son is growing strong in my belly. I am grateful for anything that comes with it."

He kissed her again, this time on the forehead, as she turned back around to look for red fabric. The shopkeeper's wife and daughter joined her, and soon, the three of them were poring over new fabric that they'd just received. It was a veritable explosion of finery, and Addax thought this might be a good time to slip away. He had a little shopping of his own that he wanted to do pertaining to their coming marriage.

"My lady?" he called to her. "Emmy?"

She had been busy chatting away with the shopkeeper's wife and daughter, so he had to call her once more before she finally turned to him.

"My love?" she responded.

He gestured to the street beyond. "I must see to something," he said. "I will return shortly. You are not to leave this stall."

"Where are you going?"

"That is none of your affair."

It was clear he had a secret. With a grin, she waved him on. "Go, then," she said. "I have plenty to keep me occupied."

She was already inspecting a red silk, and he headed out of the door. The merchant himself, a tall man by the name of Ingram, was standing next to a couple of wagons parked in front of his stall, in conversation with another man who seemed to either be bringing goods or taking them. Wooden boxes were being moved around the wagons. Addax caught Ingram's attention.

"I am in need of a goldsmith," he told the merchant. "Can you direct me to one in town?"

Ingram pointed north, up the avenue. "Up there," he said. "Next to a man who sells knives, and only knives, there is an alley that has silversmiths and a goldsmith. His shop is guarded, my lord, so you must show your purse before they'll let you in."

Addax nodded. "My thanks," he said. "What is the man's

name?"

"Eduard Goldmann," the merchant said. "You may tell him that Ingram sent you."

"Again, my thanks," Addax said. He was forced to move aside because someone was trying to pack a wooden box into the wagon right where he was standing. He noticed that the wagon was mostly full. "It looks as if someone has made a large purchase. How fortunate for you."

But Ingram laughed. "Nay, my lord," he said. "This is my brother, Neif. He is going home and taking half of my stock with him."

"Where is home?"

"Amsterdam. His wife's family has a business that makes jewelry."

Addax nodded. "Then I wish him safe travels," he said. The horses in the lead wagon were startled by something at that moment, and Addax found himself grabbing the bridle of the horse closest to him to keep the animal from bolting. He gave it a few pats in a calming manner. "This is a young horse. Too young and inexperienced for a wagon, I'd say."

"The livery sold the team to me," Neif said. "It was all they had."

Addax looked the horse over. It was strong, but skittish. He patted the animal on the neck. "I would keep a tight rein if I were you," he said. "You do not want him to run away. By the looks of him, he'd run straight into the ocean, and you might get to Amsterdam the hard way."

Neif snorted softly. "I hope not, my lord."

Addax petted the horse one last time and let it go, turning to Ingram. "Thank you for the information," he said. "I've a goldsmith to see."

Appleby was busy on this day because they had a license to hold a market every fifth day of the week, so people had come in from the countryside for the market, which consisted of an entire meadow full of farmers. The meadow itself was right next to the village square, so people were filtering in and out of the market where fruits, vegetables, livestock, and other goods were for sale. As Addax headed down the main road, he thought about checking out the horses, as he had already several and tended to collect them, but he wanted to find a goldsmith to commission a ring for Emmeline. He still had the pin she'd given him, and he wanted to have a ring made for her with the same word inscribed:

Worthy.

But he had to do it quickly, because he didn't want to take the chance that she would conclude her business sooner than expected and, in spite of her promise not to leave the stall, come looking for him.

He wanted the ring to be a surprise.

The area containing the jewelers was near the end of town that had three taverns. It was quite crowded on this day, with people drinking in the street. He could see a few Alston soldiers near one of the taverns, and he was about to turn down a small alleyway next to the man who sold knives when he saw Adonis heading in his direction. De Mora lifted a hand to him, so he came to a halt, waiting impatiently while the man caught up to him. Had he not been so impatient to get to the goldsmith, he would have seen the expression on de Mora's face.

The man looked as if he'd just seen a ghost.

"My lord," de Mora said. "I think… I think you must come with me."

Addax frowned. "Why?" he said, gesturing to the goldsmith

alley. "I have business to attend to and not much time to do it."

But de Mora didn't back down. In fact, he grabbed Addax by the arm. "You will want to come with me, I promise."

Now Addax could see that the man looked almost sick. "Why?" he said. "What am I to see?"

"Bretherdale."

"Make sense, man."

De Mora took a deep breath and pointed down the street. "Maximilian de Grey," he said. "I've found him."

Addax hadn't been expecting that. In fact, he looked at Adonis as if the man had completely lost his mind. "Are you mad?" he asked. "It's not possible."

"It *is* possible."

"But he's dead!"

But Adonis shook his head. "Nay, my lord," he said with some force. "He is *not* dead. He is at the tavern at the end of the avenue, offloading barrels of wine. I saw him myself and tried to speak to him, but he ignored me. He did not seem to know me. He does not look like himself, my lord, not at all. You *must* come."

Addax did. He took off at a dead run. Adonis caught up to him and pulled him back to a walk, but Addax was trying to push past him the entire time, as if he knew where he was going. But he didn't. He was moving blindly until they came to the last tavern on the left, one that had a sign hanging above the door that announced "the Scot's Head." It was a large, rambling, one-storied tavern, and even at this daylight hour, it had people coming in and out of it. The entry door swung open, and Addax could hear laughing and shouting. But that wasn't what caught his attention. Adonis was pointing to the side entrance of the tavern, where a group of men were offloading barrels of wine and ale. As they watched, one slipped and fell to the ground, exploding all over. The tavern keep, a burly man with a big nose and surprisingly small hands, cuffed the man who dropped it.

Addax watched as Maximilian fell to the ground, bleeding from the side of his mouth.

"You stupid fool," the tavern keep boomed. "I'll take that out on your hide!"

He kicked Maximilian in the thigh for good measure, grumbling and cursing. Astonished, Addax watched Maximilian pick himself up from the ground, wiping at the blood on his mouth. But Adonis had been right.

It didn't look like him at all.

The Maximilian he knew had kept his hair neatly cut and liked finer clothing. This Maximilian was dressed in rags. His hair was long, he was unshaven, and he had the general look of a wild man. But he was also big and strong, so he was offloading the barrels with the help of others, carrying them inside and then coming back out again as the tavern keep continued to yell at him.

Addax couldn't have been more stunned.

"Oh... my God," he breathed. "What in the hell is he doing here? Maximilian!"

He boomed the name, shouting so loudly that it echoed off the wattle and daub walls of the tavern. It startled those working on the wagon, and they all turned to look at him. Everyone but Maximilian, who was shouldering another barrel. He wasn't looking at all.

Like he'd never heard that name in his life.

"You see?" Adonis said as Maximilian went inside. "He ignored me, too. I do not think he is deaf, because he responded to the tavern keep, but it is as if he does not know his name."

Addax's initial shock was starting to wear off, replaced by rage. Blinding rage. Before him was a man who was believed to be dead, only to be found working in a tavern. For what? To pay off his drinking debt? Because he was obligated to? Because he wanted to? Addax couldn't think of a good reason as to why Maximilian would be here. Worse still, the man wouldn't answer to his name.

What was going on here?

Determined to find answers, Addax charged over to the wagon just as Maximilian came out of the tavern again, preparing to load up with another barrel. But Addax shoved one of the tavern workers aside to get at him.

"Max?" he demanded. "Maximilian, answer me!"

Maximilian looked at him with a face that was battered and sagging on one side, but there was absolutely no recognition. Nothing. He didn't even look confused. He simply reached for another barrel as the man Addax had shoved aside now shoved Addax.

"Leave him alone," he said. "Go about your business."

Adonis appeared, pushing the worker back, hard. "Still yourself, you fool," he growled. "Lay hands on him again and you'll lose them."

Adonis flashed his broadsword, and the man, who was just a tavern worker, put his hands up in immediate surrender.

"Easy, knight," he said nervously. "I meant no harm. It's just that he won't understand you."

Addax was standing beside Adonis, listening closely. "That man?" he said, pointing at Maximilian. "Why not?"

The worker kept his hands up because the knight hadn't lowered his sword. "Because he cannot speak," he said. "He hears well enough to do what you tell him to do, but he can't speak. He doesn't know anything."

Both Addax and Adonis looked at Maximilian as he took yet another barrel off the wagon and lumbered inside with it. Addax was as confused as ever.

"Do you know who he is?" he finally asked the worker. "Do you know his name?"

The worker nodded. "His name is Gorach," he said. "At least, that's what we call him. It means 'stupid' in the Gaelic, and that's what he is—stupid."

"Gorach," Addax repeated, looking at Adonis, who shrugged in a manner that suggested he had no idea what was going on. Neither of them did. Addax returned his attention to the worker. "How did he get here?"

Because Adonis had finally lowered his sword, the worker lowered his hands. "You'll have to ask Wat," he said. "He owns the tavern. Wat Glidden is his name."

"Fetch him to me," Addax said. "It is important."

The worker gestured to the barrels being brought in. "He's busy, my lord," he said. "Can you come back later?"

"Nay," Addax said. "Tell him that Sir Addax al-Kort, a knight in the service of the Earl of Hereford, wishes to speak with him. Do it now."

The man darted off. All the while, Maximilian kept coming in and out of the tavern, rolling out barrels or carrying other things—working as the man had never worked in his life, because Maximilian had never been the industrious sort. Addax and Adonis watched him with shock that had not yet diminished.

"Did you see his face?" Adonis said. "He looks as if he'd been severely beaten."

Addax nodded. "That is not Maximilian de Grey," he muttered. "I do not know who it is, but that is simply a beast of burden. The Max I knew never worked that hard in his entire life for anything."

Adonis looked at him. "And he cannot speak?" he said. "He does not know who he is?"

Addax had the same questions with no answers. All he could do was shake his head, struggling not to let his horror of the situation get the better of him. The very real horror that if Maximilian was alive, Emmeline was still married.

She still belonged to Maximilian.

The Earl of Bretherdale.

Addax was genuinely trying not to become ill at the thought. He felt nauseated with the reality that Maximilian had been found alive. He couldn't even think how Emmeline was going to react to this. A local magistrate had declared Maximilian dead without a body. Even as Addax rolled that around in his mind, he'd never heard anything so stupid in his life. No body didn't necessarily mean death. It simply meant that there was an absence of a corpse. But Addax had been more than happy to accept that and claim Emmeline, ignoring the very real fact that Maximilian could be alive somewhere.

But the truth was that he'd ignored it because he wanted to ignore it. God help him, he just wanted to be happy for once in his life. And what was he looking at now? Taking Maximilian back to Alston so Emmeline could take care of him for the rest of his life? A man who'd tried to kill her, tried to ruin her life?

Was God really so cruel?

As he was pondering the darkness the future might hold, the tavern keeper emerged from the warm, stale tavern, and he didn't look happy. The worker who had fetched him pointed to

Addax, and the tavern keeper stormed in his direction.

"What do you want?" he demanded.

Addax pointed at Maximilian, who was now swabbing out the wagon bed where he'd broken the barrel. "That man," he said. "How did he come to work for you?"

The tavern keep turned to look at who Addax was talking about, but there were a few men standing around. "Who?"

"The man you call Gorach."

That brought recognition. "Ah, *him*," he said. "Why do you want to know?"

"I may recognize him. Can you tell me where he came from?"

The tavern keeper mulled over a response before finally answering. "I found him."

"What do you mean, you 'found' him?"

"Just that," the tavern keeper said, wiping his hands off on his apron. "I was coming back from Penrith, crossing a bridge over the River Eamont, and I saw him lying on the riverbank. He was nearly dead. I brought him back here, my wife nursed him back to health, and he works for us."

Addax sighed heavily, hanging his head with the short but very plausible story. As the magistrate in Penrith had presumed, Maximilian had ended up in the river—only somehow, he'd washed onto the bank rather than drowned. He was found by the tavern keeper and brought to Appleby, where he'd been recovering for the past several months.

Indeed, Maximilian de Grey was alive.

The knots in Addax's stomach were getting worse.

"What happened to him?" he managed to ask.

The tavern keeper shrugged. "Someone beat him," he said. "They broke his skull and left him for dead, I suppose. He is blind in one eye, but he's strong. He can work. He is the best kind of worker because he cannot complain. But why the questions? Do you know who he is?"

Adonis started to nod, but Addax stopped him. "I am not certain," he lied, mostly because he didn't want the tavern keep to try to ransom Maximilian if he knew that he was the Earl of Bretherdale. "I thought I might have recognized him, but now I am not certain."

The tavern keeper looked back at Maximilian before shrugging. "Gorach!" he called to him. When Maximilian looked up at him, the tavern keep waved him over. "Come here. Hurry, lad."

Maximilian had never obeyed an order in his life, or, at the very least, he obeyed them with some reluctance. He'd never been a man who liked to be pushed around. But he obeyed the tavern keeper as if God himself had given him the order, shuffling over to where the man was standing. Addax could see that he was limping. In fact, there was so much he could see about him that was wrong. It may have looked like Maximilian de Grey, but it wasn't. Not as Maximilian used to be. But the tavern keep's explanation cleared up nearly all of the confusion. Maximilian couldn't speak, he didn't know who or what he was, and he'd ended up in a village where no one had recognized him.

Yet.

That was the key factor in all of this.

"Gorach," the tavern keeper said, indicating Addax. "Do you know this man?"

Maximilian looked Addax in the face. Addax found himself looking back, holding his breath, waiting for some kind of acknowledgement, but Maximilian simply stared at him. There was nothing in those eyes that was warm or even kind.

It was just a blank stare.

"Think," Addax said to him. "Think back to the people you have known. Do you recognize me?"

Maximilian continued to stare at him. There were several long moments where he seemed to tilt his head as if almost remembering but not quite. Addax looked at him, straight on, wondering if some distant memory might be jogged. The broken skull had obviously affected everything about him—his memory, his eyesight, the way he moved. One side of his face was even droopy, so the damage he suffered had been great. Addax found himself feeling sorry for the Maximilian he used to know, but not the man he had turned into once he married Emmeline. He didn't pity that man at all.

He wished that man had stayed dead.

After staring at Addax for what seemed like hours but in reality was only a minute or two, Maximilian simply turned away and headed back to his task of swabbing the wagon bed. The tavern keeper, Addax, and Adonis watched him go before the tavern keeper returned his attention to Addax.

"I would say he doesn't know you," he said. "But I think you know him and won't tell me. Who is he?"

Addax was still looking at Maximilian as the man picked up a rag and resumed washing the wagon. "As I said, I'm not sure," he told the tavern keeper. "But I'll be back. Make sure he does not go anywhere."

The tavern keep shrugged and headed back inside his establishment as Addax and Adonis turned away. They headed out into the busy street.

"Well?" Adonis said. "What are you going to do?"

Addax shook his head, struggling to stay logical about the

situation. *Heartbreak* didn't cover half of what he was feeling. He was terrified to tell Emmeline, terrified of her reaction.

All he could feel was devastation.

"I do not know," he said honestly, pausing as they reached the opposite side of the street. His gaze moved to the busy tavern. "He is alive, but he does not know who he is. But that does not mean someone who knew him will not recognize him and tell the tavern keeper."

"You did not tell him who he was," he said. "Why not?"

Addax cocked a dark eyebrow. "Tell the man that his mute servant is none other than the Earl of Bretherdale?" he said. "If he tries to ransom him, or worse, it will be a horrific mess, and one I do not wish to engage in, so it is best not to tell him. For now, let him think what he will."

Adonis scratched his head. "And Emmeline?" he said quietly. "What about her?"

Addax sighed faintly. "I will have to tell her."

"And what about you?"

"What do you mean?"

Adonis looked at him. "I've known the lady for several years now," he said softly. "I am not a fool. I know you were in love with her when she first married Maximilian. I know she was in love with you. It was a sad situation, I will admit. I will further admit that I never liked de Grey. He was selfish and vile. I would much rather see you married to her, Addax. If I may call you Addax. You are the husband she deserves."

Addax smiled weakly. "While I appreciate that, the fact remains that her husband isn't dead," he said. "He isn't dead, but he does not know who he is. Mayhap he never will. Do I leave him at the Scot's Head and hope no one who knew him ever recognizes him? Or do I bring the Earl of Bretherdale home? If I do that, I cannot marry the woman I love."

Adonis was sympathetic. "But even if you marry her now, the marriage will not be valid," he said. "With Maximilian still alive…"

Addax knew that. He simply couldn't believe that his future happiness was in the balance at the moment, not to mention Emmeline's. He found himself praying his brother would show up, because he needed Essien's guidance. He wasn't sure he could make the correct choice here, because he was more than willing to leave Maximilian at that tavern.

But as a man of honor, he knew he couldn't.

Honor that would cost him the love of his life.

"The honorable thing would be to bring him home," he said hoarsely. "But I must… I must speak with Emmy and tell her what has happened. We must make that decision together."

Adonis understood. "I am sorry you must. I truly am."

So was Addax. Resigned, and depressed, he shook his head. "I do not feel much like going to the goldsmith today," he muttered. "Find the escort and have them report back to the carriage. I just want to go… home."

There was nothing else he could do, and they both knew it. Perhaps that was the bitterest pill of all. As Addax turned in the direction he had come from, he heard Adonis' soft voice.

"Wait," he said. "Addax… *look*."

Addax turned to see what had the man's attention, and he could see Maximilian standing at the edge of the road, looking over at him. There were people between them, going about their business, but Maximilian was staring straight at him. Addax simply stood there, watching and waiting, wondering what was going through Maximilian's mind. He wondered if Maximilian had suddenly remembered him and was trying to figure out how and where and why. As Addax continued to watch with some apprehension, Maximilian began to cross the street toward him. He lifted an arm, pointing at him, as he walked. But then he stopped in the middle of the street and lowered his hand. His mouth began to work.

Addax was on pins and needles as one word came forth out of Maximilian's mouth.

"*Ahhhhd,*" he said loudly.

Ad. That was what he used to call Addax. Next to Addax, Adonis gasped.

"My God," he breathed. "He knows you. He *knows!*"

Addax was staring at Maximilian. He couldn't tear his eyes away. He didn't know whether to cry or run. As he stood there, debating what to do and how his life was going to change from now on, a runaway horse and wagon tore down the street, straight for Maximilian. Addax was looking at him one moment, and in the next, he was gone.

The horse and wagon had plowed right into him.

People were screaming and scattering to safety as the wagon went another few feet before breaking an axle and tipping over. The driver was thrown out, and the harnessed horses became tangled up with the twisted wagon behind them and couldn't go any further. Men were running out to grab the horses and help the driver, and Addax could see Maximilian crumpled underneath the tipped wagon.

He and Adonis rushed forward, grabbing a few of the men who had spilled out of the Scot's Head to see what the screaming was about, and ordering them to lift the wagon. Six or seven of them lifted it, including Adonis, as Addax slid Maximilian out from underneath it.

There was no doubt that the man was dead.

Just like that, Maximilian was gone. Again. But this time for good. Hands on his head in disbelief, Addax found himself looking at Maximilian, whose neck had clearly been broken. The man's head was turned all the way around on his shoulders. He knelt in the dirt beside him, suddenly feeling a horrific sense of loss. It was true that Maximilian's discovery had meant that Addax's future plans were destroyed, but it was also true that Addax had intended to do the right thing, even to his own detriment. He was resigned to it.

And now this.

He simply couldn't believe it.

Glancing up, he could see that the wagon had been driven by Neif. The young and skittish horse had apparently gotten away from the man, with devastating results. Addax found himself looking down at Maximilian once again. The man's eyes were open in death, and Addax leaned over him, gently closing them.

"Godspeed, my friend," he murmured. "I do not know what happened to you, or why, but go now. Go and be free."

"My God!" Ingram was suddenly there, looking at the catastrophe. "What happened? Is that man dead?"

He was pointing to Maximilian, but Addax didn't reply. He was looking at Adonis. "Find a blanket or something to cover him up with," he said. "Quickly."

Adonis rushed straight into the tavern as a crowd began to gather around the wagon, emerging very shortly with a coverlet he'd ripped off a bed in one of the rental chambers. He had to push his way back through the crowd to hand it to Addax, who covered up Maximilian just about the time Emmeline appeared.

He heard her cry out.

"Addax!" she gasped. "My God! Are you injured?"

He stood up quickly when he saw her standing next to Ingram. Ingram's wife and daughter were with her, but Addax went to Emmeline and hurriedly pulled her away from the snarl of people.

"Nay, love," he said steadily. "I am not injured. But what are you doing here? I told you to stay in the stall."

Emmeline tried not to appear too guilty. "I know," she said. "But the horses bolted, and Ingram ran after them. Then his wife and daughter ran after them, so I did, too. They were panicked, and I thought I could help."

He frowned. "Help with a runaway wagon?" he said doubtfully. "Honestly, Emmy. Did you think I would believe that?"

The guilt overtook her. "I was only trying to help," she insisted weakly. But then she pointed to the covered body by the wagon. "What happened?"

Addax turned to look at the blanket-covered corpse, the people still standing around it. The situation, in only the past several minutes, had changed so rapidly, and he was still trying to keep up with it. He'd just been resigning himself to the fact that Maximilian wasn't dead, but Fate had a different idea about the situation. That skittish horse that Addax had commented on had turned out to be the catalyst for his future. A future he'd worked so very hard for. The plans he'd made, the child Emmeline carried... All of it would come to fruition now. For good, this time.

The realization was enough to bring tears to his eyes.

"Em," he said softly. "There's something I must tell you."

She looked up at him. "What is it?"

"You are aware that Max's body was never found."

She cocked her head sharply in surprise. "What brought that up?"

He turned her around, moving her back the way she'd come. "There is something you should know," he said. "I've found Max."

She gasped. "You did?" she said. "Oh, Addax… you *did*?"

"I did."

"But where?"

"Here."

"In this town?"

"Aye."

"How did you find him?"

Addax decided, very quickly, that she didn't need to know all of it. Not now. It would only upset her, and he didn't want to do that, not when she was in a delicate condition. Perhaps he'd tell her all of it someday, but for now, all she needed to know was that Maximilian's body had been found and they could get on with their lives. They could live and laugh and love one another as they'd planned.

Everything as they'd planned.

Briefly, he remembered what Emmeline had said to him once when they realized their feelings for one another and knew they would never be able to act on it. They were painful and poignant words that had stayed with him. But they seemed especially important now.

I shall go to my grave having never known a loving touch or the kiss of a man I love beyond all reason. That is why I envy your parents—at least they knew what love was.

Addax knew too. And so did Emmeline.

Thanks to a pair of runaway horses, nothing could come between them ever again.

Addax told her, with as little detail as possible, about finding Maximilian in the village. He didn't tell her that Maximilian had been alive when he found him, however. That was something that would wait, details she didn't need to know at this time. He wasn't surprised by her relief, and her gratitude, and two weeks later in St. Catherine's Church in Penrith, they buried Maximilian in the same crypt as his mother and father, at the feet of his grandparents.

And with that, it was finally over.

When Essien finally arrived at Alston Castle a week after the burial, Addax told him the entire story from start to finish. It was quite shocking. But when Essien realized that his brother's happiness was now assured, with no more twists of fate or with a woman that was out of his reach—again—Essien's reaction was surprising.

He wept.

EPILOGUE

A year later

*T*HE KING HAS come!

Addax and Emmeline had known Henry III was touring the north, and they furthermore knew he was coming to Alston Castle for about a month. Word had been sent on ahead, and he was to spend one night at the castle, which sent Emmeline into a frenzy because the quiet castle of Alston had never seen a royal visitor. At least, one who came in peace. There had been years during the reign of John when the king had sent his armies to try to wrest some of the valuable ore from the mines, but he was never able to accomplish his goal. Therefore, a peaceful royal visitor was something of an anomaly.

And Emmeline was determined that everything should be right and proper.

Addax had to grin at his wife becoming so crazed over a royal visit. Given that he and the king knew one another on a personal level, he wasn't in nearly the state she was, but he was touched that the man should think enough of him to visit. In fact, when Henry arrived on a glorious autumn day, he embraced Addax as one would embrace a long-lost friend. But that wasn't the only surprise Addax was in for.

Christopher de Lohr was with him.

Christopher, too, embraced Addax, and he was quite kind to Emmeline when they were introduced. Emmeline was overwhelmed by the enormous blond earl, whose blue eyes seemed to be perpetually twinkling, especially at Addax. She could see how fond Christopher was of her husband, and he greeted Essien, now a permanent fixture at Alston, in much the same way.

Alston Castle quickly filled up with royal troops and courtiers, with de Lohr troops and men, and by evening the great hall was lively with a roaring fire, royal minstrels, and enough food to feed half of England. But Henry, Addax, Christopher, Essien, Emmeline, and a few of Henry's advisors remained in the solar of Alston, where they had been most of the day, discussing the Scots, politics, and local issues.

Emmeline couldn't have been prouder of her husband.

Addax was a born king. It was in his blood. He was thoughtful and wise, compassionate when he needed to be and fierce when the situation called for it. He hadn't ridden the tournament circuit since they had married, because the management of Alston had kept him quite busy. Under his guidance, they'd opened three more mines and built a smelting furnace, with royal permission, so they could start extracting their own silver from the lead ore. While this was going on, Essien took command of Raisbeck Castle and expanded what had been a few sheep herds for wool, meat, and income into much larger herds for profit.

The sons of Amare al-Kort were creating their own empire.

Emmeline had to briefly leave the conclave in the solar to

tend to her twin sons, Amare and Alek, because she insisted on feeding them herself and not employing a wet nurse, as was the custom. The boys were big and healthy, thriving, and she thought quite possibly that Addax was the most attentive father she had ever seen. Having lost his own father so young, he was determined to make his mark on his sons, even at their very young age. So was Essien, as a doting uncle, who was much more apt to run off with both of them and take them to "see the goats" or "inspect the horses." He insisted the boys were old enough to do what men did, much to the protest of their mother.

His behavior was both frustrating and sweet.

Clad in a red surcoat and pale shift that she'd had specially made for the king's visit, Emmeline returned to the solar, where the men were still talking. The feast was in full swing on a crisp, clear night, but the king remained in the keep, lingering over conversation and wine. When Emmeline entered, a ravishing vision of beauty, Addax met her with a cup of watered wine, taking her hand and leading her to a chair.

"Sit," he said. "Henry has something he wishes to tell us."

Emmeline sat down, looking at him curiously. Before he could reply to her unspoken question, Henry lifted his voice.

"Good," he said. "You have returned, Lady al-Kort. I wanted to wait until both you and your husband were in the room before delivering my news. It is the real reason I've come to Alston."

Emmeline looked at the man who had been king since he was nine years of age. Quite literally, he'd been a king all of his life. He was fair-skinned, with dark eyes and pale hair, and his manner, while polite, was oddly detached, as if he didn't know how to show true warmth. He was friendly with men he called his friends, like Christopher and Addax, but it was as if he'd never learned how to truly be sincere when dealing with people he loved and admired. Still, he was trying hard to be congenial, and Emmeline smiled.

"We are honored by your visit, your grace, whatever the reason," she said. "You are always welcome at Alston."

Henry held out his cup for more wine, poured by the one royal servant in the chamber. "I know," he said. "Addax and I are old friends and allies. It is good to be friends with another king, even if that king does not rule his country. Is that not correct, Addax?"

"It is, your grace."

Henry looked at him. "Essien and I had a long discussion when he and Cole came to London to discuss your marriage plans for Lady al-Kort, who was then Lady de Grey," he said. "Truthfully, I'd forgotten about your history, Addax. I knew you were the heir to your father's throne and that your uncle had turned against him, but the details escaped me. Essien reminded me of what you lost. What you both lost."

Addax was standing behind Emmeline, his hand on her shoulder. "Aye, your grace," he said. "We lost a great deal, but that is in the past. It is not something I think of, nor is it something that shapes the way I live my life. I consider myself a survivor."

"Absolutely," Henry agreed. Then he looked at Christopher. "And this is the man who helped you survive."

Christopher smiled faintly as he looked at Addax and Essien. "I remember two starving little boys in an olive grove," he said, watching them smile in return. "But once I fed them, they were like a pack of wild dogs. I could not get rid of them no matter how hard I tried. Quite annoying."

That had the room breaking into soft laughter, because they all knew that none of it was true, most especially Addax.

"It is your own fault, my lord," he said. "Once we realized that you could provide steady food, there was no possible way we were going to leave your side. In fact, I remember riding with your brother, David, sitting behind him in the saddle. We were going somewhere—I forget where—but David had a pouch on his belt that contained dried meat. When I realized that, I spent the entire ride eating all of his meat, and when we stopped and realized all of his food was gone, I told him an elaborate story about thieves who had snuck up behind him and taken only his food as I tried to fight them off. I do not think he believed me."

Christopher chuckled. "I am surprised he let you get away with that."

"He did not. I was forced to clean his boots, constantly, for three straight days, and I could not figure out why."

Grinning, Christopher could see the obvious, just as they all could. "The truth is that we grew very attached to you and Es," he said. "You became part of us. We missed you both when you went with the Thuringians, but it was for the best. We faced a great deal of hardship after that."

Henry, not to be left out of the conversation, nodded. "They were with my Uncle Richard, who was a veritable lightning rod for his enemies," he said. "But let us return to you, Addax, and the reason why I've come. I've recently been forced to confiscate property from Robert de Vieuxpont. You recall that Bretherdale was involved in selling the Scots ore? It seems that de Vieuxpont was worse than Emmeline's former father-in-law. He was providing the Scots with men and material, bringing them in from Ireland and running them into Scotland. In any case, de Vieuxpont has been banished, his properties confiscated, and he is quite fortunate I have not thrown him in the Tower of London. That leaves Brougham Castle and Appleby Castle as Crown properties, but we have more properties than we need. And more expenses than I want. I intend to give those castles to someone I trust, and that someone is you."

Addax struggled to keep the astonishment off his face. "Brougham is a magnificent castle," he said. "It is just outside of Penrith. I've seen it many times."

"It is now yours."

In his periphery, Addax could see Emmeline looking up at him, and he tore his eyes from Henry for a moment to look at his wife, who was beaming with pride. Overcome with surprise, Addax swallowed hard.

"I do not know what to say, my lord," he said. "To offer my thanks does not seem adequate."

"I am not done," Henry said. "Addax, I cannot offer you a kingdom. But I can offer you an earldom. Not Bretherdale; nay, not that one. It is not nearly as grand as you require. But Bretherdale will become part of the new earldom of Deira, which is now yours. Your lands are from Penrith to Middlesbrough, which was part of Deira in ancient times, and you have many villages and castles that will be subject to you, including Bowes Castle. That is a de Royans property, and I am certain he will not be troubled by you being his new overlord. My cartographers have drawn a map of your new earldom, so I want you to study it. You can make Brougham or Alston or even Raisbeck your seat—that is your choice—but missives are going out to your new subjects, announcing your new rule as Earl of Deira."

Addax was looking at the king with wide eyes. "My lord…

your generosity is overwhelming," he said. "Forgive me for behaving like an idiot, but I simply do not know what to say. I am ashamed that I am not more eloquent in my response."

Henry held up a hand to ease the man's sense of embarrassment. "Addax, you are a king," he said quietly. "You have married my niece, so we are joined by marriage. While I cannot return you to Kitara, I can do this. You deserve nothing less."

Addax had to sit down. In fact, it was Emmeline who stood up and directed her overwhelmed husband into a chair. As she stood next to him, holding his hand and beaming, Addax took a deep breath and tried to control his shock.

"My lord," he said, feeling a lump in his throat. "Never did I imagine I would be so honored. I am without words, but know my gratitude is limitless. I am your servant for life."

Henry was pleased with how shocked Addax was. That told him how much it meant to the man. Essien, standing on the other side of his stunned brother, seemed just as pleased for him. He was patting his shoulder and his head, congratulating him, as Henry fixed on him.

"Essien," Henry said. "There is a small fiefdom known as Binchester which borders your brother's lands near Middlesbrough. I am certain your brother would not mind having you as a neighbor, Lord Binchester."

Essien suddenly had much the same expression that Addax had. His eyes widened and his mouth popped open as an unexpected gift was bestowed upon him. Emmeline left Addax long enough to give Essien a congratulatory hug, but she had to pull up a chair for him, too, so he could sit down.

The al-Kort brothers were both overwhelmed.

Happy that he'd managed to flap two unflappable men, Henry suddenly developed an appetite and departed for the great hall. But Christopher remained, watching Addax and Essien become accustomed to what they'd been given. Nay, *earned*.

They had earned this.

Every bit of it.

"You should also know that Henry has sent envoys to Kitara to see what has become of your father those years ago," Christopher said softly. "It is a diplomatic mission under the guise of establishing a trade treaty, but the truth is that he is trying to find answers for you both. He, too, was a child when he lost his father. He thinks enough of you both to help you find closure."

Addax and Essien both looked up at him, but it was Addax who spoke. "Truly, I am speechless," he said. "I do not even know what to say."

Christopher smiled. "Say nothing," he said. "But know that this is where you belong, Ad. When I found you those years ago, it was not by chance. It was providence. You were meant to be here, in England, because I believe you are meant to be a guiding force in a country that is constantly trying to tear itself apart. I am growing older. Someday, I will be gone, but you will still be here, God willing, to help make this country what it was meant to be. A place where our children can raise their children in peace. A place where the king of an ancient kingdom brought his wisdom, and his experience, and helped make England a place he can be proud of. Nothing is ever by chance in this life, Ad. God always has a plan."

With that, he left Addax and Essien and Emmeline to ponder the turn the day had taken. While Essien eventually wandered over to the hall to celebrate his good fortune, Addax and Emmeline remained in the solar.

Emmeline had pulled a chair up in front of her husband, leaning forward to hold his hands as he struggled to accept all he'd been given. She simply sat there, watching him, a proud expression on her features until he was ready to speak. As he looked into her eyes, he felt like the most fortunate man who had ever lived. Every dream he'd ever entertained had come true. Perhaps the path to reach it hadn't been easy, but that made the victory all the sweeter.

"When I left Kitara, I thought I'd lost everything," he finally said, his voice hoarse with emotion. "I never expected anything more than to survive. But this is more than survival."

Emmeline smiled. "It certainly is," she said. "How proud I am of you, Ad. The Earl of Deira. It is well deserved."

"Is it?" he said, looking at her. "I am still trying to accept that I should be so honored. I already have everything I could have ever wanted—you, my sons, a prosperous life. Do I truly deserve it all?"

Emmeline was still smiling when she reached into the pocket of his tunic and pulled out the pin she'd once given him. He never went anywhere without it. Every moment of the day, the gold pin was with him, reminding him of the most important things in life. Reminding him of who, and what, he was. She held it up for him to see.

"What does this say?" she asked softly.

Addax could see the word, faintly. After a moment, he, too, smiled. "Worthy," he whispered.

Emmeline came off the chair, kneeling between his legs as she gazed up at him. Her hands went to his face, a face she loved so well, as she pulled him down to her for a gentle kiss.

"You are," she murmured. "You *are* worthy. Of everything."

In the years to come, the standard of the Earldom of Deira

was a red banner with a fearsome black dragon on it, and it became one of the most recognizable banners in England. As Addax had hoped, his sons went on to do great and noble things in the politics of England, with one marrying into the royal family. Another married into the House of de Wolfe. The al-Kort family became legendary, the bloodlines of ancient kings mingled with the bloodlines of the Plantagenets. They were known for their fierceness, their brilliance, and their wisdom.

Amare, the last *kaara ejadar*, would have been proud. His teachings to his young sons bore fruit not in the sands of Kitara, but in the green fields of England and beyond. His influence was felt for generations to come, and the dragon-headed dagger, carried by Addax, was passed to the firstborn son of every generation.

So was the "worthy" pin.

The Black Dragon, and the tale of Addax and Emmeline, lived on in ways they could have never imagined.

A love story of legend.

❦ THE END ❧

Children of Addax and Emmeline
(The children were given both names from Addax's culture and the land of their birth so they could choose which names they wished to use. It should be of note that all of them chose to use their first names, from their father's culture)

Amare Christopher
Alek Henry
Kaara Elizabetha
Amala Eleanor
Rami Marcellus
Taj Augustus
Kiya Isabelle
Zain Bastien
Khari David
Kader Coleby

KATHRYN LE VEQUE NOVELS

Medieval Romance:

De Wolfe Pack Series:
Warwolfe
The Wolfe
Nighthawk
ShadowWolfe
DarkWolfe
A Joyous de Wolfe Christmas
BlackWolfe
Serpent
A Wolfe Among Dragons
Scorpion
StormWolfe
Dark Destroyer
The Lion of the North
Walls of Babylon
The Best Is Yet To Be
BattleWolfe
Castle of Bones

De Wolfe Pack Generations:
WolfeHeart
WolfeStrike
WolfeSword
WolfeBlade
WolfeLord
WolfeShield
Nevermore
WolfeAx
WolfeBorn

The Executioner Knights:

By the Unholy Hand
The Mountain Dark
Starless
A Time of End
Winter of Solace
Lord of the Sky
The Splendid Hour
The Whispering Night
Netherworld
Lord of the Shadows
Of Mortal Fury
'Twas the Executioner Knight
Before Christmas
Crimson Shield
The Black Dragon

The de Russe Legacy:
The Falls of Erith
Lord of War: Black Angel
The Iron Knight
Beast
The Dark One: Dark Knight
The White Lord of Wellesbourne
Dark Moon
Dark Steel
A de Russe Christmas Miracle
Dark Warrior

The de Lohr Dynasty:
While Angels Slept
Rise of the Defender
Steelheart
Shadowmoor
Silversword

Spectre of the Sword
Unending Love
Archangel
A Blessed de Lohr Christmas
Lion of Twilight
Lion of War
Lion of Hearts

The Brothers de Lohr:
The Earl in Winter

Lords of East Anglia:
While Angels Slept
Godspeed
Age of Gods and Mortals

Great Lords of le Bec:
Great Protector

House of de Royans:
Lord of Winter
To the Lady Born
The Centurion

Lords of Eire:
Echoes of Ancient Dreams
Lord of Black Castle
The Darkland

Ancient Kings of Anglecynn:
The Whispering Night
Netherworld

Battle Lords of de Velt:
The Dark Lord
Devil's Dominion
Bay of Fear
The Dark Lord's First Christmas
The Dark Spawn
The Dark Conqueror
The Dark Angel

Reign of the House of de Winter:
Lespada
Swords and Shields

De Reyne Domination:
Guardian of Darkness
The Black Storm
A Cold Wynter's Knight
With Dreams
Master of the Dawn

House of d'Vant:
Tender is the Knight (House of d'Vant)
The Red Fury (House of d'Vant)

The Dragonblade Series:
Fragments of Grace
Dragonblade
Island of Glass
The Savage Curtain
The Fallen One
The Phantom Bride

Great Marcher Lords of de Lara
Dragonblade

House of St. Hever
Fragments of Grace
Island of Glass
Queen of Lost Stars

Lords of Pembury:
The Savage Curtain

Lords of Thunder: The de Shera Brotherhood Trilogy
The Thunder Lord
The Thunder Warrior
The Thunder Knight

The Great Knights of de Moray:
Shield of Kronos
The Gorgon

The House of De Nerra:
The Promise
The Falls of Erith
Vestiges of Valor
Realm of Angels

Highland Legion:
Highland Born

Highland Warriors of Munro:
The Red Lion
Deep Into Darkness

The House of de Garr:
Lord of Light
Realm of Angels

Saxon Lords of Hage:
The Crusader
Kingdom Come

High Warriors of Rohan:
High Warrior
High King

The House of Ashbourne:
Upon a Midnight Dream

The House of D'Aurilliac:
Valiant Chaos

The House of De Dere:
Of Love and Legend

St. John and de Gare Clans:
The Warrior Poet

The House of de Bretagne:
The Questing

The House of Summerlin:
The Legend

The Kingdom of Hendocia:
Kingdom by the Sea

The BlackChurch Guild: Shadow Knights:
The Leviathan
The Protector

Regency Historical Romance:
Sin Like Flynn: A Regency
Historical Romance Duet
The Sin Commandments
Georgina and the Red Charger

Gothic Regency Romance:
Emma

Contemporary Romance:

Kathlyn Trent/Marcus Burton Series:
Valley of the Shadow
The Eden Factor
Canyon of the Sphinx

The American Heroes Anthology Series:
The Lucius Robe
Fires of Autumn
Evenshade
Sea of Dreams
Purgatory

Other non-connected Contemporary Romance:
Lady of Heaven
Darkling, I Listen

In the Dreaming Hour
River's End
The Fountain

Sons of Poseidon:
The Immortal Sea

Pirates of Britannia Series (with

Eliza Knight):
Savage of the Sea by Eliza Knight
Leader of Titans by Kathryn Le Veque
The Sea Devil by Eliza Knight
Sea Wolfe by Kathryn Le Veque

Note: All Kathryn's novels are designed to be read as stand-alones, although many have cross-over characters or cross-over family groups. Novels that are grouped together have related characters or family groups. You will notice that some series have the same books; that is because they are cross-overs. A hero in one book may be the secondary character in another.

There is NO reading order except by chronology, but even in that case, you can still read the books as stand-alones. No novel is connected to another by a cliff hanger, and every book has an HEA.

Series are clearly marked. All series contain the same characters or family groups except the American Heroes Series, which is an anthology with unrelated characters.

For more information, find it in **A Reader's Guide to the Medieval World of Le Veque**.

ABOUT KATHRYN LE VEQUE

Bringing the Medieval to Romance

KATHRYN LE VEQUE is a critically acclaimed, multiple USA TODAY Bestselling author, an Indie Reader bestseller, a charter Amazon All-Star author, and a #1 bestselling, award-winning, multi-published author in Medieval Historical Romance with over 100 published novels.

Kathryn is a multiple award nominee and winner, including the winner of Uncaged Book Reviews Magazine 2017 and 2018 "Raven Award" for Favorite Medieval Romance. Kathryn is also a multiple RONE nominee (InD'Tale Magazine), holding a record for the number of nominations. In 2018, her novel WARWOLFE was the winner in the Romance category of the Book Excellence Award and in 2019, her novel A WOLFE AMONG DRAGONS won the prestigious RONE award for best pre-16th century romance.

Kathryn is considered one of the top Indie authors in the world with over 2M copies in circulation, and her novels have been translated into several languages. Kathryn recently signed with Sourcebooks Casablanca for a Medieval Fight Club series, first published in 2020.

In addition to her own published works, Kathryn is also the President/CEO of Dragonblade Publishing, a boutique publishing house specializing in Historical Romance. Dragonblade's success has seen it rise in the ranks to become Amazon's #1 e-book publisher of Historical Romance (K-Lytics report July 2020).

Kathryn loves to hear from her readers. Please find Kathryn on Facebook at Kathryn Le Veque, Author, or join her on Twitter @kathrynleveque. Sign up for Kathryn's blog at www.kathrynleveque.com for the latest news and sales.

Milton Keynes UK
Ingram Content Group UK Ltd.
UKHW020241010424
440366UK00012B/386